D0031782

CLIMATE of CHANGE

TOR BOOKS BY PIERS ANTHONY

THE XANTH SERIES

Vale of the Vole
Heaven Cent
Man from Mundania
Demons Don't Dream
Harpy Thyme
Geis of the Gargoyle
Roc and a Hard Place
Yon Ill Wind
Faun & Games
Zombie Lover
Xone of Contention
The Dastard
Swell Foop
Up in a Heaval
Cube Route
Currant Events
Pet Peeve
Stork Naked
Air Apparent
Two to the Fifth
Jumper Cable

THE GEODYSSEY SERIES

Isle of Woman
Shame of Man
Hope of Earth
Muse of Art
Climate of Change

ANTHOLOGIES

Alien Plot
Anthonology

NONFICTION

How Precious Was That While
Letters to Jenny

But What of Earth?
Ghost
Hasan
Prostho Plus
Race Against Time
Shade of the Tree
Steppe
Triple Detente

WITH ROBERT E. MARGROFF

The Dragon's Gold Series
Dragon's Gold
Serpent's Silver
Chimaera's Copper
Orc's Opal
Mouvar's Magic

The E.S.P. Worm
The Ring

WITH FRANCES HALL

Pretender

WITH RICHARD GILLIAM

Tales from the Great Turtle (Anthology)

WITH ALFRED TELLA

The Willing Spirit

WITH CLIFFORD A. PICKOVER

Spider Legs

WITH JAMES RICHEY AND ALAN RIGGS

Quest for the Fallen Star

WITH JULIE BRADY

Dream a Little Dream

WITH JO ANNE TAEUSCH

The Secret of Spring

WITH RON LEMING

The Gutbucket Quest

CLIMATE of CHANGE

PIERS ANTHONY

A TOM DOHERTY ASSOCIATES BOOK • NEW YORK

This is a work of fiction. All of the characters, organizations, and events portrayed in this novel are either products of the author's imagination or are used fictitiously.

CLIMATE OF CHANGE

A Tor Book
Published by Tom Doherty Associates, LLC
175 Fifth Avenue
New York, NY 10010

www.tor-forge.com

ISBN 978-0-7653-2353-8

First Edition: May 2010

Printed in the United States of America

0 9 8 7 6 5 4 3 2 1

CONTENTS

INTRODUCTION

In school I hated history classes. This was ironic, because the study of human history has been a hallmark of my later life. So what was the problem in school? It was that a school's idea of history was lists of the names and dates of kings, the dates of battles, and maybe some lists of products of the times. Things to memorize. I was never good at memorization.

So the kind of history I liked was ancient, before there were names and dates. The problem was that there were no classes in that. So I had to research it myself. But there were huge gaps. Here is a typical example: modern man emerged from Africa about 100,000 years ago. Then he expanded throughout the rest of the world about 50,000 years ago. What happened in between? It was a mystery. It aggravated me.

Now at last we have a hint: it was the climate. Mankind was spreading, but then came the Mt. Toba volcanic eruption, 74,000 years ago, of a scale we have never seen in historic times. It blotted out the sunlight and obliterated perhaps 99 percent of human life, and I think all of it outside of the home territory of Africa. Mankind had to recover and start over after that setback, from a far smaller base. This time there was no eruption of that magnitude, and he succeeded in colonizing the world, though constantly affected by the weather.

I also have a broader idea of history than conventional texts do. I see it as a process dating from when mankind separated from the apes, several million years ago. When he left the trees, walked on two feet, learned to use tools, started wearing clothing, and learned to talk. I believe that the phenomenal tool of language powered his explosive increase in brain size. That brain made it possible for him to conquer the world, once he learned how to use it.

There were other mysteries. Why did he lose his fur, so that he had to replace it with clothing? Why did human women, alone of all mammals, develop permanent breasts that weren't needed for feeding her babies?

Okay, such things have been addressed in the prior volumes, but here's a spot summary. That burgeoning brain needed to be kept cool, especially when people insisted on going out in the equatorial African sun at noon. They went out, in significant part, because few other animals could; they would die in the heat. Thus foraging was better, because of reduced competition. Walking erect helped by diminishing the amount of the body exposed to the sun, but it wasn't enough. So the loss of fur and the development of copious sweating made the skin the most efficient cooling system in the animal kingdom. *That's* what air-conditioned the brain. At night or in winter clothing was used to keep the body warm; it was easier to do that, than to cool an active furry body.

And breasts. When people walked on two feet, it was a special challenge for the youngest children, because of the constant delicate balancing act required. It would take a couple of years for them to get the hang of it, and longer to become really fleet. But a hungry lion would not wait two years before pouncing. So the mother had to carry her baby. That meant she could not run as fleetly herself, and it inhibited her foraging for food. She needed help, such as by a man. In the normal animal scheme, a male sees a female as good for only one thing. It takes a minute or so, and then he goes on about his business. How could the human female get him to stay close longer than that one minute?

Well, she found a way. She did it through sex appeal. She made herself seem perpetually breedable, so that he was constantly attracted to her, wanting to spend his minute not just once a year but several times a day. Men are hardwired to want to breed any available breedable woman, often. She concealed her estrus—that is, when she was fertile and could become pregnant, so that he could not cherry-pick his time.

But what about her breasts? Mammals use them to feed their infants, and once the baby stops nursing, those mammaries shrink back to token size and the female is breedable again. Full breasts are a turnoff, because she can't be bred while nursing. The human woman couldn't get rid of her breasts to make herself look sexy, because her unfed baby would die. Here was perhaps the most significant challenge: to convert that turn-off signal to a turn-on signal, so as to conceal her time of nonfertility—which was obvious as long as those big breasts were evident—and to make the man desire not the absence of breasts but the presence of them. A 180-degree turn.

Somehow she managed it. Maybe it was that those women who did not attract the constant attention of at least one man did not survive. So surviving boys were the sons of fathers who liked full breasts, contrary to their former self-interest. Men who bought into the fiction of breedability, though they had to know better. Thus breasts became potent sexual lures, and women used them freely to keep men close. You will see it throughout this novel: when a woman flashes her breasts, the man notices and is drawn to her. This is true right up to the present time. Men want to look at women's breasts, to feel them, to kiss them, and to have sex with bare-breasted women. The reason is historical.

But how many school history texts have that discussion? They seem to prefer to keep breasts out of sight and out of mind. I concluded that if I wanted a book to show my kind of history, I would have to write it myself. Thus this GEODYSSEY series, concluding with this volume. Oh, sure, there are some dates and places and names, but generally only to help set the scene. The essence is in the stories. I am a storyteller, and this too is part of the development of the species: storytellers kept children close and quiet during dangerous times, and helped them increase their vocabularies and their imagination, and to learn the nature of their culture. Storytellers were always historians as well as entertainers. So I am merely returning to our origins.

Each volume has its own cast of characters, usually a particular family and its romantic associations as it struggles to survive the challenges of existence. This one has a family of five siblings, three boys and two girls, who relate to a family of two siblings, boy and girl. What's different is the ambiguity of relationships: which boy of the three marries the girl, and which of the two family girls does her brother marry? Different chapters have different combinations, which may be confusing at first, but it seemed the most feasible way to explore alternative prospects. So much of human history is what might have been. We all do wonder on occasion: If only we had gone with this partner instead of that one, how much better life might be. So in this novel we explore them all.

One other thing. This time I have five settings, following five specific peoples from the time of their first awareness as separate entities to the present. These are the Xhosa (pronounced Kosa) of Africa, the Basques of Europe, the Alani of the near east, the Aborigines of Australia, and the Maya of Central America. All were eventually overtaken by the globally advancing Europeans and largely suppressed, but all retain some fraction of their original cultures. World history is not just about the Europeans, despite the impression some historians seem to have.

Thus my version of human history, here sampled for the past hundred thousand years.

1

HERO'S DILEMMA

The precise chronology of the development of modern mankind is obscure. We are "primates," because we fancy we have a prime position in the animal kingdom, but only recently—within the past million years or so—have we demonstrated much of that. Climate drove our development throughout; millions of years ago we were rain forest creatures, but when the climate changed and the forests shrank, we had to change too, or lose. So as dryness changed our habitat, we adapted to handle it. This adaptation took the usual evolutionary form: anyone who couldn't handle dryness died.

We became more flexible in gathering food, drawing on a greater variety of edible things, including scavenging meat. To get meat, including nutritious bone marrow, we had to use tools, and that made us use our brains more. Tools enabled us to manipulate our environment, to an extent, rather than being manipulated by it. Tools helped us compete with specialized animals, including predators. But it took time.

Australopithecus *started walking on two feet about five million years ago; two and a half million years ago* Homo habilis *showed an expanded brain and a smaller gut. These were related: it seemed we faced a choice whether to develop a more versatile digestive system, or a more versatile brain. Some primates chose the gut and huge teeth; we chose the brain.* Homo erectus *moved into Asia well before the moderns evolved, and was a sophisticated hunter. Spears have been found dating to 400,000 years ago, well made and balanced;* Erectus *knew what he was doing. But he seems to have lacked the fine breathing control needed for modern speech. He could probably talk, just not as readily as we do.*

Meanwhile back in Africa an even more sophisticated variant was evolving. Nothing less had any chance to displace Erectus, who had already conquered as much of the world as he cared to. For the purpose of this novel, it is assumed that modern man evolved in the Rift Valley and the region of Lake Victoria, in Africa. When the climate changed, constricting the plant and animal resources there, the growing human population could not be sustained. Some people had to move out, or all would starve. Thus a significant portion of mankind had to leave the Garden of Eden and travel elsewhere, searching for sustenance. They were not entirely pleased, as their subsequent legends suggested.

The setting is the southern merging of the divided Rift Valley, north of Lake Malawi. The time is 100,000 BPE (Before Present Era). It should be remembered that at this time the human species was virtually identical to what it is today, in everything except numbers, technology, and information. The culture may have been primitive, but a man of that day was just about as smart as a man of today, and just about as competent with his hands and language. Subsequent small changes in aspects of the brain were to make a big difference, however. There is some evidence that there were startlingly elegant harpoons and knives in this region at this time, but it is inconclusive; more likely these date from 50,000 years ago, matching the level elsewhere in the world. So "conventional" technology is assumed for this story.

•

It was the twentieth day of their journey south: both hands spread twice, in the gesture dialect. The end of the world was near, for ahead loomed the huge range of mountains that bordered it. If they did not find suitable land here, they would have to turn back, their mission failed.

Hero shook his head. He had said he was confident, but he wasn't.

People and tribes much like their own occupied all the territory they had traversed, and all were crowded and hungry. The drought had impoverished the entire region. None wanted newcomers hunting or foraging in their lands. They were courteous to the travelers, but made it plain: Not Here.

They were following the trading trail, which was marked by widely spaced piles of rocks and scraped earth and specially twisted trees. Travelers were allowed to hunt, forage, or fish along this route, but could be considered enemies if they strayed from it. Every so often they spied others watching them from a distance, so they knew that the restrictions would be enforced. It was bad luck to kill a traveler, for the spirits of the dead could be vengeful, but there were sharp limits to tolerance when times were tough.

Haven sniffed. "Smoke," she said. She was his sister, one year younger than he at seventeen years—three hands and two fingers—but a full-bodied woman who knew her mind. Her senses were sharp; she could spot a ripe fruit or hear an odd sound before Hero could. She was the apt forager, and that really helped on this mission.

Now he smelled it too. "A hearth," he said.

"A cooking hearth," she agreed. "We may have lodging for the night."

They moved on toward it, feeling better. They were used to traveling, but this was the end of the day, and they were tired and ready to rest. A native home could be very nice.

In due course they saw it. At the base of a southern mountain was the house, formed of poles and brush, thatched over with woven branches. The hearth was in front, its open fire licking modestly up, roasting a leg of animal.

There was a young woman by it, focusing on her cooking; her gender was made evident by her employment and her bare breasts. She had long hair, worn loose, just as Haven did, as an indication that she was unmated. But there was surely a man in the house, for lone women did not hunt large animals.

Hero cupped his hands around his mouth. "Ho!" he called.

The girl looked up. She spied them, and jumped to grab a spear, holding it defensively before her. The gesture was more to show that strangers were not trusted than to indicate any actual fighting ability. She had surely been aware of them, but preferred to pretend innocence. It was part of the protocol.

Haven opened her hide cloak, spread her arms wide and stepped forward several paces, then stopped. She was showing her gender by her own bared breasts, and offering to come in alone, unarmed. That was the main reason she had come with Hero: to facilitate lodging with families. It had worked well enough so far.

The girl paused, then beckoned with her free hand. Haven walked on in, while Hero stood where he was. He watched her go right up to the hearth and talk with the girl. Then Haven reached into her pack and brought out a small object, and gave it to the girl. That would be one of their brother Craft's wooden carvings. They were marvelously intricate curiosities, linked circles cut from a larger piece. Anyone could bend a small branch around and tie it to itself to make a ring, and link another such ring to it, but to link always-solid circles was a novelty that intrigued just about anyone. So these artifacts were another key to hospitality, for there was no one who didn't have some curiosity about oddities. That was part of what made a person human.

The two talked more, and then they embraced. They had decided to be friends. That meant that there would be comfortable company, food, and lodging for this night.

The girl faced Hero and beckoned. Haven had made him seem all right. He waved, then strode forward. He carried his spear and staff across his shoulders, sidewise, making it clear that he did not intend to use them. When he got close, he pushed the staff point into the ground so that the shaft stood up without falling. Then he leaned the spear against it, the stone head up. He was disarming himself, without throwing away the weapons. This was another part of the protocol of introduction. There was very likely a man hiding in the house, his weapon ready; only when it was quite clear that Hero had no hostile intent would that man reveal himself. The girl's father, or uncle, or brother. Girls of any group were generally not left unprotected.

Now he wished that his younger brother Keeper, named for the way he kept animals, had come along. Because Keeper had tamed a den of wolf cubs, after Hero had killed their mother. It had seemed ridiculous, the way he carried the tiny wolves home and struggled to feed them and protect them. But as the pups survived and grew, Keeper's craziness turned out to be savvy, because the little wolves did not run away; they remained with him, loyal to him alone. Now they were grown, and he was training them to help hunt. Others were amazed, but had to concede that there was something to it. Also, the wolves were very good at sniffing out strangers; they knew the smell of every member of the family, and tolerated them, but raised a clamor when any stranger approached. One of them would have let Hero know for sure whether there was an ambush in the house.

But it had seemed better for Haven to travel with him, for she could be friendly in a way the wolves would not. They were looking for cooperation, not antagonism. So this was not the place for the wolves. Haven had just demonstrated her usefulness, by successfully approaching this woman. Once they found new land, the wolves would help tame it.

Hero took the last few steps to join the girl. This close she looked young, not far into nubility, slender and pretty. She wore a short skirt of reeds, and simple sandals. Her small breasts did not sag, and the nipples were enhanced with red stain. Her face was rounded and sweet, and her hair was brown rather than black. So were her eyes. But her thighs were solid enough; she would be bearing children as soon as she took a man.

"I am Hero," he said, naming himself. "I am a hunter, and warrior at need. But now I am traveling, seeking no quarrel." He made the sign of peace, his head bowed, his hands spread empty.

The girl eyed him appraisingly. "I am Crenelle. I am three hands years and unmarried." She too augmented her speech with gestures, for her dialect differed from his and she wanted no confusion. She finished with a brief tug at her own hair, calling attention to its looseness.

Fifteen. That was about what she looked. A girl could marry when she got breasts, and usually did not wait long, especially if she was pretty. But the fact that she stated it, and her marital status, meant that she wanted similar information from him. Her lack of concern about the presence of two strangers indicated that she felt safe with them, and that in turn probably meant that protection was close by. He saw another spear leaning against the house entrance, and smelled man-odor. There was surely a man listening.

"I am three hands, three fingers years," he said, spreading his own right hand three times and adding three fingers. "Eighteen. I have no wife, and seek none at this time. I search for land for our family to occupy."

"There is none here. Only for members of our family/tribe." She smiled at him, more than passingly. "You lack interest in women?"

Now there was no doubt. She was interested in him as a prospect for marriage. "I have interest, but I must see to my family first. We are going hungry in the Lake area. The water is sinking. The game is disappearing. We must move to better territory." He gestured as he spoke, touching his crotch, his belly, making waves with his hand, and finally making a broad hand sweep to indicate spread land.

"It is not good here in the Mountain area either," Crenelle said. "The trees are dying. Game is scarce here too."

"Maybe we need to look farther," Haven said with regret.

"No, no need for that," the girl said quickly, surprising Hero. "We can manage, if we just get more rain."

Their gestures were gradually diminishing, as the concepts became more detailed and it was clear that their dialects were mutually intelligible. "If we got more rain, the lake would rise," Haven said. "The game would return. But there is never enough."

"Never enough," Crenelle agreed. "Yet the weather changes as it wishes, and maybe will change again."

Hero shrugged. "We have traveled far, and would like to return home. But I think we must go on until we find a land with enough rain."

"But you can't," the girl protested. "You come from the north. To the south is just mountains, and a big lake, and the lake folk are hostile. To the east and west are fire mountains. There is nowhere to go."

"This is bad news," Hero said with deep regret. "Perhaps I should talk with your brother."

"My brother?" She stepped from foot to foot, in place, making her loose reed skirt shift and reveal flashes of her thighs. She was trying to be seductive, and succeeding reasonably well, because they were good thighs, slender but firmly fleshed.

Hero smiled, masking his interest. "There are the possessions of a man here, and I'm sure you did not make this house yourself. I should meet with him before talking too much with you, lest he misunderstand my intention."

"My brother is away," Crenelle said. "He had to go to trade for dry fish."

"Then we should not be here. You do not wish to sleep with strangers too near."

"I think you are not strangers any more. Haven gave me a wonderful toy, and you I would like to know better." She put her hands to her belt thong, and drew up her skirt so as to show a clear flash of her crotch. It was no longer possible to doubt the nature of her interest. She was being somewhat too obvious, but had the right motions. His interest was indeed being aroused.

Hero glanced quickly at Haven, but she turned away. This was his problem to settle. So he addressed it directly. "I have just appeared here, and you offer me your skirt, knowing that I must go on elsewhere tomorrow?"

"I think you would make a good husband. If you married me, you could stay and hunt here."

"But what of my family? I have two grown brothers and two grown sisters, and younger siblings who may similarly have to find other territory."

Crenelle shook her head. "My people let only spouses remain. Haven could marry my brother Harbinger, and stay. I'm sure he will like her. She has a full body."

Haven jumped. "I'm not marrying either!"

Crenelle turned persuasive. "But then you could stay here. Your family would be free of two members, and the others could look elsewhere. That is better than failure."

She had a point. But Hero refused to desert his remaining siblings. "We are close. They would not desert me; I will not desert them. So

I thank you for your interest, but we must be moving on, with regret."

"You are generous," Crenelle said.

"Not generous," Haven corrected her. "Decent."

"Yes. I like you." She considered briefly, then shrugged, making her breasts jiggle. "If I were a year older, I could seduce you, and make you marry me."

"Surely so," Hero agreed. He was not merely humoring her; she was impressing him enough as it was, and the added flesh a year would bring would make her a beauty. "Now we must move on and find a place to camp for the night."

"No need; stay here, by the fire. I have food enough, this night, and my brother will return tomorrow with more."

"But I can't give you what you want, so should not take favors from you."

She looked at him with a new sort of appraisal. "You are a hunter—and warrior. You can use those weapons." Her glance flicked to the standing staff and spear.

"Yes. But never against a friend."

"Bring them here, and protect me. I get nervous, alone. There is a lame leopard who may attack."

That was fair enough. Normally leopards stayed clear of human settlements, but lame ones could not hunt well, and so could go after human beings in desperation. Hero walked to his staff, took it in his left hand, pulled the spear from the ground with his right hand, and returned. He set both down within reach. Meanwhile Crenelle was taking down the roast, which was now ready, and was using her stone blade to carve off chunks of meat for each of them. She also had some fermented berry juice to share. That was bound to be a pleasure.

They sat cross-legged around the hearth and ate. "This is a feast," Hero said appreciatively. "I hope there is some threat in the night, so that I can justify my presence."

"There may be a way," Crenelle said.

Aware that she had something other than the leopard in mind, he glanced at her. Her position caused the strands of the skirt to diffuse, showing aspects of her lightly furred crotch, surely by no accident. Haven was sitting similarly, but wore a loinskin that remained in place regardless of her legs. So did Hero. "A way?"

"There could be a storm, damaging the house. You could repair it."

"A storm would bring water," Haven said.

"Good luck, a blessing from the spirits," Crenelle agreed.

He realized that Crenelle had diverted his question, not telling him her true thought. But there seemed to be no harm in her, and he did like the view she was giving him, so he did not pursue it.

"How is it that your brother left you here alone?" Haven inquired.

The girl grimaced. "He didn't want to. But since our father died, we have had to make do as a family of two, and can't be together all the time. So he leaves the spear in sight, and I pretend he's here. So far there has been no trouble. But there really is a leopard, so I keep the fire burning all night."

"We would not have approached, if we had known you were alone," Hero said.

"Why not? You would have taken me for easy prey."

"We are not looking for prey. We want land to settle."

"You could have killed me and taken this land."

Hero laughed. "I doubt it, even were we so inclined."

She glanced sharply at him. "Why do you doubt?"

He answered her seriously. "Because you are young, but not defenseless, even alone. You carry a knife at your waist, you use it with flair, and the house is booby-trapped."

Her jaw dropped. "How did you know?"

"He is a good hunter, and warrior," Haven said. "He is observant."

Crenelle nodded. "The more I learn of you, the better I like you. You would be a good provider."

"I like you too," Hero said. "You are competent and clever, and you have nerve. Your body is most appealing. But I will not desert my siblings."

"And I will not desert mine," she said, flushing at the compliments. "Harbinger is all I have, and I am all he has."

Crenelle ate less than they did, and finished sooner. Then she brought out a small piece of bone. She put the end to her mouth and blew. Sound came out, high and sweet.

"You have a flute!" Haven cried, delighted.

"My brother sings and beats a drum. I play the bone. Our family likes music."

"So does ours," Hero said. "We listen when we hear it."

"Then listen." Crenelle applied her mouth to the bone, and her fingers to the holes in it, and played an appealing tune. Both Hero and Haven were enraptured; the girl was good at it. Her melody stirred something deep and vital.

As she played, she moved, swaying the upper part of her body to keep time. Her motion became more vigorous. Her breasts bounced and rippled, compelling Hero's attention. Breasts were always interesting, even small ones, but moving breasts were fascinating. Of course Crenelle intended to attract his gaze there, but he had no choice.

The combination of appearance and music and berry drink was having its effect. Hero was now pondering whether it would after all be possible to marry her. Of course he should not, yet it was easy to imagine holding her, loving her, being constantly close to her. She could be very nice to be with.

They completed their meal as dusk closed. Hero's head was pleasantly dizzy from the fermented juice. He stood, carefully. "I must urinate. Is there a safe region?"

Crenelle stood, putting away her flute. "I'll show you. Follow my tracks." She walked around the house, showing some dizziness herself. Possibly it was feigned, as she had drunk sparingly, but it added to her appeal: the suggestion that she would be amenable to anything he might have in mind, because of the juice. Such an effect was common enough.

Hero and Haven followed, staying on the path she showed. They knew that one trap would not be the limit; there would be several. By daylight they could have spied them, but it was chancy by night.

"Here," the girl said, and squatted, doing it herself.

Hero turned away, embarrassed by her openness. She was still trying to seduce him, and was having more effect than perhaps she knew. He wished he could simply sweep her into his arms and have sex with her.

Crenelle stood, and walked back toward the house. Haven went to the spot and squatted, drawing aside her loinskin. He did not look, out of courtesy, but of course he had seen her do it before. It didn't matter, with a sister. But it mattered with an unrelated young woman. Then she moved to the house, leaving Hero to manage his half-erect state alone. Haven well understood what was occurring, but had the grace to pretend ignorance. She had seen him similarly embarrassed before, but was discreet.

He managed, in due course, and went to the house. The two girls were entering it, stepping on one side of the threshold. Hero removed his pack, brought out his cloakskin, and lay down beside the dying fire, his staff and spear beside him.

But before he could sleep, a figure emerged from the house. Darkness was closing, but he knew by the sound and smell that it was Crenelle, not Haven. Uncertain of her mission, he lay still, with his eyes closed.

She came to stand almost over him. "I could club you where you lie," she murmured disdainfully.

His hand moved too swiftly for her to escape. He clasped her ankle. "I doubt it. You don't have a club."

She neither moved nor screamed. "So you are alert. I like that."

He slid his hand up to squeeze her calf, smiling. He opened his eyes, peering up under her skirt. "And I like that."

"Like what?" she demanded, not trying to free her leg.

"That you do not spook frivolously. It could be dangerous, in the wrong circumstance."

"Is that all you like?"

"No. But I told you, I am not seeking a wife." He let go of her calf and averted his gaze. The two actions required more willpower than he cared to admit, especially since he knew she sought neither.

She squatted, one knee projecting over his head. He couldn't keep his gaze clear. The flickering firelight illuminated her inner thigh. She was showing him, again, while pretending to be unaware of it. That enhanced the effect, for secret glimpses had more power than open ones. "I could be good for you."

He sighed, with mock dismay. He was enjoying the game, despite its pointlessness. "You will not let me sleep until you argue the case?"

"If I let you sleep, you will depart in the morning, and I will never see you again."

"Then lie under my blanket and let me feel your body, and I will listen as long as you wish."

He had thought she might demur, but she did not. She stretched out beside him and tugged the cloak across to cover her. But it was not wide enough; the other side slid off his body.

She paused, lifting her head. "You do understand that if you take me, you marry me. I am not offering myself to you, I am only sharing your blanket."

"Yes. In our tribe, a man must marry the woman he takes, if she wishes it."

"Good." She rolled to her side, came up against him, and reached down to spread the cloak so as to cover them both.

He rolled similarly, so that they were facing each other, and reached over to put his right hand against her back. He clasped her, so that neither of them was at risk of falling away. Her left hand rested on his thigh, and her breasts pressed against him as she breathed. He was of course aroused, and she was aware of that. But he made no further motion. She had said she was not inviting sex; he had to honor that.

"My brother won't marry until I do, though he is two years older," she said after a pause. "He wants to be sure I am provided for."

"But he could still provide for you, if he married."

"His wife could make me leave. So he wants me married well before he does. He is handsome; he could steal the prettiest girl, and she wouldn't scream."

"Why would she scream?"

"Some girls don't like getting raped."

"Raped! I thought you were speaking of marriage."

Her hand slid down inside his loinskin to cup his buttock. "You can do the same, you know."

"I would never rape anyone!"

She laughed, which struck him as an odd reaction. "I mean your hand. You may touch me where I touch you."

Oh. He slid his hand down her back until his fingers reached the curvatures of her warm bottom. The reed skirt offered no barrier. The flesh was tight and muscular, but also fuller than his own; she was definitely a woman. His desire for her magnified, but he limited himself to stroking her gently. "What is this about rape?"

"It must be different in your tribe. In ours, a man chooses a girl he likes, catches her alone, steals her, and rapes her. Then her family must give her to him in marriage."

"I should think they would kill him."

"No. Then she would be a widow, and unable to marry again for a year. They wouldn't like that."

"But don't they protect her from rape?"

"Yes, if they don't like the man. But if they like him, they make her go out alone so he can get her. If she likes him, she doesn't scream much. For my brother, there are several who would not scream at all. So I am a hindrance; if I don't marry soon he will lose the best of them, because they won't wait long."

Hero was appalled, but also intrigued. "Suppose the wrong man steals a girl? One her family doesn't like?"

She smiled. "Sometimes it is not easy for her to arrange to be where the one she wants can get her, instead of where the one her family wants can do it. But if she manages, then they have to accept him."

"I mean one nobody likes. A stranger, or bad man, who comes upon her unaware."

"One from another tribe," she clarified. "He must get her all the way to his tribe, where his kin can protect him, before her kin catch him. Or he can rape her immediately, and hope that they prefer to have her married than widowed. If they decide to let him have her, but remain angry, they might have one of their men rape his sister and flee without marrying her. If her kin don't know who the man is, there's not much they can do. So it's a good vengeance."

"Don't any girls marry for love?"

"Oh, yes, of course, when they get the right man. But when their families choose someone else, and watch her closely, what can she do? I have a friend, and she wouldn't go out alone when the man her family wanted was near, so he came into her house and raped her there, and none of her family heard her screams, they said. Now she is with child."

Hero considered. "We do not practice rape. Not for marriage. We punish it by killing the man, or cutting off his penis. But neither do girls always get to choose their own. Their fathers or brothers may decide. Sometimes they will choose a man the girl likes, sometimes not. But there is no violence."

"Suppose she marries unwillingly, and resists her husband?"

"She wouldn't. He has the right."

"But if she hates him, and fights him?"

He saw her point. "Then perhaps you could call it rape."

"So you are not so different from us. You just phrase it differently."

"Still, I would not. I would not marry a girl who didn't want me, and would not force her, ever."

"Would you beat her, to make her amenable?"

"No!"

She squeezed his buttock. "I like you better yet. But I would never give you cause to beat me."

He knew he should send her back to the house, before she tempted him beyond endurance. But it was difficult to give up the pleasure of her proximity, and he remained curious about her culture. "Suppose I took you, not raping you, just doing it because you were willing? That would not be rape. Would I not have to marry you?"

"You can't take me willingly. I am a virgin."

He ran his fingers into the crevice between her buttocks, feeling the heat and wetness there. "You desire me, as I desire you. If I asked, and you agreed—"

"I will not agree. You must rape me."

"I will not rape you! And I don't mean to marry you. But you are doing your best to get me into you. I don't believe you are unwilling."

She moved her hand around inside his loinskin, to the front, and found his erect member. She clasped it, clearly having no fear of it. "I want you. I want this hot stick in me. But I will not give you leave. You can overpower me and do it, but I will fight you."

She was astonishingly candid. He tried to be the same. "You have made me mad with desire for you. But I will never force a woman."

"You must rape me. There is no other way."

This had gone more than far enough. "Then return to your house now."

"No. I love it in your strong embrace."

"Then I will go elsewhere, leaving you here by the fire."

"I will go with you."

"No." He flung off the cloak and sat up, dragging free of her hand.

"Yes. You can't keep me away."

"Yes I can," he said, getting to his feet.

She got up with him, and put her arms around him. "No you can't."

"Yes I can. Now go, before I—" But he couldn't finish, for she was kissing his neck.

"What are you going to do?" she inquired slyly after a moment. "Beat me?"

"You are trying to drive me to violence," he exclaimed.

"Yes, this first time. After this there will be no need, for we will be married."

He realized that there was more to this trap than he had supposed. She was trying to seduce him by temptation or violence, and either would do the job. He needed to proceed carefully, avoiding either extreme.

He took up his staff and spear and began walking away from the house, uncertain where he was going, but needing to go somewhere. The darkness beyond the dying fire offered some comfort. She went with him, staying very close.

"Isn't this like rape, what you are trying to do?" he demanded. "To trap me into marrying you when I don't want to?"

"Yes. Sometimes that is the way of it."

"You mean that girls get men to marry them involuntarily?"

"Yes. When a girl wants a man, and he doesn't want her, if she can get him alone she can say he raped her, and then he has to marry her."

The aspects of this culture continued to be intriguing and, to a degree, frightening. "But can't someone—her mother, perhaps—examine her, and know it isn't true?"

She held up something. "Feel this."

He reached across and touched the dark object she held. It was the bone handle of her knife, rounded to fit her hand. "What of it?"

"With this, a girl can quickly stop being a virgin. She can also bruise her face and body."

And who would believe the man's innocence? "I see that girls are not defenseless, any more than your house is."

"It is true we have ways. But we seldom need them."

"You would do this to me? Knowing that I wish you no harm?"

"I will be good for you, Hero," she pleaded. "I know how to forage and keep a house. I will play music for you, and kiss you and part my legs for you whenever you want it. You will never be ashamed of me."

"Except that I am trying to help my family. I can't settle down until they are secure. Just as your brother can't settle until he knows you are placed."

She suddenly stopped walking. He paused, turning back to her. "Are you all right, Crenelle?"

"Go, before I change my mind," she said tightly. "Go."

"You are letting me go?" he asked, stupidly amazed.

"Get away from me!" There was a catch in her voice.

He remained nonplussed. "Are you crying?"

"You fish-brain! Tears are a weapon too. Get away from me now, or I will have you forever."

It was the truth. But he could not do it. "It is not safe for you out here alone. Come back to the house."

"You are too stupid to save yourself!" she cried. "So I must save you." She ran to the side, into the darkness.

He pursued her, moved by her flash of decency. He had made an analogy with her brother, and it was clear that she truly loved her brother. "Crenelle, wait!"

"Oh!" He heard her fall. She had tripped over something.

He caught up to her, and knelt beside her, dropping his weapons. "Are you hurt?"

"Don't try to comfort me. I can't save you from yourself."

He ran his hands over her body, feeling for injuries. She seemed to be all right. "We must go back to the house."

She caught his head in her hands and hauled it in to her face. She kissed him savagely. His head reeled, and his desire for her became overwhelming. They fell back to the ground, tangled together. Then she thrust his face away. "This is your last chance," she gasped. "Get away from me before you succumb. You know I can make you do it."

"I know. But maybe it would be worth it."

She slapped him. "Get away, get away, you utter fool!"

He caught her hands. "Please, Crenelle!"

"I'll scream."

Suddenly it came together in another way, and he started laughing, helplessly, still holding her beneath him.

"What is the matter with you?" she demanded. "You're about to rape me for real, destroying your commitment to your family, and you laugh?"

"That's what's so funny. You have goaded me into truly raping you—and you're trying to stop me, though it's what you want."

She relaxed, laughing herself. "You're right. This is weird. But you know you shouldn't do it. Now I'll give you a count of ten fingers to let go of me, before I kiss you again and rip off your loinskin and wrap my legs around you. This is truly my last warning. One. Two. Three. Four."

But then she paused, and so did he. For they both heard something else. In sudden silence, they listened.

It was the sound of something bounding through the brush toward them. It was an animal, a large one.

There was a snarl. "The leopard!" Crenelle cried, horrified.

Hero let go of her and grabbed for his weapons. "Stay down and quiet," he said. "I'll stop it."

She didn't argue. She went still and silent. He stood over her, his spear poised in his right hand, his staff in his left. He tracked the leopard by sound alone, and this was good enough, for he was experienced in night hunting as well as day hunting. He braced to meet the onslaught.

The creature sprang—and Hero thrust with his spear, going for the head. He felt the impact, but it wasn't right; he had caught skin rather than mouth.

The body came up against the staff, which Hero held crosswise before him, defensively. The impact shoved him back, and he fell, the leopard on top. But he shoved forward and up with the staff, pushing the cat back. He had to stop the teeth and claws from scoring.

Then the creature jerked away, dragging the spear. It fled. It had been looking for an easy kill, not this complicated fight.

"It's gone," Hero said. "Are you all right?"

Crenelle stirred. "Yes. You saved me."

"I saved myself! I shoved it off, and it ran on."

"It would have killed me," she said, shaking.

He put his arm around her shoulders. "I had to pay for my food and lodging. I agreed to protect you."

She was silent, and he knew she was crying. He drew her in to his shoulder.

"Don't comfort me!" she flared. "You know what will happen."

He nodded in the darkness. "I think I wouldn't mind marrying you, Crenelle. You have courage and good reflexes."

"I lay on the ground, terrified, and now I'm crying. That's not courage or good."

"It *is* good. You did what I told you, so I could fight it without you getting in the way. I needed to know exactly where you were, in the darkness, so I wouldn't hit you. You didn't panic. Now it's done, and it's time to react."

"If I had been alone, I'd be dead."

"If you had been alone, you wouldn't have gone out from your house."

"You're a decent man. I do want to marry you. But I have to let you see to your family."

"And you are a decent woman. You tried to protect me from myself, after you won our contest of wills. I appreciate that. Now I desire you more than before. It's not just your body; your music reached me first."

"But that's part of it. You know that."

He nodded in the darkness. "You tried to impress me, and you succeeded. I think you are as good a woman as I am likely to find. I think there is a way. Would you leave your home and join my family?"

Her head snapped up. "Yes!"

"Then maybe I will marry you."

"Will you rape me?"

"No."

"But you have to, or there is no marriage."

He hesitated, his desire for her burgeoning again. "Can't we just . . . just say I did it?"

"No!"

"But you were ready to rape yourself, and accuse me. Why not accuse me without violence?"

"I can't do that now. I owe you my life."

"Then repay me by marrying me without violence."

"I would like to, but it wouldn't be real."

He remembered something else she had said. "But you are a virgin. If I have sex with you, it's rape by your definition, isn't it?"

She brightened. "Yes."

"Then let's do it."

"Yes," she said gladly.

He stood and removed his loinskin, and she removed her skirt. They lay together on the ground. She kissed him ardently and wrapped her legs around him. Her body was hot and eager.

But when he sought to enter her, she fought him. "No!"

He stopped immediately. "I'm sorry. I thought—"

"Do it!"

He started to enter again, but again she struggled. "I don't understand."

"I have to fight you, the first time. I can't help it. That's the way it has to be."

"But then I can't do it."

"Please try, Hero. I think I love you already."

"But it's just not in my nature to do anything like that to a woman."

She considered. "Give me your hand."

He shifted his balance and held up his right hand. She grasped his wrist with her left hand. "Make a fist."

He made a fist. Then she shoved his hand violently into her face.

"Crenelle!" he cried, drawing his hand back and opening it. "What is this?"

"Do it!" she repeated. "Now you have hit me. Now I will scream. But you anticipate that, and—" She jammed his open hand across her mouth.

At last he caught on. He was stopping her from screaming.

He sought a third time to enter her, but the position had changed and he was not aligned. This time her right hand grasped his member and corrected its course. He started to thrust, and she let go and lunged to meet him, as if struggling to free herself. She twisted, and her right hand came around and up to scratch his back. Then her fingers caught his hair and yanked his face down to meet hers. She kissed him savagely, her interior muscles clenching.

He pulsed inside her, transported. He had done it. She had actually done most of it for him, but perhaps it counted.

They relaxed together. "And never again will I resist you," she murmured in his ear.

"Never again will I force you," he said. He suppressed a foolish laugh.

"We are married."

He hesitated. "Crenelle, this is not the way I—"

She cut him off with another kiss. "It is the way we do it."

In due course they disengaged, got up, dressed, and made their way back to the house. Haven was standing by the fire, which she had built up to flare more brightly. "What happened?"

"He raped me," Crenelle said.

Haven stared at her. "He what?"

"He threw me down and hit me and stifled my scream. I couldn't stop him."

Haven looked at Hero. He averted his gaze. She knew that he would never force a woman, but she didn't understand what was going on.

"I tried to fight. See, I scratched his back." Crenelle pointed to the place she had scraped him.

"So what does this mean?" Haven asked cautiously.

"So now we're married," Crenelle concluded.

Haven looked again at Hero. This time he had to speak. "She says she will join our family, and help us look for good land."

"But what of your brother?" Haven asked.

"Now he can rape his own woman, and bring her here. Before someone else gets her. There is one who wants him. She has held out about as long as she can, hoping he'd come. Now he will. They should be happy."

"That's nice," Haven said noncommittally. "Now we need to get some sleep."

"Now you can join me inside," Crenelle said to Hero. "It's more comfortable there."

"I can sleep outside," Haven said.

"No, you can be in with us. If you don't mind what we do."

Haven looked once more at her brother. Hero shrugged. She knew about sex, and was figuring out that Crenelle was not an unwilling partner. "Is there anything else I should know?"

"He also saved my life," the girl said.

Haven's lips quirked. "That too?"

"Yes. From the leopard. He fought it and drove it off. Just before he raped me."

She kept insisting on the rape, and that kept restoring his doubt. He was willing to marry her, but not to do it by a lie.

Haven nodded. "He is thoughtful about things like that."

They went inside, and Hero joined Crenelle on her mat. He had thought to sleep, but she embraced him and kissed him repeatedly, and summoned his desire again. This time she made no mock resistance. She was showing him all that she had to offer, to solidify his resolve to marry her.

It turned out to be a long night, for Crenelle was endlessly ardent. But Hero didn't mind it at all. At last she tired, and remained asleep, and he was able to sleep too.

In the morning Haven was up first, tending the fire. Hero got up and went out to urinate, leaving Crenelle sleeping. He was somewhat bemused by his new state of companionship, but not regretful. Crenelle had excited more than his passion; he believed that she would be a good wife. But the idea of calling it rape repelled him.

"You didn't really rape her," Haven murmured as he joined her by the fire. "You wouldn't, and anyway, no victim would be that passionate."

"Her culture requires rape, so we played at it," he said. "But we must not say that openly."

"She seems competent. But you know it's not binding by our culture. What made you decide to have sex with her?"

"She wanted me so much, it made me want her. And she does have a good body."

"I saw her showing you her cleft. I know that's pretty exciting for you." She was alluding to an episode with another girl, who had exposed her genital region and let him penetrate her while others watched, in a kind of game. She was right: even as a game, it was immensely compelling. Women might mock the reactions of men, but the reactions were nevertheless real, and women took free advantage of them to get their way. Women never showed more than they were prepared to have touched, because of the force of male reactions. "Well, go and have at it again, before we have to travel."

"But I don't know if I should marry her. How could I let our people think I raped her?"

Haven pursed her lips. "I see the problem. Maybe she'll agree to shut up about that aspect."

"I'm not sure. She's very insistent."

"Well in any event, you can have her now without rape. You had better do it, lest you lose the chance."

He smiled, and went inside. Crenelle was stirring. He lay down beside her and stroked her flung hair.

"I was afraid you would run away and desert me," she said. "I know you have doubts."

"Not without telling you."

"You didn't come back just for more sex?"

He was embarrassed. "Not just for that."

She laughed. "Take it."

He did, half afraid she would protest or resist, but she was fully cooperative. She had evidently meant it when she promised never to resist him again.

"West," she said as she embraced him. "Across the mountains and the lakes. I have heard there is land there that no one occupies. Wide land, so far across that no one knows its end. Much game. I know a route."

That was not what she had said before. But he could not blame her for not telling everything to strangers. "How can you know it, if you haven't traveled?"

"My father went there once, and told us all about it. I know I can guide you there."

His passion was spent, but something new was rising in him. "Thank you, Crenelle," he said, kissing her again.

"Well, I said I would be good for you."

She had indeed. "But this business of saying it was rape—"

"You and I know the truth, Hero. Does it matter what others think?"

"Why not let them think there was no rape, then?"

She shook her head. "Please, Hero. My people will not recognize it as marriage otherwise. They will say I wantonly wasted myself, and am unfit for marriage."

He appreciated her point, but still could not admit to the lie. She had indeed been somewhat wanton, but it was in her effort to persuade him to marry her.

They went outside, where they ate more of the roast. Then Crenelle prepared to go. "I will leave a message for my brother," she said. "So he will know."

"A message?"

She went inside, and emerged with two cunningly made doll figures. One was male, with a little stick for a penis; the other was female. She set them together, facing each other, and looped a length of tendon around them so that they would stay that way. She arranged them so that the male doll's arms were clasping the other close, while the female's arms were stretched out at wild angles, as if helpless to defend herself. She laid them on her mat. That seemed clear enough.

But it reminded him once again of the lie. "Crenelle, I can't—"

Crenelle faced him, her face crumpling. She was going to cry, and he couldn't stand that, as she surely knew. But this, too, was effective even when understood as a ploy. Yet how could he face his brothers Craft and Keeper, or his fiery sister Rebel, if he confessed to raping a woman?

Haven interceded. "Can you tell your people it was rape, and we tell our people it was not? If you come with us now, Crenelle, our people and yours will not meet."

Crenelle considered. "I suppose so. For a marriage this good. If Hero agrees."

They turned to Hero, awaiting his decision. He had no idea what to say.

•

The twin engines driving the migrations of mankind were surely population and climate. When folk found a good location, such as the fertile basin of the Lake Victoria region, they were fruitful and multiplied, filling their ecological niche. Then the climate would change, making their homeland less fertile while promoting other regions. The people had to move or starve, as their homelands could no longer support them. First they spread all over Africa, then across the rest of the world. Their exact routes across Africa are unknown, and probably there were many migrations over the millennia crisscrossing given territories. Most of the species remained in Africa; there is more human genetic diversity there than in all the rest of the world.

Mankind was considered to have been a hunter/gatherer for most of his existence. But this did not necessarily mean that he lacked houses. It would have been more comfortable to sleep in a covered, protected place, and to have supplies there for convenient use. Such structures might have been dismantled and moved to new sites periodically, or simply allowed to deteriorate when deserted, so that only the hearths would remain for archaeologists to find. It is also possible that most tribesmen traveled, while some remained in houses. We just don't know.

Did any cultures practice rape as a mechanism for marriage? They surely did, because some do today. Yes, we frown on it, as we do on sex with fifteen-year-old girls, but in the past nubility was the signal for sexual availability, regardless of the girl's preference. We try to impose a veneer of modesty and caution, but teen girls are still getting pregnant.

The place of music in human development is largely unknown, because sound leaves no fossils. But a 60,000-year-old bone flute was found in southeast Europe in 1995, suggesting that music was indeed part of mankind's heritage. There may have been many other musical instruments that left no traces because they were made of wood or leather. It is conjectured that music and language are closely connected, and the continuing popularity of songs of all kinds endorses this. Music may be one of the ways men can impress women, leading to sexual selection for it, but surely women can also impress men with it, especially when they dance to it. As described in a prior GEODYSSEY *novel, the arts, especially music, probably enabled larger groups of people to assemble peacefully, contributing to tribal strength. But it surely started on the individual and couple level, facilitating relationships, as shown here.*

2

HAVEN'S CURSE

One mystery is why modern mankind, having emerged from Africa to Asia Minor circa 100,000 BPE, took so long to move on into Europe, as well as remained relatively primitive in technology. The answer is probably that southern Asia was far more inviting, being warmer and closer to the African climate in which the species had evolved. Europe was cold and forbidding, and was already occupied by a formidable competitive species, Neandertal man. So the advanced mainstream human culture proceeded eastward. (Another answer is discussed in the afternote.) But there were some contacts to the north.

The prior novels of this series followed one or more characters through history, their seeming reincarnations similar in description and relationships. This novel differs in one respect: while the relationships of five siblings to each other remain constant, their connections outside the family differ. They are not really the same people, but descendants many generations removed. They may make fundamentally different decisions at the critical turning points. It is as if reality is played over, so that alternate bypaths may be explored. Thus a person who marries in one chapter may not be married in another, depending on a key decision. Or one who is undecided in one chapter may, by this device, get to live through the consequences of each side of a decision. The differences, as time passes, may become formidable.

The setting is southern Anatolia. The time is circa 74,000 BPE, not long after a savage global winter decimated human and animal populations.

•

Haven drew her fur hood closer about her face and forged on into the increasingly chill terrain. Her companion did the same. After Hero's journey south had failed to find good, unoccupied land, Haven had decided to try a trip of her own, to the north. Hero, discouraged, did not come; instead it was her younger brother Craft who accompanied her. Craft lacked the power and expertise of the hunter and warrior, but had other assets. Actually he knew more about tools and weapons than others were likely to realize, because he focused on learning how to make them. In order to make them well, he had to know how to use them. But he preferred to pretend that he was no warrior, and indeed he was not, emotionally.

They had been warned against coming here, and the warning seemed well taken. It had been cool at home in the fall; here in the northern mountains it was cold. They had found nothing worthwhile; all the good hunting and foraging ranges were already occupied. Their only hope was to get beyond human habitation and find open land beyond—perhaps on the other side of these mountains.

But crossing the mountains was not proving to be easy. There was already snow on them, and they were not properly prepared. The two of them had bundled up as much as they could, but remained cold, especially in the feet. They would have to find warm shelter for the night, or they would be in serious trouble. She was almost sorry she was traveling with Craft instead of with Keeper, because Keeper would have brought his tame wolves, and they liked to curl up and sleep next to her feet, keeping them warm. But out here in new country it was too dangerous for the wolves, because other hunters would not know they were tame. Wild wolves never came within a spear-throw of a person, but the tame ones did.

Then she saw smoke. That meant a house. Where there was one residence, there might be another. They should be able to make a deal for food and shelter this night. It was a great relief, because they had passed a number of ruined homesites, some with the bones of their former occupants scattered around. No mystery what had happened: they had starved to death in the terrible winter. Few people remained, and few animals. All had suffered horrendously.

They trudged toward the smoke. Sure enough, there was a stone and wooden structure, with a hearth in front. With luck, a friendly family lived there.

A man emerged as they approached. He was shrouded in furs, but looked tall and handsome.

"Hail!" Haven called. "Can we trade for shelter?"

The man didn't answer. He just stood and gazed at them. He held a spear ready.

Haven realized that the man might think they were enemies coming to attack. Strangers were always a gamble, and not to be trusted until something was known about them. The best way to satisfy him that they weren't dangerous was to reveal her gender. So she stopped, and drew open her fur cloak to show the mounds of her breasts under the skin vest. She inhaled. "I'm a woman. I mean no harm. My brother and I need shelter for the night."

The man looked. He nodded. In the widely scattered enclaves of their species, young women were a universal currency. A man would gamble to obtain access to a woman in ways he would not for other purposes.

They resumed motion. They came to the hearth, where the radiating heat was wonderful. Haven put her hands out to it. "Thank you! We're freezing."

The man turned and opened the bound-sticks door of his house. They ducked their heads and entered. It was dark and close inside, but warm from the fire. What a relief!

The man followed them in. He dug into a crevice and brought out sections of smoked meat. He handed them across as Haven's eyes adjusted to the wan light. She found a place to sit down, and Craft sat beside her. Then the man squatted opposite them.

They removed their packs, which were hide bags slung over their shoulders, containing their traveling belongings. That was one of the things Craft did: he made superior packs, facilitating transport of tools and food. "I am Haven," she said by way of introduction. "This is my brother Craft. We are looking for land for our siblings to occupy."

The man said something, but she couldn't make it out. Craft caught on, though. "It's a foreign dialect. He doesn't speak our language."

Oh. She should have realized. They were in the hinterlands, far from her tribe. But that was the point: they were looking for unoccupied land they could take over. Hunting and gathering required a wide range, so that the animals and edible plants did not become even scarcer. She had known that distant tribes did not speak the same language; she just hadn't thought of it. Actually the tribes were largely defunct; this would be a surviving remnant.

She tried again, this time augmenting her words by gestures. "Me Haven." She tapped her breast. "Me woman." She tapped Craft on the shoulder. "Craft. Brother."

The man tapped his chest. He repeated what he had said before. Haven still couldn't make it out. So she repeated the closest word it might be. "Harbinger? Your name?"

He nodded. Whether his understanding was the same as hers was doubtful, but it would have to do. She would call him Harbinger, hoping that he was indeed the herald of good news.

She glanced at Craft. "We should pay for our lodging."

He nodded, and dug into his pack. He brought out one of his carvings, three wood circles, linked, and proffered it to Harbinger. The man took it and studied it, curious in the way any person was who first encountered such a novelty. Then he shrugged and handed it back.

"But it is for you," Craft said, gesturing.

The man shook his head. "Naa."

"He doesn't understand," Haven said. "Maybe when we work out some mutual vocabulary."

So Craft put it away. Haven tried to engage Harbinger in conversation, pointing to things, asking their names, saying the names she knew for them. But the man seemed not much interested. He abruptly got up and pushed outside.

Surprised, Haven got up to follow him, but he gestured her back, glancing at Craft. So Craft got up and went out. Harbinger picked up the last few sticks of dry wood and set them carefully on the fire. Then he set off briskly along a path toward a distant forest.

"More wood," Haven said. "Help him fetch more wood."

Craft nodded and followed the man. She stood just inside the doorway, peering out between the spaces between branches, until they were out of sight. Maybe Harbinger had understood, but wanted help with the wood rather than a novelty item. It was true that they needed heat, for the coming evening promised to be cruelly cold.

She took advantage of her time alone to go out to urinate. There was a path to a place not far behind the house that was plainly used for such functions. She opened her cloak, drew aside her loose loinskin, squatted, then scraped some dirt over the spot. There was no point in advertising her personal odor to the local animals, who could be as desperately hungry as the people. She returned to the house.

In due course the two men returned, bearing armfuls of gathered branches. The branches were of different sizes, ranging from twigs to substantial pieces. Some were firm, some dry-rotted. So they had had to forage for them, ranging across an area. A necessary chore for a night's fire.

They dropped their loads next to the hearth. "I'll get more," Craft said, and walked back down the path. He had found a way to be truly useful.

Harbinger nodded, and built up the fire further. Then he entered the house, opening his fur cloak. Haven stepped back from the door and sat down so as to be out of his way. He closed the door behind him, and secured it firmly with a connected thong.

"But Craft will need to get in," Haven said.

The man just shrugged, standing there.

He still didn't understand her. So she tried it again, with gestures. "Brother. Craft. Door."

Harbinger nodded. "Craft. Wood."

"Yes. We wouldn't want to lock him out." She smiled, to indicate that this was humor, though she knew he would not follow the words.

Harbinger lurched forward, crashing into her. One hand pressed against her shoulder, bearing her back and down, while the other caught at her cloak, opening it. He must have fallen. She tried to help him get his support.

Then his face was on hers, for a rough kiss. His chest pressed against hers, pinning her. She felt a hand at her groin, pushing the material roughly aside.

Suddenly she realized what was happening. "No!" she cried. But it was already too late. She tried to push him back, and couldn't; he had her locked in place. She turned her face away, but that was a useless gesture, as it was not his primary focus.

His firm member found its lodging and pressed hard. She tried to kick her legs, to get out from under, but all that did was spread them wider, opening the access. Her struggles were only facilitating the dread process. The member shoved on into her, stage by stage as her struggles shifted her posture, painfully distending the channel, until the thing seemed impossibly deep. Almost instantly she felt it pulsing in the center of her body, filling her with its hot fluid. She could do nothing to prevent it. The deed was already done. She had known that this sort of thing happened, but never imagined that it could be so fast.

She relaxed, realizing the futility of further resistance. She had been raped, and that could not be undone. She waited while he faded and subsided and diminished, like a storm abating. She neither moved nor spoke.

Harbinger rolled off her and lay there, breathing heavily, not even trying to cover up his spent groin.

Stunned by the suddenness and force of it, she couldn't even cry. Instead she asked a stupid question: "Why? Why did you do this to me?" But the answer was obvious: because she was there. He had caught her alone, so he had indulged his desire.

She knew from her brothers that men were always yearning for sex. She had seen them get erections, even as children. They didn't care what she saw, because she was only their sister, and they were candid about their fascination with the subject. They let her see them masturbate, spurting onto the ground, but said that wasn't enough. Usually they tried to persuade the better-looking young women of other families to provide sex for them, and sometimes one did encounter an amenable young female.

Haven had watched once when Hero won a youthful game of penalties with a bored neighbor girl, and she had simply hoisted her cloak clear and gotten down on hands and knees, her nascent breasts assuming greater volume, her buttocks thinning and spreading apart. She had let him wedge his stiff member into her cleft from behind, teasing him all the while about his supposed inability to satisfy her. "Can't you get in any deeper that that, little stick?" It was clear that the maneuver was far more meaningful to him than to the girl, who had done it with others before. Indeed, she was happy to have the other youths watch, so they could see how little it mattered. She said she didn't see the point in it, because as soon as a boy got hard enough to get into her, he got soft again.

She was right; in moments Hero had to pull out, his member diminished. He looked embarrassed. The girl accepted it when she lost a game, because she could get good things when she won. Boys were foolish enough to bet good possessions against this brief silly indulgence, so to the girl the games were worth it. And, Haven suspected, she liked showing off her ability to do an adult act, awing her audience, male and female. To prove her superiority over any boy, by letting him do his utmost and seeing it leave her indifferent. By taking in the whole of his proudest aspect, in effect making it hers, leaving it spent and limp. Haven was indeed awed, never having realized that it was possible for a boy's big stiffened member to get all the way inside that small opening. But there was no doubt of it now.

Nevertheless Haven, though intrigued by what she saw, refused to make bets of that nature, because she didn't want to have to bare her bottom to anyone. The girl assured her that it didn't hurt, except for the first time, and sometimes felt slightly good, though she wouldn't tell a boy that. There was a sense of power in outlasting a boy, draining his potency from him.

So that was voluntary, but Haven knew that on occasion a man just took it, when he had the chance. She had been a fool not to anticipate something like this. At least she had known that it didn't last long, so the unpleasantness was brief.

Harbinger surprised her again. He propped himself on an elbow, reached out, and took her near hand. He brought it to his mouth and kissed it.

"You pretend this was an act of love?" she demanded, appalled.

His gaze met hers. Her outrage surely showed. He let go of her hand and looked away.

He had gotten what he wanted, and now he was sorry? That was hardly sufficient. But what could she do? If she made too much of a fuss, he might simply beat her up. That would hurt her a lot more than this had.

There was a sound outside. Craft was returning with more wood. Haven hastily pulled her loinskin back into place and sat up, wrapping the cloak about her. Harbinger watched her, then did the same. If she wanted to keep it secret, he was amenable. He got up and went to unwind the tendon, opening the door. He stepped outside.

Haven had a moment to herself. She reached down to check her cleft. She was raw, but not actually bleeding. She was wet, from his essence. She wiped that out as well as she could with the hem of her robe, then wiped the hem on the ground. She was in reasonably good repair.

Harbinger and Craft entered the house and settled into their places. Haven wanted to say something, to tell her brother what had happened, but she didn't. She wasn't sure how he would react. He was sixteen, and desired women, but would not countenance rape. But he was of slender build, no fighter; if he attacked Harbinger, he could get killed. Unless he paused to consider, and used one of his special weapons; then he might kill the other, and be sickened by it. So it was better to leave him out of it.

They settled down to sleep. The men were soon snoring, but Haven remained tense. How had this happened, and what was she to do now? Had she invited it by her foolishness? She had showed Harbinger her breasts, masked by the vest, making clear her gender. Could he have thought she was offering sex for lodging? But he hadn't asked, he had attacked.

Yet why hadn't she screamed? She could at least have done that. But she hadn't. He might have stopped, if she had screamed. She should have. But she hadn't thought of it in time. Her silence suggested that she wanted it, like the girl who liked the feel of a member in her, but pretended it was nothing. Was Haven a similar tease? Maybe the man had been led on by her seeming acquiescence, and been overcome by desire, and just had to do it.

Hero had said that sex had been like a great thunderclap of joy coming from his penis and spreading to the rest of him. He thought there was something inside the girl that filled him to bursting with pleasure. Maybe she didn't like it because she felt the pleasure being taken away from her body.

Certainly Haven had had no joy of this union, while Harbinger obviously had. The woman gave it to the man. If she hadn't wanted to, why hadn't she screamed? She shouldn't have had to think of it; she should have done it automatically. Why had she spread her legs instead of pulling them together? Had she really been making mistakes, or only pretending to? She wished she could talk with her sister Rebel, who was two years younger, but surprisingly knowledgeable about certain things.

She gazed in Harbinger's direction, though it was now too dark to see him. He had acted as if he liked her. He had kissed her hand. He thought she had given sex to him as a gift for the lodging. Could he be blamed? Maybe she *had* given it. Maybe she had pretended to herself that she didn't want it, but had really offered it to him, by showing her breasts and getting alone with him and not screaming. Because she knew how much pleasure she could give him, to make him glad they were here, so he wouldn't send them back out into the cold night. All she had to do was flip up her cloak and bare her bottom, as it were. Not much trouble at all, very soon over. So it was her fault.

Settled on that, at last, she relaxed again. Now the tears came, silently, copiously. She had crossed a boundary, and could never cross back, even if she never saw Harbinger again. Would it have been better to play the game with neighbor boys, and let them go into her, so she knew how it felt, so that she had nothing remaining to lose? What had she lost, really? She didn't know. But still she cried. Maybe she had done it on purpose, but now she felt the burgeoning grief of it. She had done wrong; she knew it, even if there was no rationale. The guilt of it suffused her, and overflowed from her eyes.

She woke several times in the night, her face wet. But by morning she had run out of tears. She had done what she had done, and it was done, and she and Craft would go on, hoping to find land for the family. For the two of them, and Hero, Rebel, and Keeper. That would be the end of this significant night.

Then she woke to full daylight, and both men were gone. She had finally slept soundly. But they had to get moving, so as to be somewhere good before the next night, for this region was inhospitable.

She got up, and felt the ache in her cleft. But that would heal. She went out, and the air was much colder. She went to the refuse place and squatted, checking herself more carefully. There was no doubt she had been raped; she had not dreamed it. But she wanted to get well away from here, so as to be able to bury the memory and her guilt.

She returned to the fire, which was blazing well. The warmth was wonderful. Soon the men returned, with more wood. Harbinger brought out the last of his stored meat and shared it with them, to eat at the flame.

"He doesn't have much," Craft said. "After this he'll go hungry. There's no game here at this season."

"He told you this?"

"No. I observed. It won't be good for us out there, either. I think we should stay and help him. We know some things he doesn't, about making a house secure. Together maybe we can get through the storm."

"Storm?"

"He signaled a storm. I believe him. The signs are there."

"But we can't stay!"

"Why not?"

She couldn't answer. Not without giving away her secret. Yet if they remained here, for even a few days, she would have to give Harbinger more sex. That was the price of shelter. She had done it once; he would expect it again. Boys did. It was a natural belief, on his part.

It was soon evident that the storm was indeed coming. It was looming from the northwest, over the range of mountains.

"We need more wood," Craft said, turning back to the forest. "You had better help."

Well, it was something to do. She followed them along the path. It gave her more time to make a decision, assuming she had some sort of choice. But her choices seemed to be to give Harbinger sex voluntarily, or to get repeatedly raped. Craft would try to defend her, and get himself killed. Unless she warned him, and he armed himself and did what he thought he had to do. She couldn't have that. So, until they had a chance to get away, it was voluntary sex. Voluntary in the sense that it was the best of bad alternatives.

That meant in turn that she would have to tell Craft. She hated the necessity, but could not avoid it.

They reached the forest region. The trees were mostly bare, with some scattered fallen branches. Haven took hold of the largest one she thought she could handle, and dragged it along toward the house.

The men took more time to gather choice pieces, so Haven led them back. In fact she reached the house, panting with the effort, before they came in sight of it.

"Ho."

Haven jumped. There was a person there by the hearth. She had been concentrating on her dragging and hadn't looked. Who was this?

"Wo-man," the other said, surprised. The voice was high. It was another woman! In fact, Haven recognized her.

"Crenelle," she said, amazed.

The woman stared. "Haven!"

They came together and embraced. They had met about a year ago, when Hero had made his unsuccessful trip south to find land. Haven and Hero had stayed the night with Crenelle, and the woman had been fairly taken with Hero, and he with her, but he had to see to his mission first, so nothing came of it. Haven had chided him on their way back: "You should have bedded her. She would have welcomed it." Actually he had had a night of sex with the girl, but she had insisted that he say he had done something, and he wouldn't, because he hadn't, he said. Haven had been confused.

"But she would have considered it marriage," he had replied. "I couldn't do that." He had been unable to compromise, though plainly much interested.

"She's young, but supple. Marriage to her wouldn't have been bad."

He nodded, reconsidering. "Maybe if we meet again."

So it had not happened. But Haven had come to know Crenelle somewhat in that night, adapting to her dialect, liking her. The woman was two years her junior, actually the same age as Rebel, but competent and sensible. But what was she doing here in the north?

"I live here with my brother," Crenelle answered. Her dialect made her hard to understand in detail, but Haven got the gist of it, because of her prior experience. "We moved north, looking for better land. But this doesn't seem to be it."

"Your brother," Haven said, amazed. "Harbinger?" But now she remembered: Crenelle had mentioned her absent brother, before.

"Yes. I had to go trade for supplies for the winter. I hurried back to beat the storm." She glanced at the looming cloudbank. "But why did you come here?"

"Looking for land," Haven echoed. Then she gripped her nerve and said it: "Your brother raped me."

Crenelle's response amazed her. "So you married him! That's wonderful. I wish your brother had raped me."

"Raped you! But—"

"This is how we marry. The man abducts the girl he likes and rapes her, and they are married."

More memory returned. Crenelle had wanted Hero to rape her, and he had demurred. Haven had mostly expunged that aspect from her mind. "But that's no basis for marriage!"

"Yes it is. He never rapes her again, of course; he devotes his life to making her secure. But your brother didn't like me enough to do it."

Haven had much to say, but now the men were coming up the path, bearing huge loads of wood. Still, she had learned a great deal, and her understanding was growing. Having Crenelle here would make things much better. But what a turn this was. Harbinger thought he had married her?

Harbinger spied Crenelle, dropped his load of wood, and hugged her.

Then he turned to introduce her to the others, but Crenelle intercepted that. "I know Haven. Her brother almost married me."

Harbinger turned to look at Craft, surprised.

"Craft," Haven said. "My younger brother."

Crenelle nodded. "I met her older brother. I know he liked me, but he had to see to his family first. So I lost him."

That had been only part of it. Crenelle had agreed to join Hero's family. It had been the rape he couldn't countenance.

Harbinger turned toward Haven.

"She told me," Crenelle said. "You married her."

Craft picked up enough of this to drop his jaw. "What?"

Haven made a sudden decision. "It's true. We . . . married."

"But that's not possible! There have been no—"

"It happened very quickly." She hoped he would settle for that.

"He raped her," Crenelle said proudly.

Craft stared at Haven. "He what?"

There was no avoiding it. "In their culture, a man wins a woman by raping her. It's the way they do it. She expects it. I . . . didn't realize."

"When I was gathering wood alone," he said, putting it together.

"Yes. Now . . ." She shrugged. "I'll make the best of it."

He reflected. She knew he was assessing his chances of killing Harbinger in a challenge of honor. His eyes flicked to his pack, where he had a half-length spear with a very solid and sharp stone head. Harbinger could well misjudge the deadliness of that weapon in close quarters, or suppose the youth did not know how to use it. That would be a fatal error.

Crenelle, realizing that there was more here than showed, stepped in. "It is our way. Take me similarly, if you want." She opened her cloak to Craft, in clear invitation. She wore a skin vest beneath it, but the outline of her breasts showed clearly. She had a good figure.

"It is their way," Haven agreed. "Please, Craft. We can't undo what happened. We can only make the best of it."

"By having me rape *his* sister?" he demanded.

"She's trying to make up for it, knowing it's not our way." Haven appreciated Crenelle's effort, surprising as it was. But maybe the woman was used to sex. What had she used to trade for supplies? "With the storm coming, we have to be together. This is a way to manage."

"I'm not raping anybody!"

"No need to marry," Crenelle said. "Make it a passing liaison. No fighting. No grudges."

Craft looked again at Haven. "This is the way you want it?"

She sighed inwardly. "Yes." Maybe Crenelle, having had sex with Hero without persuading him to marry her, was ready to tackle his little brother. What did she have to lose?

"You two make the meal," Crenelle said. "I brought supplies. I'll see to this." She took Craft's hand and led him inside the house.

Craft looked back once more. "You're sure, Haven?"

"Yes."

He turned and followed Crenelle inside. He knew she was buying off his outrage, but it was nevertheless a good price.

Harbinger glanced after them, then at Haven. He spread his hands. "Sorry," he said, becoming more intelligible because of her attuning to the words of Crenelle.

"You rape me—and you're sorry?" Haven flared.

"Thought you knew. Wanted."

And he had no doubt persuaded himself of that. That she really had wanted it. Haven's memory was sharpening as she remembered her prior meeting with Crenelle. Things the girl had said then now made more sense. She had spoken of rape, and said she would like to be raped. Haven had assumed it was just a clumsy word for marriage, but now she knew it had been literal. Crenelle had wanted Hero to take her by force, thus signaling his commitment to marry her. Harbinger had done just that with Haven. So it was a misunderstanding.

Yet her own unparalleled foolishness in making herself vulnerable to such an attack—didn't that suggest that she deserved it? That she had asked for it? She couldn't be sure. At any rate she was stuck for it. She could aggravate the damage, but could not undo it. Harbinger did not seem to be a bad man, overall. Maybe it would work out.

So she smiled at him. "Maybe."

He gazed at her, still uncertain. So she went up to him and kissed him.

His arms came around her. He kissed her back, hungrily, but not violently. Then one hand slid down to her bottom, outside the cloak.

"Yes," she said, willing her body not to flinch. "After they are done."

He nodded, clearly well satisfied. She was surprised to see a tear in his eye. Maybe he did have more than sex on his mind. He and his sister were, after all, regular people, with a different culture—at least in this one significant respect.

They dug out Crenelle's supplies and spread them on the ground. There were dried sections of meat and tubers, which would expand when cooked. At least they would not go hungry for a while.

Harbinger set up a woven pot that was caulked by clay outside, and filled it with water from the nearby spring. Haven put both meat and tubers in. Harbinger used sticks to fish a hot stone from the hearth, and dropped it into the pot. There was a hiss as it struck the water; then it sank down to the bottom. He fished for another stone.

"Salt," she said.

He glanced at the house. Oh—it was in there. "It can wait," she said.

They were working well together, she realized. He was doing the brutework, and she the careful work. They were getting the meal prepared. Probably he was used to doing this with his sister, but Haven knew the womanly arts as well as anyone. She had always cooked for her siblings.

When the first rocks cooled, she reached in with her hand and drew them out, and Harbinger put them back in the fire. When the water in the pot became too hot for her hand, she left the rocks there; they were doing their job.

By the time Craft and Crenelle emerged, the water was boiling and the things were cooking. Haven glanced up at Craft. He looked somewhat awed. He had never before done it with a woman. With a girl, maybe, but not a woman. Crenelle obviously knew her business, whichever man she entertained.

Haven stood. "Take over here," she said. Then she glanced at Harbinger and stepped into the house.

Inside she did what she had imagined, opening her cloak and removing her vest and loinskin. Harbinger seemed oddly hesitant, in complete contrast to the prior night. So it really was true: after the rape, it was to be voluntary. She appreciated that.

She took his hand and drew him down beside her. She opened his cloak for him, and helped him get out of his underthings. Then she kissed him and embraced him.

He entered her slowly, gently, savoring her body. She kissed him and wrapped her legs around him. This time there was only trace pain as he completed his thrust. She was healing, more than physically.

She let him finish, then held him close, kissing him again. "This way is good," she murmured.

"Good," he agreed gratefully. "You are good." He stroked her hair.

The odd thing was, now that she was acting loving, she was feeling it. She had control of the situation, and she did like being with a gentle man. She might not have chosen this one, had she had a choice, but he was handsome, and the fact that Crenelle was his sister spoke well for him. Probably it would work out. Certainly she could have done worse for a marriage. Maybe she really *had* invited it.

In any event, once the storm passed, she could leave, if that seemed best. He might consider rape the basis for marriage, but she did not.

They put their clothing back on, for the chill was coming in, and went back outside for the meal. Craft and Crenelle had it ready. They fished out morsels from the pot and chewed hurriedly, for the cloudbank was almost upon them. Haven could see the distant trees bending in the wind, and leaves were flying up.

Then the storm arrived and it was dark despite being full day, with hailstones pelting down. The wind rose, tearing at their clothing, blowing the smoke of the fire sideways across the land. They piled inside and lay jammed together, for there was barely space for four to stretch out. The two men lay on the outsides, the two women inside, sharing warmth. Haven would have liked to talk with her brother, to compare notes, if he wanted to, but this was not the occasion. There were several extra cloaks, and they spread these over the group of them for additional warmth.

"I'm glad it was you he chose," Crenelle whispered. "I knew you were good, like your big brother."

Haven didn't answer, because she wasn't sure how to react. At the moment she was more concerned about whether the wind would tear the roof off the house and leave them cruelly exposed. But the house did seem to be well made.

The howling of the storm prevented further dialogue. All they could do was huddle, trying to escape it. Their grouped bodies under the blanket skins kept them warm, but it seemed precarious.

They slept. There was nothing else to do. From time to time Haven was aware of Harbinger getting up to go out and tend the fire. That helped, for otherwise the snow would have put it out. At least there was now plenty of wood. The storm raged on, sending cold gusts of air in through the crevices. Snow filtered down onto the blanket skins. Haven knew that she and Craft never would have survived this weather out in the field.

She did not know the time of day, for her bearings had been blown away by the storm, but judging by the times she had slept and awakened, she judged it to be afternoon. Now she was awake and bored in her prison of slight warmth. She had had a reasonable night's sleep, and was caught up. But there was nothing else to do.

Crenelle moved beside her, turning over to lie on her side, facing Haven. Then she nudged slightly back, bringing her knees up and clasping them. What was she doing? Haven peered at her, and saw the face of her brother beyond the girl's neck. He was moving in close to Crenelle's back, apparently at her invitation, cupping her for additional warmth.

Then the woman began jerking, as if banging into something. Was she sick? Alarmed, Haven reached out to take her hand in a silent query. But Crenelle merely smiled, drawing Haven's hand down to touch her groin. Then up to touch her breast, where there was already a hand.

Suddenly Haven caught on. They were having sex! Like the girl on hands and knees, only Crenelle was on her side, giving Craft similar access from behind. His hand was on her breast, and his pounding entry was making Crenelle's whole body bounce.

Haven blushed, ashamed to have intruded on something private. But why were they doing it now, when they had done it just this morning?

Then that too fell into place. They were as bored as she was. And one ready way to alleviate boredom for a time was sex. So Crenelle had offered, and Craft had accepted, and they were doing it without shame. Crenelle did not seem to be concerned about getting pleasure herself; this was just a diversion, something more interesting or amusing than lying there doing nothing. She was not belittling the man's effort, but cooperating to make him feel good.

Haven considered. Well, why not? It might be hours more before the storm abated. Sex was not her idea of entertainment, but in a situation of nothing at all, it might be an improvement. There was also much to be said for keeping the man satisfied; it forestalled any other inconvenient notions he might develop. So she turned to Harbinger, and touched his groin. Yes, he had caught on too; he was already hard. She turned away from him, drew up her knees, and nudged back, as Crenelle had done. She felt much like the girl who had given it to Hero, more to show off her indifference than from any desire. In a moment his hand came to cup her breast, and his member was sliding into her. She knew she was taking it all in, for his groin bone came up against her tailbone. So she was competent that way, too. There was a certain gratification in being appreciated. In another moment, he was pulsing in the depth of her, and subsiding.

It was too fast. He had had his fun; now she would have hers. So Haven withdrew, then rolled over to face him. She pushed him onto his back, and climbed on top of him, pressing her breasts against him. He offered no resistance, not knowing her intention; as far as he was concerned, it was over. But she had something to teach him.

She kissed him, and ran her tongue into his mouth. She stroked his hair, and massaged his neck. When she tired of that, she slid off him and reached down to play with his penis, massaging it similarly. He let her do what she wished, satisfied with this novel form of play, lacking erotic ambition at this stage. She was in control, and she liked the feeling. The problem with rape was that she lacked all control.

After a while his member hardened in her hand, signaling her power to restore him to life when she chose. She got on him again, setting it carefully in her and easing down around it. She had him lie still while she moved, taking her time, wringing increasing pleasure from it. She tightened on it, and withdrew part way, and rode slowly back down to the base. She set the depth and the pace, thrusting and withdrawing, being the man. She kissed him, when she chose, and withheld her mouth when she chose. Glorious! And in due course she got her own wash of joy, jamming hard down on him, clenching, taking his fluid from him. This was the way it should be!

But eventually even sex lost its diversionary power. They had done it, and done it again, and it seemed that Craft and Crenelle had indulged similarly, and were similarly sated. Old sex lost the appeal of new sex; both desire and novelty were gone. Their bodies had to recuperate. And she needed to go out to the toilet region.

She got up, wrapped her cloak tightly around her, and went out. The storm caught her, shoving her back. She recovered her balance, hunched down, and plowed through the snow to the back. She could not tell exactly where the place was; everything was blowing whiteness. So when she judged it was right, she squatted inside her cloak and did it there.

When she returned, Crenelle went out. Then Harbinger, and Craft. That, too, was a diversion, in its fashion. But more was needed.

Crenelle came to the rescue. She brought out her little bone flute. She began to play a lovely melody.

Harbinger set up his drum, then joined in by singing the same melody. He had a good voice, and he knew words to it. Haven could not decipher all of them, but the combined effect of voice, drumbeat, and flute was lovely.

"That's wonderful," Haven said when they finished the song. She was trying to be positive, making the best of their situation, but it was also true: they were making beauty.

Harbinger and Crenelle knew many songs, and Haven and Craft

encouraged them all. Soon they were joining in, learning some of the tunes and words. It made their confinement much less burdensome.

The storm continued through the day. They kept the fire going, and remained under the blankets, alternating between shallow sleep, pleasant music, and languid sex. Three days ago, Haven would never have imagined herself doing anything like this. But if she had known it was coming, would she have avoided it? She realized that her life had already become somewhat dull, and this was a significant change. So maybe she would have accepted it anyway.

In the evening Harbinger and Craft got the fire blazing high and dropped more hot rocks in the pot, so they could eat again. Then they settled for the night.

Haven thought of something else. "We must learn to speak better to each other," she said. "We can learn words." She took Harbinger's hand and put it on her breast. "Breast," she said. "What's your word?"

"Oh, this will be fun," Crenelle said, laughing. She took Haven's hand and put it on her own breast, which had filled out since the prior year, repeating the word. Haven had to laugh at that. The funny thing was, she found Crenelle's breast interesting, and could almost imagine the stimulation it would give a man.

So they continued, and made rapid progress, because it was their only diversion between sleeps. And by morning they had a fair basic mutual vocabulary, so that they would have far less trouble communicating essential thoughts.

The storm carried through the day, but was easing as the snow piled high. The cold was intense, but the snow mounded around the house protected them from the wind, so they were more comfortable. They were riding it out.

But Craft wasn't satisfied. He was a maker of tools and a builder. He got to work chinking the cracks with mud he made from dirt and hot water. He buttressed the mud with twigs, giving it stability. This house was going to be much tighter than before.

Harbinger and Crenelle watched. It was evident that they had never thought of this, but as the leaking drafts cut down, they were appreciative.

The supplies Crenelle had brought were diminishing. She had not anticipated four people. They would have to get more—and how could they do that? The snow covered everything; there was nothing to forage. There was also no sign of game.

She stood by the fire and gazed across the landscape. And spied smoke. They had neighbors!

But Harbinger shook his head. "Other," he grunted.

"Who?"

"The Others," Crenelle clarified. "The beast men. We stay away from them."

"Surely if they make fires, they are our kind," Haven said. "Maybe we can trade with them, for food."

Harbinger shook his head. "Beast men dangerous."

But Haven would not let go of it. "We're in a desperate situation. We'll starve without help. Can these strangers be worse than that?"

Crenelle tried to explain. "They are ugly and brutish and very strong. We can't fight them. Their women are as strong as our men, and their children are like our women. They speak a different language, not like any of our dialects. They mostly leave us alone if we don't get in their way, and we try to stay out of their way. They are good hunters and deadly fighters. If we bothered them, they would kill us."

Haven looked south. "Can we trek south, until we reach one of our own settlements?" It was what she had thought of doing, once the storm abated, but now she was doubtful. The landscape was so frighteningly bleak.

"It's a long way. The ones I traded with don't have any more food, and I don't think any others do. No one is doing well here, except the Others. They like this kind of weather."

Haven looked at Craft. "What do you think?"

"I think we should try to approach the Others, in peace. Maybe they will trade."

"No!" Harbinger and Crenelle said together.

"But if we have no other way—" Haven protested.

"They kill any of our men they meet," Crenelle said. "They don't like anyone else hunting in their lands. That's why we're short of game:

we can't cross into their territory, but they can cross into ours and take what they want. So our game is scarce."

Her words rang with conviction. But Haven's life had changed so much recently that she was reckless. "You say they kill men. But not women?"

"Not women, usually."

"What do they do with our women?" Haven feared she knew the answer. But would getting raped by a beast man be any worse than a rape by an ordinary man?

"Sometimes they feed them," Crenelle said reluctantly. "Sometimes they try to adopt them, but their lifestyle is so rough, an ordinary woman can't survive it. Mostly they just ignore them."

"Adopt them?" Haven asked, amazed. "Why?"

"I think it's because they see us as children. So thin and weak. But we can't live their life. No, it's best when they ignore us."

"They don't . . . rape?"

Crenelle laughed. "They don't find us sexually attractive. Maybe they don't mistreat children."

"Then it might be safe for a woman to go to them, to trade."

"They wouldn't trade. They would adopt her or ignore her. Or maybe kill her, if she made a nuisance of herself."

"I will try it," Haven said. "I will take Craft's toys and hope they appeal."

Crenelle's face blanched. "So soon married, and you want to risk your life like this?"

"If I do nothing, we starve!" Haven flared. "If I succeed, we eat."

Crenelle swallowed. Then her jaw firmed. "I'll go with you."

They looked at the men. Both looked uncomfortable, but did not protest. It was a gamble, but things were desperate.

"Give me all your toys," Haven said to Craft.

He dug in his pack and came up with four carved links. He did not have many, because it took time and concentration to carve each one.

"You're the one who makes those!" Crenelle exclaimed. "Haven gave me one before. I still have it." She went to her own pack and brought it out. "It's fascinating. I could get to like you."

Craft shrugged, embarrassed by the compliment.

Haven had to smile. They had just indulged in repeated sex, and now they thought they could like each other? But she had done the same with Harbinger. Sex was an act; liking was a feeling. They were different.

They made a plan to go to the other camp early the next day. The two women had to go alone, because the Others would know if the men were near, and that would prejudice their case. It was a dangerous mission, they knew, for they would be in the power of the Others. But if they were successful, it meant survival.

They had been sated of sex, but the prospect of danger restored interest, and they retreated to the house for another bout. This time, mischievously, the two women assumed exactly similar positions, lying on their bellies, spread out, letting the men lie on them and do their business from behind. When the men were done, the women turned over and demanded immediate repeat performances, knowing the men could not. "Then you must do it our way," they said, and made the men go to work with their tongues, exactly where and how directed. Haven wasn't sure whether it was the delicate physical stimulation or the marvelous feeling of control, but she derived enormous pleasure.

In the morning the two women set off for the Others' camp, guided by the smoke. The day was calm, fortunately. They talked as they went, making no attempt at concealment, so that there could be no misunderstanding of their innocent purpose. They carried no weapons.

The Other camp was a crude collection of lean-tos and smoldering fires. They walked right up to it without attracting much attention. But they knew the Others were aware of them.

The Others were not tall, but were extremely solid. Their foreheads sloped back from massive brow ridges, and their noses were amazingly broad. Their breath steamed out in the manner of large animals. Their hands looked strong enough to crush rocks. They were indeed brutish in appearance, and Haven was frightened.

The two of them approached an Other man who squatted by his fire, roasting meat. But he bared his huge teeth and growled. Clear enough. They retreated.

They approached another man, but he too growled. He had a pile of stone tools he must have chipped recently. He picked one up, and the women quickly backed away. It was as if they were being taken for bothersome neighboring children, tolerated but not catered to.

Then Haven saw an Other woman, at a fire with a child who would have been about ten had he been human. He was probably younger; Haven understood that the Others grew faster. "If they take us for children, maybe a child will help," she murmured, and approached.

This time Crenelle held back, not wanting to complicate the effort. "Grunge will trust two of us half as much as one," she said.

Grunge? Well, it was a descriptive, if unkind name. Haven continued her motion, keeping it slow.

The woman stared at her without speaking, but did not make a threatening gesture. Haven smiled at her, hoping the expression meant the same in Other culture as in human culture. Then she oriented on the little boy. She brought out a wood link and held it out toward the boy. "Toy," she said. "For you." She shook the carving, so that the links shifted.

The boy was interested, but hesitant. He looked at the woman, but she gave no sign. Haven held it closer. Suddenly he snatched it away from her, so quickly she didn't see his arm move. He held it up, peering at the links, trying to figure it out. It was clear that he knew it was from a single piece of wood, but couldn't figure out how it got that way.

Haven waited, studying him. She saw that though the child was husky in the Other way, his cloak did not fit well. It was big enough, with holes cut for the arms and neck, but hung in such a way that it was drafty, letting air in through the holes. It would not be good protection in a wind. The boy surely got cold at night.

This was something she could do something about. "Let me help," she said, though she knew the boy would not comprehend her words. She did not look at Grunge, but was acutely aware of her.

Haven reached back into her pack and brought out her bone awl. She moved very slowly, for alarm at this point could get her killed. She took hold of the boy's cloak and put the awl point to it, near the edge of an armhole. He ignored her, still fascinated by the toy. The woman watched, but made no move. She surely could and would move rapidly and effectively if she perceived a threat to her child.

Haven applied pressure, pushing the awl point through the leather, making a small hole. Then she made another hole near it, and another, until she had worked her way entirely around the armhole.

Now she brought out a thin thong, and threaded it through the holes, outside, inside, outside, inside. She completed the circle, then drew the thong tight and knotted it. Now the cloak was snug around the arm.

Still no reaction from the woman. So Haven did the other armhole, and then the neck-hole, getting them all firm, but not tight, around their extremities. "Now show your mother," she said to the boy, giving him a gentle shove in that direction.

Obediently, he walked across to Grunge. She inspected the cloak. Would she realize the significance of the change in it?

The woman uttered a guttural sound. Another woman responded, coming to study the cloak. Then a third, and a fourth. They tugged at it, trying to understand the new mechanism much as the boy was trying to understand the mechanism of the toy.

Then they turned as one and looked at Haven. This was the crux. Did they understand? Would they deal?

She put her hand to her mouth, then rubbed her belly. She wanted food.

Grunge considered. Then she went into her house, and emerged with a huge frozen haunch. She dropped it before Haven and returned to her fire. She did understand!

But now there was another problem. The haunch would provide them with meat for a long time, but it was too heavy for Haven to carry. She tried to pick it up, but could not. Could she drag it? That would take a long time, even if it slid across the snow.

Grunge watched for a moment, then got up again. She bent down, heaved up the haunch, and started walking out of the camp. The boy followed.

Haven exchanged a glance with Crenelle, who shrugged. Where was the Other woman going? Did she think they had rejected the food?

Helplessly, they followed. Grunge was walking straight toward their house, though it was far out of sight. She wasn't following their trail, which had been largely covered by blowing snow. She knew where it was.

Haven realized that the woman was not stupid at all. She had known their origin throughout. She had waited to see what they had to offer, then acted when it was time. All of the Others must have known where the two women came from, and perhaps also what they wanted. They had let the women make their case.

Soon they approached the house. But when Grunge saw the two men beside it, she threw down the haunch and went back the way she had come, her child following. "Thank you!" Haven called belatedly after her.

Then the men came out to join them. Harbinger bent to pick up the haunch. He strained, then got it to his shoulder. He trod with heavy steps, feeling the mass of the burden. Yet Grunge had carried it without seeming effort.

"It really is true," Haven murmured, awed. "One of their women is stronger than one of our men."

"She could have killed us," Crenelle agreed. "Did you see how fast that boy took the toy? He could have killed us too."

"Maybe that's why he wasn't afraid of me," Haven said. "He let me punch holes all around his arms and neck."

"He will be warmer tonight."

"Yes."

The haunch lasted them for many days. All they had to do was gather enough wood to keep the fire going. The trading mission had proved worthwhile beyond their dreams.

Craft found suitable wood, and carved more toys. Harbinger studied his technique, and learned to carve similarly. Now he knew the potential value of such items.

As they used the last of the meat, and had to consider another trading mission, they were surprised again. A figure approached the house, bearing a burden. It was Grunge, with her boy in tow. Perhaps it was her imagination, but the boy looked better. Warmer clothing could do that. Haven went out to meet them, knowing that the woman would not stay if the men came out.

This time she had brought not only another huge haunch, but a pile of used cloaks. "Do," she said.

Haven realized that the Others wanted more tightening done. They lacked the technology of awl and thong, but appreciated the improvement it made. She nodded. "Yes."

Grunge turned to her son. She lifted the toy, which he now wore on a thong around his neck. "Do."

They wanted more toys too. "Yes." Haven turned to face the house. "Crenelle! Bring out the toys."

Soon Crenelle came, carrying a basket of the little carvings. There were ten of them. Haven took the basket and gave it to Grunge. "We'll do the cloaks as fast as we can. Three days." She gestured at the sun, three times.

The woman nodded, turned, and marched away, her child following. Then the men came out to fetch in the haunch and cloaks. They would be busy, but it was well worth it.

Craft had to use one of their own cloaks to cut into strips for thongs, but the trade was well worth it, because they had no problem of hunger. He used his stone carving knife to cut slowly and carefully, so as not to ruin a thong by a miscut. Harbinger wielded his awl, making holes. Crenelle threaded the thongs through and tied them in loose knots. Haven carved and cooked sections of the haunch. They actually got the job done in two days, and resumed working on toys.

On the third day Grunge reappeared, her boy in tow. Now Haven was sure he looked better. Haven and Crenelle hauled out the refurbished cloaks. "You tie them this way," Haven said, demonstrating on one. "Put it on, pull the thong tight, knot it."

The woman nodded. She clearly wasn't much for speech, though she understood it. Then she picked up the heavy pile as if it were light and trudged away.

Thus simply was trade with the Others established. The weather was terrible; more storms came, burying their house in snowdrifts. But whenever their meat ran low, Grunge appeared with another haunch, and more cloaks. Sometimes there were edible tubers too, tough but amenable to cooking. Somehow Grunge knew their situation, which spoke disturbingly well for the Others' awareness of them. Haven gave Grunge the toys they had crafted, and reworked the cloaks to make them tight. She was sure that the Other children were happier, and that many of their adults were warmer. It was a fair trade: skill for food.

Between times they foraged for wood, and chinked the crevices of the house against the wind, and diverted themselves with further novelties of sex. Haven was amazed by the way she acted, but it was the only significant entertainment available. Crenelle was a constant font of ideas, coming up with ways to tease the men, to make it a challenge. Such as hooking the women's feet to lock their legs together and lying straight, so that it was difficult to get between their thighs. Or standing, and requiring the men to touch no other part of their bodies. Or having the man achieve entry, then having to assume every other possible position, front and rear, without ever losing that entry. It could be done when the women cooperated athletically; it was harder when they did not. Sometimes they had the men lie absolutely still, letting the women do whatever they wished to them, discovering just how far they could tease them without quite making them spurt. Or they demanded that the men bring them to orgasm first; that could be a real challenge to men eager for completion, especially when the women did not help them with guidance. The men went along with it, being as bored of the confinement as were the women. Sex the men's natural way was over rapidly; this way it stretched out to fill whole days.

The winter months passed slowly. The weather didn't seem to bother the Others, whose squat bodies were solidly clothed in muscle and fat. Only the children, sometimes. On the worst day Grunge's boy was shivering despite being well bundled.

When Grunge turned to go, having dumped down the haunch and cloaks, the child started to follow, then fell. Grunge glanced back, and grunted. The boy got up and took a step in snow that was thigh deep on him, and fell again.

"That child is ill," Haven said, going to him. She reached out to help lift him back to his feet, and saw his face. It was red and wet. She touched his forehead. It was burning hot.

Haven made a sudden decision. "We must help this child. He needs rest and warmth."

"Grunge won't stay," Crenelle warned.

"But she can return for him in a few days."

"She wouldn't understand."

"Let me try," Haven said. "He'll die, otherwise."

Crenelle nodded. "I'll tell the men." She set off for the house.

Haven slowly embraced the child. He accepted it, perhaps appreciating her physical warmth, or the additional support. "Will you trust me?" she murmured. Of course he did not understand her words, but he responded to her mood, hesitantly smiling.

She faced Grunge. "He is sick. He can't walk home. Let him stay here for a few days." She pointed to the distant house, where the smoke rose from the constant hearth fire. "Warm." She embraced the child again. "I care."

Grunge just stood there. That did not necessarily mean she didn't understand, just that she hadn't decided.

Haven turned the boy around to face the house. "There. Warm. Good." Still the Other woman stood.

Haven opened her cloak, despite the bitter cold. "I am a woman," she said, showing the mounds of her breasts under the skin vest. She inhaled, and cupped them, making her femaleness as obvious as she could. The action gave her discomfort; the vest was too tight. "I will take care of a child." She turned to hug the boy once more.

Grunge abruptly turned and strode away. She had agreed!

"We go to house," Haven said. She drew her cloak back together, and took his hand.

But the moment he tried to take a step, he fell again. She would have to carry him. She put one arm under his shoulders, and the other at his knees, and tried to lift him, but he was remarkably solid. She couldn't lift him.

Then the others emerged from the house and walked toward them. Would the boy trust the men? Haven wasn't sure, so she turned him back toward her, kneeled, and hugged him close. His face rested against her bosom, and he stood quietly.

Harbinger approached. Crenelle must have prepared him. Without a word he put his arms around the boy and picked him up. Haven took hold of the child's hand, and spoke reassuringly to him as they walked toward the house.

Craft picked up the pile of cloaks. Harbinger would return for the haunch.

A place had been made in the warmest part of the house, closest to the fire. Harbinger set the boy down, carefully, and stepped back. He went back for the meat.

"You are safe now," Haven said to the child. "Warm and safe. Now you can sleep."

Then she became aware of something else. There was a smell.

She looked up. "Crenelle—" she began. But the woman was already busy with the pot, dipping a bundle of soft dry plants in the water. She had smelled it too.

Harbinger returned with the haunch. He set it in the snow beside the house; it would keep.

The smell intensified.

Harbinger and Craft decided that this was the time to forage for more wood. They set off for the forest.

The two women opened the child's cloak and worked it off his body. It was warm enough here so that he did not have to be completely bundled. Then they drew off his loinskin. Sure enough, he had soiled himself. The stuff was watery and very smelly. But Haven had seen similar symptoms before; the fever cleaned out the system, and then recovery began. She knew what to do.

They used the plant bundle to wipe the region off, pouring warm water on it to rinse it out repeatedly. The boy's torso and limbs were thick with muscle and fat; he weighed perhaps twice as much as a human boy of that height might. They progressed to his packed groin, getting the voluminous refuse clear. Then they paused, staring.

"He's a girl," Crenelle said.

"He's so solid, I just assumed . . ." But obviously she had been mistaken. She might have guessed, because Grunge was as solid as any human man.

"What's her name?" Crenelle asked.

"I don't know. I never thought to ask."

"Let's call her Cute," Crenelle decided, glancing at the girl's thick waist.

Haven laughed at the irony. A young human woman had a narrow waist that opened out into broad hips below and projecting breasts above. This torso was more like a tree trunk with massive branches. But maybe when the girl matured, she would be attractive to Other men. She could be cute, by the standard of her species.

They got her into a clean loinskin, and cleaned off her cloak. Cute, comforted by the warmth and perhaps the attention, had relaxed into sleep. Her body remained sweatingly hot, but the fever would run its course if they kept her otherwise comfortable.

The men returned with loads of wood. "This is Cute," Haven said, indicating the sleeping child. "She is female."

"She's solid like a man," Harbinger said.

"So is her mother." Haven paused, then addressed another matter. "We will need clean clothing, and more cleaning leaves. She may poop again. It's the sickness."

"We'll fetch more," the men said almost together.

Cute did poop more, but a diminished amount. There was only so much a body could contain. They kept her clean and warm, and she slept.

Night came. The work of the house went on around the sleeping patient. Haven stayed with her throughout. But in the evening she glanced across at Harbinger, lifting an eyebrow: Sex? He shook his head. He preferred that she keep Cute clean, than to take time off to entertain him. So she lay down beside the child, bracing her against the intensifying chill of the night and diminished fire. She gave her some water to sip when she woke, knowing that it was too soon for food.

In the morning, Cute's fever was down. Haven had to go out to the latrine area. When she returned, Craft was with the child, tempting her with a wooden toy of a new design: a ball in a cage. Cute smiled, liking it, but didn't actually take it.

Haven was relieved. The child was mending. She didn't know what they would have done had she died. She dipped out a small piece of cooked meat and proffered it. Cute took it and gnawed, her massive jaw crunching it more readily than a human jaw could have managed.

Then Cute frowned—and vomited it back out. It was, after all, too soon for solid food.

Cute stared at the vomit, and began to cry.

Haven sat beside the child and stroked her head. "It's all right," she murmured as Crenelle cleaned up the mess. "You're ill. Not your fault."

Later in the day, Cute was able to eat without losing it. Her fever came up again, but not as bad as before.

Harbinger settled down beside her with his drum. He beat out a rhythm with his hands, and sang a song. The child's eyes opened wide, staring at him; then she smiled and relaxed. She liked the music.

Later Crenelle settled down with her flute, and Cute reacted similarly, enjoying the melodies. They seemed to be helping her to recover. Haven was very pleased to see it. Had the child worsened or died, it would have been her fault, for she was the one who had brought Cute here.

By evening, Cute's strength was returning. The two women steadied her as she got up and went out to the place for urination. She was continent again.

This night Harbinger accepted Haven's silent proffer of sex. She went to the back of the house chamber, spread her clothing clear, and sat on his lap in a precise and special manner. His hands came up inside her loosened cloak and vest to find her breasts. By mutual consent they did not make what they were doing obvious in the presence of the child. Their winter's experience had made them proficient in almost any position, and they could do it with no seeming motion, efficiently and silently. This, too, was an interesting variant, because it was the first time they were trying to conceal it from another person.

"Thank you for singing to Cute," she murmured. She wanted him to know that she wasn't doing this just to satisfy him, but because she was pleased with him.

Crenelle, knowing the situation, sat by Cute, who was now fascinated by the new toy. She kept poking her finger into it to touch the ball, trying to figure out how it had gotten into the cage.

Cute continued to mend. She watched them working on the cloaks, and Craft showed her how to punch the holes. Even weak in her illness, she had as much arm power as he did. She liked the work, and did several cloaks for them. On the third day she helped put wood on the fire. Harbinger smiled at her, and she smiled back. She had lost her fear of alien men.

Then Grunge returned. Cute was aware of it before the others were; she had very sharp senses. She got up and ran out to join her mother. The others followed, with the cloaks they had altered.

The mother and daughter were embracing. It was the first time they had seen Grunge express emotion. Then she picked up the pile of cloaks and started back, and Cute followed. It was over.

But the next time Grunge came, there was an Other man with her. The four of them watched nervously; if he came to the house, they would have to flee. He carried a huge bundle, twice the load any human man could have handled. He dumped it down and departed, and Grunge followed him after dumping her load of cloaks. Only Cute remained, dallying by the pile.

Haven went out and hugged her. Then the chunky child ran back to join her family.

Now they looked at the bundle. It was not just meat and tubers. It was an assortment of useful things, including several nice flint-stones, small animal furs, a collection of good thongs, and a skin of fermented berry juice. That last was precious, in winter.

These were gifts. The Others were expressing their appreciation for the help rendered to their child. Grunge must have had something to say about it.

Meanwhile, Haven was in increasing distress for a different reason. Her breasts had swollen and become tender, and her digestion was queasy. Was she coming down with the illness? She confided her concern to Crenelle.

The woman laughed. "You had no blood."

Haven stared at her. Crenelle was right! She saw what Haven should have. She had not bled on her usual schedule, but that happened on occasion. Now her breasts were growing. That explained it. She had a baby inside her.

She told Harbinger. He was pleased and very solicitous. Their association had started with a rape, but Haven had long since come to terms with that. It was clear that the relationship Crenelle had with Craft, though similar sexually, was different socially, for there had been no rape. They were not married. When spring came, they would separate. Harbinger and Haven would not.

Spring did come. The snow melted in the increasing sunlight. And Grunge and Cute stopped coming.

They went to the Other camp. It was empty. The Others had gone. Apparently it was getting too warm for them.

With the departure of the Others, the game returned. Now the men could resume hunting, both because there was something to hunt, and because they would not be subject to killing if the Others caught them at it.

But it was clear that this was not a region they could live in year round. They had survived the winter only because of the considerable help of the Others. True, they had traded for it, but not all Other bands might be amenable to trading. In any event, they would not care to be dependent on the Others. They would have to return south to report that this region was uninhabitable. It was too bad.

Yet Haven was satisfied. This excursion had gotten her a decent husband, a decent woman friend, and considerable experience. She had been a relative innocent; now she was a competent adult. And she would be a mother.

Then something went wrong. She began to have pains in her swelling belly, and suffered spells of dizziness. She got short of breath, and experienced awful sieges of tightness.

"Something's wrong with the baby!" Crenelle said.

"It's just indigestion," Haven said. But she knew it was more than that.

The others made her rest and stay mostly off her feet, but the dizziness and contractions continued. Haven knew that Crenelle was right: the baby was trying to come out, and it was way too soon. She sank into depression. What would she do if the baby died?

In the course of a largely sleepless night, she came to an answer: the baby was the child of rape. If it died, it would be because the spirits knew rape to be an abomination, and destroyed its issue. Therefore the marriage based on rape was also evil, and would have to be destroyed too. She had come to love Harbinger, who was a good man despite his differences, but he had done wrong.

If the baby died, and Haven lived, she would leave Harbinger and return to her family. Then there would be nothing left of the rape. That was the only way to make it right.

That decision satisfied her, though it brought tears. She sank into sleep.

•

Europe during the ice age was simply too cold for modern man to handle, when there were better territories to occupy. So mankind expanded east rather than north, for several tens of thousands of years. Only when a combination of circumstances changed did he take over Europe. First, the climate: when the ice age eased for a time, giving the advantage to the species acclimatized to warmer weather. Second, population: when other convenient regions had been filled, and land was running out, and numbers were still growing. Third, technology: the assumption of this volume is that Africa was the source not only of all the original stocks of mankind, but also of the most advanced culture, though the final fruition of this culture occurred in Asia. More on that in Chapter 4. So Homo erectus *spread across Eurasia perhaps two million years ago, evolving into regional types, of which Neandertal—here called the Others—was one, and modern mankind spread perhaps 100,000 years ago, displacing the prior variants because he was smarter and had better technology and cultural devices for survival, such as the arts and superior language ability. This spread occurred in successive waves, noted not by the skeletal remains, which were almost identical, but by the level of technology. When the moderns had significantly better stonecraft, woodcraft, and other technologies, and the ferocious ice-age climate eased for a time, they were finally able to tackle the Neandertals in their home territory and prevail. That occurred about 35,000 years ago, and in only a few thousand years thereafter the Neandertals were gone, as were all the other* Erectus *variants who had the misfortune to occupy territory the moderns wanted. Though the climate may have eased for a time, it nevertheless remained the ice age, so the Neandertals were taken out from the situation for which they were best adapted. They were demolished during their strength, not their weakness. That suggests the power of the new order.*

Yet if modern man was as smart then as he is now, and expanded into Eurasia 100,000 years ago with an increasing population, how could he have waited more than 50,000 years before developing his arts and technology and moving into Europe? In other times, in other regions, he has shown the capacity to expand explosively, filling an entire continent within one or two thousand years. Indeed, in the past two thousand years human population has jumped from a few million to six billion. Could something have happened to set him back? As it happens, this is more than possible: human population seems to have fluctuated considerably throughout its existence. Two hundred thousand years ago there may have been 100,000 people; but 100,000 years ago there may have been only 10,000 people. So at the time mankind began to spread into Eurasia, his population may have been sparse. It surely increased rapidly thereafter, in the great new territory.

Then, a quarter of the way around the world, Mt. Toba erupted in Sumatra 74,000 years ago. This was one of the worst volcanic events in several hundred million years, spewing enormous amounts of dust into the atmosphere. It would have dropped summer temperatures by as much as twenty degrees Fahrenheit, making a volcanic winter several years long. The modern humans, adapted to warm conditions in Africa, would have been ill-prepared for this. Plant and animal life would have declined precipitously, adding hunger to the rigors of cold weather. Population would have crashed, perhaps as much as 99 percent, leaving isolated, widely spaced families or groups scattered across Asia, the survivors scratching for survival. Established trade routes would have been lined by the bones of those who had once prospered.

In fact mankind may have become an insignificant part of the landscape, extinct through much of it, as repeated severe climate fluctuations made mini-ice ages and beat them back. Similarly horrendous volcanic events occurred in America, encouraging the ice age. We have seen nothing of this magnitude in recorded history; Mt. Pinatubo dropped global temperature by only one degree, mitigating a record heating trend. The European Neandertals, however, were cold adapted; this was their kind of weather, and they expanded after taking a similar hit at the time of the Toba eruption. Until new waves emerged from Africa to assimilate the fragments and reunify the species. One of these may have been the Cro-Magnons, 50,000 years ago. Only then did the moderns resume their progress and take Europe.

This chapter shows an earlier and unsuccessful effort to penetrate Neandertal land. The more advanced folk were moving out to the fringes, encountering the physiologically identical but socially primitive prior occupants, and their impact was insufficient to transform that society sufficiently. So the tougher Neandertals prevailed, being physically better adapted to the rigorous climate of Europe. There does seem to have been some trade between the two peoples, but no interbreeding; they were different species who surely were capable of crossbreed sex, and would have tried it by raping captive women. But not of reproduction, as recent DNA typing has established. The last common ancestor of Neandertal and modern mankind seems to have been about 600,000 years ago; thereafter they went their own ways, genetically.

Why didn't the Neandertals advance their technology when they saw it in trade items, such as the tighter clothing the moderns made? For this we must understand Neandertal psychology, which is both unknown and perhaps self-evident. We resemble them in many ways. They may have been the original conservative "If it was good enough for my grandfather, it's good enough for me" folk, resistant to change, as their stone artifacts demonstrate. We do the same in certain respects. Consider the typewriter keyboard: I, being a progressive thinker, use the superior Dvorak layout. Most others refuse to change from the designed-to-be-inefficient QWERTY layout. It would pay the rest of the world to follow my example and change to the clearly better keyboard, but like the Neandertals, it simply does not. It is a similar story in weights and measures, as much of the English-speaking world clings to confusing archaic systems instead of converting to the efficient metric system. So we are not so different. Had the Neandertals been open to change, they would have been formidable indeed. But they thought they didn't need to.

Yet it may be more than that. The brain of Neandertal was as large as that of mankind, but differently configured. He did not think the same way we did. One conjecture is that he was short in the reasoning section and long in the memory section. He may have had a virtually eidetic memory for the relevant things of his landscape, with a specific name and location for every tree with edible fruit, every patch of ground where edible tubers grew, every bend in the river where fish were plentiful, and every mountain slope where berries ripened in season. So where we would say, "I found ripe apples on a tree beside the river's second tributary, an hour's walk northeast," he might say, "TreeZilch ready," and others would know exactly where to go for what, and would get there first.

He had a huge mental data base, and hardly needed the flexibility of language and thought that our kind requires. Indeed, he may not have needed the cooperation of others of his kind, so could be pretty much a loner in his territory. He seems not to have been social in the way we were; family units may have been more typical than the larger campsite shown here. He hunted, killed, and ate much more meat than we did, eating the small kills in the field. The ultimate individualist.

His tools were similar to ours, but the proportions were different; he made, used, and threw away hunting equipment at ten times the rate our ancestors did. So just as a memorized thing does not need description or figuring out—after all, you know where your house is, and what use it is to you, and so do your family members, so the directive

"Come home" needs no further definition—Neandertal needed no clarification. But this also meant that Neandertal had little need of imagination or reasoning, and was extremely set in his ways. When he established a camp, he stayed there year round, until he had hunted it out and had to move on.

Our kind, in contrast, moved around more, having summer camps and winter camps, giving the wild creatures less time to become wary. Neandertal: we out-hunted him, in the end, and marginalized him, and he probably slowly starved to extinction. He was well off for a very long time, and would probably still be in Europe if he hadn't been displaced by a cousin species with a way that turned out to be better in the end. But the advantage of our reasoning ability took some time to manifest. Not until we learned how to use the enormous potential of our changing brain did we actually prevail against Neandertal or Erectus. *It was as if we had a powerful new software program and didn't fully realize what it could do. So we were using our computer brain mainly to play games, as it were, instead of to design jet planes. Some things become obvious only in retrospect.*

There is also a question about sex. Modern mankind is virtually the sexiest creature on Earth. The only other is our closest relative, the Bonobo chimpanzee, where sex is an ongoing social event. They really do make love, not war. But the Bonobos do not have sexual literature, pictures, movies, pornography, and legal complications. They just do it without much consideration. So I think we are the ones who are most obsessed with sex. Why? Because it is to a fair degree a basic socializing mechanism. When conditions are difficult and creatures are confined without other entertainment, sex becomes paramount. It is seen in zoo animals, and it works, so long as certain rules are followed, such as not indulging with the partner of another person, or hurting your own partner. So it is a way to get through a long cold winter without sacrificing sanity. Our ancestors did not have the diversions of books or television. Thus sex evolved not merely for reproduction, but for diversion in otherwise dull times. The fact that broad power failures lead to increased births nine months later indicates that sex remains effective.

So was rape a way to start a marriage? Yes, in certain cultures, and it still is, as discussed in Chapter 1. We of a more enlightened culture prefer equality and consensual sex, but as with other aspects, often brutal power is the decisive factor. Discrimination against women is perhaps the most common social element today, as men seek and exercise power over them. So we are still not that far ahead of the Neandertals, socially, in some respects.

3

CRAFT'S STRATEGY

Modern man thrust generally eastward, driven by continuing population/resource pressure, but the terrain was formidable. The ice age held the northern regions in thrall, and many of the mountain ranges were glaciated. The climate was punctuated by sharp changes, with warm periods followed by devastatingly cold periods. The best land was by the coast and great rivers, for there the soil was richer, supporting more plants and animals, and the extremes were not as great. But there were always those who pushed into the hinterlands, driving back Homo erectus, *who had lived there almost two million years.* Erectus, *also called Archaic Man, was by this time a different species, distinct from both Neandertal and our own line. But to our ancestors, both of these other variants of mankind were simply the Others, to be displaced from the best hunting and foraging territories.*

The time is 60,000 years before the present era. The place is what is now Afghanistan, northwest of India and Pakistan.

•

"Now let me make sure I have it straight," Rebel said. "You got along fine with Crenelle, but it wasn't serious, but her brother Harbinger raped Haven and got her with child, and when the baby died, she dumped him and came home. Now you think you like Crenelle after all, so you're returning to her, even though she won't take you seriously unless you rape her, as Hero was supposed to."

Craft nodded wearily. Rebel was a year younger than he was, and actually the same age as Crenelle, but she was an entirely different creature. She was wild and beautiful and independent, and she loved danger. He had expected to make this journey alone, but she had insisted on coming with him, and actually she was good company and considerable help. "It's in their culture. They think marriage should begin with a rape. Hero wouldn't accept that, and neither did I. But I just can't forget her. So I'll try to—to rape her. If she lets me. But you had better be wary of Harbinger, unless he has found another woman to marry."

"I came along to explore new territory, and to see that you don't get into mischief, dear brother. I mean to be wary of everything."

"We are likely to be in close quarters, and Crenelle and I will be having frequent sex. That's going to give Harbinger ideas."

"Well, he won't get any ideas about me." She paused, pondering. "Remember, you made my knife for me, and taught me how to use it."

And use it she would, if so moved. Craft well understood the use of any weapon he made, but hoped never to use one against a human being. Rebel, in contrast, could use a weapon with enthusiasm, when she felt it necessary.

The region was becoming familiar. Craft hoped that Crenelle was still there, and still unmarried. Otherwise his long journey was for nothing. He wished that he had realized how he felt, before leaving her. But of course he had had to see Haven safely home.

"And there's a tribe of Others in the area," Rebel continued. "You traded with them, and helped one of their children."

"They enabled us to survive the winter," Craft agreed. "There's no need to fight them."

"Yet most of our kind calls their kind beast men, and tries to drive them away."

"They are just living and hunting and taking care of their children, the same as we are. We should have no quarrel with them."

"Is it true that their children are as strong as one of our women, and their women are stronger than our men?"

"Yes, I think so. At least the ones we met."

She shook her head. "That's hard to believe."

"Best to stay clear of them, regardless."

In due course they came to the familiar house. "I should approach first," Craft said. "Lest Harbinger think you are Haven."

"I will let him know I am not," she said firmly. Rebel was fiercely independent, and seemed to be afraid of nothing. Craft worried about her, for that reason. She was, after all, a woman, lithe and healthy, but without the bones and musculature of a man. An extremely attractive girl. But maybe it would be all right.

He put his hands to his mouth and called "Hoooo!"

In a moment the door pushed open and a figure emerged. It was Harbinger, by the stance.

"Remember, he's a decent guy," Craft said. "But he does believe in marriage by rape."

"Remember, I'm not like Haven," she retorted. "If he tries to put something into me, he'll find it in the cook-pot in a hurry."

He didn't pursue the matter. She was not joking. She was indeed not like Haven, in much the way fire was not like water. At age seventeen, she had already had adventures that those who did not know her would hardly believe. But he would not tell; it was part of the pact between them.

By the time they reached the house, both occupants were standing outside. Neither moved or spoke. Craft had thought that Crenelle might run to meet him, but she was staring at Rebel. Both of them were. Belatedly he realized: they knew this wasn't Haven, and so thought he might have taken another woman as wife. No Haven for Harbinger, no Craft for Crenelle. That was only half correct.

So he introduced Rebel first. "This is my little sister Rebel. Haven is not returning, but I am. Rebel likes adventure."

They relaxed. Now Crenelle stepped up to embrace him. "You know what you have to do," she murmured.

"There has to be another way."

She pushed him gently away. "We'll see."

Meanwhile Rebel braced Harbinger. "You raped my sister. Try to rape me, and you die."

He shrugged, not taking it seriously.

"She means it," Craft said quickly. "Best to stay well clear of her."

"Then what adventure is she here for?" Crenelle asked, seemingly bemused by the girl's boldness.

"I want to see the horses," Rebel said.

Harbinger shook his head. "We can't get close to them. They spook readily, and they run fast."

"My brother Keeper could get close to them," she said. That was true, but in a way they would not understand. Keeper had a very special way with animals. Indeed, he had rescued and raised three wolf pups, who were now formidable assistance in the hunt, because they could range out beyond a herd and drive it back toward the hunters. But Keeper was young yet, sixteen, and this did not seem to be the occasion to bring the tame wolves.

"I have a new hunting technique in mind," Craft said.

"It won't help if we can't get within spear-throwing range," Harbinger said.

"It will help us get within that range."

The man nodded, interested.

"We are tired from traveling," Craft said. "Let's rest and eat, and then we can discuss it."

They did that. Craft had been gone only two months, and it was now summer, but he felt older. He was eighteen now, a full man, thanks in large part to Crenelle.

And she was up to her tricks. She sat across from him, cross-legged, letting her thighs show, reminding him of the joys he could find there. When he had come here with Haven, Crenelle had intercepted him and given him immediate sex, to divert him from any problem with her brother. Her offerings had been phenomenal. He had expected to have sex with a woman at some point, but even in his fondest imagination had not dared aspire to one like Crenelle. She was beautiful, talented, and ardent, and though they had agreed that their relationship was not serious, he had loved her from that first encounter. He couldn't even call it a seduction; she had simply taken him inside, thrown off her clothing, removed his, and swept him into her embrace. She had known he would do what she guided him to do, and indeed he had. Thereafter she had given him sex many times, and in many ways, teaching him all he would ever need to know about the subject.

But when Haven lost her baby and decided to go, he had had to go with her. She was not strong, physically or emotionally, after that loss. So he had seen her back to the family, then turned around and returned to Crenelle. He had expected to come alone, but Rebel had another notion, and he could no more deny her imperative than he could Crenelle's.

They had agreed that if he returned, it would be to marry Crenelle. Now he had done so. But he still had to negotiate the hurdle of the manner of winning her.

Crenelle caught his eye, and delivered a measured smile. He knew that she would not give him any free sex on this occasion. He would have to take it by force, the first time. He wasn't sure he could. Not because of any effective resistance on her part; she would make sure her resistance was insufficient. But he simply was not constituted to rape any woman, even in pretense. No man of his family was.

Yet those parted thighs were driving him crazy. Her legs seemed more fully fleshed than before, more rounded, more desirable. He knew she would keep doing it, tempting him unmercifully, making him desperate for sex, until he could hold back no longer. She was sure she could make him do it. Maybe she could; he wasn't so sure. She hadn't been able to make Hero do it, but Craft was not as decisive as Hero.

After the meal, they got down to business. "Here is my plan," Craft said, clearing a place on the ground. "Here are the mountains; here is the level range where the horses graze." He drew lines to mark the places, making a map.

"It looks like dirt to me," Harbinger said.

The man had his talents, but was not strong on imagination. "Think of a bird, a hawk flying high above us. Now think of seeing through that bird's eyes as it peers down looking for prey. This is the lay of the land."

"The land," Harbinger repeated dubiously.

Craft tried again. "Or think of climbing the mountain and looking from the cliff. The trees look tiny, and the winding river resembles a snake. You can see where the horses graze, here." He marked the place with a little crude horse figure.

"By the river," Harbinger agreed, getting it.

"It's warm enough to swim in now," Crenelle remarked, making a swimming motion with her arms that made her breasts flex. They too seemed to have filled out somewhat, but that was probably his frustrated imagination.

Rebel smiled, appreciating the private contest. She was well familiar with the nuances of sexual interplay, and quite capable of doing something similar herself, if she chose. Haven was a circumspect, cautious woman, who had surely submitted to sex reluctantly, the first time; Rebel was incapable of submitting to anything, any time. Rebel had no fear of sex, merely of ever being subservient.

Craft forced his eyes back to the map. "If we go after the horses, they will flee to the north, and we will never catch them."

"That's why we don't hunt horses," Harbinger agreed.

"But if we arrange a special course for them, we can divert some into a trap," Craft continued. "See, here is the old dry chasm where the river once ran, before it changed course. Any horses that run into that can't run out of it, except by turning around—and then they would have to run past us, within our spear range."

"No horse would be fool enough to run there," Harbinger said.

"I think some might—if the herd were spooked, and there was not room for all to run in the main channel."

"But there *is* room," Crenelle said.

"There is room now, but there won't be when we act. We'll put up a baffle—"

"A what?" Harbinger asked.

"A wall. Here, in the narrow part of the running channel." Craft marked the place. "Some horses will pass on one side, and escape; some will pass on the other side, and be diverted into the chasm. Then we will close in on them."

"How will we make a wall?" Crenelle asked, leaning forward to peer more closely at the map. By no coincidence her well-formed breasts hung close to his face. He had caressed those breasts so many times, and wanted to do it again. If he reached across and grabbed her, she would scream and haul him into her. They would land across the map, and her legs would be wrapped around his body, preventing his escape, while she continued to protest the ongoing rape she fondly imagined. Harbinger and Rebel would merely watch knowingly. It would be Crenelle's victory—and his. Yet he could not do it.

The others were looking at him, with similar quarter smiles. Craft had been staring instead of answering. He closed his eyes for a moment to get the breasts out, and answered the question. "We can use sticks and hides."

"But the horses will run right through them," Harbinger protested.

"I don't think so, because they will think the wall is solid."

Harbinger lifted a skin and shook it. "Nothing will think this is solid."

Craft shrugged. "I think they will."

Harbinger hesitated. Craft knew that the man thought the hunting plan to be nonsense, but also that Crenelle wanted to keep Craft here until he succumbed to her charms. Harbinger wanted his sister to marry the man of her choice. So he demurred. "We'll see."

They got to work on the baffle. Craft made a framework of thin, strong sapling sticks, and cut small holes in the hides so that they could hang on the sticks. "We will have to dig holes to put the stick in, so the wall will stand," Craft said.

The work took two days. They slept in the house, and Crenelle came to join Craft, but he refused to let her be naked under the blanket with him. He knew she would wrap herself around him and cry rape. She did not protest; she faced away from him and curled up, her posterior an easy target should he be so inclined. He would have the whole night to reconsider.

Harbinger slept on Crenelle's far side, and Rebel slept the other side of Craft. Rebel was fully clothed, and her stone knife was in her hand;

there was no doubt at all that she was sleeping alone. The difference between her demeanor and Crenelle's was complete.

In the night Craft woke to find Crenelle naked against him, nudged against his side. He pushed her away and turned over. He wished they could be together as they had been before, but she wouldn't allow it, without marriage, and neither would he, really.

He returned to sleep, and woke to find her up against him again, this time half across him, one thigh over his thighs. He moved her away again, and turned away once more.

A third time he woke. This time he was clasping her from behind, his left hand on her left breast, his right passing under her head to rest across her mouth, his exposed groin tight against her bottom. Clench two hands, thrust forward with groin, and the rape would be complete. She would struggle—hardly at all. But she had not given him leave, no matter how artfully she had arranged the two of them while he slept, so it would be rape.

He disengaged, but realized that this was likely to continue indefinitely. Every time he slept, she set up a new connection. Each one was harder to break. Yet he felt that if he was going to rape her, it should be a real rape, not a mere pretense—and he wouldn't do that. What was he to do?

Rebel stirred. She reached out and touched his shoulder. She knew what was going on. She would help, if he asked her. He rolled toward her—and she quietly climbed over him and settled between him and Crenelle.

After that his sleep was undisturbed. But he still dreamed of Crenelle. His sister couldn't protect him from everything.

In the morning they took turns rising and going out to the latrine area. Crenelle returned with her hair straggling down across her breasts. She wore much less, in this summer warmth, and what she did wear concealed things only passingly. Rebel continued fully garbed, but she was evidently warmer than she liked.

Then they ate from the pot and went back to work on the baffle. It was nearing completion. It was in several sections that could be set up independently.

"It will be best if there is a storm," Craft said. "So they are nervous."

"But they spook faster when they are nervous," Harbinger said.

"And when they spook, they run," Crenelle said. "As fast as they can."

"Precisely. When they run fast, they don't take time to pause and think. They just go forward, one following another."

"I think there will be rain tomorrow," Crenelle said. "Perhaps a storm."

"Then we should set this up before then. In the night."

Crenelle made a girlish groan. "I can think of better things to do by night."

"Marry me without rape, and we'll do them."

"We did them last winter, and you didn't marry me."

"And Harbinger raped my sister, but they didn't stay married," Rebel put in.

"And if he catches you off guard, and rapes you, will you stay married to him?"

"He won't catch me off guard, and if he does, he won't return with his member attached."

Harbinger winced. He had made no approach to Rebel, yet she acted as if he were a constant menace. It probably didn't help that she was a strikingly beautiful girl, with a figure easily the match of Crenelle's, and wild fair hair and eyes. She had demonstrated her ability to captivate any man she chose, even as a child, but had married none. Now her attitude was discomfiting Harbinger and angering Crenelle.

"Nobody's going to rape anybody," Craft said.

"We'll see." Crenelle returned to her work.

"Will the horses smell our traces, and stay clear?" Rebel asked.

"Not if it rains. Anyway, we've hunted there often enough, so our smells are there. It's us they fear, not our smell."

They prepared carefully for the night. It was clear, and there was a fat moon, so they had enough light to see by. They carried their loads of stakes and hides down to the horse trail, and set them up where Craft indicated. They had to dig into the ground with one stake, to make holes, and pound on its end with a stone to make them deeper, then set in the baffle stakes and tamp them tight. The job was a bit clumsy, but Craft thought it would do. Would this work? Now that the test was close upon them, his fear of failure increased.

Harbinger had worked well, despite his disbelief in the project, and so had both girls. The two men had worked together much of the time, and the two women, to avoid the complications of mixed genders. But when they finished, not long before dawn, Crenelle fell in beside him. "If it works, will you marry me?"

He couldn't answer that.

"There are other men who might find me worth raping," she persisted.

"If you desired one of them, you would have made him do it already."

"You're too smart. Which is why I want you."

"Hero isn't known for being smart."

"Hero is strong. That's good too."

It was a valid point. "If you had been willing to marry him without rape, you would have had a child by him by now. If you are willing to marry me without rape, it will be the same."

"I could have had a child by you already."

That made him curious. "How did you prevent it?"

"I can tell when a baby is ready to be made. I avoided it, with you."

"How?"

"Do you remember when we played the game of mouths and tongues?"

Craft was amazed. "To keep my seed out of you! I thought it was just for variety, to keep me entertained. I never realized."

"There was no need for you to know. Rebel surely knows too."

He glanced across at his sister. "Do you?"

"No," Rebel said shortly. That was odd; usually she had provocative opinions on everything.

The dialogue lapsed. They reached the house, but were too tired to sleep immediately. Rain started, nicely timed, but its noise outside was distracting. So Harbinger and Crenelle brought out their instruments and made music. Harbinger beat his drum and sang, and Crenelle played her flute.

"Oh, my," Rebel murmured. "It's beautiful. How can I hate them now?"

"Why should you hate them at all?"

"Because of what he did to our sister, and what she will do to you."

"I want to marry her!"

"She will squeeze you dry, you fool."

He shifted the subject. "Harbinger's not a bad man. Haven loved him. But when the baby was cursed, she couldn't stay."

"The child of rape. Of course the spirits punished it." Then, oddly, she joined in the singing. Craft hardly understood his wild sister.

As dawn came, they sank into sleep. This time Crenelle did not torment him; apparently she was too tired to spare the energy.

By midday the horses were in the pasture, having passed the baffles. A storm was building up. This was ideal. They gathered all their spears and walked quietly down, staying out of sight of the herd. They crossed the river, which was rocky at this stage, and paused.

The herd was grazing to their north. Several horses were gazing alertly toward the intruders, well aware of their presence. But horses knew which predators could run fast enough to be dangerous and which could not, and their spooking range varied accordingly.

The storm had continued to build during their descent, turning the sky dark. The horses became skittish, not liking it. They milled about, uncertain whether to cut short their grazing.

"Now!" Craft cried.

The four of them spread out, each of them yelling and waving a spear in each hand. The nervous herd spooked immediately. In a moment it was in full flight north. They followed, losing ground but continuing the noise.

The animals came to the baffles and avoided them. Most passed left, the way they had come, but a few were unable to crowd in and had to pass right. This led them to an alternate trail that went to the canyon. Before they realized, they were in it, and the rest of the herd was pounding away in the distance.

The four humans ran up to the baffles, remaining spread out, blocking off the channel. Now they no longer yelled; the trap had been sprung. The horses had only one way out: past the people.

They continued to advance. Four horses were in the canyon, milling frantically. Fine fat animals. "All we need is one," Craft said. "We need to be sure of that one."

"The first one that comes within range," Harbinger said. They moved slowly on in, Harbinger and Craft leading, the two girls close behind.

Suddenly one horse made a break for it. The animal charged toward them, while the other three paced uncertainly. But it lost its nerve, and skidded to a halt, turning back.

Harbinger threw his spear. It was a long, hard shot, but a good one; the spear struck the animal in the flank. It squealed and bolted, dragging the spear.

The three others were spooked by their companion charging toward them. They galloped outward, directly toward the people. "Let them go!" Harbinger cried.

They stood as the horses passed on either side, almost close enough to touch. Then they closed on the wounded one. Rebel ran up to give Harbinger one of her spears.

The animal tried to run past them, but both Harbinger and Craft hurled their spears at point-blank range. Both struck the horse in the chest. It squealed again and stumbled, trying to turn away. Blood came out, but the animal was still afoot, now dragging three spears.

They followed it, herding it back into the dead-end chasm. Suddenly it whirled and lurched, directly at them, making them scramble out of the way lest they be trampled. Neither man was in position to use his second spear.

But Rebel thrust hers as the horse passed, wedging it just behind the foreleg. It squealed again and plowed into the ground.

The men recovered and ran up to finish it. But there was no need; the animal was already dying. Rebel's thrust had mortally wounded it.

Harbinger turned to her, amazed. "You *do* know how to use a weapon!"

"Somebody had to," she retorted. But she was clearly pleased, both by her success and the compliment.

They set to work butchering the creature. They used their stone knives to cut and hack off the legs, which had good meat that could be readily carried. Then they carved off as much of the surface meat as was feasible. There was really too much of the horse for them to take completely; they would leave the carcass for scavengers. It had been a successful hunt.

"You were right," Harbinger said, excited by their victory. "They went by without knocking down the wall, just as you said. Then they couldn't escape us. We can hunt this way, now, and always get a horse."

"When they return," Craft agreed, quite pleased by the success of his ploy. "But they may not return soon."

"They will return. It's good grazing here by the river." Then he glanced speculatively at Craft. "You threw fast and well. You are no novice with a spear."

Craft shrugged. It was not a side of his nature he cared to show, ordinarily. It was necessary to fully understand the use of a weapon in order to make it well, so he practiced carefully, and was competent. He liked fathoming the ways of tools and weapons, and wished he could spend more time studying them. But he was no warrior. He lacked both the muscle and the spirit.

Well satisfied, they hauled their meat up to the house. Then they took down the baffles, so as to save their elements for future use.

When Rebel worked beside Craft, she commented on another aspect. "You did well, inventing the baffles. It's too bad you can't spend your whole time inventing things."

"Yes. But there are so many other things to do."

"If I could go out and hunt all the time, I'd be glad to let you stay home and make things."

He sighed. "But you can't. And I can't. We both have other tasks. Everyone does."

"Everyone does," she agreed. But she seemed thoughtful.

Dusk came before they were done. Crenelle and Rebel put some of the new meat into the pot, and in due course served up good portions.

They all ate well, and then sang well, and retired for the night. The two women slept in the center, but this time Rebel was beside Harbinger rather than Craft.

However, they were all worn out, and sleeping was all they did.

In the morning the two women were up first. Craft heard them talking as they set more meat on the fire to roast. They seemed to be quite compatible now. "It's time to decide," Rebel said.

"Yes."

"You know he'll never commit if you don't force the issue. Men don't."

"I know. But what will you do, if I take him?"

Rebel shrugged. "I haven't decided."

"You don't hate my brother anymore."

"He does intrigue me. But if Craft doesn't stay, neither will I."

"So you won't be my enemy, either way."

"That held you back?"

Now Crenelle shrugged. "It holds him back. Maybe now he'll commit."

"Maybe. But I think some concession will be required. Nobody in our family likes rape, especially considering the way it angers the spirits."

"Maybe I can compromise."

Their dialogue lapsed. Craft suspected that they had meant him to overhear. It was true: He had returned to marry Crenelle, but there had been constraints. He didn't like the rape aspect, or Rebel's antagonism to Harbinger. But there was more: He wasn't sure he liked this northern life. He had had a winter of pleasure with Crenelle, but he would much rather have that pleasure in a warm climate. He knew she liked this territory, and now that he had worked out a way for them to hunt the horses on the plains, she would want to go on north, following the herds. That would mean more cold winters.

Harbinger stirred, so Craft stirred too. They got up to join the women.

They ate. Then Crenelle made her move. "Craft, it is time for us to decide. Are you going to marry me?"

"I want to. But—"

"Harbinger and I will go north, following the horses. Come with us, and I'll let you take me without rape." She smiled, somewhat sadly. "That's more than I did for your brother."

This was awful. She was conceding a key point—and he still wasn't sure. "I don't think I want to go north. I want to take you south, into warmer lands."

"Then you will have to take me by force. I will fight you." She paused. "But after the first time, I will do whatever you say. I will go south with you."

"And what of your brother?"

"My sister and I stay together," Harbinger said. "If she goes south, so do I."

Rebel looked at him, but didn't comment.

Crenelle returned to Craft. "So which is it to be?"

The moment of decision was upon him, but he had no idea what to do. He couldn't rape her, even though he knew she wanted it, but neither did he want to commit to life in the cold north. So his choice was really between marrying her and going north, or going south without her. Neither prospect appealed.

Climate, it seemed, was his destiny. He needed a compromise, but did not see one.

•

Mankind spread across Asia, but was more thinly spread in Siberia. The earliest evidence dates to circa 67,000 years before the present. As elsewhere, he hunted the large game animals, horses included. Yes, today we think of horses as steeds and pets, but before that they were prey. Erectus *seems to have been on the way out, probably outcompeted for resources and marginalized until he was gone.* Erectus, *like his cousin Neandertal, was well suited to endure, but he had a limitation that was to prove critical.*

4

REBEL'S DREAM

Mankind moved across southern Asia, crossing India and Indochina and coming up against the Pacific Ocean. The ice age lowered the sea level, making what we call land bridges in several parts of the world, but in human times there was always a gap between Asia and Australia. However, at times Sumatra/Java/Borneo and the Philippines were connected to Indochina, and evidences of mankind there date back as far as 50,000 years ago. That is the time of this setting. The place is by the shore of the Sulu Sea, which today separates the Philippine Islands from Borneo, but at that time was a great inland sea some four hundred miles across. Climate does, to a fair extent, determine the outlines of the land; when it changes, the land changes.

Erectus *was resident throughout Eurasia for more than one and a half million years, but his population was relatively sparse. Man for man,* Erectus *was more than a match for modern man, physically, and he was by no means stupid. But the superior technology, communication, and foresight of the moderns made them more formidable. Why didn't* Erectus *develop such things in similar fashion? Perhaps because his brain was as significantly different from that of mankind as his body: of similar size, but differently proportioned, as described in Chapter 2. On the other hand,* Erectus *and Neandertal did hold their own for about 50,000 years after the moderns invaded their territories, so it took more than a better brain to do the job. The key to victory may have been as simple as a better idea, late in coming, but ultimately overwhelming in its cumulative impact.*

Plus one other thing: the first tamed animals. Genetic evidence now indicates that the dog descends from the wolf, and was first domesticated perhaps 100,000 years ago. Until relatively recently no effort seems to have been made to modify its appearance; the dog looked just like a small brown wolf, but ran with men. It proved to be a great friend.

Note: in this context, the term "beest" means any large beast of prey, as in wildebeest.

•

This time it was Rebel who was returning, with her younger brother Keeper. And Keeper's dogs.

For Keeper had a way with animals. When Hero had speared a wolf bitch, Keeper had sought out her den and found the pups. He had taken them in and cared for them, and Haven, softhearted, had helped. The others thought this was crazy, but the pups grew up into tame wolves that looked to Keeper as their pack leader. Keeper, at seventeen, was a slight man, gifted with neither the power of Hero nor the expertise of Craft, but now the three wolves were always with him, and while they sought no quarrels with others, they bristled and growled warningly when there seemed to be any threat to him. Recently he had found another litter, and was raising a second group of animals, so that he could breed them together and have more. At this point, a number of other people were interested. Haven was caring for that second litter, while Keeper traveled with the first.

The area was easy to locate, because the brother and sister lived on an island in the sea. All they had to do was follow the coast until they spied it. The sea was so big they could not see across it, but Rebel understood that it was entirely surrounded by land. That was hard to imagine!

They came in sight of the isle. It was a rocky projection from the water, about a hundred and fifty paces from the shore. Nestled among the stone spikes was a structure of rocks, gravel, wood, hide, and brush:

the house. The only access to it was by boat, for there were crocodiles and large snakes in the vicinity.

"I like that," Keeper said, gazing at the residence. "No one will sneak up on that residence."

"That's the idea," Rebel agreed. "The Others don't use boats, and they're the main threat." She took a stance on a projection of land that reached out partway toward the island. "Keep the dogs quiet while I hail them."

Keeper cautioned the wolves, who were suspicious of strangers, and Rebel put her hands to her mouth and called, "Ho! Harbinger!" She was afraid he would be gone, or have found another woman. She had hardly encouraged him during her prior visit, after all.

Harbinger emerged, and stood with his bare toes touching the water. He recognized her, of course. "Come to quarrel, Rebel?" he called.

"No. I come to marry you."

He shook his head, knowing better. "What of Craft?"

"He didn't come. This is my younger brother Keeper. And his dogs."

The man stared at the animals. Aware of it, even from that distance across the water, they began to bristle. "Don't stare at them," Rebel called. "That makes them angry. Ignore them."

"Dogs?" he asked, averting his gaze to a degree. "They look like odd wolves."

"They *are* wolves," Keeper said. "From another region, so they don't look the same as the wild ones around here. These are smaller, and brown, and tame. But not friendly until they know a person. So just let them sniff you, and they will gradually accept you. You can tell when they are friendly, because their tails curl upward and their ears perk up too."

Harbinger looked doubtful, understandably. So Rebel made a demonstration. "Here, Brownback," she called. One of the dogs perked up his pointed ears and ran to her, tail wagging. She stroked his head, and he licked her hand. He was her chief foot-warmer, and she always gave him tidbits from her food. He was the boldest of the three, sharing her adventurous spirit.

Now Crenelle emerged. She had evidently held back, until sure of the visitors. She cupped her mouth to call. "How is it you come, and not Craft?"

"I had a wild change of heart. He didn't." Rebel glanced to Keeper. "This is Harbinger's sister Crenelle, who almost married Craft. But it didn't work out."

"I know," Keeper said. He was here nominally to protect Rebel, and with the dogs he was quite capable of doing that. But she suspected that he was more than slightly curious about Crenelle, about whom he had heard from all four of his older siblings.

Crenelle seemed just as curious about Keeper, but wary. Twice she had been ready to marry his brothers, and twice they had left her despite being greatly attracted. Keeper was a year younger than Crenelle, so was of less interest, but Rebel knew the woman was not one to let any possibility pass by without close inspection.

Harbinger squatted and drew a boat out from under the house where there was a low channel. He held it while Crenelle stepped in and took her place at the front, kneeling. Then he climbed into the back. Both lifted stout paddles and stroked the craft forward across the water.

Soon they reached the landing. The dogs drew forward, their ears laid back. "Don't move," Rebel said. "Just stay there in the boat."

Both Harbinger and Crenelle looked uncomfortable. "If you will sit still while the dogs sniff you, they will let you be," Keeper said. "But don't make any sudden gesture that might be taken as a threat to me."

"Tame wolves!" Crenelle said. "I never saw that before. What do they do?"

"They protect us," Rebel said. "And they help us hunt."

"The Others don't let us hunt much," Harbinger said darkly. "Anything larger than a rabbit, and they will come for us."

"But aren't you protected by the island?" Keeper asked.

"Not against a siege. They could make a raft if they wanted to. They know how, but don't trust large waters. It's better not to give them cause."

"But there were no Others here before," Rebel protested.

"They returned. They range widely. Once we traded with them, but I think the Other woman who did it died. Now they merely tolerate us."

"Well, if I am to marry Harbinger, I'll want more hides than rabbits provide," Rebel said.

Harbinger didn't speak, so Crenelle did. "Get in the boat, come into our house. Settle by the fire, and we'll talk."

"We must bring the dogs," Keeper said.

"Put the wolves in the boat with us? They wouldn't like that any better than we would."

"They have been in boats before," Keeper reassured her. "They know your smell now, and understand that we are friends. It will be all right."

Rebel got carefully into the boat behind Crenelle, and Keeper got in ahead of Harbinger. They laid their spears on the boat's floor. It was a close fit, but they made a space between them. Then they gestured to the dogs. In a moment all three had scrambled into the space.

Silently, Harbinger and Crenelle paddled the craft around and back out to sea. It floated low in the water now, but was strongly made and not in danger of sinking. The dogs peered out across the water, evidently enjoying the experience.

They crossed to the island. There was a snug harbor there, just wide enough for the boat, holding it steady. Crenelle stepped out, then held on to a bar on the house and extended her free hand to Rebel. Rebel stood and got out, steadied by the hand, and stood beside the boat. Then she signaled the dogs, who scrambled out to join her. After that Keeper and Harbinger got out, and Harbinger slid the boat the rest of the way under the house.

Keeper looked around. "Is there anything dangerous on the island?"

"Nothing but us," Crenelle said cheerfully. "It's barren."

Rebel hoped her wince didn't show. "Go," she said to the dogs. They bounded away, gladly exploring the terrain.

They went to the hearth on the other side of the house, where there was an open region, and Crenelle produced some dried rabbit meat and some fermented juice. Also some scrap bones for the dogs as they returned, who quickly warmed to her. The woman was not stupid; she appreciated both the danger and the help the dogs could be to her and her brother, so was already cultivating them in much the way she cultivated men.

"Now we need to understand each other," Crenelle said. "When you were here with Craft, you didn't let my brother near you. Are you teasing him now?"

Rebel shook her head. "I know how he raped my elder sister. No one will ever rape me. I thought it best to make that clear at the outset, lest blood be shed. But then I heard him sing."

"Ah." Crenelle glanced at her brother. Then they brought out the drum and flute, and sang and played. Rebel loved it, and saw that Keeper was also rapt. Of course Crenelle was also doing her thing with the bouncing breasts and partly glimpsed crotch, so he had plenty to occupy his attention. But the dogs were also listening, surprised. Maybe it sounded like howling to them, which was no bad thing.

"Yes, like that," Rebel agreed when they were done. "I realized that there was more to you both than hunting and foraging. And you do those things well too."

"Still, you can understand why my brother is wary of you." Crenelle held a tempting bit of bone and sinew out toward the nearest dog, Whitepaw, who was similarly wary. The implication was that Harbinger might be amenable, given sufficient reassurance.

"I need to explain two things," Rebel said. "The first is that I will always be my own woman. I will not be raped, I will not be dominated. But the man I marry will find me good company, and competent."

"You brought down that beest," Crenelle agreed, referring to a prior hunt when Rebel had wielded a spear like a man. "You can use a weapon."

"I can use a weapon," Rebel agreed. "And I like action. So I can be good for a man who doesn't mind an aggressive woman." She got to her feet, and removed her cloak. In this warm weather she wore no underclothing, so for the moment she stood naked. She turned in the light of the fire, showing off what she knew was as good a body as they were likely to see. "Very good."

She saw Harbinger's tongue run around his lips. He did appreciate her physical qualities, as she intended. Crenelle was good at impressing men, but Rebel knew she herself was better, when she wanted to be. She sat down, remaining nude, and folded her legs under her. Everything was in plain view. Her brother, knowing her, ignored it, and the dogs hardly cared.

But she did need to explain. "The music impressed me, and I began to reconsider. But it was time for Craft to stay, or go, and when he went I had to go with him. I thought I would forget, or find another interest. But instead of fading, the feeling grew, until I knew I wanted Harbinger. But on my own terms, of course. So I have come to accomplish this."

"You say you want to marry my brother," Crenelle said. "You know that we require a rape to start that. Harbinger expects to rape his bride, and I expect to be raped by my groom. This has been a point of difficulty between us. Your brothers didn't want to rape me, and you don't want to be raped by my brother. So we are at an impasse." Meanwhile, Whitepaw had finally yielded, and taken the bone from the woman's hand. The dog was being secondarily tamed.

"Why can't you just change that difficult aspect?" Rebel asked.

"Why can't you?"

It was an apt retort. She had no apt counter, so she changed the subject. "Now about the Others. If they won't let us hunt, we'll have to be rid of them. Are there many here?"

"Three men," Harbinger said. "Two of them have women who don't hunt or fight, and the third may be a brother. They have territories, just as we do, and this land by the lake is theirs. If we could be rid of them, other Others would probably leave us alone, because we would have won the territory."

"Now we have two men," Rebel said. "And two women. And three dogs." She stroked Brownback, and saw that Whitepaw now accepted Crenelle's touch on her back. "So we outnumber their three men."

"We don't," Harbinger said. "They are faster and stronger than we are, and can throw their spears farther. Even if we wounded one, we would not dare close in for the kill, because of their power. We would need two men to their one, to fight them, and even that would be uncertain. Three to one would be better."

Now Keeper spoke. "We discussed this with Hero and Craft. They agreed that we could not match the Others in a physical contest with even numbers. But they said the Others are stupid about planning ahead, and that's where we can prevail."

"Plan all you want to," Harbinger said. "But two men and two women can't match three Other men."

"It may not be easy, but with the right tactics, we should be able to do it," Keeper insisted.

But it was plain that Harbinger was not convinced. Neither was Crenelle.

"I think we'll have to show them," Rebel said. "Harbinger, how far can you throw a spear?"

"Accurately? To that rock." The man indicated a stone several paces distant.

"And how far can an Other man throw?"

"To *that* rock." Harbinger indicated one several paces farther. There was a steep dirt bank beside it. "So we would be dead before we could hope to score."

Keeper stood. He picked up his spear, together with a stick about half the length of the spear. He held the stick beside the spear, as if preparing to throw the two of them together. "The bank, not the rock," he said. "I don't want to ruin a good spear." He took careful aim, and hurled them at the farther bank.

The stick unfolded and dropped down, not flying. But the spear sailed for the bank, and scored on it at about a man's chest height. The point was embedded in the dirt; it was a good hard throw.

Harbinger's jaw dropped. "You are smaller than I am, and less muscular. How can you do that?"

Keeper held up the short stick. "This is a spear-thrower my brother Craft made. He learned it from another craftsman. He taught me and Rebel how to use it, so that we would be the equals of those who are of stouter physique than we are. It enables us to throw a spear significantly farther than we could otherwise, because it has the effect of extending the arm. Of course we had to practice; it takes time to master the technique." He paused, glancing sidelong at Harbinger. "Do you think this will help against the Others?"

Harbinger remained amazed. "It might. Can—?"

Rebel stepped up with her spear and throwing stick. She hurled the spear at the same bank. It struck lower, and with less force than her brother's had, but still would have hit and injured a man at that range. The thrower gave her power no woman could otherwise muster.

"Could I . . . ?"

Rebel handed him her stick, while Keeper went to recover the two spears. "You will need some help to manage it, the first time."

"I don't need help!"

"As you wish." She watched as he took his spear from Keeper and tried to fit it to the throwing stick. It didn't work; the spear and stick fell apart immediately.

"This doesn't—"

She smiled. "Because your spear isn't made for it. Try mine. It has a hole for the hook."

Harbinger shut his mouth and let her exchange spears, and fit the hook on the end of the throwing stick into the depression in the end of the spear. Then she showed him how to grip the two together, and make a special hurling motion that allowed the stick to extend the reach of the arm double and add force to the throw. She stood close before him, guiding his right hand with her left, gratified by his confusion of manner and gaze. She was still naked.

He tried it. The spear missed the bank and plowed into the ground.

"I prefer the old way," he said, disgruntled.

"It does take time," Keeper agreed. "We put many spears into the ground before we got the hang of it. We hope that this will make us both competent to help in the campaign."

"What campaign?" Harbinger asked.

"The one to secure this good region for us. To drive the Others away."

"You two may be able to throw your spears well, but that doesn't make us a match for three Other men."

"You forget the dogs," Rebel said. "They will attack the Others, on Keeper's command."

Harbinger was surprised again. "They will?"

Rebel smiled and dragged a small log to lie before the nearer rock. Then she stepped back.

Keeper touched the lead dog, Brownback. He pointed at the log. "Attack!"

All three dogs charged for the log, growling and biting savagely at it.

"Quit!" Keeper called.

The dogs left off the attack, and returned to him, their tails wagging.

Harbinger nodded. "This becomes impressive."

"One other thing," Keeper said. He turned to Rebel. "Rebel, if you would."

She smiled. She took up her spear and made a threatening motion toward the dogs. They immediately growled and scattered.

"They know the danger!" Crenelle said, surprised.

"Yes. I don't like my animals getting hurt."

"Truly impressive," Harbinger said.

"If you marry me," Rebel said, "my brother will train some dogs for you, who will obey your commands and no others." She set down the spear, and Brownback returned to her for stroking.

"But you will not be raped."

"Indeed I will not," she agreed. "But there may be a way, if you are interested."

"I am interested. You are a fine-looking woman. But—"

"But there is a catch," she said. "I am barren."

He stared at her. "Impossible!"

Rebel returned to sit by the fire, and the others settled down around it, letting her handle this her own way. She was privately pleased that he could not believe that a body like hers could be infertile. "Do you really wish to know?"

Harbinger nodded. "You rejected me before, and I stayed clear of you, because if I raped you, you would hate me and try to maim or kill me. Now you return and tell me you wish to marry me, but will not be raped, and are barren. You parade naked before me, inciting my lust. I doubt I will ever see a more desirable woman than you are at this moment. If you are angry with me, and wish to make me suffer, you are succeeding. I would take you this moment, if you told me you truly wanted it. You wouldn't even have to resist, as long as you didn't cooperate. But I fear you want me to try, and you will sweep up a knife and try to gut me, because I gave you a pretext. So I can't touch you or trust you. But I admit you are torturing me, and I want to know why."

There was the ring of sincerity to his words. She liked him better than ever. But she had to tell him the truth. "Then hear this: I was angry with you before, because you raped my sister Haven. But she never condemned you, and I think would have stayed with you, had her baby lived. As I came to know you, I understood about the rape; it is your way. Apart from that you are a good man, worthy of marriage. But just as you will not marry without rape, I will not submit to it."

She took a breath. Now came the hard part. "Part of the reason I refuse to be raped is that I thought I would never marry. Because no man would want me. So I made a thing of it, pretending that it was I who was refusing to be dominated by a man. But as I came to know you, I came to like you. To want to marry you. That is why I am preparing for the pain of being rejected by you. Because I am indeed barren. I know it. I have tried with more men than I can name, more times than I can count, more ways than I can remember. I can get any man I choose to have sex with me, and he will not leave off until I tell him to, being endlessly potent, though he cry for mercy. I confess I enjoyed showing my power over men at an early age. Before I had breasts I could get men into me, when I tried. After I got breasts I didn't even have to try. At first I feared getting a baby in my belly; then I thought I deserved it, for being wanton, and would have to marry whichever man put it into me. But at last I realized that no man could put a baby into me. It would have happened by now, if it were possible. I am eighteen, and have been doing it since I was ten, with grown men as well as youths. Most of them have fathered children elsewhere. So I am barren, and if you marry me, you will never have children. I will never remain home and passive; I will be out helping you explore and hunt, in my fashion.

That is the punishment the spirits will visit on you for taking your pleasures with the likes of me."

She took another breath, and stroked Brownback. Harbinger was immobile. "So if you will not marry me, I will understand. In that case you can have me without rape, knowing it is not marriage, by your definition, and in due course we will part company, as has already happened twice with my brothers and your sister." She cupped her breasts, then stroked her spread thighs, once more calling his attention to her assets. "Everything is as good as it looks, and I am no timid child. I have not shown you this merely to tease you; I will deliver in full measure. I will wear you out in a manner my sister could not. When we sleep, I will wake you with passion. When I am bored, as I often am, I will turn to you for something novel. When we go out on a hunt, I will give you silent sex while we lie in wait for an animal. It will never be dull. But if you still wish to marry me, we shall have to address the matter of how it can be possible, given our incompatible strictures about the initiation of it." Now she was done.

There was a silence. Crenelle and Keeper stayed well out of it, though Rebel could see by the way they both fidgeted that her discussion had turned them on. She feared she had turned Harbinger off, however, and she truly regretted it, because she really did like him. But she couldn't marry him on a false pretense. He had to know the price of the joy she would bring him. He had to know just how aggressive she was, in sex and other things. That had already driven away a number of otherwise amenable men.

At last Harbinger spoke. "If there were deaths elsewhere, orphaning children, would you adopt them?"

She had never thought of that. She *could* have a family, by such means. He had come up with the answer. In so doing, he was agreeing tacitly to marry her, when it could be arranged.

"Yes." And she had similarly agreed to marry him.

There was another silence. The decision had been made, but they still didn't know how to accomplish it.

"I think you could kiss him," Crenelle said. "As long as he doesn't touch you." Keeper nodded agreement.

"How can I kiss him without touching him?"

"Like this." Crenelle shifted her position. Then she leaned over and kissed Keeper, with no more than their mouths touching. He was so surprised he froze, which helped make it work. Crenelle completed her kiss and resumed her former position, looking a bit smug. "You touch him, not he you."

Good idea. Rebel got up, went around to Harbinger, bent down, and kissed him languorously on the mouth. They did not embrace.

Then she fetched her cloak and donned it, concealing her body. The time for temptation was past. "Now we must plan the campaign," she said briskly, glancing at her brother.

Keeper nodded, coming out of his trance, and began speaking, describing the strategy Craft had instilled in him. And slowly Harbinger's doubt converted to agreement.

That night the men slept on one side, the women on the other, with Keeper and Rebel adjacent. Neither Harbinger nor Rebel wanted any misunderstanding in the darkness, and though it was evident that Keeper found Crenelle highly intriguing, the woman was just as evidently less interested. She had vamped him on general principle, but had now turned off the glimpses. He just wasn't enough of a man for her. That was too bad, because Keeper was sensitive and loyal and competent with animals and plants, a good man for any woman.

In the morning they completed their preparations and went out on the campaign. The women bound up their hair and smeared dirt on their faces, trying to make themselves look more masculine, because the Others would not fight women. That did not mean they had no use for them, but the use was not kind. A straight fast death was preferable.

They took bolos, which were thongs weighted with solid bones, and one spear each. Then they set out for the nearby beest pasture, without the men. They used the second boat that was normally tied on the other side of the island, kept in reserve. They landed where Crenelle indicated, and hid the boat in bushes. The rest of this mission would be on foot.

In due course they reached the pasture, where a fair herd of beests was grazing. The beests paid them little attention, knowing the difference between human beings and Others. Only the Others had hunted them hitherto.

They selected a suitable calf who had strayed a bit too far from its dam. They walked slowly toward it, so as not to spook it prematurely. Its ears twitched; it was aware of them, but not yet concerned enough to leave its good grazing patch.

They went into confusion mode: they separated, and when the beest turned its head toward one, the other advanced. The motion was always at the fringe its vision. In that manner they were able to get within bola range.

Finally the beest spooked. But as it leaped to join its dam and the herd, Rebel threw her bola. Her aim was good, and the three weighted cords wrapped around the beest's hind legs, entangling them and bringing it down. It struggled and kicked, and the bola dropped away—but then Crenelle hurled her bola, entangling it again.

By the time it got free of the second bola, they were upon it, thrusting with their spears. It squealed as Crenelle stabbed it in the haunch, but the sound cut off as Rebel got it in the throat. It kicked wildly, thrashed its head about, bled copiously, and died.

Meanwhile the herd spooked, and charged away from there. Rebel knew that would alert the Others, who understood the habits of animals. She felt a cold chill, but had confidence in their plan. They recovered their bolas and tied them to their waists.

"We make pretty good hunters," Crenelle said with satisfaction as they drew their knives for the butchering. "I hope you do marry my brother."

"I have something in mind," Rebel said. "Are you interested in Keeper?" She knew the answer, but wanted to promote her brother's case, because Crenelle would make a good wife for him.

"I can't say I am. He's too young, and hardly taller than I am."

"But he does have a way with animals, and he understands plants."

"What's to understand about a plant?"

"If you get sick, he knows which ones can help. If you can't find regular forage, he knows which ones can be eaten if properly harvested and prepared. He has helped others that way."

"All of which makes him seem like an old woman."

Rebel shrugged. Some women didn't appreciate gentleness or foraging ability in a man. It was stupid, but she understood it, because she was one of those women. She was Keeper's sister, and felt a kind of responsibility for him, but were she not his sister she would as readily dismiss him. Only as his sister could she appreciate his worthwhile qualities. Crenelle was Rebel's age, and could hardly be blamed for being less impressed with a younger man. Yet the two would indeed be good for each other.

They proceeded with their butchery, stripping the good hide and dismembering the carcass. These things took time to do properly, and they took that time, though Rebel was suppressing the urge to flee. She knew that the Others would be on their way.

Indeed they were. Three men came striding across the plain, not trying to conceal themselves. They had spied illicit hunters, and were coming to punish the poachers.

"Take what you can, and flee," Rebel said tersely.

"To the nearest forest," Crenelle agreed.

Rebel bundled the hide, and Crenelle took a haunch. The rest they had to leave. "It seems a shame to do all this work, and leave it to the Others," Rebel said.

"But if our plan is successful, we'll be able to come back for it."

They ran. The Others were now uncomfortably close. But the women had gauged it so that they would be able to reach the forest first. If they miscalculated, there would be mischief indeed. But it had to be played close enough to allay suspicion.

Soon they were panting, and the Others were closing the gap. "Ditch the meat!" Rebel cried.

"Ditch the hide!" Crenelle retorted. But in a moment they both dumped their loads in the interest of increased speed. Perhaps the stuff would distract the pursuers.

It didn't. The Others were well aware of what came first: dealing with the enemy. Now the sound of their rough breathing was audible, as they continued to gain.

The two women reached the forest and got under the cover of the trees. The Others came right after them, having no fear of trees. They were frighteningly fast on their feet. In a moment they would catch hold of the women. They might even catch on to their nature, and commence raping designed to inflict maximum pain and injury. It was probably just a spook story, but Others were said to have ripped human women open by the size and force of their penetration, leaving their hips disjointed.

There was a thud and a scream. Rebel turned her head to see. One Other was down, and the two remaining were pausing, glaring around to locate the source of the mischief.

That was Harbinger's spear. He had hurled it from ambush and caught the Other in the side. Now he was lifting another spear. There was no sign of Keeper or the dogs.

The two Others charged the man. That allowed Rebel and Crenelle to slow, catching their breath. The first part of their plan had worked; now the three Others were two. The third man was not dead, but he was evidently not in any condition to fight.

Harbinger hurled his second spear. His aim was good, but the Other dodged it. Now Harbinger had no spear, while the Others still had theirs.

"Get out of there, brother!" Crenelle whispered. She knew, as Rebel did, that Harbinger would be no match for even one armed Other.

Harbinger turned and fled, with the two Others in pursuit. He could run faster than the women could, so the gap between them did not close rapidly. The Others did not throw their spears, preferring to run him down rather than risk a miss of an unevenly moving target. Others were very conservative fighters, and deadly because of it. Meanwhile Rebel and Crenelle were making their way swiftly through the forest to the next planned rendezvous. Because one Other down was not enough; they needed to take out another, before they could feel confident of victory.

They came to the spot, and hid behind a large tree, holding their bolas ready. The man was leading the Others in a wide circle back to this spot. This was the second ambush point. It was a natural path passing between large trees.

They heard the men coming. Harbinger was running well, and Rebel admired that, but the Others were running better, and were now close behind him. Soon one would throw his spear, and it would score.

Then the three dogs charged out from the opposite side of the path, growling. They passed right by Harbinger and closed on the Others. They were trained to attack only strangers, and their night with Harbinger had made him familiar.

The Others paused, plainly astonished. Wolves did not attack men! But they readied their spears to handle this new menace. Here, again, their caution proved this value: they were ready for this unexpected menace.

A spear flew from the side. That was Keeper, using his spear-thrower from out of sight. The range was too far and it missed, but it made the Others pause again. Another enemy? How many were there? That gave the dogs time to close on them.

The Others were no cowards. They held their spears, facing the dogs. But when they made ready to throw, the dogs growled and scattered. The Others stared, surprised again. This was not wolf behavior.

"Now," Rebel murmured. The two women emerged from concealment as the Others were facing away. They were quite close, because of the choice of location and cover. They threw their bolas at the nearest Other.

One bola wrapped around the man's head and arms. The other wrapped around his legs. He made an exclamation of amazement and dismay, fighting the strange attacker. The dogs, seeing him incapacitated, turned and charged from three directions.

Keeper emerged with his second spear. He hurled it at the entangled man, who was unable to dodge. The spear caught him in the chest. He groaned and went down. The dogs pounced on him, going for any likely spot. He was done for.

The third Other stared for a moment at Keeper, not understanding the mechanism of the spear-thrower. Then he hurled his spear at Keeper. But he was beyond effective range, and Keeper was alert; he was able to dodge it. The Other had made a tactical mistake, being distracted by the odd attacks.

The Other drew his knife and charged Keeper. But Keeper called to the dogs, and they left off their attack and bounded back toward him. Meanwhile Harbinger was running back, his own knife drawn, and the two women were also advancing. Because the women were emulating men, this made the group seem like four men and three wolves closing on one man.

The Other, realizing that the odds had changed, reversed his course and ran back the way he had come—right at Harbinger, who tried to turn and orient. The Other was on him in a moment, striking with his closed left hand, hard, more rapidly than a man could move. Harbinger was rocked back, jarred but not hurt. He tripped and fell on his back.

The Other ran on so swiftly that none of them could stop him, or catch him. He was gone. Keeper did not let the dogs pursue him; they were likely to get killed by themselves.

"But we got two of them," Rebel cried with satisfaction. She caught Harbinger, who was just sitting up, and kissed him hard on the mouth. Then she was up and away, leaving him bemused.

"I think now they will leave," Crenelle said. "Not just because one man is not enough to hold the territory. Because of the way we did it, with the bolas and the dogs and the spear-thrower. They don't understand these things, and they avoid what they don't understand. That third one will carry the word back, and they will go."

Harbinger nodded. "These are good things."

Well satisfied, they saw to the mopping up. The entangled Other was dead in grisly fashion. They stripped him of anything useful and left the body there for his kin to find. The other Other was alive, but gravely wounded; Harbinger dispatched him with a swift spear throw from close range. They stripped him similarly, and went on to recover the beest hide and meat. It had been a very good day.

They hauled the meat to the boats, now able to take all of it. When Rebel worked beside Keeper, she spoke quietly to him. "Would you like to have Crenelle?"

"Yes!" There was evidently no doubt in his mind.

"I may be able to steer her to you. Take whatever she offers."

"I will. She's—she's almost as good as you are."

Rebel flushed, caught by surprise. But it was a fair comparison, for she and Crenelle did seem to have more than age in common. If Keeper desired a woman who was similar to his wild sister, Rebel was flattered.

By the time they got everything back to the house, the day was fading. They cooked and ate some of the meat, and settled down for the night. Harbinger, fatigued from his hard running, was the first asleep. He was lying prone, snoring, with only his cloak as a cover.

Rebel caught the attention of the other two and made a signal of silence. Crenelle and Keeper looked at her perplexed, and did not speak. This had been a day of such adventure that they were perhaps numb to one more oddity. Rebel took thongs and knelt beside the sleeping man. Slowly, carefully, she lifted his arms behind him, and bound his wrists together. Then she did the same for his feet. She made sure the knots were secure; he was helpless. And still sound asleep.

Keeper and Crenelle watched, not comprehending her purpose. Crenelle's hand was on her knife; she would act if Rebel threatened actual harm to her brother. Brownback lay quietly, but he was watching the woman; he knew what a knife was, too, and he would attack it if it came near Rebel. But for the moment Crenelle was mostly curious what the point was. Keeper, however, was just beginning to understand that this related to what Rebel had told him privately.

Then Rebel stripped away her clothing and approached the sleeping man again. She put her hands on his shoulders and turned him over. She tore open his loose cloak, laying his body open to view. His eyes flickered open.

"Now you are mine," she said, taking hold of his penis and kneading it, forcing it to react. She knelt and brought her face to his, kissing him. "You are helpless. I will possess you, and you can't resist." She lay against him, pressing her torso against his, flattening her breasts against his chest. "You can do nothing. You are subject to my will—this first time."

Now Crenelle caught on. She licked her lips, half smiling.

Then Rebel set herself on him, and guided his erect penis into her. Brownback watched, but was aware that the woman was not the one being attacked. The dogs had seen sex often enough, and didn't care.

Rebel pushed down with her belly while kissing him again. "I am raping you," she said, lifting her body slightly, then jamming down hard. "You may struggle, but you can't escape me. I will have my will of you."

And in a moment she did. She felt him pulsing within her. That sensation set her off, and her own climax came, long and slow and delicious. She kissed him repeatedly, savoring it. He did not try to avoid any of it.

When at last she cooled, he was limp. But she wasn't quite through with him. "Now I will release you, if you promise not to flee. This rape has been accomplished, and we are married. Do you accept it?"

For the first time, he spoke. "Yes." He had accepted the reverse rape in lieu of the regular one. *She* had not been raped, and never would be.

She got off him and rolled him back over. She untied his hands, and then his feet. She glanced across at Crenelle and Keeper, almost hidden in the darkness. "And you two witnessed this. Rape and marriage. It is done."

"Yes," Crenelle agreed, her voice sounding awed.

"Yes," Keeper said, similarly awed. He had seen his sister indulge in wild moments, but this was beyond any past exploit.

Rebel lay beside Harbinger, holding his hand. She had accomplished her primary purpose. What about the secondary one?

"Do you want me to rape you similarly?" Crenelle asked Keeper, humor in her voice.

"Yes."

"Forget it. You will have to do your own raping. I am not that desperate."

"I almost could, if you wanted it."

"No. You are too young for me. But that scene got me hot. I will be with you, this night, without marriage."

"Yes." No hesitancy there.

She started to embrace him, but the third dog, Toughtail, growled warningly. "You will have to put aside the knife," Keeper said.

"Done." Crenelle set her knife down beside Whitepaw, who eyed it warily.

Then the two of them were at it, while Rebel lay beside Harbinger.

So she had indeed succeeded there too, to a degree. She had known Crenelle would like the reverse rape, and be sexually excited by it. There really was no person for her to turn to except Keeper. But women were unpredictable, so Crenelle's decision had been in doubt.

"Do you want more?" Rebel asked Harbinger.

"Not right now."

"You don't mind that I'm barren?"

"Not now."

She snuggled against him, and they slept. In the night she dreamed, not of sex, but of what they had accomplished. They had organized in a way the dull Others could not, and used all their resources to conquer their enemy. Because of weapons made by Craft and taught to herself and Keeper. Craft could make anything he set his mind to. But he lacked the time to do a lot, because of the other requirements of living.

But suppose he could spend his whole time doing what he loved, making things? How much more could he accomplish? Suppose Hero could spend his whole time hunting and fighting; how good at it would he get? And Haven, who liked cooking and other dull chores; suppose she could cook all the time, freeing women like Rebel to do what they most liked? She could dance naked all the time for gaping men, making them eager to plumb their mates. What a wonderful life it would be!

But it was only a dream, impossible in real life. She turned over and wandered into other dreams. But she did not forget this one.

In the morning Rebel woke Harbinger by rubbing against him until he reacted, and they had more sex. Then she broached a key question: "We can't stay here; it's not our way. Do we travel north or south?"

"North," he said. "I like cold winters."

"I like hot summers."

"I don't want to fight you. You might rape me again."

"No, only the first time. After that you can't resist."

"My sister will travel with me, wherever I go. Will your brother travel with you?"

"Yes. And my other brothers will join us."

"Then let them decide."

Rebel was amenable, so she called across to the other pair. "Hey, stop whatever you're doing and answer this: Do we travel north or south?"

"North," Crenelle's muffled voice came. There was laughter in it.

"South," Keeper said.

This was going to be a problem.

•

Mankind went both north and south from there, and probably west too, in a returning ripple intersecting the already-populated areas. North took him along the coast of Asia, through China and eastern Siberia, and ultimately to the Americas. South took him across the sea to New Guinea and Australia, and later to the myriad Pacific islands.

The actual pace of the development of technology is uncertain, because very little other than the stone tools and weapons survived the dissolution of time. But there were surely equivalent advances in woodworking, leatherworking, and weaving. The bola was known at this time, and the atlatl, or spear-thrower, could have been known too. Certainly modern mankind displaced Erectus, *who faded from the world despite having dominated it for almost two million years. Probably because the technology and planning of the moderns made them superior warriors, and shrewder users of natural resources.*

At this time the full flowering of mankind's culture and technology had not yet occurred. That was to be brought about not long thereafter, however, by a single significant idea that took some time to gain acceptance. This was Rebel's dream: organized specialization. To share resources to such an extent that many members of a band could concentrate on what they were best at, without being denied food or shelter or the pleasures of the opposite gender. This idea may seem obvious to the folk of today, but could hardly have been obvious to those who had survived all prior challenges by being consummate generalists. It was never grasped by Erectus *or Neandertal, though they did have the rudiments. Four hundred thousand years ago they could make fine balanced wooden spears, and chip hand axes efficiently from large anvil stones. But that was as far as it went; they left the axes lying on the ground when through with the specific task for which they had been chipped. What mankind did was a special type of specialization, accomplished by adult individuals within the framework of an organized culture of a supremely generalistic species. The social revolution preceded the technological one. Any human person could assume any specialist role, and become proficient therein.*

In contrast, an animal will always live the type of life for which it is destined by heredity. A young rabbit will not become a predator, and a tiger will not survive by grazing on grass. Some species, like the ants and termites, do have specialist members, but they are locked in to their roles, the queen always laying the eggs, the warriors always guarding and fighting, the workers always working. Bee workers seem to be able to assume some different roles in the course of their lives, but they will never become swimmers, or scholars, or entrepreneurs. Neandertal specialized physically for the cold climate of Europe, and thereby limited himself. Erectus *adapted to his own terrain, never feeling the need to change his environment much. Only human beings, with the ultimate tool for generalization, the reasoning brain, can specialize in everything. Because of that discovery, mankind became rapidly far more efficient in most of his pursuits, improving his safety and food supply, enabling him to increase his population enormously.*

When the idea of specialization became accepted, it had a profound effect on human society. In fact, it led to the relatively rapid improvement of all the arts and crafts. For the first time there was leisure to develop the crafts as arts rather than occasional diversions. Stone knappers advanced their technology, and painters became highly proficient, and hunters developed their skills beyond anything possible before. Not only did they do more, they did better, perfecting tools to make other tools, learning to use symbolism well beyond that of word = object, a process leading ultimately to the computer age.

Thus the age of the generalist gave way to the age of the specialist individual, protected by the generalist tribe. By 40,000 years ago mankind was in full leap forward, on the way to the remarkable accomplishments we see today. Mankind has not changed much physically or mentally in the past hundred thousand years, but has instead developed social dynamics and sophisticated technical mechanisms that have changed much of the environment to suit his inclination. All because of an idea that may have originated in southeast Asia, and rippled out to the rest of the globe, reaching Australia, Europe, and Africa, transforming the entire human culture, and the world. Rebel's dream.

Meanwhile, the dog really does turn out to be man's oldest and best friend. Probably first domesticated in Africa, the tamed wolf traveled with man wherever he went, including Australia as the dingo, and North America as the Carolina Dog, with ginger-colored coat and fox-like face, which may be closest to the original stock. The enormous variety of types dates from relatively recently, perhaps the last 20,000 years. But surely the dog was serving man well throughout, and might indeed have been the difference that enabled mankind to oust the relatives of Erectus *from dominion of the world. A human man might have been puny compared to* Erectus, *but a man and a dog would have been more formidable.*

5

KEEPER'S QUEST

Obviously mankind made it to the American continents; the question is how and when. An oddity is that there are indications of his presence in South America before there are in North America, though his only feasible access was via Asia, Siberia, Alaska, and North America. Could he have come by water? This was theorized in Volume III, Hope of Earth, *but there are counterarguments, and the case is uncertain. For example, the same ice that blocked off Alaska extended to the western coast of North America. Boats would have had to slide along up to two thousand miles of ice to pass that barrier. Unless families could subsist solely from the sea for months, this seems impractical. So it seems more likely that they came overland, or along the coast at the same time as the glaciers retreated enough to leave the natural shore exposed.*

During the last ice age, so much water was taken up by the ice sheets that the sea level dropped by as much as four hundred feet. This exposed land in many parts of the world, such as off southeast Asia as we have seen, and between Asia and America. Specifically, between Siberia and Alaska. What is now the shallow Bering Sea was then the broad arctic plain of Beringia. It was cool in summer and frigid in winter, covered with grasses, shrub birch and sedge. Herds of animals migrated across it seasonally, seeking better pastures beyond it. It was bounded gradually on the west by Siberia and abruptly on the east by mountainous ice. The ice was an effective barrier; there is no evidence that mankind or other creatures crossed it in either direction until it melted, ending the ice age.

It is an irony that the same time that Beringia was open so that it could be crossed, the ice was thickest, so that it could not be crossed. When the ice receded, the sea advanced. So for 50,000 years there was always a barrier, either of water or ice, except for one time, 11,000 years ago, when there was an avenue of opportunity that allowed mankind to pass through and colonize America. But that's a later story. This one is about life on Beringia itself, 20,000 years ago. The setting is that part of Beringia that touched what are now the Aleutian Islands that trail off southwest of Alaska. The Cordilleran ice sheet covered the mountains of south Alaska, extending down the Aleutians, so that for a time that seeming wall of ice reached well beyond mainland Alaska, and became the border of Beringia itself. The land north was actually clear of ice all the way to the Arctic Ocean. This was not because it was warmer—it was cold enough—but because there was not enough moisture there to sustain a glacier. Thus there was the seeming anomaly of land to the north, and ice to the south. It was essentially an east-west barrier, not a north-south barrier. In the summer it might have melted back a little, forming fissures and drainage channels, and in winter it would have frozen again to its former extent. That marginal flow should have encouraged vegetation at the fringe, attracting grazing animals. There could have been an enduring human residence there, but for the purpose of this story it is assumed that there were only occasional explorations.

•

Keeper gazed at the wall of ice. It was huge and ugly, with patches of dirt and sand embedded, irregularly reaching toward the land. The edge was slushy, for the daylight sun melted it. But it froze again at night, as far as it could, and the war between sun and ice continued. Keeper was fascinated by the slow dynamic interaction.

"Ugh," Crenelle said. "Now we've seen it; can we go?"

She did not share his interest. He knew he ought to seek a woman who was more compatibly inclined. But he adored Crenelle, and had to try to win her. She was beautiful and healthy and infinitely appealing, and she was close, because of a family connection. She had given him his first experience of sex, and of love, and even if it wasn't returned, he was bound.

"But this is different," he argued. "So much ice, extending so far beyond anything we know. Don't you want to see the far side of it?"

"I don't even want to see this side of it," she retorted. "It's the ugliest thing I've seen."

He glanced at her. Perhaps it made sense that a woman as lovely as Crenelle should hate ugliness. Her appearance was a stark contrast to that of the ice. Even bundled in her bison hide shirt and pants, she was esthetic. The only match for her in beauty was his sister Rebel, the same age. But in other respects the two were quite different.

"If we found a way around it, there might be good land," Keeper said.

"And there might not." She turned her head. "What do you think, Hero?"

"I'm not smart enough to think," Hero said affably. "My brothers do it better."

Hero was a nice guy. He was powerful, but gentle with people. And despite his claim, not stupid. He knew that Keeper wanted the company of Crenelle—wanted, in fact, to marry her—so he had agreed to come on this day of exploration.

Because Crenelle's interest was in Hero. In fact, Crenelle had met Hero first, and had sex with him, but then wouldn't marry him because he wouldn't announce that he had raped her. It was evident that she still would like to marry him, but Hero's attitude hadn't changed; he would neither rape her nor say he had. So though Keeper knew that Hero found the woman just as fascinating as Keeper did, Hero would not touch her. Instead he tried to facilitate things for his little brother. So he had come on this exploration, thus tacitly persuading Crenelle to come too, giving Keeper that extra chance.

"You never try to take anything from your brothers," Crenelle complained. She was surely aware of the reason Hero had come, but she was caught in much the way Keeper was: If she wanted his company, it had to be on his terms.

"Or my sister," Hero agreed affably.

"She got *my* brother."

They laughed, but there was an edge to it. Their sister Rebel had indeed married Crenelle's brother Harbinger, and the two seemed well satisfied. But that made it more evident that Crenelle herself had not married any of the brothers, despite coming close more than once. Yet that business about rape was a problem for all of them; they didn't believe in it. If Crenelle had softened enough on that point, she could have had any of the three.

Meanwhile, Keeper was studying the edge of the ice. "Look at that," he said.

"What, more ice?" Crenelle inquired disdainfully.

"A mammoth print!" he said, excited.

She frowned. "All I see is slush."

Hero looked, his hunter's eye quickly deciphering the obscure mark. "You're right. In fact, there's an occasional mammoth path here."

"Yes. He must come here to chew the ice when he's thirsty. A lone bull, big."

"How can you tell?" Crenelle asked, her disdain fading. She knew that discovery of a mammoth was a significant event.

"By the size of the foot. Only a male could be this big."

"And a bit lame," Hero said. "Which is why he comes here instead of trekking to the water hole to the north."

"He's getting old," Keeper agreed. "I think we can take him."

Crenelle shook her head. "All this you know—from a single indistinct print?"

Both men turned looks of feigned surprise on her. "Of course," Hero said. "Isn't it obvious?"

Keeper saw her stiffen with anger, realizing that they were teasing her, but immediately stifle it. She was trying to entice Hero, not quarrel with him. If only she felt that way about Keeper!

They returned to the camp. The three dogs bounded out to meet them, tails wagging. They had been left behind, because it was hard to explore anything quietly with canine company. The other family members were there too, preparing for the evening meal. Haven had a big pot of boiling horsemeat, while Rebel twisted tufts of waste sedge into knots for the fire. The main sedge stems made good baskets, and mats for sleeping on, but there was always dry refuse. There was so little of anything on this bare plain that they had to make do with whatever offered.

"We found a mammoth," Crenelle said.

Craft raised an eyebrow. "Do you have it in your pack?" He was working on an arrow, shaping the split end to hold a stone point firmly.

"No, she must have eaten the whole thing already," Harbinger said. "It's a wonder she isn't fatter than she is."

"A print. By the ice," Crenelle said. She was by no means fat, which was why they teased her about it.

Interest grew. "Mammoth meat would be good, after all the horse and bison we've been chewing," Rebel said. She glanced at Keeper, knowing that he was the expert on this. "Is it huntable?"

"I think so," Keeper said. "It is large and old and lame, and alone. Such a creature is never a sure hunt, but if we plan well, we may succeed."

"What's it doing by the ice?" Rebel asked.

"The grass grows better there, because of the water from the melt, and maybe the dirt it dumps down. But mainly for the ice it can chew for drinking. It's as good as a water hole. So it has all it needs right there close by, and doesn't have to travel much. He's probably not far off, maybe in an alcove in the ice."

"So we can locate it without much trouble," Craft said. "And drive it against the ice, instead of having to entirely encircle him."

Harbinger shook his head. "Mammoth aren't like horses. It'll retreat only so far. Then it'll charge. That's mischief."

"We'll have to organize carefully," Craft said. "Select our terrain, drive him as far as we can, then use arrows, thrown spears, and finally stabbing spears. Better if we can prepare a covered pit, but he's probably too wary for that."

Haven looked up. "You speak as though we'll hunt him just ourselves. Four men can't kill a mammoth."

"The main tribe is two days' march distant," Craft reminded her. "If we want that mammoth, we'll have to take him ourselves. There's a lot we could do with it. Meat for a month, tusks to carve, bones to build a house with. If Keeper thinks we can handle it—"

"I'm not sure," Keeper said quickly. "A bull mammoth's unpredictable. It might be too much for us by ourselves. Four men—"

"And three women," Rebel reminded him.

"I don't want you getting trampled by an elephant!" Harbinger said.

"Oh, pooh! We're not going to run under its feet, you know."

"But when it charges—"

"Maybe Keeper should study it some more," Haven said. "To make sure it's not too much for us. We don't want to lose any people."

"Good idea," Craft agreed. "Meanwhile I can prepare heavy arrows."

"And a heavy bow," Hero said. "The farther we can stand from that creature, the better off we'll be."

"I'll do what I can," Craft said. He glanced at Keeper. "So why don't you same three go out tomorrow and track the mammoth, and we'll prepare for the hunt here."

Keeper appreciated that. Craft had had his turn at Crenelle, and lost her, just as Hero had. He still liked her, just as Hero did. But he regarded it as Keeper's turn. If Keeper failed, then the matter would be open for reconsideration.

"I feel as if I am being herded," Crenelle muttered.

"You don't have to go," Keeper told her.

She flashed him a smile. "I am my own woman. I will go. It isn't as if you are inferior. Just young for me."

He was eighteen and she was nineteen. He couldn't change that. She was the only woman he would ever want. He would accept her company on whatever basis she allowed.

So it was decided. They settled down to their meal of horsemeat, and to their sod shelters for sleep. Harbinger and Rebel shared a shelter, and Haven and Crenelle were together, and the three brothers had the third. The dogs curled up together wherever they chose. When one of the brothers finally married Crenelle, they would make another shelter for two.

When one married her. Keeper thought about that every night, wishing he could be the one. Had she married either of his elder brothers, he would have had no such dreams, for the three of them did not impinge on the privileges of the others. But neither relationship had worked out, so now she was his for the taking—if only he could take her. Theoretically she would be his if he raped her, but he could no more do that than his brothers could. There had to be some other way. If only he could think of it.

As if tuning into his thoughts, she appeared, or rather her voice did, in the dusk that passed for night. In the summer the sun never quite set; it just hovered above the horizon as if reluctant to depart. So Crenelle had no trouble walking across. It was a nightly ritual. "I don't suppose any of you men have changed your mind?"

How he wanted to answer! But he couldn't. It was Hero who did: "Nobody's going to rape you, Crenelle."

"Not even token?"

"Not even token," Craft said.

"Are you sure?"

It was Keeper's turn. "Yes," he said, wishing it were otherwise.

"Think of the joy your sister is giving my brother at this moment. I could give similar joy to you, if you just had the gumption to take it."

"I know it," Keeper agreed. How he longed to have that joy of her!

She departed silently. Keeper wondered if his brothers were as regretful as he was. He thought they were.

•

Next day the three of them packed cuts of horsemeat and tools and set out for the ice. Keeper was glad Crenelle was coming, though he knew it was still for Hero rather than for him. But if he could somehow win her, he knew she would be true to him thereafter. She was a good woman, perfect for a wife. Just with that one thing about how a marriage should be made. She wanted to be taken, violently. She seemed less certain than she had been, but still she hadn't softened enough to yield on that matter. Otherwise there would have been a marriage long ago.

It was a fair trek across the tundra, and a dull one. The ground was almost level, with sections of shallow swamp with tussocks. No plant rose above knee height. The seven of them were able to survive here only by hunting the large animals that trekked across in quest of better grazing elsewhere. Now and then they started a rabbit or a bird. Meanwhile clouds of black flies accompanied them. All of them wore a tonic Keeper had squeezed from certain herbs, that discouraged flies and mosquitoes. Otherwise life here would have been unbearable.

"Let's play a game," Crenelle suggested. She was clearly bored, and she did not take boredom lightly, any more than Rebel did. "A contest, and a prize. Whoever spies the first sure sign of the mammoth being close by—what would that be?"

"Fresh dung," Keeper said.

"Fresh dung. Whoever spies that wins a kiss from me. Agreed?"

She was trying to get Hero to kiss her. But Keeper would have an equal chance. "Agreed," he said for both of them.

"And whoever first spies the mammoth itself, wins me for the night. One night only, no obligation." She paused. "Agreed?"

And she wanted to have sex with Hero, hoping to persuade him to marry her, her way. She was very good with sex, as they both knew. Such a night would be persuasive indeed. But again, Keeper had an even chance. "Agreed."

Hero was silent. "That binds you both?" she asked, making sure of the bargain. She didn't want a contest only Keeper could win.

"Agreed," Hero finally mumbled.

"And you will really look?" she persisted.

There was a pause, but an answer had to be made. "Yes."

"One would think the prize was not worthwhile," she said, affecting dismay. She well understood the reason for Hero's reluctance: that he wanted to be fair to his brother. The real contest was between her need to be raped, once, and their need never to treat any woman that way. Her need to have it bruited about, and their need never to be accused of any such thing. Eventually one side or the other would break down and give way to a sufficient extent. But at this point, none of them knew which side that would be. Rebel had found a way around it, with Harbinger, but Crenelle evidently didn't care for that.

She must have been pondering the same question, for she came up with an answer. "And whoever kills the mammoth can demand any favor of any of the others, and the other must agree. Any favor at all."

This was especially interesting. Did she mean that the winner could require that she marry him without rape? Or was that something other than a favor, by her definition? And why did she say "any of the others," rather than just her?

Keeper had to ask. "You are the prize for the first two. Do you mean that someone else might be the prize for the third?"

"There is something I could not openly agree to," she said, "so I won't say it. So I make it more general. Maybe there is something you really want your brother to do."

Now Hero spoke. "Suppose I won—and asked you to marry my brother?"

She was silent for a time. Keeper could appreciate why. Hero, not known for cleverness, had nevertheless come up with the hole in her offer. She was hoping to get Hero, by having him win her without rape, but she might wind up with Keeper regardless of who won.

Finally she spoke. "I was thinking of a favor for the winner, not a favor done for someone else. I think it would have to be direct."

And she had found a repair for the hole. Her reasoning seemed fair enough. And of course if Hero won, he would not have to require her to marry him. He might simply ask for another kiss. So it wasn't tight. But if Hero won, it might indeed seem that he had a right to take her. Ultimately, she had to go to the man she wanted to go to. Anything else would be like another form of rape. So while Keeper desperately wanted to win her, he saw that this was not the way. Which meant that if he won, he would have to ask some other favor.

"Agreed?" she prompted.

"Agreed," Keeper said.

Then, after a pause, Hero agreed also.

They reached the mottled wall of ice. Once again Keeper marveled that such a thing existed. How huge it was! Where was the end of it? Was this the end of the world? Where it got too cold for land, and turned to ice? So there might be nothing beyond it. Yet there was the sea, and it went on past the ice. How he longed to explore that!

"I just thought of something," Crenelle said. "Suppose *I* spy the turd, or the beast? What prize do I get?"

"Then you get to keep what you have found," Hero said.

Keeper bit his tongue to keep from laughing. His brother had scored again.

"Thank you so much for your generosity," the woman said, making a noise as if spitting out something distasteful. "There's nothing I'd rather have than a fresh mammoth turd."

"It would grow some very rich plants," Keeper offered.

Meanwhile they were tracking the huge creature. Its trail was not hard to decipher, as it had been grazing as it went, tearing up whole sedge plants to chew on. The ground near the ice was damp and a bit mushy, and there were a number of plain prints. At one point there was a clear ice slick, where the animal had stood against the wall and gouged out clean ice to slake its thirst.

"Good idea," Hero said, and broke off a sliver of ice for himself. The others did the same. Water was not necessarily easy to come by, in this dry level land.

Hero, first to resume travel, paused. "I see it," he murmured.

They joined him. Sure enough, there was a fresh pile of manure that could only be from the elephant. He had won the first contest.

"Here is your prize," Crenelle said, pleased. She stood close to him, took his face in her hands, angled it to suit her, and gave him a firm and lingering kiss.

Keeper looked away. It wasn't just jealousy, though that was a component. It was that they did make an appealing couple, and Hero surely was more deserving of her favor than Keeper was. He was older, and larger, and stronger, and better in hunting and combat. And she plainly desired him. Keeper was simply in the way.

But he couldn't let go. Crenelle was too appealing a woman. He would probably lose her, but he would do it by failing, not by giving up.

They moved on, carefully, for it was their mission to spy the mammoth, not to spook it. They needed to learn its habits and trails, so as to know how to hunt it effectively.

Hero had been leading the way, but now he slowed. He bent over, reached inside his legging, and scratched. Itches were chronic; bugs got inside clothing, seeking whatever section of flesh was not protected by the repellent juice. Keeper went on ahead, not waiting, rounding the bend of the ice wall.

There was the mammoth. "I see it," he breathed, awed by the grandeur of the beast. It was feeding on a richer patch of brush, not paying attention. Mammoths had few if any natural enemies, apart from man, so tended to be careless. This one was huge and shaggy, twice the height of a man, with enormous twisting white tusks and a trunk that reached down to touch the ground. Its feet were massive stumps, while its eyes were relatively tiny. What a creature!

"So you do," Crenelle said, coming to stand beside him. "You will have me for the night."

So he would. He had forgotten that for the moment. But now he realized something: Hero had paused at a most propitious time. But for that stray itch, Hero would have been the first to round this bend and spy the quarry. Hero, seasoned hunter that he was, must have known, and deliberately given the first sight to Keeper. Giving him Crenelle, for the night.

He hoped she didn't realize that. But he feared that she did. Should he tell her to give the night to his brother? Keeper wanted her so much, but it was complicated.

"No, I'll do it," she murmured, reading the doubt on his face. "He wants you to have it."

"Sorry," he said, his emotions uncomfortably mixed.

They studied the mammoth, and spied out its paths. By evening Keeper had an excellent notion of the creature's habits, and concluded that they could indeed take it.

That night Haven came to share lodging with her brothers, yielding her place to Keeper. He joined Crenelle, still mixed in emotion. This night was a gift of Hero, with whom Crenelle would rather have been; how could he reconcile that with his own presence here?

"Let me make one thing clear," she told him as she got them both naked under piled blanket skins, and got Whitepaw comfortably settled by their feet. "It's not that I think you are inferior. You're not. Your way with animals is wonderful. I just always thought of marrying someone older than I, rather than younger. So I don't take you as seriously as perhaps I should. I know it's your turn. If I hadn't been so insistent on a rape, I could have married one of your brothers long ago. So I am obliged to give you a fair chance, not just because your brothers want it, but because you deserve it in your own right. So here it is: fight me, rape me now, and you will win me."

"I can't do that," he said, ashamed.

"I won't even resist. I will just lie here unmoving, telling you no, that I brought you here for nothing, making you angry."

She was making it so easy! But he was still unable. "I can't."

"You can't," she agreed. "Any more than your brothers could. And I don't care to do what Rebel did with my brother. Very well; we'll do it the easy way. For this night only." She rolled into him, and put one leg over his, pressing against him. "Come into me, you hesitant suitor."

He did. But he wished he could have made even the semblance of a rape, and won her, her way. He felt so inadequate, even in the throes of the delight she gave him.

They slept, sated yet not satisfied. Being with her like this was sheer joy, yet hollow because it was so much less than it should have been. He wondered whether he would dream of performing the rape she demanded, and wake to know it wasn't true.

He woke at night, and found her sleeping curled, facing away from him. Desire sprang anew: he could still do it. He could grab her as she slept, and penetrate her cleft before she could react or resist, and it would be rape. She would wake to find it accomplished. He would never have a better chance.

He put a hand on her hip and moved in close. She continued to sleep, not responding to his touch. Her flesh was soft and evocative. He knew exactly where to go. His hard member was right there at the aperture, ready for the thrust. In a moment he would be inside her, and it would be done.

But he didn't. He couldn't take a woman without her consent, even if she had given her consent for her nonconsent. He just couldn't.

"Damn!" he muttered.

"Damn," she echoed.

"You knew!" he said, chagrined.

"Of course I knew. How long do you think I have been here like this, waiting for you to wake?"

"I'm sorry."

"Well, go on in, so it's not a total waste."

He did so, and it was phenomenal. But he had forfeited his chance for the real accomplishment.

"You're a decent man," she said. "I respect that, really, Keeper. It's just that . . ." She shrugged, and he felt the motion all the way inside. "But if you catch me asleep again, don't hesitate. Because after tonight I'll be back after Hero. You know that."

"I know it," he agreed.

They finished and slept again. He hoped he really would wake to find her truly asleep, and have the courage to take her, but he knew it wouldn't happen.

He dreamed she was bestriding him, in the manner they had seen Rebel do with Harbinger. He woke to find that she was, but she did not take it the last step. "I can't do it either," she said, disgusted.

He laughed, without much humor. "Do it anyway, so it's not a total waste."

She set him in her, and lay on him, squirming, forcing him to spend. "This is ridiculous."

"I think we really would be good for each other, if we could find a way to marry."

"It would be good with any of the three of you," she said seriously. "And I mean to have one of you, some way."

"Some way," he agreed.

They slept again. This time neither woke. Keeper was disappointed to discover that dawn had arrived, and the camp was stirring. Crenelle had given him several chances, and he had squandered them all. As he had perhaps known he would.

They got up and dressed. It was time for the hunt. Maybe, he thought despairingly, he would be the one to make the fatal thrust, and win a complete favor from her. Yet even then, he knew, he would not be able to ask her to set aside her requirement.

Craft approached him. "I have made a new bow that I think will work well for you. It's larger than usual, and requires a longer arrow, but has more power. For this hunt, we need power."

"Yes," Keeper agreed somewhat tightly. He was excited by the prospect of the hunt, but apprehensive too, because he knew how dangerous those huge beasts could be. "But shouldn't you or Hero be the one to use it?"

"Hero will use the spear-thrower, which gives a harder thrust than any arrow. Haven will keep him supplied. I will make sure of all the weapons. You will do better with the arrows, knowing exactly where to put them."

"In the eye," Keeper said. "That mammoth is so big and fleshy that we'd have trouble reaching its heart even if it stood still and let us try for an hour at close range."

Craft laughed. "And it won't do that!" he agreed. "So you try this bow, and see if you can hit an eye."

Keeper tried. He set up a hide target thirty paces distant and drew the first long arrow. The feel was strange, but the draw was smooth and strong. He had to exert more power than he was used to, but seemed better able to do that, with this powerful bow. Craft knew what he was doing, as usual.

He sighted along the arrow and loosed it. He scored on the target. It was almost as if he had thrust the arrow there with his hand, from up close. It had gone right where he aimed it.

He tried again, and scored again. This was indeed a fine instrument, and these were fine arrows. But could he score on a moving monster's tiny eye? He doubted it. Not with one arrow, or two.

But Craft had made ten arrows. That might be enough. That had to be enough.

They moved out. Keeper called the dogs, and they bounded along ahead of him, happy to be participating. Crenelle fell into step beside him. "I'm your spear carrier," she said.

He was thrilled, but doubtful. "I thought you'd prefer to help your brother, or—"

"Rebel's helping Harbinger. Haven's helping Hero. I'm helping you. Craft made the assignments. He knows what he's doing. This is serious business."

Keeper nodded, gratified. They were still arranging things so that he could be close to Crenelle, and she wasn't objecting. He might be the least of the brothers, but they kept peace in the family by being fair to each other. It was still his turn, it seemed.

But if he failed to kill the mammoth with a shot through the eye, his turn would be finished. Then Crenelle would go to one of his brothers.

They reached the wall of ice and spread out. They did not try to go silently, for the mammoth would soon enough be aware of them. They would harry it and try to drive it into the sea, where it would be much easier prey.

They spied it, foraging against the wall. They spread out, barring its escape to the plain. Whichever way it ran, it would have to pass a man. If it didn't run, they would close in, but leave a channel along the wall.

Hero and Haven, at the northern side, started hooting. The mammoth lifted its head, gazing at them. It didn't understand small creatures that acted as if they were dangerous. It backed away, then turned and strode along the wall toward the south. Exactly as they wanted.

Harbinger and Rebel paced it, not making noise as long as it was going the right way. Craft followed them, carrying a bundle of spears.

Keeper waited. He was south of the mammoth, and would let it pass, because the sea was not far beyond. The ice and the sea: that was the trap.

But the beast was too canny to be herded far. It suddenly turned and charged Harbinger. Now Rebel sounded off, ululating. The mammoth, surprised by this new sound, turned its head to look at her.

Harbinger hurled his spear. He had grown proficient with the spear-thrower, and the shot was good. The spear struck the beast's shaggy shoulder and lodged.

The mammoth squealed in pain and rage. It whirled and started north, the spear bobbing. The wound had to be painful, but not critical.

Hero flung his spear. This struck the animal on the head, between the eyes—and bounced off the heavy bone there. That was the problem with an animal this massive. Flesh wounds didn't stop it, and neither did bone wounds.

But it did cause the mammoth to change direction again. It ran south, while the women gave Harbinger and Hero second spears. They pursued the creature, spear-throwers lifted, ready to throw again when there was a suitable target.

"Here it comes," Crenelle said. There was a catch in her voice; she was nervous, if not frightened. But she remained beside him, holding his spare arrows.

"I'll try a shot," Keeper decided. Herding the animal was fine, but if he could take it down as it passed, that was better.

He waited until the mammoth was between them and the wall. Then he drew and loosed. The arrow struck the animal's wrinkled ear. He had not allowed sufficiently for its motion.

Crenelle handed him another arrow. He nocked it and drew—as the mammoth suddenly turned toward him, pausing. It started toward him.

He loosed another, but this time hadn't allowed for the turning head. The arrow broke against a tusk.

Now the mammoth decided that he was the enemy. It trumpeted and started toward him.

Crenelle gave him another arrow. Then she stood, setting down the arrows. "It's going to get by us, and escape onto the plain. I'll drive it back."

"Don't get close to it!" Keeper cried.

But she was already in motion. "Go, go, go!" she screamed, waving her arms.

But this time the beast did not spook away from the noise. It had been injured several times, and was in a frenzy. It oriented on her and charged.

Keeper's vision became preternaturally clear. There was the woman. There was the mammoth, twice her height and enormously more massive. Its whitish tusks were coming at her like twin twisted spears.

He loosed. The arrow struck just below the right eye and lodged in loose flesh. The mammoth tossed its head as if flinging the nuisance away, and continued its charge.

Keeper snatched up another arrow. He had time for only one more shot before the monster trampled the woman.

He drew and aimed, but the target wasn't right; even a perfect shot would glance off the bone of the eye ridge. He held his fire, cursing.

Crenelle, realizing that it wasn't working, stopped. She tried to turn to flee, but wasn't going to make it in time.

Then the head turned slightly, bringing the eye into line. Keeper loosed the arrow before he knew it.

Suddenly the arrow was in the mammoth's eye, embedded deeply, penetrating to the brain. The creature's knees buckled and it tumbled to the ground, just short of the woman. It struggled a moment, its tusks tearing up turf. Then it relaxed.

"It's dead!" Crenelle cried. "You got it!"

"Great shot, brother!" Hero called as he ran up.

Keeper felt weak and shuddery. It was the best shot he had ever made, and he doubted that he could have done it again. Superior skill had come to him in his moment of most desperate need. Because otherwise the woman he loved would have been killed.

Crenelle came to him. She embraced him and kissed him. "You saved me," she said. "And you have won whatever you wish from me. You killed the mammoth."

Keeper remained in a numb state. He knew she would marry him, without rape, if he asked her now. But he knew that wouldn't be perfect. So he went for his second ambition. "Come with me, to explore the ice," he said. "To go to the other side."

She looked at him. "I thought you would say something else."

"I don't think you want something else."

"But to demand of me what I don't want to give—that's rape."

He saw her rationale. "But I'm not a rapist."

She sighed. "Indeed you are not. Then I will go exploring with you."

"We'll all go," Hero said. "As soon as we butcher this animal and store the meat. We won't need to hunt again for months. We can take time to explore."

Crenelle hesitated. "I think he wanted to travel alone with me."

Craft arrived. "You can't go into the ice alone. You'd die. It has to be an organized excursion."

She nodded. "He's right, Keeper. But if you want to ask something else—"

Keeper found his voice. "No, that's good. I'm glad to have us all go. It will be safer and better."

She shrugged. "Maybe something good will come of it."

All of them were now standing around the fallen mammoth. Craft began organizing the butchery, which was no simple task.

•

Several days later they set out on the exploration. All seven of them were going, using three boats. Hero and Crenelle shared Keeper's boat, while Harbinger and Rebel were in another, and Craft and Haven in the third. Each craft carried a ballast of supplies: piled fur cloaks, sections of roasted mammoth meat, spare spears and arrows, and enough dry sedge twists to start a fire. Just in case they didn't get beyond the ice. Because they knew this could be as much of a challenge as killing a mammoth.

There was also one dog riding in each boat. The dogs had been nervous about this at first, but when they realized that all the people were going, they didn't want to be left behind. Whitepaw was hunched by Crenelle's feet, in the center.

Keeper was thrilled to have their support, and to be undertaking the exploration at last. He wanted desperately to marry Crenelle, but this was his second desire, and to have her participating made it almost as good. And perhaps he would still find a way to win her.

They paddled along the wall of ice as it descended into the sea. The ice did not like yielding to the water, but the sea was so deep that there was no alternative. There were gouges in the wall where the waves had eaten it out.

When the ice submerged, they paddled on into its territory, following the wintry shoreline east. The ice rose up in a shining cliff that leveled off high above. So they had not gotten around the wall; they had merely followed it around a turn. They still didn't know what was behind it.

There was a commotion in the water. Keeper watched closely, and was able to see what it was: seals. Seals were swimming near the wall, catching fish. There were also gulls flying low, inspecting the waves for something worth catching. Whitepaw was interested; she was losing her concern about the deep water and was sniffing the breeze.

The ice wall was interminable, seeming to have no end. But then it curved north. It was, however, no end; another wall came in from the east. The walls did not meet; they moved north parallel to each other.

"A river!" Keeper exclaimed. "This is a river, flowing into the sea. The ice walls follow its shore."

"It must flow from land," Crenelle said. "Maybe we should follow it to find that land."

Keeper was pleased to agree. The ice seemed determined to wall off the entire sea, but the river might rise above it, and they might reach the land beyond by following it.

They paddled up the river. Soon it narrowed, with the walls of ice closing in. There was more of a current, so they had to paddle harder to make progress.

The walls on either side came closer, until there seemed hardly to be room for the river. They leaned out over the water. Then they touched, forming a tall cave with the river in the bottom. Keeper was not the only one who stared, finding this fascinating. Ice covering over a river, not by freezing its surface, but by arching above it.

Still, the river had to flow from somewhere. So they continued to follow it, entering its huge cave. The wind died down, and the surface of the water became calm. This, too, was strange; the sea was always restless, with waves constantly going somewhere. This river was relaxed.

The arched ceiling thickened, cutting off more of the light from above. But some still came through, making the ceiling seem to glow.

They had reed torches, but those were for emergency use. If it got too dark, they would have to turn back. That would be too bad; Keeper was enchanted, and wanted to follow this quiet river to its source.

Whitepaw woofed. They looked where she was looking, and saw a seal swimming past the boat. It went to the edge, where the ice wall rose, and climbed out onto land.

Land?

They steered the boat there. Sure enough, there was a sliver of land. The ice had retreated just enough to expose some of the river's natural bank. This was the first actual land they had seen since rounding the sea corner.

The seal was gone, but it had done them its favor by showing them the land. They paddled up along it, and saw an opening in the ice. A trickle of water flowed from it. A tributary stream, making its own cave in the monstrous mass of ice.

Whitepaw sniffed the air, then scrambled to get out of the boat. "No!" Keeper said sharply, and the dog paused.

"Don't be silly," Crenelle said. "Do you want her to poop in the boat?"

Oh. "But she might get lost," Hero said.

"Then I'll go with her. I have to poop too."

This was a detail Keeper hadn't thought of. How could they spend days in the boats, caught between ice and water, without any trench to bury their dung? So he kept his mouth shut as dog and woman climbed from the boat and disappeared into the tributary cave.

Soon Crenelle returned. "This is interesting," she said. "You'll want to see, Keeper."

So he climbed out, leaving the boat to Hero, and followed her into the little cave. "This winds around like a regular cave," Crenelle said. "Only it's all ice. And Whitepaw smells a breeze."

"That means it connects to the surface," Keeper said.

"Yes. So maybe we don't have to follow the big river all the way up. Maybe this little one will take us to the other side of the wall." She followed the dog into the farther reaches of the cave.

Keeper, excited, returned to let Hero know. "Maybe it leads out," he said. "We'll check."

Hero nodded. The other two boats were pulling up to join him. They could all uncramp here for a while.

Keeper turned and went back after Crenelle. There was no question of losing track of her; there was only the one winding cave.

He walked along it, setting his feet on the narrow banks beside the trickle flow. At spots the cave became tight, as the sculptured ice closed in from the sides, but then it opened out again. He was exhilarated; this was exactly the kind of exploration he had craved, without knowing the precise form it would take. A cave of ice!

He squeezed through another bind, and came to Crenelle and the dog. "This is as far as I can go," the woman said. "Whitepaw can go farther, but I'm afraid to let her. If she fell in a freezing hole, how could we rescue her?"

Keeper nodded. "I love this, but we mustn't take bad risks."

She didn't move. She just stood there, leaning against the ice, gazing at him.

Oh. She could not get out until he did, clearing the way. The passage was now too narrow for anything but single file. He began to back out.

"You could ravish me here, and I would not be able to escape," she remarked. "No one would hear my screams."

He paused, startled by her thought. "Whitepaw would protect you."

"Not from you."

He wasn't entirely sure of that; she had befriended the dog with the same energy she befriended men. But it didn't matter, for he would never attack her. "You will never be in danger from me."

"You could pin me against the ice and wedge my legs apart."

She was so suggestive! Merely arguing the case got him sexually excited. "I couldn't get past your thick clothing." For she wore stout fur leggings under her cloak, as they all did, and a warm loinskin. It was all protection from the cold, as were her gloves, hood, and foot bindings, but effective against other kinds of intrusions too.

"Yes you could. Come here."

Bemused, he reversed course again and approached her. There was just room for them, both standing, their fronts touching, with the dog in the smaller continuation of the cave.

She opened his cloak, and her own. She adjusted her loinskin. "Bring it out."

She really was ready to do it! The air was cold, but their merging cloaks provided warmth between them. He drew his own loinskin aside, freeing his erect member.

She took it and guided it. Sure enough, she had made an access there. He felt the warmth of her groin.

"Are you sure you don't want to do this by force?" she inquired.

"I wish I could."

She guided him farther, and adjusted her body to accommodate him. "One day I will lead you to this point, then deny you. Then you will be unable to stop yourself."

"But don't you see," he said, frantic with desire for her. "To make me do that would be to violate my belief. I would be—be less of a man."

"I do see," she said. "That's why I haven't made you do it. But maybe someday, maybe as a seeming game, you will be able to." Then she moved onto him, taking him inside her.

"Oh, Crenelle," he breathed as his body plunged deep into that ecstatic warmth. "I love you."

"All three of you love me. But I can marry only one, unfortunately."

And that one could be him—if only he could make himself take her by force, one time. And he could not.

He realized that he had told her that he loved her, but she had not spoken love in return. She had expressed interest in all three brothers. She was honest about that: she would marry the one who raped her, and surely be true to him thereafter. Within that framework, she was taking turns with them, trying to achieve that rape. She had given him several chances, and he had failed each time.

It was such a stupid thing to bar his prospective lifetime of happiness with her. All he had to do was take her without her given permission, one time.

"Why do I suspect that your mind is elsewhere?" she inquired.

It was time to disengage. "I want so much to do . . . what you want. I wish I had done it this time."

"When this trip ends, and we return to the plain, your turn will be over."

"I know it," he said, ashamed.

She kissed him. "I do like you, Keeper. You saved me from getting trampled by the mammoth. But you must win me." She drew back, and they came apart, that small necessary amount.

They put themselves back together, and then made their way back through the winding tunnel to the main river. Whitepaw scrambled past them and went ahead to let the others know.

"It narrowed until we could go no farther," Keeper reported when they arrived. "Maybe a larger river will take us all the way through."

"It is getting late," Hero said. "We need to camp."

"We can anchor the boats here," Haven said. "And use the cave for refuge."

They did so. There were several small tributary caves, and what they deposited there quickly froze. Craft hammered a wood spike into hard ice, and tied a fiber rope to it to anchor the lead boat. The second boat was tied to the first, and the third to the second, so that none could become separated. Haven made a small fire in a stone bowl set on top of a section of mammoth meat, and the heat from that bowl thawed and cooked the meat below it. They ate well.

They slept stretched out in the boats, with blanket furs below and above them. Crenelle slept between Keeper and Hero, drawing heat from their bodies but favoring neither. That was one reason she had given him sex in the tunnel, Keeper realized: so that there would be no question of it at night in the boat, where there was no possibility of rape. She was very practical about her imperatives.

He dreamed of following a tunnel through the ice until it emerged on the far side of the wall, where there was a beautiful, warm bright land. Crenelle stepped out of her furs and ran naked in the sunlight. "Catch me!" she cried invitingly. So he stepped out of his own clothing and ran after her, and caught her. This time he knew he could do it! But as he turned her around to face him, he saw her face. It was Rebel.

He woke, appalled. He had no hankering for his sister! Yet the two women were the same age, and similar in form. It would be easy to mistake one for the other, from behind, even naked. He wondered whether his brothers suffered similar confusion. Rebel, in her quest to prove her fertility, had seduced every man she found except her brothers, and sometimes, playfully, she had seemed almost to want to try it with them. Maybe she was just practicing her technique, assuming provocative exposures, asking them whether this was more tempting than that, sometimes shielding her face so that her body became nameless. Sometimes he had wondered just how far such a game might go, if followed up. But they had known it was forbidden, and Keeper had been ashamed of the reaction such sights and conjectures had stirred in him. Just as they knew rape was forbidden. Maybe that was the connection: the equation between the forbidden sister and the forbidden act. Barred not because the woman objected, but because it was simply wrong.

The dream shook him, but perhaps it had brought him to a better understanding of his problem. Still, he saw no solution. Unless—this might be nonsensical, but maybe not—Rebel herself would have an answer. He resolved to tell her about the dream, when he had a chance to talk to her alone.

But as it happened, he had no chance to talk to his sister alone. She was in a different boat, and had different chores to do. He was unable to find a pretext. Frustrated, he realized he would just have to wait.

They paddled upstream. Keeper had the front paddle, and Hero the rear one. Crenelle, in the middle, was idle, so she brought out her little bone flute and played. The sound echoed around the huge ice cave, amplifying and modifying itself before fading. The effect was weird and alluring.

They came to another offshoot cave, this one larger. There was a fair flow of water from it, confirming a larger stream, though tiny compared to the main flow. Maybe this one would lead them to the other side of the wall.

They stopped, and Keeper, Crenelle, and Whitepaw set out to

follow it. The stream coursed along the base, uncovering sand and rock, while the ice formed a twisting niche beside and above it. Whitepaw was thrilled; she definitely smelled a trail.

The trail was rising, at times steeply. That was the way they needed to go, to get out of it. The stream twisted back and forth, as if seeking a better route, and sometimes formed small rapids or even waterfalls.

As they went, the wan light from above gradually brightened. They were definitely approaching the surface, and the size of the tunnel remained large enough so that it seemed unlikely to close.

Crenelle paused, and turned back to face him. "I think this is going to make it through," she said. "I wonder if we should tell the others, so they can come too?"

He realized that she was right. If this led out of the ice, it might still take long enough to be a long trip. It would be better to tell the others now, instead of going all the way and having to come all the way back. "Yes. But you don't have to go; you can go ahead with Whitepaw, and I will go back."

"No, this is your exploration. You must be first through. I can go back."

"We can both go back," he said. "I—I may have something to say to you." Actually it was Rebel he wanted to talk to, but it concerned Crenelle.

She opened her cloak partway. "You do have me alone here, and helpless. Are you finally ready?"

He averted his gaze. "Not exactly. Actually I wanted to talk to my sister about it."

"Rebel? She can't do anything for you I can't."

"I—I think she might. This time."

She made a decision. "We will both go back, and you can tell me what Rebel can do that I can't." It was a challenge.

He hesitated to agree, but she and Whitepaw squeezed by him and started down the winding passage. He had to follow, speaking to her back. "It—she—I wanted to tell her my dream."

"You dreamed of her?"

"Not exactly."

"Tell me."

"I—I don't know whether that would be smart."

"Now I definitely want to hear it."

"But it might make you embarrassed, or angry."

She glanced back at him. "Not as much so as denying it to me."

He was in for it now. He should have kept his mouth shut. He would alienate her either way. "I suppose—if you insist."

There was a pause. "I promise I won't be angry," she said.

That might be worth something. "I dreamed last night that we followed a tunnel, as we are doing now. You were leading. It came to the end of the ice, which stopped, just as the wall stops on the near side, suddenly, and there was a wonderful open land, with trees growing."

"I like this dream so far."

"You got out of your clothes, because it was so warm, and you ran out across the land. I saw your bare bottom, and I wanted you. You called 'Catch me!' to me."

"I definitely like this dream. Was my bottom pretty?"

"Oh, yes!" He looked at Crenelle's real backside as he spoke, trying to picture it bare. "I got out of my clothes, and wasn't cold at all, and I chased after you. You ran fast, but I ran faster, catching up."

"I was letting you catch up."

"Yes. I knew that this time I could . . . could . . ."

"If you can't say it, how can you do it?"

He forced himself. "Rape you. Because I knew you wanted it. And you were so beautiful. I was . . . my . . ."

"Your penis was hard."

"Yes. But when I caught you, and turned you around, you . . . I . . ." He couldn't say it.

"You still couldn't do it?"

"Not exactly. You . . . you weren't—"

"I was willing. You know that. But of course I said I wasn't."

"You weren't Crenelle," he said doggedly.

She stopped abruptly. "What?"

"You were Rebel."

"Suddenly I don't like your dream."

"I know," he said, dejected. "I think I know what it meant. I wanted to talk to Rebel, and get her . . . her advice."

She resumed walking. "What do you think it meant?"

"That you were forbidden."

"How could I be forbidden?"

"Because I have to rape you to take you, and rape is forbidden."

"Why should I turn into Rebel?"

"That's complicated."

"Tell me anyway."

He explained about Rebel's sexuality, and his occasional interest in it, especially when she bared her body and hid her face. And his shame in being so tempted, when he knew that she was his sister, and therefore forbidden.

"Now I see!" Crenelle said. "Sex with Rebel would be like rape, even if she wanted it."

"Yes." It was a relief to have her understand.

"So raping me would be like sex with her."

"Yes. Like raping her, and she would slit my belly open and cut out my penis and throw it in the fire."

Crenelle laughed without humor. "I begin to understand your reticence better. It's not just decency; it's fear. But how could you not recognize her before you caught up? Maybe I ran behind a tree, and she ran out instead, playing a game."

"No, I saw you all the time. You became her. From behind I couldn't tell."

"We looked that similar?"

"Yes, when I couldn't see your face."

She paused again, but this time didn't turn. "You couldn't tell me from Rebel, if you didn't see my face or hear my voice?"

"If you wore her clothing . . . or were naked, I think."

"You think?"

"I haven't ever seen you naked."

"But we have had sex!"

"In clothing, or under covers in darkness. I have never seen you naked in the open, as you were in my dream."

"Have you seen Rebel that way?"

"Yes. Mostly when we were children. But she didn't always cover up when she got breasts."

"I think you filled in her body for mine, in your dream, because you had seen hers and not mine."

Keeper's mouth dropped open. "That must be what I did."

"It's too cold here, or I would show you my body. We're not the same."

"You look very similar in clothes."

"Similar, yes. But she is leaner and firmer than I am. In fact she has a better figure, if you like the athletic type. I am softer, with more on my bottom. My breasts are lower."

"I wish I could see," he said sadly.

"I wish you could too. Then you would know that we are not the same, and that you could rape me without raping her. But why would you have told this dream to her?"

"So she could tell me how to get around it. She is very practical about sex."

Crenelle considered. She reached back to catch her loose brown hair and tuck it inside her cloak so it didn't show. When she spoke again, her voice was different, more like Rebel's. "Pretend I am she," she said. "Look at me from behind and think of me as her. Say to me what you would say to her. After you have told her of your dream, and interpretation."

"But—"

"I think I know how she would answer you. We have become close, not just in age and outline."

"I—I'll try." This was strange, almost like the dream. There Crenelle had become Rebel; now she was doing it awake. The absence of hair helped; Rebel's was wild and fair, and it was easier to picture it when Crenelle's hair didn't show.

"Do it." She resumed walking.

He followed, and she did strongly resemble his sister, especially with her voice masked. She said that her bare body would be different, and perhaps she was right, but her clothed body with her hair covered left only the very similar outline. "Rebel, I know Crenelle isn't the same as you. But you are so similar that I—in my dream I saw you as the same. I think that's what stops me from taking her by force, even when she invites me to. It would be like attacking you. But she won't marry me otherwise. What can I do?"

"You need to realize that we *are* different women," she replied. "Age and size are but two aspects of more complicated creatures. We don't think alike, and we don't look alike in the faces."

"I know that. And usually I don't confuse you. But in my dream—"

"You fitted my bare body to her image, and soon it brought in my face too. You must not do that. Focus on her face. Don't avert your gaze when you approach her."

"Do I do that?" he asked, bemused.

"Yes you do. Especially when you want sex. You go with her in the dark, or from behind, and in daylight you look away."

"How could you know that?"

"She has told me. We share secrets. She knows about Harbinger's sexual faults too."

He considered that, and it seemed true. His shame about the association, the effort of rape, made him unable to meet Crenelle's gaze when there was a question of closeness or sex. But could he reverse that? Could he actually peer into her face when having sex? When trying to have forced sex?

"Your silence says you are in doubt," she said.

"I am. I think you're right. I should look into her face. But I still don't know if I could rape her."

"All you have to do is have sex with her when she hasn't agreed to it. She won't resist you the way I would."

"I wouldn't ever try that with you!" he exclaimed, appalled.

"Next time you get her alone, stare into her face and do it."

"I will!" he said with sudden resolve. "The next time! In fact, right now! Let me see your face."

"Too late," she said, drawing her hair back into view. "We are there." Indeed, they had just come into sight of the boats. Whitepaw was bounding ahead to greet them.

And would he be able to do it some other time? Once again he had messed up his chance. He should have decided earlier, and stopped her before they completed their trip back. Instead he had been so absorbed in the dialogue that he had been unaware of their approach to the camp. Now he had lost his chance. Again.

"We think this goes through to the other side," Crenelle said to the others. "So we came back to fetch you before going all the way."

Keeper found this strange, and realized it was because he had not quite stopped picturing her as Rebel. She had indeed responded much as his sister would have, which showed how close they could be. But she had also given him the key, and now he thought he could do what he had to do, when he had the chance.

"We're resting," Rebel said, sounding almost like Crenelle's imitation of her voice. "Hero can go with you."

Hero heaved himself up. It was a matter of pride with him not to need rest, even after a half day of hard paddling. "Yes, I'll go."

They reversed course again. Crenelle fell in between them, as she was in the boat. Whitepaw ran ahead.

This time the trip seemed faster, because it was more familiar. They knew where to put their feet, to avoid splashing in the stream, and knew where the ground was solid. Soon they were back to the point where they had turned around.

The passage around the stream continued to narrow, but never got really tight. It was as if someone had used it before, though this seemed impossible. They were the only people to have entered the wall of ice. They would have seen the leavings of any others.

One place was awkward, where the water cascaded down so steeply as to be a virtual waterfall. They would have to get wet to go up the center, so they chipped carefully around the edges to make footholds they could use to brace against and straddle the stream of water without touching it. It was an awkward maneuver, but effective, and soon they were all above the drop. Hero, the last to ascend, handed Whitepaw up to Crenelle; the dog thought this a great adventure. She moved ahead again, eagerly sniffing the way.

The stream moved up through a series of bubble-like caves in the ice. Keeper wondered how they had formed. He liked to understand all the mysteries of nature, and pondered them wherever he found them. His best guess was that sometimes there was more water flowing, and it backed up and spread out, carving out round channels. Then when there was a smaller flow, the water swirled around in its chambers and drained on down, leaving beautifully carved ice. This meant that this was not always a safe path, and might not be safe at the base either. There could be a torrent of water washing out everything.

The light above brightened, indicating their approach to the surface. At last they emerged, and stood on a great mountain slope, a valley of ice. The sun beat down from above, brighter than Keeper had seen it before. In fact it was painful.

Crenelle stood beside him, blinking. "We must be standing closer to the sun," she said.

"I think its brightness is because of all the ice," he said.

"It hurts my eyes."

"Maybe we can shield them." He drew his hood close around his face, so that it was like peering out through a tunnel. Crenelle did the same. It was awkward, but did relieve some of the strain. Hero, the strong one, merely squinted.

They climbed the slope, trudging through slush, to reach the nearest crest. As they came to it, and got a broader view, it became awe inspiring.

They had actually emerged in a high valley, a catch in the slope. To the east the mountain of ice rose up majestically high; to the west and north it rose less. To the south it fell away toward the sea, where they knew it abruptly dropped down to the water. A small cleft showed in the distance: the river opening they had paddled up.

This was not a wall of ice. It was an entire landscape of ice. There were no trees, no rocks. Just ridges and furrows of ice, and some huge crevices, big enough to swallow a man.

"We'll never get beyond this," Keeper said, dismayed. "The world is ice."

"At least now we know," she agreed. "We have come to the end of the world we can live in. Beyond is just endless ice."

He turned to gaze back into the minor valley. "The sun melts the ice, a little on the surface, and it flows down through its channel. It must re-freeze at night, or when there is a storm. This river may exist only in summer, when there is enough melt."

"You really understand such things."

"I try to. But there's so much I don't understand, I'm not sure I'll ever catch up. Such as why the world ends in ice."

"It has to end in something. We wouldn't want all that ice on the plain."

"I wonder whether it's the melt from this ice that makes the sea. So the warmer center of the world draws from the cold edge of it."

"It must."

They stared out across the amazing edge of the world. Keeper saw that it was smooth in some sections, while rent with large fissures in others. It would not be good to fall into one of those.

"Ho!" Hero called. He and Whitepaw had gone exploring over the ridge, just out of sight.

They ran to join him, fearing some mischief. But he was merely calling their attention to what he had discovered: a huge white bear.

The beast stood at bay, staring at them. Hero had his spear and bow, of course, but Keeper and Crenelle had only their knives. Even the more deadly weapons would not guarantee victory over a bear this size; they were deadly antagonists. They didn't need it for meat; they had plenty of mammoth meat. So there was no point in fighting it unless they had to. But what was it doing here atop the ice?

"The river path!" Crenelle exclaimed. "The bear uses it. To get to the seals and fish."

That was surely it. Something had made that path, and it must have been the bear. So they had been following its trail—as Whitepaw had known. Now they had caught up to the bear, and the bear didn't like the intrusion.

The bear took a step toward Hero. Hero took his bow off his shoulder and nocked an arrow.

"No need to fight it," Keeper called. "We're on its path."

Hero paused. "Path?"

"The stream path," Keeper explained. "Its way to food. It must have a den in the ice, then go below to fish."

Hero smiled. "That must be it! Bears have their paths. We're lucky we didn't meet it in the cave!"

"Yes. And maybe we should leave it alone now, so it won't attack."

"That may not work," Hero said seriously. "We'll have to go back down its path to join the others, and it won't like that. It may come after us."

"Bad place to try to fight it," Keeper said. "No room to maneuver or escape."

"Best not to chance it." Hero paused, then came up with a heroic solution, as was his nature. "You and Crenelle go back now. I'll hold the bear off, giving you time to get clear and warn the others."

"But that will put you in danger!" Keeper protested.

"Danger is my business. I'll kill or disable the bear if I have to, but I think I can distract it, or lead it a chase elsewhere. Then, when I know you are clear, I'll come down."

"With the bear chasing you?" Crenelle asked. She was not trying to be funny; her face inside the hood was drawn.

"I've had experience. I won't start down if it's too close."

Keeper exchanged a glance with Crenelle. "He does have experience," he said doubtfully.

"And we do have to get back," she said, as dubiously. "I don't like this, but maybe we have to."

"Yes," Hero agreed. "Tell the others to have the boats ready, in case we have to leave the ledge quickly." Then he faced the bear and waved his arms. "Grrrr! Back off, snowhide!"

The bear actually did back off slightly. But it was obvious that it would not be balked long. They certainly did not want it to precede them down the stream.

"We'll go," Keeper said. "But take care."

"Take care," Crenelle echoed. Keeper knew this was as hard for her as for him. Hero was his brother, and the man she would like to marry. What would they do if he did not return?

They waited briefly, while Hero baited the bear, leading it to the side, away from the stream. When man and bear disappeared beyond the ridge, they moved toward the stream.

"Whitepaw!" Crenelle said suddenly. "Where is she?"

"With Hero."

"Maybe that's best. She'll know to be careful. They will help each other." But it was clear that she didn't like risking the dog either.

They reached the stream hole. Crenelle slid down into it first, then called back to him when she was clear of the opening. He went down. It seemed dark, but that was because of the extreme brightness outside. His eyes would soon adjust.

They moved as rapidly as they could, walking where it was close to level, and sliding where it was steep. They got splashed a bit, but not soaked, and it was worth the gain in speed. Should Hero come after them in a hurry, they did not want to hinder his passage.

They reached the waterfall. "That bear must just slide down it," Crenelle said. "Its fur sheds the water."

"Yes. And when it climbs up, it can let the water bounce off its head. It's fat enough to handle cold water, as the seals do."

"This is a bear's world."

They did not try to emulate the bear. They stepped carefully down, using the footholds. "I hope Hero has time to do it carefully," Keeper said.

"And to lift Whitepaw down."

They resumed speed below the waterfall. The light seemed to be fading, but that might be imagination as they got farther from the surface. In any event, they would have been able to move mostly by feel.

They reached the juncture with the larger river. "We're back," Crenelle called.

There was no answer.

Surprised, they saw that the others were gone. Only their own boat remained anchored.

"They wouldn't leave us," Crenelle said, a trace of uncertainty in her voice.

"They must have decided to do some exploring on their own,"

Keeper said. "They thought we would be away longer, so there was no reason to wait here. They should be returning soon."

She brightened. "Yes. Nothing happened to them, because they carefully untied the other two boats. Maybe they looked for a better place to fish, or to camp for the night."

"Yes." But he shared her slight nervousness. It wasn't comfortable to be this much alone as night approached, especially with Hero in danger.

"I'll get some meat from the boat," she said. She took hold of the cord, drawing the boat in toward her, and raised one foot to step into it. The boat rocked, pushing away, disturbing her balance.

Suddenly her other foot slipped out from under her. She screamed as she fell, unable to catch herself. Keeper lurched forward, but it happened too fast. She dropped into the water before he got there.

He was there immediately, catching her arm, pulling her out as she scrambled to help herself. In a moment she was out of the water and lying on the bank.

"You'll freeze!" he said. "We must get you into dry clothing."

Crenelle did not respond. Alarmed, he tried to lift her to her feet, but she was limp. She was unconscious.

Half panicked, he tried to bring her to. He shook her, but she just sagged. Her face was turning blue. Maybe she had choked on the water. He laid her down, turned her over, and slapped at her back, trying to get the water out. "Oh, Crenelle, it's my fault," he said. "I should have been holding the boat steady."

She just lay there. She seemed to be breathing, but she was too cold.

"Clothing," he said. "In the boat. Anything. To get you dry and warm. Quickly."

He went to the boat, pulled it in, and reached across to get hold of one of the hide blankets. He tossed that on the ledge and grabbed another, and another, until he had them all in a clumsy pile. Then he set to work changing her. He turned her over again and opened her sodden cloak, stripping it partway off her body. He half lifted and half turned her, getting the cloak the rest of the way off. Then he tackled her leggings, and her undergarments. The job seemed interminable, with every piece hanging up on every part of her. But finally he had her naked.

He spread out a blanket, then lifted her up clumsily and put her on it. He got another and put it over her. He piled the others on, making a mound over her. But she still seemed too cold, and she didn't wake.

"What am I going to do?" he asked the air. "You need warmth, quickly. There's not time to make a fire."

The question brought its answer. Body heat, as it was at night. He lay down beside her, but the piled blankets got in the way; he knew that none of his heat was reaching her. He had to get right against her, his warm skin against her cold skin. So he stripped away his own clothing, then got under the covers with her, naked.

He embraced her. Her skin was icy. He pressed against her, trying to warm her, but she seemed to be cooling him faster. Yet what else could he do?

"I know how to get hot," he said. "For a little while. Maybe that will be enough."

He kissed her cold lips, then her cold breasts. Even like this, she was attractive. He worked up his sexual desire for her. "I will heat you from outside and inside," he said as his groin responded.

He found the place and pushed into her. It wasn't completely comfortable, but it was feasible. She wasn't as cold inside as outside. He squeezed against her and kissed her, feeling new warmth coming to his skin, going to hers. He drew back his face to stare at her face. "I know exactly who you are," he said. "And I love you, Crenelle. I can't let you die of cold."

Then his eruption came, forging into her belly like boiling water. "I give you my heat," he panted. "Wake, and be warm, beloved!"

She stirred. Her eyes opened. "You did it," she said.

"I got you warm!" he agreed happily. "Oh, Crenelle, I was so afraid you wouldn't wake."

"You raped me."

He tried to draw back, horrified. "I—"

"I never told you yes. I was unconscious."

"But I wanted only to get you warm. I—"

"You raped me."

He started to protest. Then he realized what she meant. He had had sex with her without her permission or cooperation. That was rape. That meant they were married. At last.

"I raped you," he agreed.

Now she kissed him. "Warm me some more, my husband. I'm still very cold."

He was glad to oblige.

When she felt warm enough, they separated, and she donned skins and furs as new clothing. He got dressed in his own clothing. Her color had returned, and she seemed to be feeling better.

Then the two other boats returned. Haven spied the scattered wet clothes. "What happened here?" she called.

"Keeper raped me," Crenelle said.

Haven gazed at the scene. She well understood the significance. "It must have been quite an occasion."

"It was. We are married now."

"Where is Hero?"

They had forgotten him! "We went to the top," Keeper said. "There was a big white bear. Hero distracted it so we could get back safely. Then—"

"And he's not back?" Haven tied the boat behind the other, and drew it to the bank.

"He was giving us time," Crenelle said. "He should return soon." But she was looking nervous again. "This passage—it's the bear's trail."

"Then we had better go elsewhere," Rebel said from the third boat. "After we make sure Hero is all right."

Craft and Harbinger were already stepping from the boats and checking their spears.

"I don't know how well spears will work," Keeper said. "The passage winds around, and there's not much room at the sides."

"Better than arrows, I think," Craft said.

There did not seem to be a better course of action. Keeper fetched his own spear. "Whitepaw is with him. He hoped to lead the bear astray, then follow us back. I know the way; I'll lead."

They let him. He felt guilty for leaving Hero there, though it was what seemed best. He forged along the winding passage, his hands against the walls for guidance in the gloom, wishing it could have been done some other way. Had he been having sex with Crenelle while his brother died?

Then Whitepaw came bounding up. He knew her by her sound. That meant that Hero was close behind. "Hero!" Keeper called. "Are you all right?"

"I'm not sure," his brother's voice came back.

"The bear—is it after you?"

"No, I don't think so. I don't hear it."

It was fairly dark now, which would make it hard to see, apart from the twists of the passage. "You aren't injured?"

"I think I can't see."

Keeper didn't like the sound of that. "You are hurt in the eyes?"

"No. Maybe it's just too dark."

"I have a torch," Craft said, coming up behind. He had lit one, and its light flared brightly.

Soon Hero stood in the illumination. "Can you see this?" Craft asked.

"By the smell, you have a torch. I don't see it."

Hero was looking in the wrong direction. He was indeed blind. What had happened?

"Was it bright out there?" Harbinger asked from farther back.

"Brilliant," Keeper said. "Crenelle and I had to shade our eyes from it."

"I heard of a man who spent too much time in the sun in winter," Harbinger said. "The brightness got in his eyes, and he couldn't see for several days."

"That must be it," Hero said. "I looked all over, leading that bear, to be sure I didn't step in a crevasse or off a cliff. I tried to squint, but the brightness hurt. I ignored it and led the bear away from the tunnel. Then I circled around and returned to the tunnel, but I couldn't see it. Whitepaw led me to it. Then I was all right, because I could feel the sides."

"We must get you home," Craft said.

"I'm not injured. I just can't see."

"You won't be much good in combat or on a hunt if we don't get you home where you can get better," Craft pointed out.

They reversed course and led Hero the rest of the way back. The women had the boats packed and ready. They got in and shoved off. There was no point in waiting for the bear to arrive.

The trip by torchlight was relatively swift, because they were going downstream. Keeper wasn't easy about the prospect of entering the sea at night, but it did seem best to get Hero home as soon as possible, so he could rest and recover in safety.

But as they reached the open water of the river, they were buffeted by strong winds, and the water got rough. "There's a storm!" Harbinger said.

They wanted no part of that! They turned the boats and paddled back upstream, getting away from the storm. They would have to spend another night under the ice after all.

"We don't need to go home because of me," Hero said. "I can paddle well enough, and do other things, as long as someone tells me where. It's easy, here in the boat." Indeed, he was doing most of the moving of the boat, while Keeper guided it by paddling on one side or the other.

"You're right," Crenelle said reassuringly.

Maybe it was better this way. Hero back home would have to be largely idle, and he wouldn't like that. Here in the boat or in the gloom of a tunnel, he was at less of a disadvantage. If Harbinger was right, the blindness would last only a few days.

"We can make camp at another ice cave," Keeper said. "Now we know how the ice protects us from a storm. It's better than a lean-to. We can fish, extending our supply of meat. It should not be difficult."

"It should not be difficult," Crenelle agreed. She smiled at him, and he realized that she was thinking of more than camping. They were, after all, married now.

•

Mankind did not make it to North America 20,000 years ago. The ice was impassable, considering the technology of the time. The melt described would have been a fringe effect limited to summer. As it was, human penetration to North America proper may have been a fairly close call, as mentioned in the forenote, because as the ice age ended and the continental ice shelves retreated, the melt from them returned to the sea, raising it to its present level and covering Beringia with water. Perhaps only the easternmost fringe of mankind's population remained in Alaska as the sea rose year by year to inundate the plain. That fringe probably followed an extending ice-free corridor between the Laurentide ice sheet that covered most of Canada and the Cordilleran ice sheet that covered the western fringe of Canada and the southern fringe of Alaska. This corridor was just east of the Rocky Mountain range, and may have been ten to fifty miles wide and a thousand miles long.

The evidence of human passage is scant; in fact, were it not for the incontrovertible indication that human beings did make it to North America, the balance of evidence would have indicated that no such passage was made. As it was, it must have been swift, with perhaps a small band moving through in as little as a year, leaving no traces. It was no easy passage; they might have followed the Yukon River east, then had to cross the Mackenzie Mountains to reach the lee side, then bear south between the endless glaciers. It could have been a migration of desperation, through a channel providing little sustenance. Perhaps enemy tribes cut off their return to the more fertile lowlands of central Alaska, so they had to go forward into the unknown, or starve. So they gambled that the corridor did not lead to oblivion. Until that tribe emerged below, and discovered a world more wonderful than any imagined. It was surely one of the more remarkable breakthroughs of human existence. The rest is prehistory.

But there are mysteries beyond this. There is growing evidence of human occupation of South America dating from before the ice sheets retreated, and some evidence of scattered North American sites. Where did these people come from, if not from Beringia? The obstacles to passage before the ice-free corridor opened are so formidable that it is difficult to believe that any human colonization could have occurred. A boat culture might have done it, staying to the shoreline and not penetrating to the continental interior. Maybe a bad storm blew those boats far enough south to find the end of the ice, and they were unable to return to tell their fellows. Or perhaps the ice-free corridor opened at prior times, briefly, allowing a trace leakage of human beings. Neither of these prospects seems likely. Yet if the evidence of earlier settlement holds up, some such explanation will be necessary. At present it is a mystery that archaeologists would dearly like to resolve. The best present lead is from cores drilled in the continental shelf off the Queen Charlotte Islands along the west coast of Canada. These cores show that this area, which is now more than 450 feet below sea level, was above water 14,600 years ago. There was a wide flat corridor leading south, with herbs and pine trees. So this made human passage much easier. This could account for the presence of people along the coasts of America more than a thousand years before conventional dates. But the evidence is that there was ice across Alaska throughout this period, as shown in the story. How was that passed? Perhaps there were a few islands off the lowered coast that the ice could not reach, so that at certain times boats could hop from one to another, until they reached the Pacific corridor. The southward progress of such boat people might have been a mere intermittent trickle, compared to the later land corridor trek, but it might have happened. The key is surely associated with Beringia in some manner, for the immensity of the Pacific Ocean makes a more southern crossing even less probable. Like the fabled Atlantis, Beringia existed long ago, and sank beneath the sea, a victim of climate change. Unlike Atlantis, it was real.

6

HUNT

Fifteen thousand years ago, Africa was similar to the way it is now, though in the intervening millennia it was warmer and wetter. Mankind had spread throughout the continent, just as it had through the rest of the world, except perhaps for the Americas. The ice age had not ended, but was slowly weakening.

Between the shrunken rain forest and the expanded desert was the broad savanna. Nomadic tribes crossed this, looking for sustenance. The setting is central Africa south of the Sahara. At this time the size of stone implements was decreasing toward what is called the microliths, or much smaller blades. This was not because anyone ran out of stone, or made smaller weapons or tools, or hunted smaller animals, but because they were learning how to make better use of smaller stone chips that would otherwise have been wasted. They dulled the reverse edges so they wouldn't slice the wrong things, and mounted them in wood. In this manner they could put one, two, three or more microliths in a single tool, and have a better instrument. They could make a sickle, or an adze, or spear with special projecting barbs, more efficient for its specialized task. This was another aspect of the technology that spread across Europe, Asia and Africa.

Chapter 1 ended with a decision to be made: would Hero marry Crenelle, accepting the implication that he had raped her? The following chapters pursued the consequences of his refusal. This chapter follows his life the other way: he did marry her, and his siblings joined them and remained in Africa instead of traveling into Eurasia. Five years have passed in their lives since Chapter 1.

•

"Daddy play."

Hero woke to the voice of his daughter. Tour was four years old, and the cutest girl in the tribe. He could never say no to her.

He sat up. Crenelle was outside the hut; he heard her working there. He had overslept, though he had no excuse; it had been several days since the last hunt.

Tour was holding a top. It was a rounded chip of wood, a knot, pointed on one end. She liked to watch it spin, but her little hands were not as strong as his; he could make it spin much faster and longer.

He got down beside her, took the top, and turned it rapidly between his spread hands. It dropped to the hard earth floor and stood there, whirling firmly. Tour watched it, her eyes large and bright, her black hair straggling across her dark face as she concentrated. She just loved the motion. He in turn loved seeing her while she was fascinated. His fascination was with her fascination.

The top slowed and wobbled. Tour was just as interested in this aspect. Her tongue touched her lips as she focused. Hero wasn't sure what it was about the motion that so intrigued her, but it was enough to know that it did.

The top finally fell on its side, rolled a bit, and stopped. "Dead," Tour said solemnly.

That was what she thought? No wonder she preferred to make it live. He picked it up again and gave it another spin. She could watch it as long as he could animate it.

Playing with his daughter always reminded him of her mother. Crenelle liked to play with an object of similar size, but it wasn't wood. Indeed, from it had come the child, in a manner of thinking. Crenelle had insisted on being raped, and though that was counter to his family's way, he had finally compromised by letting her tell her tribe he had raped her, the first time. She in turn compromised by not telling that to *his* tribe. It had been a small sacrifice that brought him great reward. He loved Crenelle, for all that she was the one who had chosen him, on the basis of his hunting prowess, rather than his choosing her. She entertained him endlessly on the bed, and was competent to handle the foraging and household chores, and of course she had brought him Tour.

Crenelle entered the room. "Craft is coming," she said.

"Uncle Craft!" Tour said happily. He had made the top for her. Maybe he was bringing another.

Crenelle went back out, to tell Craft to go on in. For reasons Hero did not follow, she normally remained well clear of his brother.

Hero gave the top one more spin, and stood, awaiting his brother. Craft had been checking on a potentially awkward situation, and was surely coming to report.

Craft entered. He glanced at the child. "I'll go out!" Tour said, quick to catch the hint. She knew when adult business was happening. She picked up the precious top and dashed out.

"The chief died this morning," Craft said. "He designated Bub to be the next chief."

"That must not be," Hero said. "Bub resents our family, and will do us mischief the moment he has power."

"True. But if no one contests it, he will take the office once the burial ritual is done."

"What are we to do?"

"I talked with Rebel. She said you have to contest for it. If you are chief, we will have no problem."

"But Bub won't fight me. He knows he'll lose."

"I talked to Keeper. He said there's another way."

"How can I fight a man who won't fight me?"

"By going on a challenge hunt. If you go out alone, with just one man as your second, and succeed really well, the elders will have to designate you as chief instead. Because it is supposed to be the bravest and strongest man of the tribe, not just the one the old chief favored."

"But who would be my second?" Hero asked. "Most of the men are afraid of Bub, and for good reason—he carries grudges."

Craft nodded. "He does. But he already has a grudge against our family, so one more won't hurt. I will be your second."

"I don't want to be chief."

"You can designate someone else to be chief, if you step down. If you win the contest."

Hero wasn't happy with this, but knew that his brother spoke truly. He would have to do it. "When?"

"Now. The burial will be in three days, after the chief's spirit has safely left his body. You must win your challenge by then."

"What must I hunt?"

"The ultimate: a male lion."

Hero sighed. Ritual challenges were limited to spears and knives. This was a severe restriction for single combat with a beast as formidable as a lion. "I must tell Crenelle. She won't like this."

"I will fetch weapons." Craft departed.

Thus quickly it was decided. They simply couldn't afford to have their family be subject to the ill favor of the next chief.

Crenelle returned. "I heard," she said, sparing him the necessity of telling her. She stepped into him and kissed him. "Don't get yourself killed, my love. I don't want to have to marry your brother."

"He is coming with me."

"There's another brother."

He wasn't sure how serious she was, so just held her without speaking. It was true that when a man died, one of his brothers was expected to marry his widow, so as to be sure she was provided for. But would she want to marry Keeper? He was a year younger than she was. Still, he did on occasion bring over a puppy for Tour to play with.

Now that he thought about it, it occurred to him that it was odd that neither of his brothers had married. It was not because willing women were absent. What were they waiting for?

Crenelle quickly packed his pack with food and a firepot. Then she bore him to the bed and made love to him, efficiently and well. She had always been good at that. "Return to me, Hero," she whispered in his ear.

"I will try." But they both knew that it was no simple mission he was going on. A group of men could take a lion, but it was chancy at best for a single man, especially if the lion pride was near.

Craft returned, his own pack on his back and a number of weapons in a harness hanging at his side. "I have told an elder," he said. "We will be watched."

That meant that scouts would be out, observing what they did, without helping or interfering. Hero would be disqualified if Craft did anything other than support him or tend his wounds. But if he were successful, the news would be around well before he returned to make his claim.

And if he died, Keeper had better get over to his house with the dogs to protect Crenelle and Tour, for Bub would send his minions there to burn their house—punishment for Hero's temerity in challenging him. Keeper well might have to marry the widow quickly, to make an end to the threat. For by the code of the tribe, Bub would have no grievance against Keeper or his family. Enmities existed, but even a chief had to be wary of going counter to the code.

They knew where there was a pride of lions, and walked swiftly that way. Prides came and went; this one had moved into the area in the last month, so not much was known about it. It wasn't safe to spy too closely on a pride. But it surely had an adult male, and that was the animal Hero had to kill. Craft would be allowed to scare off the grown females, if he could, so long as he took no part in Hero's battle with the male.

Hero had never tackled a grown lion before, alone; no one had. That was why it was a worthy challenge. He had driven off a lioness on occasion, when she came too near his kill, but that wasn't the same. Oh, a female lion was formidable enough; but he had not had to pursue and kill her, which would have been a different matter. He wasn't sure he could do it. But he would find out.

"Do you ever feel fear?" Craft inquired as they walked.

"I fear for my wife and child."

"For yourself."

"I am wary of the animal I must face."

"I think that is not the same."

Hero shrugged. "I do what I must do. If fear stopped me, I would have to abolish it."

"That is why you are a great hunter and warrior."

"Not if the lion wins," Hero said with gruff humor.

They crossed a ridge, and entered the wide valley of the lions. The male was likely to be lounging near the den, while the females ranged out hunting. With luck he could settle with it before a female returned.

They knew where the cave was, because it was the only one suitable for lions and had been there as long as anyone could remember. They approached it. There was the lion, alone, lying before the entrance, gazing in their direction. It knew they were coming, but had no fear of them. Perhaps that was just as well, because if it fled, they would have trouble even catching it, let alone dispatching it.

Craft handed him a second spear, for once the contest began, there would not be opportunity. This one had extra little stone barbs behind the main head, so that it would cut coming out as well as going in. The first spear was more straightforward, heavier with a larger stone. It was intended for a quick straightforward kill. The second was for finishing off the animal if it were wounded or otherwise not yet dead. But either could be used either way, at need. Hero removed his pack, as he needed to be free to move quickly. Then he marched forward alone to challenge the lion, both spears ready.

The lion lifted slowly to his four feet, surely wondering what business this two-footed stranger had here. But there was a limit to its patience. When Hero came too close, the lion roared and made ready to charge.

Hero stopped and waited, bracing himself. He was now within range, but wanted to be very sure his first throw would score, for he might not get a second one.

The lion charged, then stopped and roared again. It was merely a feint, to make the other flee. But Hero did not flee; instead he hurled his spear.

It was a great shot. The spear went right into the lion's open mouth and stuck in its throat from the inside. The animal stood there, casting his head back and forth, not realizing that it was doomed. It might not be a lethal strike, but it would not be hard to finish off the creature with the second spear.

Suddenly there was a roar from the side. "A second lion!" Craft cried, chagrined.

Hero whirled, bringing his second spear about. But, caught by surprise, he was not fast enough. The lion was on him before he could throw. All he could do was try to fend it off with the spear. Too bad he had lost his heavy spear; that would have been better for this.

The lion leaped. Hero tried to scramble back out of the way, but lost his balance and fell on his back, his spear held above him. This nevertheless caused the lion to miss him; only one paw came down on his left shoulder. The claws dug deep. Then the lion was off him, catching its own balance, skidding on the ground and turning for another charge.

Hero scrambled back to his feet. He brought the spear about, but again lacked time to throw. So he stabbed it at the lion's neck. The blow was glancing rather than penetrating. Hero stabbed again, and this time the point lodged in the lion's chest without sufficient force. He was not being effective.

The lion batted at the spear, shoving it aside. In a moment it would get its balance and launch at his throat. Anticipating that, Hero swung his spear back sideways, trying to use it as a baffle. But he knew that would be ineffective. So he grabbed for his knife with his left hand, though it was a relatively puny weapon.

The lion reared up, batting again at the spear. It didn't realize that the weapon was relatively ineffective sideways; it had felt the sting of its point and was wary. This distraction was Hero's chance to retreat.

Instead, Hero leaped forward, shoving the spear shaft in the lion's face. The creature was so surprised it fell over backward. Hero bashed at it with the shaft, striking legs and snout, trying to slice flesh with the barbs. This was nuisance rather than deadly force, but until he got the chance to make a proper spear thrust it had to do.

The lion twisted to get its feet under it. But Hero's forward momentum carried him onto it. As it tried to rise, he landed on its back. He stabbed, his left arm circling its body, his hand coming in from its front, going for its neck. This time he scored, glancingly; blood welled up on the fur.

"Yaaaaa!" Hero screamed, flush with his success of the moment. His mouth was near the animal's ear.

Startled anew, the lion scrambled up and bounded away. Hero had inadvertently spooked it. It slowed, and turned to face him again, considering another attack.

"Yaaaaa!" he repeated, and took a threatening step toward it.

The lion didn't know what to make of this strange aggression. It turned again and fled. This time it did not stop. Soon it was gone.

"Well done!" Craft said. "You scared it off."

"I was lucky." Hero went to the first lion, who was still trying to get the spear out of its body. He used the knife to slit its throat, and in a moment its struggles ceased.

Then he felt his shoulder. The contact with the second lion's paw had been brief, but there was significant damage. The claws had penetrated deep, and now that the heat of action was fading, his shoulder was freezing up. The pain was burning and continuous. He realized that it was just as well he had used his knife quickly, because he would not be able to use that arm for a while.

"Let me see that," Craft said, addressing Hero's shoulder. "Haven gave me some balm. I don't know whether it will be enough."

They cut off the lion's ears and tail, evidence of the killing, and started back. Of course the word of his accomplishment was already spreading, but this would make it official. The rest of the body they left for the carrion eaters.

"I thought there was only one grown male in a pride," Craft said.

"Maybe they were brothers."

Craft nodded. "Brothers stick together."

They walked at a brisk pace, though the sun was hot. Hero was sweating more than usual. He drank water from his water skin, but his thirst remained.

It wasn't long before the pain of the shoulder spread down the arm and across the chest. Hero didn't say anything, but Craft knew. "That lion's spirit is in you, biting inside."

"Haven will fix it." As he spoke, he wondered why he hadn't said Crenelle. She was, after all, his wife. But it had always been his sister who had ministered to his hurts, from childhood on, and now in his pain it was her comfort he sought.

"Haven will fix it," Craft agreed. "Keep walking."

Hero realized with dull surprise that he had stopped walking. He resumed, but his feet were feeling heavy. His left shoulder had turned numb, and his arm just hung.

At some point Craft took hold of his right arm and urged/guided him forward. He must have slowed or stopped again. The heat was overwhelming, though the sun was descending. He had drunk all of his water, and Craft's too, but the thirst raged on.

He saw himself as if from a distance, trudging along. His body was hairier, his spear was more crudely crafted, his face was strangely slanted back, but he was moving well. He was tracking a lame leopard who had eaten a child. For centuries the big cats had preyed on Hero's people, and there hadn't been anything to be done about it. But Hero had grown larger, and learned to walk on two feet all the time, so that he could carry things with his hands, and what he carried was a weapon. Once, when a leopard struck, his kind had dropped to four feet and run to the nearest trees for safety. But now there were fewer trees, and the spaces between them were greater, so such escape wasn't as easy. But with weapons it was possible to fight off the leopard. So they spent more time on the ground, and when a leopard stalked one of their children, they went after the cat. A rabbit could not do that, but men were bigger and stronger, and had clubs and knives, and could throw rocks. After a while most leopards concluded that there was easier prey elsewhere, and left them alone. But sometimes one did strike.

The leopard had fled to the sun-hot plain. But Hero followed it, in his continuing vision. He could go farther into the sun, and stay longer than his people had before, because he was larger now, and had a nose. It poked out from his face, and cooled the air he breathed. His father was smaller, and hairier, and had mostly two holes in his face for breathing. His father couldn't handle as much heat. But Hero could, so now he was chasing the leopard.

He crossed a river, and paused to drink deeply. No matter how much water he sucked, his thirst remained. Then he went on after the leopard. He could stride for a long time. He knew he was getting closer, for the cat's tracks were fresher, and were dragging more. The leopard was tiring. It wasn't used to getting pursued.

At last it turned at bay. Its eyes glowed as it snarled, trying to scare him off. But he was here to avenge an eaten child. It was the rule: any creature that ate a child was killed. That was to make the world safe for children.

He strode directly toward it. The leopard sprang. He jabbed the spear point at it. The cat couldn't stop. The point sank into its chest, but not deeply enough. But the pressure did cause the leopard to miss him, landing to the side.

The cat whirled, snarling. Hero stabbed it again, going for the neck. The leopard tried to spring again, and this time he shoved the spear forward hard, through the neck.

The cat pulled back, and Hero pulled back, and the spear ripped out of its flesh, leaving splinters. Blood spattered. Then he jabbed again, and again, until he got an eye. That blinded it somewhat.

The leopard kept fighting, and Hero kept jabbing. At last he got the point directly in the neck where the blood was. The blood pulsed out, and the creature sank down and died.

"We're almost there."

Hero opened his eyes. The vision dissipated. There was no leopard. They were in sight of the hut. Crenelle was coming out, with Tour. Then he knew he would be all right.

•

Hero's vision was of his distant ancestor, Erectus, *who had emerged from his ancestor* Homo habilis *perhaps two million years ago. As the climate fluctuated violently, in the throes of the ice ages, the tropics may have changed more than the arctics. It is true that the poles spawned ice sheets that covered enormous areas and dragged the sea level down several hundred feet, changing the configurations of the continents. But the tropics were hardly bypassed. They became drier, and the rich jungles shrank, sometimes to relatively tiny islands. So instead of covering most of central Africa, they became little enclaves at the equatorial coasts and by the Rift Valley. Since the richest diversity of life forms was in those rain forests, this had considerable effect on the creatures of those forests. Then the warmer conditions returned, and the jungles expanded again. This happened over and over, so that no species could count on a consistent environment. Tropical life was whipsawed by the irregular changes, and many species went extinct. Those that survived best were the generalists: species able to get along in diverse habitats. In this manner,* Erectus *emerged from* Habilis, *distinguished mainly by larger size, a larger brain, and a nose. The size enabled* Erectus *to stand up better to enemies that had overwhelmed his ancestors. The brain enabled him to better make and use tools like the spear and hand ax. And the nose not only protected his lungs from the harsher, dustier air of the dry times, it processed the water in his system. When he inhaled, it moisturized the dry air, making it more comfortable, and when he exhaled, it recovered some of that moisture, so it would not be lost from the body. This was why* Erectus *was the first of the hominids to become independent of the jungle: he conserved enough of his water to enable him to range far enough out to find another water source.*

Our species evolved in wet conditions, and was at first poorly adapted to the drier plains. The animals already there could run up to four times as fast, had short light-reflecting fur, matured in two or three years, and could sustain higher body temperatures. They did not have large, delicate, heat-generating brains. Slow moving, slow developing, unarmored, pitifully weakly clawed and toothed, two-footed creatures like us were at a serious physical disadvantage. We had to run from tree to tree, or from forest to forest, seeking security from the predators and glaring sun of the savanna. Because mankind sweats to cool himself, his water is at a premium; his kidneys and bowels recover much of it at need, and so does his nose. Part of the price of this was the excrescence in the middle of his face, the nose, a redevelopment of the snout these apes had lost. Modern mankind was unable to do without it, so we too are blessed with this anomaly, along with our embarrassingly naked skin. But that sweating skin became perhaps the most efficient cooling system in the animal kingdom. Erectus *used it to good advantage, salvaging his precious water in whatever other ways he could. We, too, conquered the world thereby. We owe it to the awful variability of the ice ages, that alternated jungle with savanna, tundra with ice sheets; once we could handle that, we could handle almost anything.*

7

AMBUSH

Perhaps 22,000 years ago there were tribes in Central Asia. Some moved on to Beringia, as shown, while others remained in Siberia, continuing there for 10,000 or more years. One culture resided at a site called Mal'ta, in the Yenisey Valley just southwest of Lake Baikal. The time is 13,000 years ago, at Mal'ta.

In Chapter 3 Craft was given the choice of raping Crenelle and bringing her south with him, or yielding to her desire to go north so that he could marry her without rape. In Chapter 4 it was apparent that he had done neither, so lost her. But in this later reality he did go with her, and found the harsh northern climate to his liking after all.

•

"I must forage for supper," Crenelle said. "The boys are yours for the afternoon."

Craft nodded. Their twin boys were sleeping, but would soon wake; his wife was leaving now so that they wouldn't fuss.

He watched as she walked down the center of the longhouse, past the hearths of the other families, toward the opening at the end. The house was dug partly into the ground, with sod walls buttressed above by stretched skins. Other women, Haven and Rebel among them, were going out similarly, making a party of several. It was women's work;

Haven liked it, but Rebel didn't. But until Rebel found a man to marry, she had no choice but to assist the other women.

Meanwhile he worked to shape burins, which were routine tools yet uncommonly useful. They looked like slivers of stone, and they were that, but also much more. A good burin was as worthy as any other tool, because it was a tool to make other tools.

Suddenly it burst upon him: Tools to make tools! This was the secret of mankind. Not just utensils, but devices to accomplish many other things. Animals were specialists, growing formidable teeth or claws or hoofs or tails or whatever, to do what they needed to do. People grew none of these things, and were at a disadvantage when it came to competing with an animal on its own turf. But people made tools, and the tools enabled them to more than match the animals. A bear could stun an animal with one sweep of its great paw; a man could stun the animal with one swing of his solid club. A snow tiger could disembowel a creature with a snatch of its sharp claws; a man could do the same with a sharp knife. A badger could delve rapidly into the ground with its digging claws; a man could match it with a digging stick. A wolf could tear open the throat of a deer with its fangs; a man could do it with an arrow or knife. A man by himself was not much, but a man with the right tool—and a weapon was a tool—could do anything an animal could do. Tools made the man.

In fact, there were many kind of tools. The poles, and the thongs they used to tie poles together to make a roof support, were tools for construction. The sod they dug to make solid walls for their houses was a tool to shield them from the weather. The brush they used to thatch the roof was a tool.

He glanced at the low fire Crenelle had left in the hearth. Fire was a tool too! A most useful and versatile one. It could scare away a predator, or cook meat, or heat a house, or make light to see at night. It would be hard to make it through a winter in this climate without the help of fire. People used tools, of many types, and so became masters of the land.

Bemused by his revelation, he contemplated the burin, thinking of the way this bit of stone, as a representative of all tools, had changed the way people lived. Without tools, where would people be? He couldn't answer.

The boys stirred. "Daddy!" Dex called, getting up.

"I am here."

"Where is Mommy?" Sin called.

"She is out foraging."

"Awww." Then both came over to see what he was up to.

Craft held up the burin. "This is a tool. It makes other tools." He doubted the boys would appreciate the full significance, but it was never too early to learn the use of a tool. "Take it."

Dex took it. Craft gave another burin to Sin, and took a third one for himself. "Here is how to make a needle. First we split a section of antler." He demonstrated, laying the antler on the floor and holding it in place by setting his foot on one end. Then he lodged the point of the burin against a thin crack in the antler, picked up a pounding stone, and banged it against the end of the burin. The point sank into the crack a bit, wedging it wider. He struck again, widening it farther. Finally he managed to split it lengthwise.

The boys were fascinated; they hadn't realized that antler could be split. Dex transferred his burin to his left hand and took a stone with his right. "Gently," Craft cautioned. "If you miss, you'll hurt your hand."

Sin took his burin in his right hand and a rock with his left. The two boys were pool-reflection images of each other; their hair curled in opposite directions, and they used opposite hands. Crenelle had tried to get Sin to use his right hand more, but the boy was resistive; only his left would do. Seeing how it was, they let him be, though there were members of the tribe who thought that preferring the left hand was a sign of possession by an evil spirit. Nobody said anything, because the boy's uncle Hero was chief, but if there ever came a time when Hero was not chief, there could be mischief. Craft had seen others glancing across from their hearths, their gazes lingering a bit too long on Sin. That was a disadvantage of communal living; there were no secrets.

Craft gave each boy one of the split sections of the antler. "Find a crack, and pound, the way I did," he said. He took another antler and demonstrated.

They tried, but the antler fragments skidded out from under. "Hold it with your foot," Craft advised. "But don't hit your toes with the rock."

They tried again, but couldn't get it. Their patience was as small as they were, so Craft ended the session before there was injury or tears. "Watch me, today. Tomorrow you can try again." He split the two halves, and split them again, until he had several thin slivers of antler.

"Now to make a hole in it," he said, taking up one sliver. He held it down and dug very carefully into one end with a smaller, sharper burin point. This could not be rushed, or it would split the sliver again, and that would spoil it. The boys were losing interest.

It was time to change the subject. "Let's do some carving instead," he suggested.

They were happy to agree. Needles might be boring, but animal figures were interesting. Craft brought out his stone knife-chips and three sticks of wood. "What shall we make this time?"

"Mammoth!" Dex exclaimed as he snatched up one chip.

"Moose!" Sin said, taking another.

They were too ambitious. "Can you carve the trunk?" he asked. "Or the tail?"

They sobered, realizing that such details were beyond them. "What about a bird?" he asked. "With its wings folded."

They nodded. That should be feasible. Such a figure would be mostly rounded.

"Start with the head, at the end of your stick," he said. "Very carefully."

They concentrated. They weren't apt, but were able to round off the ends of their sticks somewhat, which counted for heads. Craft started a similar one, trying for a recognizable owl. His brother Keeper was of course much better at carving animals and birds, because he loved them so well.

There were footsteps outside, and a woofing sound. "Uncle Keeper!" Dex cried, and scrambled up to intercept him. Sin did the same, using opposite feet to get up.

In a moment Keeper was there, with the three dogs, entering at the end of the longhouse. The boys dropped their sticks and chips and hugged each dog in turn, and the dogs licked their faces, liking the attention.

During that distraction, Keeper spoke his business, in a low voice. "A message boy came from Hero. He has encountered a raiding party of the Green Feather."

This was serious. "He'll need men and weapons," Craft said.

"Yes. Men are going there now. But they have only their own weapons. We'll need to get extra ones to him as soon as we can."

Craft glanced around. "But what of the dogs? The Green Feather eat them. And the boys—"

"We can't leave them here," Keeper said. "The Green Feather might raid this house."

Others were coming to a similar conclusion; there was a stirring as the news spread. The longhouse was an easy target, and an obvious one, because often women were in it while the men were out, easy prey. They couldn't defend it; the Green Feather would simply hurl a fire spear into the roof, then pick off the people as they fled the fire. The men would be killed, the women raped and then killed if they resisted too much, and the smaller children would be adopted as slaves. Unless the enemy was defeated and driven away before it could get close.

"We'll have to take them with us," Craft decided. "Do the women have the word yet?"

"The runner went out to find them. They'll be coming back soon."

"We can't wait for them. Hero needs those weapons immediately."

"Yes." Keeper snapped his fingers, and the three dogs came to cluster around him.

Craft doused the fire. "We must go take weapons to Uncle Hero," he told the boys. "You stay close and quiet."

They nodded together, understanding when something was serious. There were times when silence was the price of life; it was among the earliest lessons any child learned.

Craft had a separate alcove where he stored newly made weapons. These were reserved for the chief, and this was an occasion for their use. He quickly bound ten spears together and gave them to Keeper to carry. Then he bound several stout staffs similarly, and gave them to another man who appeared. Finally he took four bows, and as many arrows as there were, stuffing some into his backpack along with the remaining cords, and bundling the rest in some tough hides. It was a heavy load, but they could afford to leave none of it behind for possible acquisition by the enemy.

As they left the longhouse, the women were returning. Crenelle and Rebel hurried up and took bows and some of the arrows. Normally women did not fight, but both of these had made it a point to learn the rudiments. Crenelle was determined to protect her children from any threat, and Rebel liked violence.

The other families were scattering into the landscape, finding their emergency hiding places. Craft's party couldn't afford that luxury; they had to get the weapons to Hero. They started out as rapidly as their burdens and the smaller steps of the children permitted.

They left the longhouse behind, walking north to find Hero's party. They took advantage of the cover of the trees growing on the slopes, but still had to cross a good deal of open sections. Craft was not at all easy about this, but they had no choice. If there were Green Feather scouts in this area, there would be mischief.

Rebel lifted her chin, sniffing the air. The dogs did the same, the hair on the necks lifting somewhat, confirming her concern. She had fine senses, and in fact was a fine figure of a woman. "We'd better hurry," she murmured.

They hurried, but their burdens and the children still limited them. Craft was not at all easy with this. His sister was not given to false alarm. She must have winded Green Feather in the area. The last thing they wanted was to be caught as they were by an enemy party.

"We've got to move faster," Rebel said, slinging her bow across her back. She picked up Dex.

Crenelle didn't argue. She picked up Sin. Both women started running.

An arrow flew just ahead of them and landed in the ground. It was fletched with a green feather.

"Warning shot," Craft said. "They've got our range."

"They want us to stop and surrender," Keeper agreed.

"But we can't let them take us," Crenelle cried, well understanding the consequence of that. She might have wanted her marriage to begin with a friendly rape, but she didn't want the hostile rape and brutality of the Green Feather.

"How many of them are there?" Craft asked.

"Four," Rebel replied tersely. "You go for that copse; I'll lead two of them astray." Before Craft could protest, she set Dex down, threw down her bow, then stripped her jacket, baring her breasts. She ran in the direction the arrow had gone. There could be no mistaking her gender or her desirability.

Keeper touched Brownback. "Go, Rebel." The dog took off after his favorite person. He could complicate her capture, assuming the enemy caught her. But Keeper doubted they would; Rebel was as fleet of foot as she chose to be. She would run just slow enough to satisfy them that they were gaining, then give them the slip when they were far afield.

It worked; in a moment they saw two enemy men setting off in pursuit. Two, because the men knew that after they caught her, one would have to hold her while the other raped her. They wouldn't shoot her or club her senseless, because she was too pretty; they wanted to enjoy her whole and screaming. She had made sure they understood. They might also suspect that she was the only one really worth raping, so was trying to flee alone.

Craft shoved his bundle of arrows into Dex's arms, then picked up the boy. "Go!" he cried, and they lumbered toward the copse. Two remaining Green Feather pursued, but did not fire; they were satisfied that they had the quarry trapped.

Yet with only two, how could they be so certain that the two fleeing men would not turn and fight on an even basis? That didn't make sense. So this must be the advance contingent of a larger enemy party. There might be four more men coming up behind. So it would be the purpose of the advance party to locate and pin down the quarry, waiting for greater force to dispatch it.

An arrow thunked into Craft's back. It didn't hurt, because it had struck his pack and lodged without penetrating to his flesh. "Ooh!" he cried loudly, and staggered. But almost in the same breath he reassured the others. "I'm not hurt, but they won't know that. Better to have them think I'm injured." He set Dex down.

Keeper came close to help him walk. They staggered, almost dropping their remaining burdens. It was a good show. If it fooled the enemy, the Green Feather would be less alert for some sudden move.

Still, it wasn't safe to try to go beyond the copse, burdened as they were; arrows in the back could take them down at the enemy's will. The others weren't wearing packs; it had been sheer luck that the arrow had struck Craft. They would have to try to defend themselves and their cache of weapons in the island of trees, until Rebel notified Hero where to find them. Time would be on their side, if they could hold out long enough.

They reached the copse. It was small, but the foliage of the trees was thick enough to put the center into shadow. "We need a strategy," Crenelle gasped as she set Sin down.

Craft nodded. "There will be four or six men coming in after us, soon. We need to surprise them."

Keeper nodded. "They'll shoot the dogs first, and try to capture the children. They know we'll be helpless if the children are hostage."

"I have a notion," Crenelle said. "Set up a mock group in the center. When they close on that, ambush them."

His wife was smart, and he respected her judgment. But he didn't follow this. "Mock group?"

"They know we are three adults and two children. If they spy those, they won't look too carefully elsewhere." She took Keeper's bundle of spears and untied it. She jammed two spears into an old rotting stump, then got cord from Craft's pack and tied some brush against them so that it stood about head high.

Now Craft caught on. She was making a dummy! It wasn't much, but if come upon by surprise here in the gloom, by those whose eyes were adjusted to the bright light outside, it might do.

Soon all of them were making dummies. Dex and Sin made stick models of themselves, while the adults perfected two male and one female models. Spears and brush, cord and skins—would it be enough?

"They can't be silent," Crenelle decided. "Or motionless. I'll tend the injured one. You two hide the children and dogs, and set an ambush."

"But you can't risk—" Craft began, appalled.

She stripped off her shirt, becoming bare-breasted in the manner Rebel had. She was thicker set than Rebel, and her breasts had grown with nursing; the effect was striking. "They won't shoot me. But you be ready."

Craft and Keeper hustled the children to either side, and lifted them into trees with cautions about silence. The dogs slunk out of sight, on Keeper's orders. Then the two men hid in the brush, holding their bows with arrows nocked. This was a desperation ploy, but surely unexpected. At least it should enable them to get some slight advantage they wouldn't otherwise have.

Crenelle played her part, ministering to the wounded dummy. "This is awful," she lamented. "You could bleed to death. But I don't have anything to bind your wound, even if I get the arrow out." Would anyone question why she was attending him bare-breasted? With luck the men would be too busy staring to wonder about that.

"If only I had some water to wash it," she said loudly. "Hey, other Man, can you fetch me some?" She didn't need to use names, because few of the Green Feather understood the home dialect. They should just pick up on the essence, that the woman was tending to the injured man, distracted, and that she was a buxom prize.

"No, it's dangerous out there," she said in a lower tone, speaking for the balky other man. "Get it yourself."

"Get it myself!" she screeched indignantly. "What do you think I am!"

There was a giggle from the tree where Dex was hiding. Craft shushed him. If the enemy caught on too soon that the children were not in the center group, they would be alert for a trap, and would foil it.

"Then give me a kiss," the other man figure said.

"Here your brother's dying of blood flow, and you want a kiss?" she demanded.

"Yes, that's wrong," the other agreed. "Make it two kisses."

There was another stifled giggle. Crenelle was putting on a nice show, complete with humor. He had not realized before how apt she was at it. Of course she told the boys stories all the time, so knew how to do it, but this was surprising.

"Oh, all right," she agreed with bad grace. "For two skins of water."

"For one," the figure said. "A second skin will cost more."

"More!" she cried, outraged again. "What more?"

"A squeeze of your breast."

"A squeeze? For water? How dare you!"

"For milk, then."

There was faint choking in the tree, as the laughter threatened to burst out. The children liked her stories too well.

Then Craft saw a shadow between two trees. An enemy man was sneaking in. This show did not have much longer to run. The moment they caught on—

"You are impossible," Crenelle reproved the dummy figure. "If it weren't that my husband is dying, I wouldn't do this." She moved toward the dummy. Now Craft saw that she had also removed her skirt, and was naked.

Another dark figure appeared between two other trees. A second enemy man was revealing himself. This was amazing carelessness.

Crenelle shook herself, making all her flesh jiggle, and addressed the other dummy. The two enemy figures stood still, watching. Craft realized that they must understand more of the language than he had anticipated, and had become foolishly fascinated with the drama the woman was enacting. Would she kiss the demanding brother?

Then it seemed that the dummy lifted an arm and touched her body. "Get your hand off!" she cried, slapping it away.

Was that a Green Feather chuckle?

Then there was a whistle. Suddenly both visible men aimed their bows, drew, and fired arrows into the dummies. There had to be a third man, that Craft hadn't seen, because at least three arrows struck.

Crenelle screamed, though she had not been hit. Of course not; the last thing the men intended was to kill this luscious woman. They were advancing on her, smiling with grim anticipation.

Craft loosed his arrow into the back of the nearest man. Almost simultaneously, the one nearest Keeper groaned and fell. Meanwhile Craft was nocking another arrow and orienting on the region where the third man had to be.

In a moment that figure came clear, because it was moving, turning to retreat. Craft loosed his arrow, and the figure cried out and fell.

"There's one more," Crenelle cried, throwing herself to the ground so as to get out of the way. "There." She pointed.

The fourth man cursed, drawing his bow. Then Keeper's arrow caught him in the chest, and he went down.

But was that all of them? They had to be sure, because Craft and Keeper could be ambushed as readily as they had ambushed the others.

"Whitepaw, Toughtail," Keeper snapped. "Find!"

The two dogs leaped out of hiding and circled the copse, questing for enemy scents. In a moment they found one, and ran in pursuit, their noses down.

A shape loomed before the dogs. Craft oriented on it, waiting to be sure it was an enemy.

It drew a bow, aiming at a dog. That sufficed. Craft loosed his arrow, catching the man in the belly. He groaned and sagged. Then the dogs were on him, tearing at his throat.

That was the last of them. By the time Craft had made certain that all four Green Feather were dead, Crenelle was clothed again. He was almost disappointed; her charade had been intriguing, as had her body. He had of course possessed that body a thousand times, but in this unusual context it had assumed more startling allure than ever. She had done it, of course, to distract the enemy men, but in the process she had also distracted him, and perhaps Keeper.

That made him wonder, passingly. He had always assumed that if something happened to him, Crenelle would seek to marry Hero. He was, after all, the chief, and a fine, strong man. But might it be the younger brother instead? No, that seemed just too unlikely. Keeper was after all only twenty, a year younger than she was. Craft couldn't imagine her ever marrying him.

They made ready to resume their trek to deliver the weapons to Hero. But the dogs sniffed the air, and paced nervously.

"I think there are more enemy in the region," Keeper said.

Craft nodded. "We were lucky to escape without injuries. Best not to risk it again. We'll have to hide here until it seems safe."

"Then we'd better bury the bodies," Crenelle said.

They got to work. They were carrying weapons, not digging tools, but Craft was able to fashion two approximate spades from branches. Tools were always a great help, even imperfect ones. They excavated shallow pits beside each of the fallen men, Crenelle and the boys stripped the bodies of anything useful, interesting, or valuable. This was a good education for the lads. Nothing should be carelessly wasted. Then they rolled the bodies in and scraped the earth over them. The point was to conceal the fact that there had been a battle here, and to alleviate whatever smell might develop.

Burying was tedious work, and by the time they had finished, it was getting late in the day. The dogs remained nervous, which meant that Green Feather remained in the area. They would have to remain here the night, trusting that the morning would be better for completing their mission.

Crenelle foraged, checking around the copse to find edible fungus, tubers, leaves, and roots. Keeper helped her, for he knew more about plants than anyone. There would not be much in this limited section, but they did not dare go beyond it. Craft hoped they would find some water, too, for thirst was growing in him, and surely in the others too. It would also be chilly at night, for they did not dare start a fire.

Meanwhile it had fallen to him to watch the boys. So he produced stone knives, and found suitable sticks for carving. "We were doing birds," he said. "Let's make nice ones for your mother."

They agreed with young enthusiasm. He knew that whatever they carved and presented, Crenelle would welcome as wonderful. But it was good practice regardless of its merit, for carving birds should help them develop skill that might later be employed to carve useful tools.

In due course Keeper and Crenelle returned, and while the woman set about doing what she could to make a palatable meal without fire, Keeper considered the boys' carvings. "Very good," he said. "I wonder if I could do as well?"

Keeper set about carving a stick, and it was clear that he knew what he was doing. But he pretended to be unsure. "What shall I make?" he inquired.

"A bird," Dex said.

"A girl," Sin said.

Keeper pretended perplexity. "What bird? What woman?"

They hadn't thought of that. "A big hawk," Dex decided.

"Mommy," Sin said.

"All right." He worked vigorously, shaping the image in the soft wood.

Craft and the boys watched, curious which it was actually to be: bird or woman. Either kind was acceptable, but obviously it had to be one or the other.

They saw the head of the bird form. So it was to be a bird. Dex smiled. But then the breast of a woman developed. And indeed, it became a hawk-headed woman. Now he was working on the hips and thighs, with the legs trailing into the wood, the feet not yet emerged. Keeper was indeed good at this. Evidently he considered a woman to be another type of animal, so he could render her well.

"It's ready," Crenelle said.

Keeper stood and presented her with the bird woman. "This is for you," he said. "By order of your sons."

She stared. Then she laughed. "That's me, all right! Woman-breasted and birdbrained."

The boys laughed, agreeing. It was no affront to have the wisdom of a bird; a bird goddess was very smart. And the breasts were indeed like hers.

The meal was far from perfect, but the mixture of things was edible, and even the boys did not complain. They all knew that she would have done much better if they had had their normal foraging range.

They settled down for the night. Crenelle lay down with a boy embraced on either side, and Craft gathered leaves and mounded them over all three for warmth. Then Craft and Keeper took turns standing guard, for the Green Feather were treacherous and might come upon them when they least expected it. Craft was first, and Keeper made his own pile of leaves beneath a tree and slept.

After an hour, Crenelle stirred. She opened her eyes and looked around. Craft went over to reassure her. "No enemy near."

"Good. But what I had in mind was a friend." She raised her hand, and he caught it and helped draw her neatly out of the leaf-bed, leaving the two boys sleeping undisturbed.

"I know it's not fun out here," he said as she came into his embrace. "You have coped very well."

"As have you, my love." She looked around. "But we should be quick, if you don't mind."

"And silent," he agreed, understanding her. She was offering him fast one-sided sex, not seeking any pleasure for herself other than that of giving him pleasure. Some other time she would demand far more from him, and he would gladly oblige, but this was not the occasion. "When you distracted the Green Feather, I thought you were the most lovely creature I had ever seen."

"I knew you were watching too," she said. "I wished death for them, and passion for you."

"Both occurred."

They walked to a tree, and she stood against it and embraced it for support. He stood behind her and reached around to caress first her breasts inside her jacket, then her buttocks under her trousers. He drew the trousers down just enough, and brought his member up to her bottom until it lodged in her warm cleft. She pressed back and he pressed in, until they were perfectly merged. He wanted to hold back, to prolong the delight of her soft posterior, but she mischievously clenched on him, and he climaxed immediately. Yet even one-sided as it was, with no pretense of gratification on her part, he found it transporting.

"Oh, Crenelle," he breathed in her ear. "I love you so!" For answer, she tightened her buttocks, squeezing him lingeringly in her fashion.

Thereafter she returned to her bed, and he returned to his guard duty, much refreshed.

In due course he woke Keeper, and lay down to sleep in Keeper's bed of leaves.

In the morning they knew they would have to go on, because thirst would not allow them to remain here another day. Fortunately the two dogs were relaxed, so it seemed safe.

They detoured from the direct route just enough to intercept a stream they knew of, and eagerly slaked their thirst. Then they moved on with greater strength.

They reached Hero without further event. He was holed up in a rocky fort with a number of men. They had balked the Green Feather to a degree, but had not been able to go out and fight openly because they were short of spears and arrows. Now that was changed. They organized for a counterattack to drive the Green Feather out.

Rebel was there, with Harbinger and Brownback. The dog greeted his siblings enthusiastically, and so did Rebel. "I made it here, but couldn't go back," she said. "They would have followed me, and you already had enough trouble."

"We killed them, thanks to Crenelle's distraction," Craft said.

She drew back the jacket she had gotten, as if to show a breast, lifting an eyebrow. He nodded. She understood the nature of the distraction. She had surely used it on Harbinger, in the night, too.

Hero was pleased to learn that the enemy force had been depleted by four men. That definitely gave the home force an advantage. Craft knew that they should be able to kill many enemy, and drive them well away from the homeland. It was an uplifting prospect, for they owed the Green Feather many bad turns.

•

Mal'ta represents the easternmost range of the "Venus" figurines that were known across Asia and Europe. The Mal'ta figures were not obese in the way of western images, but were definitely female. They also did birds, and some bird-women, as described. The figures that survived were in ivory and stone, but surely there were many others in perishable material.

Craft's revelation about the importance of tools to make tools was a true one. Only mankind does this to any significant extent, and it has led to considerable technological sophistication, as modern radios, submarines, and CAT scans show. The breakthrough of human specialization facilitated this, so that individuals like Craft could, through the ages, develop ever more intricate variations.

The evidence is that bad as warfare is in the present, it was worse in prehistoric times, being more brutal and with fewer ameliorating conventions or means to save the wounded from infection and malaise. Chronic warfare probably served as a significant limiting factor for population. Only in relatively recent times has population increase become phenomenal, so that mankind is displacing other species all around the globe.

After this time, there was a series of significant climatic changes that affected all the world, and this region. Steppe alternated with woodlands, until the end of the glacial period about 10,000 years ago. Then it changed rapidly and drastically. Rising sea levels swallowed Beringia and much of the northeast Siberian coast. With the warming came more diverse animals: cattle, ibex, sheep, red deer, roe deer, moose, reindeer, wolf, red fox, brown bear, wolverine, and arctic hare. The mammoth, bison, and horse disappeared in that region.

The people survived. But eventually they moved or were driven west, emerging to history perhaps as the Iranian peoples. One of these was the Sarmatians, and one of three Sarmatian tribes became known as the Alani, or Alans. It is the Alani we shall be following.

8

REVELATION

The development of what we call civilization proceeded at a different pace in the New World. When the hunter/gatherers got past the ice barrier and colonized North and South America, perhaps twelve thousand years ago, they continued this lifestyle in most of the continents until historic times. Where they did change, it occurred only gradually, without any abrupt shift to the settled life.

The first domesticated plant seems to have been squash, dating back to ten thousand years ago. This did not lead to settling. Maybe they cultivated it in selected fields paralleling their migratory routes, and let the fields lie fallow when too distant to attend. Maybe they planted the seeds, then visited the fields at harvest time. There might have been considerable losses to the weather and animals, but enough might have survived to feed them when they arrived.

Beans were cultivated in the South American Andes, and potatoes, but these did not move to central America for some time. Teosinte would later be adapted into maize (corn) and became a major crop staple. But in Central America in early times it was squash, and maguey—otherwise known as agave, or the century plant—whose thick leaves were roasted slowly, then chewed. It was harvested at the time it went to seed, so that human use did not interfere with its reproductive cycle or diminish its numbers. Acorns were leeched to remove the tannic acid, making them less bitter, so that they could be ground into flour.

But by 5,000 years ago, there seem to have been no regular settlements.

The setting is the mountains of Central America, southwest of the Yucatan peninsula, about a hundred miles north of the narrow waist of southern Mexico. The time is 5,000 years ago, or about 3,000 before the Christian era.

•

The three of them set out on foot, as no river went the way they were going. Brownback, the most adventurous dog, was well satisfied to be along to guide and protect them. Keeper was ill at ease, and so was Haven; neither of them liked the mission they were on. But neither seemed to have much of a choice.

They made their way down the mountain path, headed for the distant sea. The journey would take them five days, and be wearing on their bare feet. They carried some supplies in their packs, but would forage along the way for most of their food.

The first day they concentrated on conserving their strength and making good progress down the sometimes steep slopes. When they crossed a stream, they drank deeply, so as to conserve their waterskins. It was a nuisance carrying water they did not drink, but if they got caught away from a stream or lake, that would make a difference. Close to home the terrain was familiar, but that would change.

As evening came, Keeper guided them to a protected copse he knew of, where a spring flowed from a small cave. The cave had been the lair of a panther, but recently the big cat had died. The smell of it remained in the cave, keeping most other creatures away, so the hole was empty. That made it safe for savvy visitors to use.

Haven settled in, foraging for wood while Keeper and Brownback went to check a nearby slope where maguey grew. He was in luck; the largest was sprouting, sending up its seed stalk. "This one we can harvest," he said to the dog. "After they go to seed, they die anyway, so we are not taking anything away from this natural garden."

Brownback wagged his tail in agreement, though he didn't much like maguey.

Keeper drew his knife and used it to cut off two of the large tentacular leaves. Brownback's ears perked, and he sniffed.

"I hear it too," he said. "A good-sized rat. If you can catch it, you can have it. Go!"

The dog was off immediately, pursuing the rat. There was a scurrying sound in the brush, then a crashing, followed by a squeak. Soon Brownback returned, carrying the rat in his mouth. He had his supper.

Keeper carried the maguey leaves back to the cave. Haven had a little fire going. The dog settled down by it, satisfied to consume his rat and then snooze. They cut the leaves into segments, poked sharp sticks through them, and roasted them over the fire. This took time, as it had to be done slowly, cooking without burning.

"Are you satisfied?" Keeper inquired of Haven as they sat there holding and turning their segments.

"You know I'm not."

He nodded. "Is there something else to do?"

"I don't think you would care for it."

He knew what she meant, but preferred to have her tell him. "What would that be?"

She shook her head. "That's not for me to say."

"Can you say why she wants this?"

"I know, but can't say."

He had an idea. "Tell me a story."

"A story?"

"Of . . . of Brownback, and his sister Whitepaw, and his wife, whose name I don't know."

Haven smiled. "I don't know either, so I will simply call her the bitch."

Keeper hoped his wince didn't show in the darkness. "Yes."

His sister was contrite. "I shouldn't have said that. I'm sorry."

"No, sometimes I agree with you."

"I'll call her Fairtail."

He shrugged. They both knew that the name did not change the reality.

"Many years ago, when the spirits were new and the world was fresh," Haven began, in the standard manner for a story, "there was a dog named Brownback. He was one of a litter of three males and two females. They all got along reasonably well, until they met two other dogs, Blackeye and Fairtail. Brownback's sister Whitepaw got raped by Blackeye, and lost her litter, so left him. Then Brownback mated with Fairtail, and she had a female pup. But maybe she liked his brother Toughtail better."

There was the ugly suspicion. Keeper had married Crenelle, and their daughter Allele was two years old. That much was fine. But his wife seemed to be too interested in both his brothers, with whom she had had affairs before marrying Keeper. He remained very glad to have gotten her for his wife, but that continuing flirtation bothered him. He had never spoken of it, but if Haven has seen the same thing, that was confirmation.

"And what of Whitepaw?" he asked her. Whitepaw was Haven, in this story, though in real life the dog preferred Crenelle.

"She came to like Blackeye well enough, and would have stayed with him, had their puppy survived. But the spirits showed the curse of the commencement of their union by destroying the baby, and Whitepaw had to go. Blackeye then married her sister, Leanbelly."

Keeper choked. What a name! For Rebel had never gotten herself with child, and remained lean in the belly.

"Blackeye thought they might adopt a pup, but they didn't find any they liked well enough. He began to look at Whitepaw again, knowing that her belly would not remain lean. However, she would neither risk another cursed baby nor make mischief for her sister. Still, Fairtail noticed, and concluded that her brother would be better off if Whitepaw were gone. Since the wife of a married dog has authority over the husband's unmarried sisters, she told Brownback to take her to a far place and leave her there."

"And he could not tell her no," Keeper concluded. "Because he loved her, and because it was her right. But he did not relish it."

"She knew that."

The maguey was done. They took their hot pieces and began chewing on them. They were quite fibrous, but there was nourishment between the fibers, and patient chewing worked it out. It wasn't the most delightful meal, but it would do.

They had covered the territory. Except for one thing. "What else could they do?"

Haven considered. "There might be a larger consideration. Blackeye might in time give up on Leanbelly and seek another bitch anyway. Perhaps one outside the family group. Then Whitepaw would be exonerated, and not need to be elsewhere."

"So it would be all right not to take her away," he said.

"Or so it might seem, later," she said. "Though it would perhaps annoy Fairtail at the time, and make things more difficult."

This led into the other ugly aspect. "Yet if Fairtail had interest in one of Brownback's brothers—"

"It might merely make her stray sooner rather than later."

Surely so. But where would that leave him? He did love Crenelle, and couldn't stand to lose her any sooner than he could avoid.

Haven understood. "It is only a story," she said. "What do dogs have to do with people?"

All too much. But he let it go gratefully, not wanting to pursue the painful alternatives further.

They finished chewing their maguey, drank some water, banked the fire, and retired to the cave to sleep.

Next day they resumed travel, descending into a winding valley, pacing a stream for a time. But the stream meandered in the wrong direction, and they had to leave it and the valley and climb over another mountain.

On the fifth day they reached the village that was said to be looking for wives. The first thing Keeper noticed was the smell. The whole village stank. Even Brownback seemed to wrinkle his nose. The second thing was the barbaric accent of the people here; it was hard to understand their speech.

But they made their way to the head matriarch, the woman who had the authority to put women with men. She gazed intently at Haven, saw the fullness of her breasts and thighs, and nodded. At age twenty-four she was no young bride, but she would do. "I will bring three men to feel her," she told Keeper. "You may turn down one, or two, or three, but I will not bring more." Haven, of course, was not consulted; she was an unmarried woman, without rights.

"I will consider them," Keeper agreed.

"In a quarter day," she said, making a signal with her arms to indicate the portion of the day that would pass as she located the men.

Keeper nodded. It was noon now; that would put it in the afternoon.

"Go to the shore," the matriarch suggested. "They will give you fish there."

Keeper thanked her, and they departed her presence. They made their way to the harbor area. The smell intensified, but the natives seemed not to notice it. Then they spied piles of rotting fish heads all along the shore. That was the source of the smell.

"Do you like this village?" he inquired, knowing the answer.

"No. But I would not like any village away from my family."

"These men she will bring—give me a signal how you feel about them, and I will honor it."

"Thank you. I will blink my eyes once for satisfactory, and twice for unsatisfactory."

That would help. But he remained disturbed. "You know I don't want to do this."

"I know." She could have said much more.

A man was cooking gutted fish on a stone grate over a fire. He glanced up, recognized them as strangers, and knew their business. He gestured, offering them baked fish. They accepted, and talked with him as they ate.

His name was Baker, because of his employment, and he was garrulous. That was fine with them, as they wanted to learn as much as they could about this village and its prospects for a woman marrying into it. Haven flashed him an encouraging smile every so often, and that was enough. They got used to his accent, just as they got used to the oppressive fish smell. Keeper guided the dialogue to topics of interest to them, and they learned about the ways of the village.

One routine question brought a surprising response. "Do you have many foreign visitors?" For if there were fairly regular contact with neighboring peoples, it might be easier for Haven to stay somewhat in touch with her family. Visitors could carry news.

"Sometimes," Baker said as he piled roasted fish on a wooden tray and put new ones over the fire to roast. "Mostly like you, bringing wives, or with things to trade. But there was one we hardly know what to make of. He washed up in a boat, half starved and mad with thirst. He spoke an unintelligible language. We got him back to health, and he learned to speak a few of our words. He said he was from the south, far away, and had been blown north by storm and current. But we knew he was mad."

"From the south?" Keeper asked, interested. He had never traveled far in that direction; in fact this was his farthest extent. "There is land beyond the sea?"

"Oh, yes. The shore curves down and around and goes on endlessly; our fishermen have never seen the end of it. They say it has no conclusion. There are surely people there, beyond our ken. Mad ones."

"Why do you say he was mad?" Haven asked.

"Because of what he said. He said there was a desert, and behind it steep tall mountains, greater than the ones here. That they grew something they called potatoes, and had long-necked animals as beasts of burden. I'm no expert on tubers or animals, but I know there are no such things as he described."

Now Keeper was fascinated. "I *am* conversant with plants and animals. Perhaps I have seen these. Can you describe them in more detail?"

Baker did, and soon Keeper had to admit that he knew of no such things. Baker took that as confirmation of the stranger's madness, but Keeper suspected that the man had been telling the truth about the strange things of his land.

In due course they returned to the matriarch. "Here is the first man," she said, indicating a gruff old man. "His name is Grubber. He is a scavenger." She turned to the man. "This is Keeper, who offers his sister Haven."

The man approached Haven. His odor preceded him; he must have been grubbing among the rotting fish heads recently. He was wrinkled and potbellied, and wore a habitual scowl. Keeper did not need to look at his sister for any signal; he knew the prospect of marriage to such a man revolted her.

Grubber reached out and squeezed one of Haven's full breasts. She had the grace not to flinch. He drew up her skirt to uncover her bottom. "She'll do," he said.

"What happened to your prior wife?" Keeper asked.

"She ran away."

"My sister is not for you."

Grubber turned away, unsurprised. He was surely accustomed to being rejected by women.

Another man approached. He was big and muscular. "This is Maul," the matriarch said. "To marry this woman."

Keeper didn't wait for the man to feel Haven. "I think not."

"Not?" Maul inquired, looking dangerous. He took a step toward Keeper, but Brownback growled, warning him off. The man could surely handle the dog, but it would be an ugly scene, not worth it, since the decision was Keeper's to make regardless.

"The third man will be here in the morning," the Matriarch said as Maul stalked off. "Come back then."

Keeper was learning caution. "What is the third man's name?"

"Pul. He is a warrior."

"Why isn't he married already?"

"Never found the right woman. But I think he would like this one." She turned away.

They walked back into the forest, preferring to get away from the oppressive smell. "Pul could be all right," Haven said.

"And he could be another bad one."

"I think she was showing the worst first, to make her real choice seem good in contrast."

He hadn't thought of that. "But is any man of this village good for you?"

She shrugged. "What choice is there? I should have stayed with Harbinger when I had the chance."

"And had the spirits take another baby? No, I think you did right. No problem of that, with Rebel."

"Which makes a problem," she reminded him.

"Haven, nothing about this seems right. I don't want to see you ill-married, or to lose you from the family, and I know you don't want to go."

She shrugged. "I wouldn't stand in the way of family harmony, even if I could."

They ranged out, finding a suitable tree to camp under for the night. "If you had a single wish for the spirits to grant, what would it be?"

"For my baby to have lived," she said immediately.

"But that would mean you would still be married to Harbinger!"

"Without the curse of the spirits," she agreed. "Maybe it is that curse I wish to be rid of. My life has not prospered since then."

"But you were blameless! Then and now."

"I let myself be raped. That was blame enough."

He pondered. "Had it been Rebel, she would have killed him rather than be raped. Then he would have married no one."

She spread her hands. "Perhaps it worked out as it had to be."

"You are so gentle, you blame no one but yourself. Now Crenelle is driving you out."

"She has the right. Were I married to her brother, and she single, I would have authority over her. It was perhaps my folly that led to this."

She would not even blame Crenelle. But Keeper did. He loved Crenelle, but what she was doing was wrong.

They slept. In the night he dreamed. He was walking south, along the shore. He walked and walked, traveling an enormous distance, more than he could cover in two months of waking walking. He came to the land of the mad stranger. There were people growing the strange edible plants called potatoes, that grew from eyes. He picked up a potato, wanting to take it home and grow others like it, but it opened an eye and looked at him, and he lost his nerve and put it back. He walked through a mountain village, and saw fat little rodents called guinea pigs running around their houses, underfoot; all the people had to do was pick one up and prepare it for eating. Then he saw a llama, a strange animal like a solid deer with a long neck and woolly fur. Its head lifted up so that it looked him in the eye from his own height.

Startled, he woke, and realized that it was indeed a dream, based on what Baker had told him. Of course it might not be true; the folk who lived south probably farmed the same crops and hunted the same animals they did here. But it intrigued him mightily, and he wished he could visit that rare land and see for himself. But that would require an arduous journey, perhaps by boat, risking storms. He couldn't do it; he had a family to support.

And in support of that family, he had to put his sister into exile in a stinking village.

When morning came, they foraged for fruit to eat, then returned to the village. Matriarch was there, but the man wasn't. "He should be on his way," the woman said. "Do what you wish, meanwhile."

They went back to the shore, accepting the squalor and smell as the price of it. This time they saw two fishermen working in their boats, not far offshore. They had a net, and were seining it through the water, hauling it up laden with fish. They grabbed the fish they wanted, and dumped the others back into the water.

"Little ones," Baker said. "No point in harvesting them. Let them grow until they are big; then we'll eat them."

"The way we leave squash until big enough," Keeper agreed. It hadn't occurred to him to do it with fish, however.

"But they are throwing back some big ones," Haven said, peering at the boats.

"Trash fish," Baker explained. "Inedible, or bad tasting. Sometimes bits of waterlogged wood. They're sorting out the catch."

"Sorting out," Keeper agreed. An idea simmered, but did not quite take form.

A little boy ran up to them. "Strangers!" he cried, addressing them. "Pul is here!"

It was time. Keeper did not look at his sister as they walked to the matriarch's station.

Pul was a large, muscular man, not handsome but not mean-looking. He eyed Haven appraisingly as they approached.

"You'll do," the man said. Men were quick to make up their minds, especially when the woman was well formed. Haven, at age twenty-four, was not young, but she had very good breasts and thighs.

"Why are you single?" Keeper asked.

"I like a woman, but she likes another man better," Pul said. "Can't think why; he's scrawny."

"Is he smart?"

"Pretty much. What has that got to do with it?"

The man couldn't see why a woman would prefer a smart man to a strong one. And it was true, some woman didn't. Crenelle, maybe. Was he going to be able to hold on to her, even if he let Haven go? She wanted Hero.

Haven kept silent, but he knew she wasn't thrilled with this man Pul. He might be all right, but Haven was not a stupid woman, and would be somewhat stultified even if Pul were gentle.

Keeper thought of the fishermen, throwing away the bad fish. That was what he was trying to do here: throw away the bad men. He didn't like Pul, and didn't want the man to have his sister. Also irrelevantly, he thought of the teo weed, with its hard little seeds; it was so much work to gather them, though they were edible. If he could just throw away the bad ones, and keep the good ones, and have a better harvest later . . .

And why not? Each plant's seeds produced more plants of its own kind. Suppose he reversed it, and ate the small hard seeds, and threw away the nice big ones: putting them in the ground, where they would grow more plants. More big-seed plants. Would he have more good ones?

Suddenly excited, he wanted to get home and try it. But then he became aware of a silence. The others were looking at him.

"No," he said abruptly. "I will take my sister home."

Both the matriarch and Pul looked at him, astonished. They had thought he would have to take this final offering. And maybe he should. But he couldn't do it to Haven. Even if it meant he lost Crenelle.

In any event, he had something else to occupy him now. The

prospect of planting good teo seeds excited him. Who could say what might come of this?

Soon they were walking back toward the mountain. When they were out of sight of the village, Haven grabbed him and kissed him hard. "Thank you, little brother! But why did you do it? You know the mischief this will make."

"I know," he agreed. "But I have seeds to plant."

•

The first tiny cobs of maize appeared 5,000 years ago, adapted from teosinte. It was a long, slow process, for teosinte in the wild was nothing like modern maize, now called corn in America. The seeds were on small brittle stalks, which shattered as they matured. But when the transition to large soft seeds on cobs was made, it was to transform New World agriculture, and later the world's, for maize was destined to become one of the major food crops of the planet.

So was the one Keeper didn't quite believe existed, the potato. That eventually became the *leading food crop in the world. But there is no evidence that the potato made the transition from South America to Central or North America until relatively recently. Similarly the llama remained where it was. As a result, the South Americans progressed to the settled life and civilization earlier than the Central Americans did, though in this case the climate would have permitted an earlier transfer.*

9

DECISION

Neolithic farming spread across Europe from east to west, reaching the Iberian peninsula (now Spain and Portugal) circa 6,700 years ago. There does not seem to have been any wholesale genetic replacement as the farmers moved in on the hunters and foragers; the various populations simply merged. This does not necessarily mean that there were no cultural clashes. The change just may have been slower and more subtle than outright conquest.

The setting is northern Iberia, the foothills of the western Pyrenees. The time is 4,100 years ago.

Haven shook her head. There simply wasn't enough left to eat. It had been a lean summer, and now they faced the fall and winter without adequate stores. Something had to be done.

She discussed it first with Crenelle, as she also had a child. Adults could suffer through when they had to, but it was awful to do it to children.

"You're right," Crenelle agreed. "We can't make it through the winter."

"What are our alternatives?" Haven knew them, but didn't want to speak them.

"We can't stay here. We'll have to go. But where?"

Where else? "We'll have to go to your people,"

Crenelle was grim. "Tour can't go there."

"Anywhere else is doom. The drought is all over."

"All over," the woman agreed.

"And you know the people."

"I know the people. Yet . . ." Her eyes flicked toward her daughter, who was playing with Haven's son in the corner. Tour was seven, Risk six; they got along well together.

But each had a problem. Risk had almost died at birth, and remained somewhat infirm. Tour had seemed healthy, but recently had started twitching unpredictably. It seemed harmless, and family members understood, but could incite ridicule by outsiders. Maybe it would go away. But until it did, Crenelle did not like to expose her daughter to the cynosure of strangers. Haven hardly blamed her.

But they were in crisis. Crenelle and Harbinger knew the ways of their people, as Haven's siblings did not. It should be possible to find refuge among the Traders, while it would be very difficult elsewhere.

"It really doesn't show much," Haven murmured. "And we can shield her. It actually doesn't bother most folk, once they understand."

"Not among our people. They would call it spirit possession, and seek to kill her."

"Your people are so backward?"

"They think they are forward. They try to clean out bad spirits."

Haven shook her head. "Maybe if we swathe her in cloth, as for the chills, when she is in public. She's a smart girl; she'll cooperate."

Crenelle sighed. "We'll have to risk it."

It would be up to the men to make the formal decision, but the informal one had just been made.

•

Six of them set out for the coast, leaving only Keeper to care for the remaining farm animals and plants. There was food enough to sustain one person, and of course he had unparalleled ability to forage from nature. He would be there when they returned in the spring. Should there be a problem he couldn't handle, the neighbors would help, and of course he would help the neighbors. A number of them had already departed, driven by the common malaise of the drought. Every farmer understood, and the more who left, the better it would be for those remaining.

They walked from the cleared section of the farming village and entered the deep dark forest that surrounded it. Haven had mixed feelings about the forest. When she had to enter it alone, it frightened her, yet she knew that it served to protect her village from hostile intruders. There were paths through it, but these were deliberately obscure in places, to foil strangers. A clear path would lead to a dead end in a swamp, or terminate at the trunk of a huge tree. The true paths followed patterns that only native villagers knew. Armed strangers could readily be ambushed long before they found the village.

It was a lot of work to slash and burn a section of forest, but the process yielded extremely fertile soil for their fields. But after a time the fertility decreased, and then they had to clear new fields. It was an ongoing process, that meant they could never truly settle down. There were also animals to be hunted, but they too faded after a time. The forest fed them, but made them work hard for that food.

Protection and fear; food and work. The forest was everything. On the whole she liked being in it, if not walking through it. Now they were leaving it. There was a peculiar pain in that, despite the necessity.

Tour was walking beside her. She was a pretty girl, and Haven liked her much as she would have liked her own daughter. She had never had another child; the difficulty of birthing Risk had stopped her body from making more babies. Perhaps that drew her closer to her brother's child.

"It's so big," Tour said, referring to the forest. "It scares me."

"Me too, dear," Haven said. "But it's a good forest."

Tour made a sound like a hiccup. Haven didn't have to look; she knew the girl was having a fit. They tended to come on her when she was nervous or uncomfortable or afraid. Spirit possession? No, just something wrong with her body. Haven reached out with her right arm and caught the girl's right shoulder, bringing her in close. Nothing needed to be said. Comforting the girl also made Haven feel less depressed.

By nightfall they were on a wider path, forming into a trail that was used by several villages. They camped at a shelter that was for common use. There was a stream nearby, and a raised platform that enabled them to sleep off the ground. They made a fire and sat around it, three men, three women and two children, and Harbinger and Crenelle played music and sang, making them all feel better. None of them liked leaving home.

In two more days they reached the coast, where there was a town. Haven felt an eerie familiarity, as if she had been here before, though of course she hadn't. She had visited neighboring villages, but never seen the sea or any settlement this size. She didn't like it.

"Now I've been away from town for most of a decade," Crenelle said. She was explaining to the women, while her brother was explaining to the men. "But there are things that don't change. We'll have to check in with the chief."

"The chief?" Haven asked. The Farmers had no such offices, but knew that the Traders did.

"His head of staff. Or whatever official is delegated to harass newcomers. The chief himself is seldom ever seen; his officials do the routine work. Now here's the thing: those men have power. They can pick a man out of an immigrant family and kill him, and nobody can tell them no. They can pick a woman out and rape her, and she had better not offer any resistance. So we don't want to look attractive."

Haven was beginning to appreciate why Harbinger and Crenelle had preferred to live at the fringe of the Trader culture, and marry Farmers. Crenelle was attractive enough to attract male eyes, and when she was younger she would have been a prize to be used.

"So we'll be plain," Rebel said, adjusting her hair to be more messy.

"Be plain, not ugly," Crenelle said. "We want to pass unnoticed. Mostly they don't bother with immigrants; I just wanted you to know the risk. This is not the occasion to assert oneself."

"Is it really necessary to go to the chief?" Haven asked. "Couldn't we go to a smaller town?"

"We could, but the Traders have suffered the same drought the Farmers have, so there's not much there. The capital town has the supplies from the ships, so is independent of the drought. Besides, there are advantages."

"There need to be, if we risk execution or rape," Rebel said dryly.

"If we pass muster, we'll have good lodgings and good jobs, and will be under the protection of the chief. That could make for a nice winter."

"And there are more jobs for foreigners," Harbinger called across to them.

So they had to take a risk, to achieve a better situation. That was ever the way of life. But Haven wished they could have stayed on the farm.

"There will be a language problem," Crenelle continued. "You know how much trouble we had understanding each other at the beginning, until my brother and I learned more of your language. Now you'll have to speak Trader, and that will be awkward."

"We do know enough words to make ourselves understood," Haven reminded her.

"Yes. But you will never speak fluently, so it's best to avoid speaking whenever you can. There are those who would take advantage of you."

"Cheating us," Haven agreed.

Crenelle looked thoughtful. "That, too." She looked at the children. "You kids speak it more fluently than your elders do. But maybe better not to let on."

The two children nodded. Crenelle had spoken her language to them from the outset, and they had learned it readily. The rationale had been straightforward: in case they ever faced the situation they did today.

The road wound up to the palace, which was a huge rambling wooden structure braced by stone pillars and angled posts. It wasn't aesthetic, but Haven could see that it was solid; it would not blow down in any likely storm. It was surrounded by a palisade, and there were guards watching from towers buttressing the wall of pointed stakes. She was beginning to appreciate the security provided by the protection of the chief.

They approached the front gate. There were two guards armed with copper swords. That suggested the wealth of this establishment. She knew that a stone ax was more effective than a copper sword, but much easier to obtain, so of course a chief would look down on it. So this was ostentation rather than defense. If there were a real attack, they would surely bring out the axes and bows and spears soon enough.

"Halt!" a guard cried, assuming a stance that barred the entrance.

They stopped. A man came out of the gate tower. He was unarmed, but well garbed, evidently an authority. "What is your business here?"

Harbinger took one step forward. "Sir, we are Farmers looking for work for the winter."

"You're no Farmer," the Trader retorted. "You're Trader."

"I am a Trader married to a Farmer," Harbinger said. "Here is my wife." He gestured, and Haven stepped forward, her head bowed. "And son." Risk stepped forward, similarly submissive.

The Trader peered at Haven. "Peel back that cloak, woman; let me get a look at you."

"Do it," Harbinger murmured tightly.

Haven opened her cloak, revealing her bloused bosom. She knew she was a well-formed woman; she would arouse suspicion if she tried to conceal it.

The Trader nodded. "I see why you married Out. She's solid." He glanced around. "Who are the others?"

"My sister." Harbinger gestured again.

Crenelle stepped forward, looking the guard in the eye. "Yes, I am Trader, married to a Farmer. Here is my husband." Hero stepped up. "And daughter." Tour joined them.

"Open your cloak, girl."

This was bad business. Tour was only seven, but was a very pretty girl, promising to be a lovely woman. She could be attractive to a certain type of man. Crenelle was keeping a straight face, but Haven knew she was nervous and angry. And if Tour suffered a twitching fit, what then?

Fortunately the Trader's attention was already moving on. "And these others?"

"Brother and sister of our spouses," Harbinger said. "We are entitled to bring them, because they are blood kin to our children."

"How many will work?"

"Five. One will mind the children."

"Which one?"

Haven indicated herself. "I."

The man nodded. "Wait outside. I will send a party to guide you to your quarters and acquaint you with the nature of your work." He glanced across all of them. "You will work hard and well, of course."

"Of course," Harbinger agreed quickly.

They retreated from the gate somewhat. They did not speak to each other, as the guards or supervisor could have sharp hearing. They were being admitted, but Haven was by no means sure that all was well. Why had the Trader wanted to look at her? And at Tour? To assess them as prospects? Or just to show his power? Maybe it was just as well that he hadn't gotten a good look at Rebel; she had managed to remain inconspicuous.

In due course two men came out. One was massively muscular, the other lean. These would be the guides. Haven hoped that was all they were.

"Hello," the lean man said, in passable Farmer language. "Do you understand me?"

Surprised, all of them nodded. "You have been among our kind," Craft said.

"Yes. When we needed food, and had things to trade. We have always gotten along well. Your folk have always treated us fairly. I am Ned, and this is my big brother Sam."

Haven could appreciate why they had gotten along well; Ned was being very nice.

"Two of us were Traders," Harbinger said. "We married Out."

"So did I," Sam said. "My wife Snow is a Farmer."

This was looking better yet. "From what village?" Haven asked.

Sam named the village. It was a distant one they had had no contact with. Still, Haven felt encouraged.

"You will have to be in the newcomers' lodgings at first," Ned said. "They aren't good. But our sisters will help you get settled. Follow us."

They followed him to a different, smaller gate, and through it. This time the guards did not challenge; the group had been checked in.

Within the guarded compound was a cluster of large buildings close to the larger palace. They entered one. Inside was a huge array of posts and sections, with women working in many. There was the smell of smoke; there were a number of hearth fires burning, with the smoke wending to the ceiling and finding its way out through vents. There were other smells, as seemed inevitable when this many people were in close quarters.

"This is yours, for now," Ned said, indicating a dirty alcove. "You should be able to get better quarters in a few days; it depends on the favor of the authorities, which in turn depends on how well you work."

"I was afraid of this," Crenelle muttered. "This is the stinkiest hole. But we won't stay here long."

"I'll fetch our sisters," Sam said, evidently feeling awkward about the matter. He departed.

"Tomorrow Sam and I will take you to the grave," Ned said.

"The grave!" Haven exclaimed, appalled.

He smiled. "You misunderstand. The chief is old, and looking toward his death. We are building a burial vault, for him and all his attendants. It will be a rare privilege to be interred there. But first it has to be constructed. I helped design it, and Sam and I are working on it. We need more manpower, so are glad to see you folk arrive."

"That's why you were assigned to us," Craft said, catching on. "You need the labor."

"Yes. I should clarify that not all of it is physical labor. We need supervisors—men who can make sense of awkward complications. And women to bring food and supplies out on a fairly constant basis, so the work can proceed apace. It's really a pretty ambitious project, because the chief doesn't want his grave to be inferior to those of prior kings. So we hope to do a really good job."

"We can work well," Craft said. "I have designed and built houses. I realize that's not the same—"

"But it's an excellent start," Ned agreed. "You will understand the dynamics of buttresses and arches."

"Yes. And of materials organization."

"Now I know we'll get along," Ned said enthusiastically. He looked up. "Ah, here are our sisters."

Two young women were approaching. One was heavyset, the other slender but not pretty.

"Here is Flo," Ned said, indicating the heavy one. "And Jes. I will leave you in their hands for now. But you must be ready to work at dawn tomorrow."

"We will be," Craft promised.

There were brief further introductions, as all the members of the family were identified. Both sisters turned out to speak fair Farmer language.

"You will need a fire," Flo said, taking charge. "I'll show you where to get wood."

"I'll help," Rebel said. Crenelle nodded; she would watch the children, as she often did.

Flo led them to an open court where dry wood was piled high. "They bring their leavings here," she explained, "and anyone who needs it can use it. This is a good meeting place for women." Indeed, several other women were there, selecting sticks of wood, and Flo nodded to them.

"One thing to beware," Flo murmured as she drew on a small log, not looking at the other two. "The officer who interviewed you, and summoned us, is named Bub. He's not bad unless he wants something, and usually what he wants is sex from prettier women. Stay clear of him if you can. Do not speak of this openly."

Haven and Rebel nodded. They had already suspected as much. This was a vindication of Flo; not only did she know their language, she was truly helping them to get along.

They returned with three armfuls of wood, which should do for their immediate need. Crenelle and Rebel were cleaning out the filthy stall with Jes's help. "But at least you know the worst," Jes said. "They start all newcomers here, so they will appreciate better quarters when they get them."

Haven looked around as she set down her wood. "The other women—are they friendly?"

"They would be if they could afford it," Flo replied. "Don't count on them." She glanced briefly at Risk and Tour. "Keep one of your own with your children, always. Especially the girl."

"Make her less pretty, if you can," Jes added quietly. Crenelle, overhearing, nodded.

Fair warning, indeed.

"Tomorrow, after you work, you will be issued food," Flo said. "Tonight you will have to cope on your own."

Soon the two women left, and the family settled down to a meal from their scant supplies, and to sleep. There were fleas and mosquitoes, but they were used to them. The worst, perhaps, was over; they had been admitted, and would have lodging and work. Then in spring they could return to the farm for a better season.

Haven woke before dawn, as she normally did, and kneaded bread for the family. Minding Flo's warning, she conducted the children and the dogs to the slop trench for natural functions. They did not protest; they knew it could be dangerous among strangers.

Sam and Ned arrived at dawn to conduct the men to the working site. Not long after, Flo and Jes came to show the women their jobs.

Haven and the children, left alone, got to work cleaning the stall. They scraped away the layered dirt and scrubbed the posts. Women in the other stalls glanced across incuriously; they were evidently accustomed to dirt. Haven's impression was that these were not bright or sensitive females. That probably accounted for their presence in this dump.

A well-garbed man arrived, trailed by a humble woman. Haven recognized Bub, the admitting officer. He spoke in the Trader language, too rapidly for her to follow. She paused in her work, looking at him with calculated blankness.

"My lord Bub says that it is a shame to see an attractive woman like you confined to a lowly barracks like this," the woman said in Farmer.

So she was the translator. But what was this about an attractive woman? Haven could be attractive when she chose, but she had not made an effort today, and indeed, was sweaty and grimy from her labors here. "I don't understand."

Bub glanced at the translator woman. "Take the children to the kitchen for some good food."

"No you don't," Haven protested. "The children stay with me."

"They will not be harmed," the woman said. "Believe me, it is better."

Something was up. Reluctantly, Haven nodded. Risk and Tour straightened up and walked to the woman. She would have to hear what Bub wanted to say to her privately.

The man wasted no time, once the others were gone. "Want you," he said in pidgin Farmer.

There could be no misunderstanding, but she made the effort. "Maid work?"

He reached forward and caught the hem of her skirt, lifting it up too high. "Sex."

She pretended astonishment. "Me? I'm ugly."

He caught her shoulder and drew her toward him. She did not resist strongly, wary of angering him. He clasped her breast with his other hand. Then he reached around her and clasped a buttock. "No. Good body."

She drew back as far as she could. She had been raped once, and though that had worked out, she didn't care to repeat the experience. She knew she could not afford to provoke this man. So she tried to talk him out of it. "No. I'm married."

"No tell."

A private affair? That was hardly an improvement. "No."

He nodded, undismayed. "Move good place."

So he was bargaining. They could have better quarters if she acceded to his desire. But it was a bargain that repelled her. "No."

"Men good jobs."

That didn't move her. "They already have good jobs."

"No."

Too late, she realized her mistake. Bub was the one who assigned the jobs. He could send the men to bad jobs, or prevent them from getting employment entirely.

Bub saw she was coming to understand it. He upped the ante. "Women good jobs."

And what was a bad job, for a woman? She hardly cared to know. But how could she accede to his awful demand?

"Children—" he began.

"No!" she said fiercely. "Don't threaten the children!"

But of course he had already done so. "Come."

"No." But she had the sinking feeling that she couldn't make it stick.

He spread his hands inoffensively. "To see. No more."

"No more," she agreed, hating even this partial acquiescence.

He took her possessively by the elbow and guided her through the barracks and outside. Of course everyone could see this, and would think she had agreed to be his mistress. But Harbinger would believe the reality, and that counted more. What would that reality be?

He brought her to the palace compound. Here rugs hung on the walls and fine stones made the floor. The residential chambers were closed off by wood and stone, with quiet passages leading between them.

He paused to draw aside a curtain. Beyond was a beautiful chamber with a solid stone hearth and separate chimney, wooden benches, and raised sleeping platforms piled with bright pillows. The room was huge, with a high ceiling, and it opened onto at least one other chamber beyond. This was surely the residence of a prince.

"For you," Bub said. "Your family."

She shook her head, unable to believe it. He was cruelly teasing her.

He understood her doubt. "Ask others," he said. "Now go. Tomorrow, decide."

She made her way back the way they had come, hardly aware of her surroundings. She knew she couldn't accept his offer, but the wonderful residential suite dazed her. For the family to live in that . . .

She found herself back in the stinking hole that was their present residence. The woman was returning with the children. Haven felt guilty for forgetting the children even briefly, but they seemed to be all right.

"The kitchen!" Tour said. "So much food!"

"We got sweetbread," Risk said. "So good!"

Bub hadn't had the children harmed, but bribed. Showing her what he could do for them. How could she tell them that there would be no more of this?

"Don't oppose him," the woman said in a low tone. "He will make it terrible for your family. Do what he wants, until he tires of you. Then he will let you go, if you are circumspect, and you won't suffer."

"How do you know?" Haven asked, torn.

"I was his mistress, three years ago. I wore fine gowns and precious perfume. I was beautiful. As you will be; he has rare judgment in that respect. He likes lovely women, and he makes them so, in privacy. He recognized your potential when he saw you yesterday. Now my status is reduced, but my family is secure and I am not worked hard. I can leave if I want to, without suffering. So can the others, once he tires of them. Just be discreet, and you will prosper."

"And if I am not . . . discreet?"

"Then you had better escape to the hills, before he kills your children."

A cold hand clenched Haven's gut. This was a Farmer woman; she had no reason to deceive another of her kind. Yet the situation was intolerable.

"The chief—does he know of this?"

"Oh, yes. Sometimes Bub brings him an especially appealing girl. He doesn't care, as long as order is kept."

Haven felt another chill. "Girl?"

"The chief likes them young. Beware." Her eyes flicked toward Tour. "That one is pretty enough. Believe me, it is better to keep Bub happy. Then he will protect you."

"You–you are married?"

"Yes. My husband knows. He hates it, but he knows the penalty for balking. So he pretends not to know. That is the way it must be."

This was even worse than Haven had feared. Probably Bub had told the woman to tell her this, but that didn't make it any less real. The family could prosper, or suffer horribly, depending on Haven's decision. What was she to do?

The woman touched her arm. "I know your pain. But it must be. Unless you flee immediately."

"We can't go back. There's a drought."

"So it was with us. Bub makes sure his prey is secure before he strikes."

"The others here in this barracks—they would all know. They saw me go with him."

"None of them will tell. They know they would be tortured to death as traitors."

So it was a conspiracy of silence, governed by fear. Haven had not much liked the idea of coming here, but had thought her fear of the unknown was probably exaggerated. Now she knew the opposite was the case.

"This is awful," Haven said.

"I am sorry. Your children are very nice." The woman turned and walked quickly away.

Haven wrestled with the problem all day, but could come to no decision. She was torn between intolerable evils. What was she to do?

Late in the day the woman returned. "Your people have worked well," she said. "You will be fed well. But remember why." She departed.

It proved to be so. Hero and Craft were tired but satisfied; they could handle the work. Crenelle and Rebel were pleased; they had helped carry food to the crew working on the grave during the day, including their three men, and it had actually been pleasant. They had seen women toiling in far more menial chores, and were glad to have avoided that.

But Haven knew they would not avoid that, and worse, if she did not do Bub's bidding. Did she have any choice?

The food from the kitchen was excellent; it really needed no additional preparation. Everyone was pleased, except Haven, who knew its price.

She saw Tour go to her mother and whisper in her ear. Crenelle looked sharply at Haven. Oh, no—the child had told about the meeting with Bub! Haven hadn't thought to warn her not to. But maybe it would be possible to conceal the larger portion of it; the child had no inkling of that.

But Crenelle did. She signaled her brother, who nodded. Then he spoke. "The crisis is upon us," he said. "We must have a family meeting."

"No!" Haven cried. "The children—"

"They belong to the family too," Harbinger said. "They must know."

"But this—"

Crenelle looked at her. "Bub wants you for his mistress," she said.

Hero and Craft jerked upright. "What?" Hero asked.

In this dreadful revelation, Haven could think of only one thing to say. "How could you know?"

"We are of this culture," Crenelle said. "We recognize the signs. We thought we had escaped the penalty, but now we know better. Tell us what he said."

It was almost a relief to let it out. "He wants me to be his mistress. If I am, the family will prosper and have a wonderful chamber in the palace. If I balk, it will be terrible." She looked up through tear-blurred eyes. "But how could I ever do it?"

"You can't," Crenelle said. "And neither can I. But Rebel can."

"I couldn't ask her to—"

"I can do what the family needs me to do," Rebel said. "We can prosper, or we can suffer."

"But I'm the one he approached," Haven said.

"But I can take him from you, sister," Rebel said.

She surely could. Haven knew herself to be a handsome woman, but Crenelle was prettier, and Rebel prettier yet. "But I'm the one he has access to. I can't leave the children."

"I think you will have to join me as a serving maid," Crenelle said. "Rebel will care for the children."

"We can manage by ourselves," Tour said.

Haven felt a chill, remembering what the Farmer woman had told her of the king's interests. She couldn't repeat that, though.

Crenelle nevertheless understood. "Gossip has it that the chief likes children."

Wanly, Haven nodded.

Crenelle turned to her daughter. "You do need to be with one of our adults. Both of you."

"Why?" Tour asked challengingly, as Risk nodded. "If they like children, what harm can come? We had a fine time in the kitchen today."

"Because if you are not protected, one of the Trader men could take *you* for sex."

Tour started to laugh, then froze, realizing that this was not humor. She knew what sex was, and knew that children might see it but not participate in it. She surely had played innocent sexual games with other children, but never gone the full route with a man. Then she started to twitch.

Haven was closest to her. She reached out and pulled the girl's face into her bosom, comforting her. No one else gave any indication of awareness.

"I will protect the children," Rebel said, and it was clear that she meant that in more than one sense. "I will see that we get the good lodging and good work."

Craft glanced sidelong at her. "What if he reneges?"

"Then I'll castrate him."

Hero smiled, grimly. "Give us time to get well out of Trader territory, first."

"Of course."

No one laughed. Even Tour nodded slowly.

Thus it was decided, to Haven's immense relief.

Next morning, Rebel remained "home" and Haven went with Crenelle and Flo and Jes. The other two women looked surprised, but didn't comment. So Haven did: "We concluded that I could do a better job here."

"We didn't see Rebel as the nurturing kind," Flo said.

"She isn't."

"Tell me if this is not my business. Something happened?"

Haven decided that it would be better to have her real reason privately known, than a mystery. "Bub wants me for a mistress."

Flo shook her head. "I was afraid of that. You can't escape him this way; he'll make it hard for your whole family until you acquiesce."

"We think Rebel can handle it."

Flo nodded. "She is a remarkably comely women. But why would she be willing to undertake such a chore?"

"We are a family."

"I think I like your family. I hope it works."

"It surely will," Crenelle said. "Rebel is talented."

"She will have to be. Bub is a bad man to cross."

They went first to the kitchen. It was an impressive place, just as the children had said. Several men and women worked to cook whole animals, and there was a huge hearth over which they baked bread.

"We'll eat here, while they set up our order," Flo said. "We get the scraps, but they're good scraps; I'm on good terms with the baker."

So she was. They were given a pile of broken pieces of bread and pastries, not sightly, but fresh and very tasty.

"Any time you want, you can eat here," Flo said. "Once they know you. Just appear, and they'll give you the scraps, which are always fresh. I come here too much." She patted her hips, which were ample.

"But why are they so generous?" Haven asked.

"They want to be sure we don't steal any of the food we take to the workers," Jes explained. "So they make sure we're not hungry. It's important that the workers get their due."

Soon the workers' rations were ready: four large wicker baskets piled with bread, hunks of roasted meat, vegetables, and crocks of drink. Flo, the stoutest, took the heaviest, which was the drink, and the others took the remaining baskets. Haven got the meat, and Crenelle the bread. The baskets were heavy, but manageable. They carried them out of the kitchen to the gate, and then on down a path into the forest.

It was some distance, and Haven's arms grew tired, though she was accustomed to carrying things. This was not rough work, but it was indeed work. She was relieved when they paused to rest, and she could stretch and limber her arms.

When they finally arrived at the grave site, she was impressed anew. She had pictured a secluded glade with some overturned earth, though she knew it was a bigger project than that. The reality was a huge construction site with perhaps a dozen men digging a cavity in the ground big enough to hold a Farmer village. Several enormous stones were lying around the edges, somehow brought here for this purpose though Haven had no idea how mere men could have moved them.

"Smile and hand out your wares freely," Flo said as they came to the tables set up for this. "It's no secret that the thought of being fed by pretty women helps motivate the men. Don't favor your own men too freely; it spoils the effect."

Haven smiled and gave out the chunks of meat to each man who passed her basket. When Hero came, she winked but did not give him a larger piece. He nodded, understanding. None of them wanted to imperil their positions; they were still very new to this work.

Soon all the food was gone. They picked up their empty baskets and carried them back along the trail. They did not dawdle; the supervisors knew how long this job took, and would not tolerate malingering.

Four more baskets were ready when they arrived. They hauled these out to the grave site. The distance was far enough so that a significant part of the day had passed by the time they got there, and the men were hungry again. It seemed that the men were fed as often as feasible; this was important work.

It soon became routine. As she toiled with her basket, Haven pondered their situation. Had Rebel been able to satisfy Bub, so that his wrath would not fall on the family? Rebel was a beautiful woman, and sexually talented, but Bub had chosen Haven and might well be angry at her avoidance of him. He could punish them readily enough by doing nothing, letting them remain in the foul quarters they had started in. Would he do so? Or would he demand that Haven herself come to him, not any substitute? It was pointless to worry about it, yet she did.

Toward evening they delivered their last load and returned. They would normally be allowed to take scraps home for their families, Flo said. But this time the head cook shook his head. Haven and Crenelle could not take any.

Haven's heart sank. It was happening. The punishment was starting.

"Not necessarily," Crenelle murmured. "Some food could have been sent already." But Haven was not much reassured.

"We had better check on this," Flo said. So she and Jes accompanied them to the barracks.

Their stall was empty. Rebel and the children were not there, and neither were their scant belongings. Haven's dread intensified. How bad was this?

A guard approached. "Your quarters have changed," he said abruptly. "Follow me."

"That has to be an improvement," Jes said, wrinkling her nose. But Haven still was not much reassured.

The guard led them to the lovely suite she had been shown before. There were Rebel and the children. Risk ran out to hug Haven, and she hugged him back, her relief overflowing. It was all right!

"We'll leave you now," Flo said, smiling. "You seem to have found much favor." She and her sister departed.

"I hoped it would be this way," Crenelle whispered. "I knew that if anyone could do it, Rebel could. But these things are never certain."

The men had not yet returned. That gave the women a chance to compare notes while the children settled down for the night.

"What happened?" Crenelle asked Rebel.

Rebel smiled. "What I do, I try to do well. I made myself attractive and waited for his visit. And do you know what? He wasn't even surprised. He said, 'You are the one I wanted, but I knew you would fight if I chose you directly. So I arranged it so that you would choose it.' And I said, 'You disgusting schemer! You put poor Haven through that for this?' And he said, 'Does that anger you?' And I said, 'Yes!' And he said, 'And what will you do about it?' And I kissed him. And he said, 'I love a woman with fire. Now show me what you can do.' So I showed him." She gestured around the chamber. "Here is the result."

"He knows you hate his scheming, yet he wants you?" Haven asked, bemused.

"That's the way he wants me," Rebel said. "I have to give him credit: he found a way to make me come to him. He's a sharp judge of women. I hadn't known he was looking at me, when we came here."

"And can you carry it through?" Crenelle asked.

"Yes. The price is right. The family, the children—this secures our winter. And the best part is that I'll never have to marry him, or even spend too much time with him, because his wife would object. It's a limited engagement."

Haven's relief continued, but it was tinged with disgust. Bub and Rebel were cynically using each other. But it did indeed secure the family and protect the children.

•

That was the way of it, as fall passed into winter. The children loved it, for they were well treated, and they understood about being circumspect. Sometimes they were actually in Bub's suite when Rebel went for a tryst, but they said nothing. Haven found that she liked carrying food; it gave her a chance to see the men several times in the day, and she still was with the children at night.

The work on the passage grave went well. Craft had always been good with tools and designs, and he consulted with Ned and found ways to improve the design. The chief was pleased with the progress.

After a month, when there was a heavy rain that made the grave site too soggy for work, Haven and Craft were allowed to take time off to visit the farm. Haven knew this was really another reward for Rebel's cooperation, but it was one she gladly accepted.

"It's actually a good life," Craft remarked as they walked along with the three dogs. "But I wish I could believe that we achieved it on merit."

"We do have merit," Haven said. "But I agree with you. When spring comes, I'll be glad to go home."

The forest was as deep and dark as ever, but now it seemed friendly. This was where her people lived, protected and sustained by that forest. The dogs were thrilled to run through it again.

Keeper greeted them and the dogs gladly. News had circulated, so he had known they were doing well, but he was lonely. The animals were lean though in good health, but the harvest had been poor. There was no question: the family was better off where it was.

They set off on the return trip next day, for they had no time to loiter. Haven's feelings were mixed; she hated leaving Keeper, and was sorry to see that the rain had not come to this region, where it was so much needed. But she was glad again that the family had found such a good situation among the Traders.

"If he had insisted on you," Craft inquired as they walked, "would you have done it?"

"I would have had to," she said grimly. "You know, I had been concerned that Rebel might have an eye on my husband, and he on her. But she is certainly coming through for me now, and for all of us. She can do what it would pain me to do."

"I must admit that I find Crenelle a most attractive woman," Craft said. "Of course I would not—"

"Of course."

"But I can't help dreaming what it would be like to embrace her. So I can appreciate how Rebel must feel. I agree: she has really come through for us all."

That was the case. Haven knew she owed her sister much. Maybe it was true that Bub had wanted Rebel all along, but maybe he merely believed that after she set out to impress him. Certainly he was satisfied with her now, and all of them were reaping the benefits. It seemed best to leave it at that.

Haven was glad to return to the family, despite a lingering unease about the reason for their good fortune. There was another component to her muted distress, but she couldn't quite figure it out.

When spring came, they were still doing well. And the farm remained in drought. They couldn't return yet; they would starve.

There was another complication. "He is tiring of me," Rebel told Haven. "He doesn't know it yet, but I see the signs. It is his nature to desire what he can't have; he doesn't truly care for any woman. So I'll be free in another month or so, or when he spies another fetching damsel. But I think the family is secure; Craft and Hero are doing good work, and the working crews like you and Crenelle."

Haven nodded. "We can stay, and have a good life. But something bothers me about it."

"We're losing our sense of the farm," Rebel said. "The children, especially. They like it here perhaps too much."

That was it! That was what had been nagging Haven all winter. Not that there was a problem here, but that there was not. They were doing too well, and becoming loath to give it up. "Our culture—we are in danger of becoming Traders," she said. "Of losing our individuality. That would be awful."

"Yet if we can't go back until the rain comes—"

"That's the problem," Haven agreed. "We have to stay here. But at what cost to our identity?"

"We've always been close as a family," Rebel said. "And as a culture. Our family isn't breaking up."

"But we are in an alien culture—and liking it too well."

"I've got confidence in us."

"I hope you're right. I don't want the children to grow up as Traders."

They stayed. The passage grave wasn't finished, but Craft had made a good impression with his construction expertise, and was transferred to the Trader shipbuilding enterprise. The Traders had come from the sea, and though they had been long settled on land, they had never forgotten their heritage. Trading vessels still came into port regularly, but the ships were getting old and unsound, and more needed to be built.

Soon Hero and Harbinger joined Craft, for there was plenty of moving and assembling to do. None of them had had prior experience with watercraft of this size, big enough to hold twenty to fifty men, and were interested. Then the women brought food to them at the building dock, and the family was together again, in its fashion. It was good work for them all.

Another appealing girl appeared, and Rebel lost her position as mistress. But by then the family was well established on its merits, and was able to retain its lodging and position. Rebel faded gracefully from Bub's presence, saying nothing. He ignored her, not interfering; her silence bought his silence, and it was convenient for them both.

But the children were growing, and Tour was getting prettier. They tried to keep her out of sight, because they never knew when one of her small fits would come upon her. Haven worried that the girl's dawning beauty or her malady would get her into trouble. They garbed her in masculine fashion, not to conceal her nature but simply to mask her appeal. That was, however, a temporary expedient. It was time to return to the farm—but they couldn't. Not until the drought ended.

They stayed the second winter, and it continued well. Keeper, unable to overcome the relentless drought, finally had to join them among the Traders. Now they were all together again. But what of their farm?

In the spring of the third year, the rains returned. They could go home!

But the men now had excellent positions, and were loath to give them up for the risky nature of farming. Rains, like droughts, were unpredictable; suppose they returned to the farm, and the drought returned? It seemed better to remain here, at least as long as things were going so well.

"But don't you see," Haven argued. "We are becoming Traders! We are losing our Farming traditions."

They listened, and were swayed. They valued their Farming culture, and recognized the threat to it. They decided to make an application to the chief to return home.

That meant talking to Bub, who represented the chief in matters of immigration and emigration. That in turn meant that Rebel would make their case, for she retained an amicable relationship with the man. This should be routine.

When Haven and Crenelle returned from their day's labors, they found Rebel in the suite. She was not smiling. Something was wrong.

"We can't go," she said.

"They value the men's work too much?" Haven asked, with a sick fear that that was not the reason.

"The chief went after the wrong girl-child," Rebel said grimly. "This one rejected him—and her family has power. But they will let it be, if he swears never to touch another child."

"But what has that to do with us?" Crenelle asked.

"The chief must take a grown woman as his next mistress. The queen is as much concerned with scandal as anyone; she prefers him to have an adult mistress, rather than a child. Bub recommended me. It is a position of much favor."

"But you can't accept," Haven said. "We wouldn't be able to go home!"

"And the chief is a toad," Crenelle said.

"I can't decline."

"We could simply leave," Haven said. "Immediately."

"No."

"I know the way Bub works," Crenelle said. "What is his threat?"

"You won't like this."

Crenelle paled. "Tour?"

"If I do not cooperate, Bub will advise the chief of her availability. If the chief suffers the price of scandal, he will have no restraint, and will take her openly. She will become hostage to our cooperation, and we will not be allowed to leave."

"Maybe if Bub realized her condition," Haven said, "that would make her unattractive."

"He knows her condition. He is more observant than I realized. He saved the information until such time as it should become useful to him. If he tells the chief, she will be executed as spirit-haunted."

"Either way, my child loses," Crenelle said grimly.

"Unless I intercept the chief," Rebel said. "I have to do it."

"You have to do it," Haven agreed reluctantly.

"I will do it. But you will have to help make me look young. Very young."

They understood. They worked on her hair, and on her mannerisms, so that she could become innocently flirty in the way of a child. She had to make an impression on the chief that would satisfy him, and therefore satisfy Bub. In order to protect Tour, and their family. It was the only way.

Haven knew Rebel would succeed. But it did mean that they would not be able to return to the farm. Not this year. Their decision had been made for them, ironically. In time this business with the chief would pass, and they would be free. But would they still decide to leave? It had been a close decision this time, and might go the other way a year or more hence. And what would that mean for the future of the family? How could they retain their culture in the face of the blandishments to which they would be subject by the favor of the chief? Haven dreaded the answer.

•

As it turned out, things changed. The Megalithic culture, here referred to as the Traders, had dominated this region, and indeed, western coastal Europe, for some one thousand, seven hundred years. But their absorption of these particular immigrants, called the Farmers, resulted in their gradual dominance by the culture of the Farmers, which was more enduring than their own. For the Farmers defended their way of life and their cultural identity with a remarkable persistence. They remained in this section of Europe, sometimes expanding, sometimes driven back, but always themselves, increasingly distinct from those around them. Indeed, they remain there today. They are known as the Basques.

10

LANGUAGE

Erectus *does not seem to have reached Australia, though there are patterns of holes drilled in stone that seem to predate the arrival of modern mankind. Pending the solution to that mystery, the human presence on the continent seems to date from about 50,000 years ago. People soon spread all across the region, though resources in the interior were sparse.*

One region that could have supported a human population in the central desert is today known as Alice Springs, where a mountain range meets a lake almost in the center of the continent. This makes it an edge zone, where there is a greater variety of species than exist in normal zones. The red gum tree supports many kinds of insects, birds, and mammals, and kangaroos graze in the fields. The time in one sense is about two thousand years ago: the year zero. In another sense—

•

Rebel woke to a headache. She opened her eyes, and found the scene blurry. She felt her head, and her hand came away damp. She blinked to clear her vision, and saw that her fingers were coated with brownish red. Blood—from her head.

It was too much to assimilate at the moment. She relaxed, closed her eyes, and sank back into unconsciousness.

She found herself in Dreamtime. This was a special state of being.

Time separated into four phases: the future, the present, the past within living memory, and the distant past. At the far end of the distant past was the Dreamtime. It was the primordial period, when the ancestors traveled across the world, shaping the landscape as they went. The time before the great flood that washed away the previous landscape.

Dreamtime was also a state of being that extended across the other phases, so that sometimes people could reach it, through ritual or magic, and briefly become their ancestors. They could thus liberate their powers for a while, and recreate the great journeys of their forebears. The logic of Dreamtime was not that of the normal world. There were no paradoxes or confusions there. Great distances could be covered in minutes, or a short walk might require many hours.

So Rebel walked the strange yet somehow familiar landscape, intrigued by its oddities. It was too bad that the flood had wiped it out, yet that had made possible the terrain that she lived in. She pondered the several explanations for that awful flood. Some said that ancestral heroes known as the *Wandjina* had caused the flood, then sent each to their own countries in the new landscape. Others believed that a blind old woman named Mudunkala had emerged from the ground carrying three infants. Maybe she had not impressed others, but as she walked across the barren wastes to the islands, water had bubbled up from her tracks, so voluminously that it raised the level of the sea itself and separated one land from another. But perhaps the most authoritative version was that the rainbow, in the form of a great serpent, made the flood, so that it would have a compatible place to sleep. That serpent was believed to exist still, hiding in the deepest pools. Woe to anyone who disturbed it!

Rebel loved it here, but she could not stay. Her own realm was drawing her back. Reluctantly she let herself be hauled to the present. She felt the water of the flood flowing from her head as she passed through it to reach her own phase.

This time when she woke, Haven was there, sponging off her head. Rebel was relieved to see her; Haven was very good at taking care of children and ill people. In Dreamtime Rebel might be gloriously healthy, but in the present she was an invalid. She opened her mouth to speak—but was unable to put together the words. They simply wouldn't formulate.

Haven spoke. It was a liquid stream of sound, completely unintelligible.

Had she returned to her own realm? It seemed real, especially in its discomfort, but this was supernatural.

Rebel tried again to speak, but somehow the words were like stones she couldn't grasp. They slipped away before she could organize them. This was frustrating, but again it was too much to handle immediately. She closed her eyes and faded out.

Each human band had its own wandjina, or ancestral spirit, represented by its totem animal. Some wandjina were very powerful. There was Biljara the Eaglehawk, and Wagu the Crow. They were the ones who had initiated the matrimonial laws, outlawing a man's marriage to his sister, and establishing the degrees of kinship in which marriage was proper. The community was divided into two moieties associated with the participants of the ancestral marriage, and thereafter individuals were allowed to marry only into the opposite moiety. Children could belong to either, depending on local custom.

But Eaglehawk and Crow were not necessarily on friendly terms. Sometimes Crow tried to trick Eaglehawk, or work other mischief. Once Crow killed Eaglehawk's son and tried to blame someone else, just as a joke. But Eaglehawk lacked a sufficient sense of humor, and discovered the truth, and buried Crow with the body.

But before Rebel could locate one of those spirits and plead for some insight into her situation, she was summoned back to her own realm. This was frustrating, but could not be avoided.

The third time she woke, her headache had retreated somewhat, and she seemed to be clean. Haven had made her comfortable. At the moment she was alone, so she tried to speak to herself. The words still wouldn't come. It was as though she had no language.

Haven entered the chamber. Rebel saw now that it was actually a cave. In fact she recognized it; it was one the two of them had discovered years ago, and kept secret. A retreat that they could go to, that no one else knew about. Haven must have brought her here to mend.

But how had she gotten this way? She couldn't remember. So she tried to ask her sister—and the words evaporated before she could catch them.

Haven spoke again, and again it was gibberish.

Rebel made another effort to speak, trying to force the words out. But all that happened was a frustrated groan.

Haven said something, and by the intonation it was a question. Rebel spread her hands to show her confusion.

Haven asked another question. Rebel put on a blank look.

Haven looked at her with dawning astonishment. "?" she asked.

Rebel shrugged. She could hear her sister perfectly well, but couldn't understand her. She was pretty sure Haven wasn't speaking a foreign language; how could she have so suddenly learned it? So it had to be Rebel herself who couldn't understand it—or speak it. She had lost her language.

Slowly comprehension came to Haven's face. "!" she said.

Rebel nodded. She was pretty sure her sister had come to the same conclusion.

Haven thought for a moment, then backed off, put her hand to the ground, and smoothed a section of the dirt. Then she took her forefinger and drew a circle. She drew another, smaller, beside it. Then she made a series of lines, extending from the large circle and connecting it to the small one.

It was a simple figure of a human being, with sticklike arms and legs and a funny face. Rebel smiled, recognizing its nature. This she could understand.

Then Haven added a little line between the legs. A penis, making the figure male. Rebel nodded. It was a relief to achieve some sort of communication at last.

Then Haven added wavy lines, signaling hair, and a heavy line across that hair. All at once Rebel recognized the man: the one who had been clubbed on the head during a fight. She couldn't find his name, but remembered how he had been rather crazy for some time after that. Apparently the knock to the head had addled his common sense. The injury healed soon enough, but it took far longer for his personality to return to normal.

Then Rebel caught on to Haven's purpose in drawing the figure. Yes, this had happened to her! She had been hit on the head—she couldn't remember it, but her blood-matted hair was proof of it—and it must have addled her sense too. Or at least her language.

She touched the figure, and nodded, touching her own head. She was crazy because of the injury.

Haven nodded. She formed her right hand into a loose fist and raised it to her face, as if drinking from a cup. She raised an eyebrow in query.

Yes, Rebel was thirsty. So she made a similar fist and drank from it.

Haven went to the side of the cave and picked up a closed gourd. She poured it into a leaf cup, and brought the cup to Rebel. Rebel drank thirstily, gulping it down immediately. Haven filled it again, and this time Rebel drank more slowly.

Haven put her fingers to her mouth, as if conveying something here. She bit at an invisible fruit, and glanced at Rebel.

Rebel nodded. She was hungry. Haven went to the side of the cave, and opened a hide bag. She brought out a ripe fruit and brought it to Rebel. Rebel took it and bit into it, satisfying her hunger.

Then she needed to urinate. She gestured to the appropriate section of her body, and Haven nodded. Haven helped her stand and supported her while she wavered dizzily, waiting for the resurgent headache to fade. Then they went out of the cave, into the bright light beyond, and to the bushes nearby.

That was enough; she was tired. Rebel returned to her bed and lay down, and slept. She was feeling somewhat better physically, and much better emotionally, because she had established communication with Haven. Now she understood what had happened to her, and that gave her direction. She needed to discover who had done it, and why. The spirits of Dreamtime would know, if they cared to tell. But this could be complicated.

There were not just primordial ancestors of human clans in

Dreamtime. There were also ancestral plants and animals, as well as sacred rocks, wells, and ritual areas of great power. Hostile or trickster spirits might also be present, as they were in the real world. Such spirits might empty a fine bees' nest of its honey just before a person could harvest it, or inflict some awful disease or curse, or kill a person, ignore her, or teach her a new way to dance or hunt. Everything depended on whether the spirit was beneficial or evil or merely capricious, and on how it was approached, or perhaps on what mood it was in at the moment. A person could approach a spirit the wrong way simply by not recognizing it, and the spirits could masquerade as anything, so it could be tricky indeed. Rebel would be better off to approach none of them, than to accost one the wrong way.

She paused to consider, as this was best done *before* she encountered a spirit. She believed those of Dreamtime were similar to those of the real world, so that should be a guide. In the real world, the Wurulu-Wurulu stole honey by using bottlebrush flowers tied to sticks to empty the nest. They also caused mischief by putting their own paintings over those left by ancestral heroes. So probably she didn't want to approach one of them. There were the Argula, who were associated with evil sorcery. They painted distorted human figures in rock shelters and sang evil curses into them. That wouldn't do either. Then there were the graceful Mimi, who lived in cracks on cliff faces, and left their own paintings, which were said to predate the flood. They were not inimical, but could inflict sickness or curses if they were angered or suddenly surprised. Sometimes folk found a wallaby that seemed tame; that made it likely to be a pet of a Mimi, so it was left alone rather than hunted. That was perhaps the best prospect. Then there were the Namorodo, associated with shooting stars, so thin that they were no more than skin and bone held together by sinew. They traveled at night, flying through the air with a swishing sound and killing with their long claws. If a dead person's spirit was captured by a Namorodo, it could not rejoin the wandering totemic ancestors, but became instead a malevolent spirit wandering through the brush.

So she should seek a Mimi, hoping not to surprise it. Then, if she pleaded prettily enough, it might give her the information she wanted.

She set out, moving through Dreamtime at mysteriously variable speed, sometimes flying without wings, sometimes walking without moving her feet. It wasn't really by her volition; the dream terrain took her where it would, how it would.

Then she found a Mimi. It was in the form of a wisp of mist rising from a crevice in a cliff wall. She halted respectfully before it, giving it time to see her. After a while it curled toward her, acknowledging her presence. "O Mimi," she pleaded. "I beg you, tell me what I must know."

The Mimi considered. Then it spoke, with a voice like that of a moth. "Kungarankalpa." It faded away.

Rebel woke. She understood that word! It was the Seven Sisters. They were ancestral heroines of the north, who fled south to escape a lustful man named Nyiru, who wanted to rape the eldest sister. Their path across the continent was marked throughout, crossing the territories of many clans. East of Uluru was a string of claypans and rock pools, evidence of their passage. West of Atila they had camped for the night, building a windbreak which became a low cliff. In the morning they dived into the ground, emerging again at Tjuntalitja, a sacred well. But Nyiru watched them from a nearby sandhill. From there they walked to Wanakula, a rock hole collecting water. Then to Walinya, a hill on which they built a hut and camped again. That hut became a cave in a grove of wild fig trees, and one of the fig trees, standing apart, was associated with the oldest sister, the one fleeing the rape.

Nyiru watched until night, when he thought they were asleep, then burst into the hut. He was going to possess the woman he desired, and the others couldn't stop him. But when he landed on her body, he found it to be a pile of brush and leaves. Meanwhile, the sisters were escaping through a low opening in the rear of the cave. No chance to catch them by surprise; they had anticipated his move.

The Seven Sisters finally made their way to the southern coast, where there was a great gulf reaching into the land. There, still fleeing Nyiru's implacable pursuit, they plunged into the sea. The shock of the cold water caused them to jump into the sky; they weren't accustomed to the chill of the southern waters. They became the constellation Kurialya, called the Seven Sisters. But Nyiru still chased them, and his footprints also marked the night sky, his toes becoming three bright stars nearby. He did not seem to have caught them, but if those three bright toes ever moved to the seven faint ones, that would be evidence of his victory.

Rebel considered. She was the younger of two sisters, so the legend didn't seem to fit. But the Mimi had named it, so it had to be relevant. Her larger family consisted of seven, including her sister, three brothers, husband, and husband's sister, who was about her own age. Maybe that was it. But Haven was the elder sister, and nothing had happened to her. So it still didn't fit.

Well, she would have to ask Haven. Except that they couldn't talk. That was a continuing frustration. Anyway, Haven wasn't here right now. So there was nothing to do except ponder it alone.

She wasn't sure whether it was a dream or a vision, or both, but was sure it wasn't reality. If it was another aspect of Dreamtime, it was a strange one, as it matched none of the legends she knew. She was among monkeys, or rather apes, who dropped from the trees to the ground and scrambled across it, four footed. But this was awkward, because their feet were made for grasping branches, and they had to walk on knuckles. Also, there was danger on the ground, from predators like lions and leopards and hyenas and canines, as well as ornery hogs and buffalo and rhinos and elephants. It was difficult to eat enough on the ground before being driven back to the trees for safety. They needed to grab handfuls of food to take back to the trees, to be eaten at leisure—but that was hard when running on knuckles. So they specialized, making their hind feet more solid so they could support more weight, and the forepaws more delicate and mobile so that they could grasp and hold food more competently. Of course it was awkward climbing a tree with the hands holding food, so there had to be compromises, but this still worked better than the old system. Soon they were walking, striding, and running on two hind feet all the time, using the front feet for carrying or climbing, depending on the need.

But going two-footed led to endless complications. It straightened out their bodies, making it possible to mate face-to-face. Rebel did it many times, intrigued by her new ability to see her partner during the act. It made her front as interesting to males as her rear, so she developed frontal attractions, because there were advantages to being able to hold a man's attention from any position. It provided her with greater control than she had had before, and that was nice. But it also made it harder for children, because they took time to learn the art of balancing on two feet, and had to be carried until they did learn. Carrying a baby had the same problem as carrying food: it limited her options, making it harder to climb trees or to forage. She couldn't do them all at once, and that made survival harder. She needed help.

She solved that by intensifying her ability to attract and hold the interest of a man. Then he protected her and her baby, and got her food. Thus families were founded. But this required better social skills as well as foraging, sexual, and baby-raising skills. There was so much to learn and remember, and much of it could be learned from the experience of others. So she grew a larger brain, becoming smarter, to handle this more complicated two-footed life on the ground. Still, there were limits to observation of others, because the things she needed to know weren't always happening when she needed to know them. Some of them were rarities, like getting burned by the fire from a volcano; it was better if someone who had experienced that, however long ago or far away, could tell her what it was like. But how was that to be done, with no way to express it?

Other species didn't try. But hers did. They started showing and telling each other about things that existed or happened far away. To do this they needed to discover symbols: words or gestures that stood for other things. This was the hardest concept to grasp: that what was being indicated was not here but elsewhere. A hungry lion was in the valley, an angry river was flooding its banks, a fruit tree had just ripened. But those who were able to grasp the concept had a better chance to avoid the lion or river, and to reach the tree before others got its fruit. Thus a concept improved survival.

Once that started working, it got better. Those who were quickest to master concepts lived better and had more children. They became more facile at the art of elsewhere. "Good berries, that way," Haven said as she pointed. Haven was in this vision, while she had not been in Dreamtime. "Bad leopard." So Rebel knew she could get food, but would have to watch out for the leopard. She warned Haven's son Risk, and went in the indicated direction. The leopard was there, and they had to leap for a tree. The leopard could climb a tree, but not as well as people could, so it did not pursue them there. But when the leopard left, they dropped back down and reached the berry patch and feasted. They had avoided danger and gotten their bellies full, because Haven had told them about both.

Rebel woke. The dream had seemed so real, and now reality seemed dreamlike. She was in a cave, and Haven was there. She wanted to tell her sister about the good berries and the bad leopard, but knew she couldn't; she had no language, here in the cave. In the dream she had a very simple language, but that was vastly better than this. Haven also had a son, as she did not have in life. How could that be explained?

In a way, Rebel faced the same challenge here as she had there: to communicate efficiently with her sister. In the hot forest and field she had had just a few key words: the thing she was talking about, like berries or leopard, and modifications, like good or bad. But those had done the job. She had avoided the leopard and eaten the berries. She had survived, thanks to communication. Now she needed the same, to understand her present situation. For Haven surely knew it, if she could only tell it.

Haven spoke, and again it was a liquid and rather lovely flow of sound, with breaks and inflections and nuances and meanings, all of which were lost on Rebel. She spread her hands to show her continuing bewilderment.

Haven smiled sadly. She pointed to her mouth: food?

Rebel nodded, then pointed to her crotch: she had to pee. Gestures worked well, for immediate things.

Haven helped her walk out of the cave. Rebel was feeling better, or less worse; her headache had faded to moderate, and there was very little new blood in her hair, and she walked with greater steadiness. She was recovering.

But what had happened? How had she gotten bashed on the head? Why had Haven dragged her to this cave, instead of home to her husband, whose name she could not yet recover? She trusted her sister, and knew that Haven would never do her ill. There had to be good reason. But what was it?

She would learn the answers when she learned to communicate better. Maybe she could follow the route her dream ancestor had taken, establishing simple words for simple concepts, and modifying them. Yet what word could stand for the whole of her unknown situation? She was unable to address it until she had developed a more competent language. One that went well beyond pointing to mouths or crotches.

Haven showed Rebel what she had brought: fruits and nuts. Rebel reached for the nuts, but Haven stopped her hand.

Oh—those were poison nuts. She could not name them, but she knew their nature. They had to be soaked to wash out the toxin, before they could be ground and baked into excellent bread. Rebel nodded. She poured some water into an open bowl-shaped gourd, then put the nuts into it, starting the soaking process.

Haven nodded, satisfied that Rebel remembered the food if not the language. She would not poison herself by eating the nuts prematurely. Haven must have found them and brought them directly here, trusting that there would be time and competence to process them. She was correct. Rebel was not in good condition, and could not speak, but she could handle this chore; it was time-consuming rather than demanding.

She ate the fruits that Haven had brought, pondering. Then she tried. She leaned over to draw a picture in the dirt. She tried to draw herself, but wasn't very effective, so she pointed to herself and to the figure and glanced at Haven.

Haven understood. "Rebel," she said, pointing to the figure and to Rebel.

"Re-bel," Rebel said, forming her mouth around the unfamiliar word. Then she drew another figure, more solid. She pointed to it and to Haven.

"Haven," her sister said.

"Ha-ven." The name of her, the sound of it as unfamiliar as the name of herself. She focused on the two words, trying to remember them. Rebel, Haven, Rebel, Haven. It was a beginning.

Rebel drew a male figure. "Re-bel . . . ?" How could she ask?

But Haven understood. She drew two figures together, male and female. "Rebel–Harbinger."

So that was her husband. But it still didn't tell how or why she had gotten bashed and brought here to recover alone. Neither did it explain the relevance of the legend of the Seven Sisters.

Haven had to go; it was clear she couldn't stay long in the cave. Rebel hoped to learn why, as soon as their communication improved. This limitation was truly frustrating.

However, she had made progress. Now she was tired again, so she lay down and returned to sleep.

Her strange dream vision returned. Now she and Haven were larger, with projecting noses. They had developed a huge vocabulary, almost every word identifying a person or a thing. Every significant tree had its name, which distinguished it from all other trees. Every key fork in the river, every unusual rock formation, every useful place of shelter from the elements, including especially caves.

They were foraging for edible tubers near the edge of their band's range. There should be good yams in this ground. When they found one, they would leave the top of the tuber attached to the tendril so that the yam would grow again, and later they would be able to harvest another from the same place. They would also spit out fruit seeds into the debris of fish and shellfish remains, as the rotting compost was very good for new tree growth, assuring more fruit trees in the future.

Then Rebel caught a whiff of a foreign scent. Male, and not one of their own. "Alien!" she said.

Haven understood immediately, for the word described foreign intruders, who were by definition dangerous. Both women dived for cover behind nearby trees, alert for the aliens.

It turned out to be a scouting party of two Green Feather, brutish neighbors who constantly invaded Family territory. The Family men needed to be warned right away.

Rebel saw Haven back away from her concealing tree, warily watching to be sure the aliens did not spy her. But in so doing she tripped over a fallen branch, and tumbled backward.

The aliens heard the sound, and recognized it as something not of nature. Both turned and oriented on it.

Rebel realized that it would not be possible to avoid these brutes. They were muscular and swift; they could outrun the women.

Haven realized it too. "Rebel go Family!" she cried, and scrambled for the most climbable nearby tree.

Rebel didn't answer or move, for either could give away her presence. Haven was acting as a diversion, so that the enemy men would not realize there was more than one girl.

The two men quickly charged Haven's tree. Haven screamed and climbed it as rapidly as she could, her bare legs flashing below her belly. She had good legs, firmly fleshed, perhaps her best feature, and from the base of the tree the men could see up between those legs. The men stood and gazed upward, fascinated, though in truth there was not much to be seen in that shadowed region. Men were dull witted about such things; they would freeze and watch any woman who showed or seemed to show more than the usual flesh, even if they were well familiar with the anatomy.

Haven's necklace snagged on a branch and came apart. It fell down, leaving the woman naked. The men continued to stare up, licking their lips.

Rebel realized that Haven had exposed herself on purpose, to distract the men, so that Rebel could escape unobserved. In practical terms, a woman in her necklace showed just as much flesh as one without it, but in social terms there was a significant difference. A woman who divested herself of her ornaments was signaling her availability for sex, and one who was spied by a man in that state was sure to be approached, even if it was an accident. In fact many men actually preferred accidental views to deliberately presented ones, and hardly realized that women seldom really showed more than intended. The Green Feather men were caught; they desired her.

But her ploy was dangerous. Soon one of the men would climb the tree to fetch her down, so they could both rape her and drag her back to their own camp. But this would take time, because they would not want her to fall from the tree and be killed before they had their turns at her. Dead women were no fun. The men would have to catch her and drag her down, branch by branch, a complicated process. They might have hurled rocks until they knocked her out of the tree, had she not shown them her legs and crotch in the absence of her necklace. Now their suddenly aroused lust limited their options. They wanted her whole and healthy.

Rebel turned and sneaked away from the scene, knowing that Haven had given her time to bring help. She needed to get the men of the Family here before the Green Feather brought Haven all the way to the ground.

When Rebel was clear of the scene, she ran with all her speed. She was slender and healthy, and could move well through familiar territory.

In moments, it seemed, she was at the home base. "Greenfeather!" she cried. "Sweettuberpatch! Haven!" They understood. With three words she had identified the enemy, the place, and the problem.

For she would not have come so breathless and excited unless there was bad trouble, and naming the Green Feather identified the nature of it.

Where the scattered Family members were she didn't know, but suddenly Hero was on his way to the sweet tuber patch, and Craft with additional weapons, and Keeper with his wife Crenelle and three eager dogs. Rebel followed, clasping her own favored weapon, a sharp stone knife. Harbinger was beside her, concerned for her welfare. She flashed him a smile to show she was all right.

When they got there, the climbing enemy had just reached Haven, and had hold of her ankle. The man on the ground took one look at Hero and fled, leaving his companion to his fate.

The man above looked down, and realized he was in trouble. But he didn't dissolve into despair. He drew on Haven's ankle, lifting her leg out from the tree. He could send her hurtling to the ground.

The Family men paused. If the Green Feather man killed Haven, they would kill him, for he had no escape from the tree. But they didn't want Haven to die.

"Truce," Hero called. It was a word that transcended cultures. It meant that the combative parties would disengage without fighting. It was normally honored, because without it there would be situations nobody could resolve.

"Truce," the Green Feather man agreed. He let go of Haven's ankle. Hero and the others stepped back, putting their weapons at rest. Each side had backed off a stage. The dogs growled, but obeyed Keeper's signal to stay clear.

The man descended the tree. Haven remained aloft. The man reached the ground and walked away. He might have wanted to run, but he was demonstrating that the truce protected him. The Family men stood unmoving.

Only when the Green Feather man was gone did Haven start down the tree. The Family men went up to it to help her. She embraced Hero, relieved to be safe. Then she turned to Rebel and hugged her too. Haven had provided the distraction that enabled Rebel to escape; Rebel had brought the help that saved Haven. The Family had protected its own, as it always did. Usually it was Rebel who distracted, and Haven who went home; this time their roles had been reversed, but the outcome was the same. Three words had done it.

Rebel woke. All the members of the Family had been in that dream. They had worked together to save Haven from the enemy. The elder sister, threatened with rape. But here in the cave it was Rebel who had suffered, and Haven helping her. Had the Green Feather attacked again? Were there three words to clarify the situation?

In the language of the dream, the words had all been things: the name of the enemy, the name of the place, and the name of the Family member in trouble. Context clarified the rest. Even the term "truce" was a thing, meaning that nothing would happen. It took more understanding to handle truce, but could be done. But here in the cave, more was needed. Rebel could not formulate the language she once had known, but remembered that it had contained other types of terms. Such as modifiers, to show whether a thing was good or bad or nice or nasty or near or far. As with the good berries and the bad leopard. It also had terms that were not things, but that connected things. So it was possible to tell where one thing was in relation to another, or how one thing affected another. Enemy attack Haven. Rebel eat berries. She needed those connectors.

She cast about for such words. How could she generate them, when she had no way to make Haven understand?

Haven heard her stirring, and came from the deeper recess of the cave. She made an incomprehensible query, and Rebel shook her head to indicate that it still made no sense to her. But she went immediately to the dirt drawing pad. She sketched herself, then drew a circle around it to indicate the cave. "Re-bel—" she started, but lacked the word to continue. How had she come here? What had happened? Without the words, she couldn't ask. What a limit the lack of language was!

But Haven understood. She pointed to the line. "Cave," she said, identifying it. "Rebel in cave. How?"

"How," Rebel repeated, knowing by the inflection that this was the key word.

Haven frowned, suggesting that the matter was not simple. Then she started sketching figures. "Rebel," she said as she drew. "Harbinger." She circled the two. "Married."

Rebel nodded. She had already learned that, and they had been married in her dream.

Haven drew another male figure. "Bub." Rebel experienced a chill; she had heard that name before, in some sexual connection. Haven drew a third figure, herself, and then a line from the Bub figure's face to the Haven figure's crotch. "Bub want Haven."

Rebel studied the figures. Bub threw a spear at Haven? No, not from his face. Bub looked at Haven? That must be it. And this man Bub was not her husband.

Haven made it plainer: she drew an erect stick at Bub's crotch. For sexual excitement. So it wasn't just a look, it was desire.

"Haven no," Haven continued, erasing the figure so that Bub had nothing to look at or desire in that direction. "Then Bub want Rebel. Rebel no."

That made sense. Rebel was married; what would she want with a strange man? She nodded.

Haven grimaced. Now she drew another male figure beside Bub.

She did not name that one, so Rebel realized that this was just a helper, not important in himself. What were they up to?

Haven drew the Rebel figure again, right in front of the two men, and facing away. "Men seek Haven, but catch Rebel," she said grimly. She drew the second man's arms holding Rebel from behind, and moved the Bub figure in front of her. "Rape Rebel."

What were they doing? She didn't know the word, and couldn't grasp why one man would be behind her and one in front of her.

"Rape," Haven repeated. She drew in the erect stick penis, this time touching the Rebel figure's crotch.

Now she understood. Forcible sex! She wouldn't tolerate that.

But if one man had held her, while the other did it, she must have had no choice. Bub had wanted the elder sister, but settled for the one he could catch. Still, Rebel could have killed them right after it.

Haven redrew the figures. "Bub hit Rebel," she said. She drew a club in the man's hands, and touched the Rebel figure's head. He had bashed her and knocked her out! That was why she hadn't gone after them with her knife.

"Drag Rebel away," Haven said. She drew the figures again, showing Rebel being dragged across the ground by her feet. "Left for dead." The figure was shown in a gully.

Raped her and killed her, so she couldn't tell. That was the way of brute men. But she hadn't died, and that would be their undoing. As soon as she recovered.

Haven drew another female figure, herself. "Haven miss Rebel. Look for Rebel. Find scuffle marks." The words weren't intelligible, but Rebel got the gist of it. Her sister had searched for her, and found her in the gully, and managed to get her to their secret cave.

So now she knew, and she had learned several key words. She was recovering, and in due course would have her revenge. She would find this Bub character and kill him.

Satisfied, she relaxed, and realized she was hungry. The nuts were not yet ready; she would have to rinse them and soak them again, then dry them and grind them between stones to make flour. But Haven had brought millet. Millet was good, but hard to harvest in any quantity at one time; the wild grains tended to ripen at different times, scattered in distant patches. So they would cut the grass when the seed was full but the stems remained green, and store it while it ripened. Then they would thresh it, so that all the seed fell to the ground in one place. It was a lot of trouble, but the dry regions had spread during the drought, becoming better for millet. Haven had found some almost ripe millet that could be threshed now. So they got to work on it, and before long had a fair pile. They pounded the seed between stones and wet it, making a paste they could bake over a small fire. They finally had some fresh bread to chew on.

Rebel had a thought she wouldn't have cared to speak, even if she had the words. She was married to Harbinger, but now was away from him. Haven could see him often. Would Haven take advantage of that? No, of course not; Haven was her loyal sister. But was it possible that she was tempted on occasion? What about Harbinger? Rebel could bear him no babies, while Haven could. Haven had almost done so, once, before breaking with him. What memories of that might they both be harboring?

Rebel pushed the thought from her mind. Haven wouldn't do any such thing, she was sure. It was just her own illness and helplessness that made her worry foolishly. After all, wasn't Haven taking good care of her, here in the cave?

Haven left, and Rebel slept again. This time her dream was not of herself or her family, but of great groups of people. This must be the time after Dreamtime, but still very long ago, when people were spreading out to occupy the land. Some went north, and some went east, and some stayed south. The northerners settled in cold lands. They developed a huge vocabulary, with specific names for everything of interest to them. They hardly needed connectors; they weren't interested in interactions between words, just in the words themselves, with some modifications. The good berry patch and bad leopards were enough for them. This worked well enough, but required a prodigious memory, with a big head to contain it.

The easterners traveled far, meeting many new challenges. They settled in warm lands, or in mountainous lands, or in cold lands, or by the shore. They developed connections between terms, so that they could describe more complicated interactions. Because of this, they needed fewer terms, and did not have to remember as much. But they did just as well.

The southerners remained in warm lands. They developed a new class of words to describe things that didn't happen. This was confusing to the northerners and easterners, and they had nothing to do with it. But these new terms facilitated understanding of things that might have been. Storytelling came into existence. Children listened raptly to the adventures of men and women who didn't really exist. They dreamed of things that had happened long ago, or were happening far away, or that might happen in times to come. Of things that could happen, if something were different from what they knew. They developed imagination. Useless as this seemed, it nevertheless improved their command of language, and made them better able to cope in an increasingly complicated society.

But this didn't make sense, she realized as she woke. The south was not warm, it was cold; the warmth was in the north. So this aspect of Dreamtime seemed reversed. If it was really Dreamtime. Maybe in the period after Dreamtime, the nature of things changed, and then changed back again in recent times.

But direction didn't matter as much as substance. She now knew that the bad man Bub desired the elder sister, but had actually raped the younger one. She was that one. She didn't know why the men of her family weren't going out to kill Bub for that insult.

Well, she was obviously in that branch of people who had imagination. She should use it to figure out why.

Haven arrived, with more food. She had a bag of roasted moth abdomens. What delight! Rebel knew how the moths were caught and prepared. In the summer they swarmed to the heights of the distant mountains to aestivate. They piled high in crevices, layer upon layer, where they could be gathered. A fire was made on a flat stone base, and when the embers were swept aside, the rock remained hot, and the moths were dumped on it for cooking. The dust and ash were winnowed out, leaving the abdomens, each the size of the last digit of a little finger.

They were delicious, and made folk fat and sleek. But they could be obtained only by trading with distant tribes, and were a rare treat in this location. Somehow Haven had gotten some, and here they were.

Rebel ate them avidly. They were just the thing for strength for recovery. Then she saw that her sister wasn't eating. She paused. "Eat?"

Haven shook her head. "For you."

But Rebel insisted that her sister share, and then Haven did eat a few. Rebel knew Haven loved the moths as much as she did, but was trying to help Rebel mend.

Soon they talked. They were developing a larger mutual vocabulary, and Rebel was beginning to remember words. The dreams had helped her, giving her inspiration and direction, and maybe her head was healing inside too. "Bub want Haven, rape Rebel," she said, setting the base for further clarification. She strained for a moment, and captured the key word: "Vengeance?"

Haven sighed. "Not yet."

"Brothers do?"

"Not yet."

"Why?" There was one of the key concept words, that separated mankind from the cousin species. The others settled for what and how; her own kind sought when and if and why. The terms of imagination.

Haven frowned. "Hard to tell." She meant it was difficult to explain, because it was complicated and they lacked the words.

But Rebel insisted on knowing. She had no memory of the event, but might bring it back by hearing what Haven knew. A bad man had gone after the elder sister, but unlike the legend, had caught the younger one. That much was clear; Rebel surely had not been fleeing, not realizing that she could be in danger too. But if they knew who did it, why wasn't vengeance already being accomplished?

Haven tried. "Brothers work with Bub's clan."

It took a moment to assimilate the statement, but she was getting better. "Why?"

"Drought. Family hungry. Need food."

It took another moment to get "drought," but it came. A prolonged period of dryness, that shriveled plants and starved animals. She remembered: it had indeed been very dry. They lived near a lake, and that helped, but they foraged well beyond it, and out there the land was suffering. Turkey, geese, and bird eggs were sparse, and the wallaby and kangaroo were ranging elsewhere in search of better grazing. Rebel and Haven and Crenelle had been going out in the dugout canoe to fish with hook and line, while the brothers went after fish with spears. But even the fish were getting scarce, as if they too felt the dryness. It might be better, hunting and fishing elsewhere, but they were limited to their territory, on pain of keeping the peace with the neighboring clans.

So they had made a deal with a neighbor, the men agreeing to join its hunt across larger territory, for a share of the kill. Rebel remembered now, as Haven described it. The women had done the same, assisting the foraging and gathering. It wasn't ideal, but it was better than going hungry.

Then the neighbor subchief had approached Haven. He liked her look, and wanted her as a mistress. She had demurred; she wasn't married, but he was, and she didn't much like him anyway. He had made it clear that the family could prosper if she obliged him and kept silent about it, and that the family could suffer if she did not. She wanted no part of it, but did not tell others in the family, because they needed the work. So it was that she didn't tell Bub outright no, but did try to avoid him. The brothers got work, because Bub knew that if he sent them away, Haven would go too, and he would lose his chance. He was trying to play her in gradually, to convert her, so that she would willingly do his bidding. He evidently had some experience at bending women to his way.

But still she eluded him, and he was getting impatient. When Haven and Rebel switched places in the foraging line, so that Bub discovered the younger sister where he had thought to catch the elder, he must have been angry. Perhaps in frustration, or maybe as a warning to Haven, or maybe just because she was there, he had taken Rebel. She must have fought, so that he knew there would be trouble, so he tried to kill her. At least that was the way Haven recreated the scene; she had not been there.

Rebel nodded. She would have fought.

So Haven had rescued Rebel, after finding her in the gully. And saved her life. But she still hadn't dared tell the others, because she knew they would seek immediate vengeance, and that would get them exiled or killed.

"First," she said, "we must get you well, physically and mentally. You are improving, but you remain weak, and your speech is not back to normal."

"I know it," Rebel said, for she had to struggle to comprehend that speech. At least she was able to; connections were evidently being made in her head. Her comprehension seemed to have recovered to about the extent her body had: maybe halfway. "But why not home with Harbinger?"

"Because then Bub would know you survived. There would be trouble. If he even learned you are in this cave, he might seek to kill you, so you couldn't tell. But if you get well, then we can handle him. So it must be secret, until we are ready."

"While our brothers and Harbinger work for Bub?" Rebel asked, appalled.

"Yes, so as to give no notice. So that when we are ready, we can kill him."

"As the Seven Sisters would have killed Nyiru," Rebel agreed, liking it better. "Had they been able to."

"Yes," Haven agreed grimly, understanding the reference. "If they had been able to catch him unawares."

"And does Harbinger know I survive?"

"Yes, we all know. But all of us pretend we don't know where you are. Bub says you must have run away, not liking to work hard."

"The liar!"

"Of course. We express doubt, but since we are supposed not to know, we merely hope you will return. So things are uneasy, and there is no sign of you. And I still avoid Bub, though it is not easy."

Rebel chafed at the restriction, but knew her sister was right. It was better for Rebel to remain lost, until she was well again, and until the drought ended. Then—ah, then!

Yet she couldn't quite suppress that nagging concern. Was this the truth? Did Rebel really need to remain sealed away from her husband all this time? She knew her worry was foolish, yet could not completely abolish it.

She slept again, and dreamed richly, learning to talk more perfectly. When she woke it was true; her language was returning rapidly. As time passed, her head and body mended, and she was whole again. Haven visited frequently, usually at night, bringing what food she could scrounge without being obvious. Rebel suspected that much of it was Haven's own food, that she had pretended to eat but actually hidden, and hoped her sister wasn't starving herself. She brought assorted fruits, taro, arrowroot, coconut, and nuts. And of course they had the processed poison nuts, now detoxified.

One night Rebel woke, aware of a presence. It wasn't Haven. She clutched her knife.

"Rebel."

"Harbinger!" she cried with glad recognition.

Then they were embracing. "Haven said you were well enough now," he said. "So I came alone, secretly." He sounded uncertain.

"I am well enough," she agreed, embracing him and spreading her legs. She hadn't realized how hungry for him she had been. She wrapped her legs around him and drew him in, welcoming his ardor. It wasn't just because of the time they had been apart; it was that sometimes a man would reject a wife who had been raped. Considering the way their own relationship had started—

But there was no rejection, only passion. He was bursting inside her. She was relieved and delighted, milking him of all he had to give. But another part of her was neither forgetting nor forgiving the injuries she had experienced, though she still did not remember their actual occurrence.

In due course, they talked. He confirmed what Haven had said. They were all working with Bub's clan, because the drought hadn't ended. The work was good, but they hated it, not least because they knew what had happened to her. But the moment the drought ended, they would not be bound. Then they could deal with Bub.

"Meanwhile, what of Haven?" Rebel asked, suspecting that the situation with her was worse than she had admitted. Rebel had borne this foolish concern that her sister might be thinking of getting back together with Harbinger; obviously there had been no such design. But the real situation was just as bad.

"She can't continue much longer," he said seriously. "One of us is always with her—Hero, Craft, Keeper, or me—but Bub tries constantly to isolate her. He needs our help with the hunting, and of course his wife watches him, so he can't be obvious, but if the drought doesn't end soon, he will find a way to catch her alone."

So she had been correct: Haven was in more trouble than she could handle much longer. "And if the drought does end soon?"

"Then we won't need him," Harbinger said grimly. "We will kill him and go."

"But he won't need you either," Rebel pointed out. "Then he'll simply rape Haven, as he did me."

He evidently hadn't thought of that. "We must kill him first."

"We can't do it openly," she said. "For the same reason he can't do his desire openly. The clans do not allow murder or rape."

"But he has done the one, and we must do the other."

"Let me do it," she said. "When the drought ends, I can appear. I am the one he raped; I have the right to vengeance."

"But you can't—"

"Yes I can. If I surprise him alone, with my knife ready. Let Haven lead him to me."

She felt his nod in the darkness. "He would follow her, if he thought to finally catch her alone."

"Yes. And he doesn't know I'm alive. So he can know that all our family is accounted for, yet be surprised."

"It is right," he agreed reluctantly. "But you must make sure you kill him."

"I will make sure," she agreed grimly. "Meanwhile, stay close to her. Protect her." That was her penance for doubting her sister's loyalty.

Soon he had to leave, lest he be missed, even in the night. They could afford to give no hint that Rebel was alive and almost well. She kissed him, much cheered. Not only did she have the reassurance of his continuing love and desire, she had a clear plan to achieve her vengeance on Bub.

Near morning Haven came, with more food. "I can't stay," she said. "It's hard to take food without it being missed. I fear Bub is suspicious."

"Yes he is." It was a man's voice at the entrance. It was Bub! "I wondered why you were sneaking out at such an odd hour, so I followed you."

Rebel's shock crystallized. "Flee, sister!" she cried. "There is no help for me anyway."

But Haven hovered near, unwilling to desert her charge.

"Go!" Rebel hissed.

"You can't escape," Bub called. "There is no other exit from this cave." His voice was closer. He was tracking them by sound, and he was alone. Obviously he had no fear of women.

Haven retreated, realizing that Rebel had something in mind. She knew Rebel was far from helpless, having by now recovered almost completely.

Satisfied, Rebel grasped her knife. She groaned, then spoke to the man. "So you come to finish the job you started," she said, making her voice sound weak. "You raped me and almost killed me, and now you want to do it again."

Bub moved cautiously forward, feeling his way, still guided by her voice. "No. I doubt you are very appealing in your present condition. I will simply kill you, then at last get to rape your sister."

"You monster!" Rebel gasped weakly.

He came close. "Keep talking, wench. This time I will make quite sure of you."

"Oh," she wailed. "You would never be able to do this, were I healthy."

"Too bad for you." He leaned over her. She was tracking him by his voice, as much as he was tracking her by hers. Apparently it hadn't occurred to him that two could play this game.

She reached out with her free hand and found his leg. She hauled hard on it, making him stumble. As he lost his balance, she sat up suddenly and stabbed upward with the knife.

She was aiming for the groin, the most fitting target, but got him in the belly instead.

Or the loincloth; her knife snagged in it. She tried to wrench it out, but Bub was jerking back, and her knife was yanked from her hand.

This was trouble. He had more muscle than she, and was not just recovering from injury. He could and would kill her this time, if she didn't find a quick way to prevent it. But what could she do?

Even as she struggled mentally to devise a strategy of combat, she was acting physically. She flung her arms out and found his legs. She grasped his ankles and hauled on them, trying to pull him down. But the effect was to draw her body into him.

Well, maybe that would do. He was bending forward, reaching down. She knew he would stab her with his knife in a moment. She had to keep active. She clung to his ankles, rolled halfway on her back, and kicked up with one leg, trying again for his crotch.

She missed, again. Her foot jammed into his belly. But this had an effect. It pushed him back, breaking his balance, but he couldn't step back to recover it. So he fell, with an exclamation, landing hard on his back. She heard the knife skitter away across the cave floor. Good—she had disarmed him.

But she needed that knife herself, for she couldn't outwrestle him. She let go of his legs and launched herself in the direction she had heard the knife go. But he was reaching for it himself. She flopped prone on his extended arm and shoulder, pinning them to the ground. She reached beyond, casting for the knife.

But his fingers were already grasping it. She was too late. She had to get away, if she could. She twisted, trying to scramble clear of him, so she could lose herself in the darkness. But his other arm came across to cover her legs, pinning her.

She wrenched herself around, trying to get to her feet. But his arm clasped her legs, and she fell back across his body, this time with her head on his belly.

"I've got the knife," he said. "I can kill you now. But if you stop fighting, I'll merely rape you, completing what I didn't do before. You're a lot healthier than I thought."

She paused. "Didn't?"

"Don't you remember? You fought so hard I had to bash you instead. Then I thought you were dead, and dead women lack appeal, so I threw you away. But now I am reminded what a fine body you have." His hand worked its way up her thigh to her bare buttock, and squeezed. "I'll let you go, after, if you behave."

She had not been raped! Only bashed, costing her her memory of the occasion. What a relief.

But she couldn't trust him. Once he had his will of her, he would kill her anyway, and then kill Haven too, to prevent them from talking.

"Do you agree?" he asked, running his fingers in between her buttocks. She was aware of his penis stirring in the darkness; he was getting an erection, spawned by his exploration of her taut bottom. Her thighs were not as thick as Haven's, and her buttocks were less fleshy, but men had always found them supremely interesting. "I want your word."

He knew her word was good, though his wasn't. But if she didn't give it, he would simply stab her through the back until she died. What choice did she have?

"Haven too?" she asked, forcing her body to relax, though that encouraged his traveling hand. At least that was a considerable distraction to him, perhaps putting him somewhat off guard.

"Her too," he agreed as his questing fingers found her cleft. His member was now quite hard; she felt its radiating heat near her face.

Rebel held herself still and physically relaxed despite her revulsion at his touch and obvious lust. Her sex appeal was making him negotiate, and that gave her brief respite. She realized that his statement was ambiguous. "To let her go."

"After I rape her," he agreed, trying to work a finger into her. The angle was wrong at the moment, but he would soon correct that. He knew she resented his intrusion, and that surely excited him yet more. Just as many men preferred to get illicit peeks at women's normally hidden flesh, some men liked to ravish unwilling women. "I mean to have that plush body."

Rebel wondered whether she could leap free without getting stabbed. She was pretty sure she couldn't. But it seemed to be a choice between getting stabbed to death now, or after he raped her. He was already working his way into the rape. The irony was that his own bared genital region was within her easy reach, but she lacked any desire to explore it in retaliation. A further irony was that she might have been interested in having an affair with him, had he not tried to rape her; he was an interesting man, in his abusive fashion. Had he come to her with an offer, instead of—but of course she was married. So there was nothing there. She had to escape him.

Then she saw a way. It would take nerve and control, but was her only chance.

"Well?" he demanded, trying to twist his hand around for a better angle. He was almost there; she knew it better than he did.

"No." She remained quite still

He moved the hand with the knife. She knew it was poised to stab into her back, severing her spine with the first strike. "Are you sure?"

Suddenly she moved. She swept one hand across his belly, finding his hot, throbbing penis. At the same time she hunched forward, bringing her face there. She took the end of his member into her mouth, setting her teeth firmly but not biting down, while her hand took a solid hold on his scrotum.

Bub froze. He realized that he could quickly incapacitate her with one stab of the knife—but not before she bit off his penis and crushed his testicles. She would die, but he would be castrate. Even if he then managed to catch and kill Haven, so as to prevent the secret of his deed from getting out, he would never rape another woman.

Rebel could not speak, but didn't need to. She squeezed slowly, giving him a hint of what was coming. She didn't much care how she hurt him, and he knew that. She had nothing to lose.

"Truce!" he gasped.

She released her pressure just slightly, and waited.

"I will let you both go," he said.

She began to squeeze again. She noticed that his penis was not losing erection; he found her hold on his anatomy exciting despite its threat.

"Without rape," he added quickly. "I will simply depart, saying nothing."

Rebel eased up, then began to squeeze again.

"I take your silence to mean agreement to the truce," he said. "You will let me go, if I let you go."

She eased up slightly with her hand, but nipped slightly with her teeth.

He knew what she wanted. "Here is the knife." He moved his arm slowly across, until his hand touched hers. His fingers relaxed, letting the knife drop to the ground. Her fingers clasped it, and carried it beyond his reach.

Only then did she lift her head, releasing his member. But she clasped his scrotum a bit longer. "Get your hand out of my cleft." That seemed ironic, considering where her own hand was.

The hand withdrew. Now at last she felt a softening in his penis, as he accepted the fact that he would not be raping anyone this hour. It was a better signal of his intention than his words were.

She loosened her grip without giving it up entirely. "Remain still while I get off you. If you move, I will use the knife."

"Agreed." He knew she was not bluffing. She would be fair, but would strike where it counted if he gave her reason. It was the only way to handle a man like him.

She held the knife ready, let go of his member, and rolled off him. She got to her feet and backed away. "Now go. We will not speak of this if you do not."

"Agreed." He rolled to his feet and walked to the mouth of the cave.

She remained still, watching his outline against the pale light of dawn beyond the cave, and following him with her ears too. She needed to be sure he did not wait outside in ambush.

He did not. She heard his footsteps departing the area. She went to the mouth of the cave, peering out to make sure. She saw his retreating back.

"He's gone," she said to Haven. Now at last she could truly relax. She felt weak; she had not recovered as far as she had thought.

Haven came from the deeper recesses. "How did you make him go?"

"I got hold of something he valued more than my life, or yours." Rebel took a breath. "He's gone—but I think it will not be safe for our family any more. We'll have to go—now, drought or not."

"Yes. And you can't stay in this cave, now that Bub knows about it. I wish I'd been more careful, so that he hadn't—"

"He was bound to get suspicious. You couldn't take such good care of me without risking discovery."

They picked up their things and stepped out of the cave. It was a glad yet sad moment: Rebel's long confinement was through, but at the cost of the welfare of the family.

Rebel felt something. She paused. "What is that?"

Haven stopped. "What?" Then she felt it. "Rain! It's starting to rain! Our Wandjina has come to our aid."

Their ancestral spirit, associated with their totem animal, the wallaby. Wandjina were not all-powerful, but did what they could when they could. Now, just in time, theirs had acted.

"The drought is ending," Rebel said. "Now we can survive on our own."

"On our own," Haven agreed thankfully.

•

We don't really know the history or interpersonal relations of the Australian Aborigines before the white man took over their continent. But their diet and legends are as presented here. They did not have pottery or the bow and arrow, as these things seem to have been developed after they crossed to Australia, but did have the spear, atlatl, war club, and boomerang. They did not practice formal agriculture, but did preserve yam plants and spit fruit seeds into fertilized ground as described. So they understood the principles of planting and nurturing, and surely would have taken it farther had it been expedient. They did just fine, until the more advanced technology of the Europeans intruded.

Rebel's dream visions were of two kinds: Dreamtime legends existing among various Aborigine clans, and re-creations of the ancestors of humankind. They were correct in essence, if not in detail; she tended to fill in details she knew in her present, such as dingo dogs, that had not been domesticated two million years before. She was tracing the development of her species, in her fashion, as she sought to recover her faculty of language.

The thing that most clearly distinguishes mankind from all other species on Earth is his giant brain, monstrous for a body his size. Theories for its development abound, and there may be no consensus, but the evidence is growing that it was symbolic language that powered the brain's ascent. When our ancestors diverged from the chimpanzees, they started out with similar mental capacities. But Australopithecus may have stumbled on a better way to get along: the first organized verbal symbols. Many animals have verbal expressions for danger, pain, warning, comfort, alarm or whatever, and these can be considered symbols, as a cry of pain is not the pain itself. But they are fixed; the animals do not organize or manipulate them. They never say, "If you get bitten by a rattlesnake, you will be in pain." They don't have language. Neither did our ancestors, originally, but somewhere along the way they took the step that led to the first very simple language. It may have consisted of all proper nouns, with each significant tree or rock or path given its special name. It may have developed adjectives to qualify those nouns: the good *berries, the* bad *leopard, making communication more flexible. They may have discovered prepositions: leopard* in *the berry patch, fruit* under *the tree. That may have led to verbs: the leopard* is *in the berry patch. We don't know how it developed, just that it did. Slowly, over the course of millennia, of eons, true symbolic language developed. Because even the simplest language was immensely more complicated than mere animal sounds, it powered an enormous increase in the size of the brain. This in turn forced other significant compromises, such as the reduction of body fur and promotion of sweating as a cooling mechanism, because that burgeoning brain had to be cooled. But it was worth it, because with superior communication came superior intelligence and group organization, leading to the eventual conquest of the world by mankind. Appreciation of symbolism also brought the arts, including storytelling, which encouraged further development of language.*

And so our species became what it is today, distinguished by its huge brain and its appreciation of all the arts, powered by the gradual development of ever more sophisticated language. There are no simple languages today, but there were two million years ago.

11

LEGEND

The mountain range of the Pyrenees served as an effective barrier to invasions in either direction. On occasion conquests were made, but generally the lands to the north and south were in different hands. In 711 AD the Moors defeated the Visigoths and took over the Hispanic peninsula. In 732 they pressed on north into France, but were balked by the Franks, and settled down in Spain. But schisms in the Muslim realm weakened it, and the Basques were among those peoples able to maintain a fair amount of independence. To the north, the Franks consolidated their power in France, and established control over the Basque territory north of the Pyrenees.

In 768 AD Pepin, the king of the Franks, died, and left the kingdom to his two sons, one of whom was Charles, who was interested in enlarging his domain. But the Moors were too strong in their territory for him to attack without a secure base in Spain. In 777 he received a surprising visit: a Moorish delegation petitioned him for help in a rebellion against another faction. In exchange, Charles could have the city of Saragossa, a stronghold in northern Spain. This could be exactly the base Charles needed to displace the Saracens, striking a blow for Christianity, not to mention increasing his own power. He quickly agreed, and in the summer of 778 sent two armies south. These were formidable forces, 40,000 to 70,000 men in all, with their supporting apparatus, surely sufficient to push back the Moors if given a suitable base of operations. Charles led one force himself, crossing the Pyrenees and occupying the city of Pamplona in Navarra. The second force took a longer route around the eastern edge of the mountains and down to Barcelona. There was no significant resistance, though the folk of the countryside did not like the intrusion.

The setting is the Basque territory of Navarra, 778.

•

Haven and Keeper were in the city of Pamplona when it happened. The city was Basque, but under the control of the Moors. The Moors were tolerable as long as they didn't try to press their heathen religion on the natives. They were here to trade for supplies, staying with their friends Flo and Jes. Jes's husband was rich and generous, which helped.

"The Franks are coming!" Jes exclaimed, having gotten early news.

"The Franks?" Haven asked, amazed. "How is it possible?"

"Suleiman Ibn al-Arabi, the governor of Barcelona, invited him. The cities are not fighting at all."

"Well, we Basques don't want the Franks here," Haven said. "We prefer our independence."

"We certainly do," Flo agreed warmly. "But I think we had better keep our mouths shut while the Franks are here, as we have no army to oppose them."

Haven nodded. When the Moors made an alliance with the Franks, it would be folly to challenge them. But she knew her countrymen would not like this development at all. "I think Keeper and I had better get home before the Franks arrive." Not that they would be able to do much; the Basques' basic level of organization was the family, above which was the gens, which was a group of several families, often united by intermarriage. Beyond that there was no political unity. So their gens would spread the word of the invasion, but it would be remarkable for the Basques as a whole to unify sufficiently to field an army capable of resisting the Franks. However, they might be able to take steps to avoid mischief, such as by hiding their supplies of grain.

But it was already too late, for one Frankish army was coming through the mountain pass at Roncevaux, close by the city. They would have to pass right by the column to get home, and that would be mischief. A foreign army was a foreign army, always hungry for food and sex, and hardly choosy about how they obtained them. The supplies Haven and Keeper had just obtained would be the one, and Haven herself would be the other, if they were caught.

"I think you and Keeper had better remain with us," Flo said. "Until the Franks pass on toward Saragossa. You can pretend to be regular citizens of the city."

That did seem best. The Franks should merely pass through Pamplona, raiding its supplies, but not having much time to do significant damage. If they laid low, they should be all right.

The Franks arrived a day later. It was a significant army, with tens of thousands of men. The city offered no resistance, pretending instead to welcome the invaders. That way, there should be no burning or killing. Armies were normally less damaging to nominal friends than to outright enemies.

The Franks were led by their King Charles, together with a number of his nobles. They quickly took over the best portion of the city, ousting the occupants or converting them to servants. Jes's husband's estate was pre-empted by one Hruodlandus, the Prefect of Brittany. He wasted no time making his demands known: the very best flesh for his table together with a competent cook, a winsome servant wench for his bed, and an experienced servant man to tend his horses.

All the members of the household were required to present themselves for assignment. Jes's husband Ittai was the first in the line. He spoke Frankish, so the prefect addressed himself to him, not deigning to attempt the local language. Haven did not understand his words, but did not need to. Ittai would translate. As host, it was his duty to make the appropriate assignments. As long as he did a satisfactory job, his house would not be burned and his wife would not be raped.

The prefect was, to Haven's mind, a typical foreign soldier. He had that Frankish look about him despite being worn from rough travel. His leather armor was soiled with sweat and dirt, as was his short brown beard. He eyed the assembled people coldly and, she thought, with utter disdain. Just because they were civilians. Just because they were not Franks.

There was a brief dialogue in the foreign tongue. Then Ittai turned to Haven. "You and Flo will supervise the kitchen for the prefect." He turned to Keeper. "You will tend the prefect's animals. I have promised him only the very best personnel and provisions."

And in so doing, he was protecting both his guests from molestation. Haven appreciated the gesture. Certainly she was competent to cook, and Keeper was more than competent with animals.

The other assignments were made, and then they were dismissed to their various posts. If they needed further instruction, Ittai would see to it personally, so that there would be no need for any directives from any of the prefect's men. That was part of what made it safer.

Haven and Flo went to the kitchen. It was technically Jes's kitchen, but Jes much preferred to be out and around, so it was really Flo's kitchen. Haven loved it; it was completely competent. Flo hardly needed any help, but the prefect hadn't challenged the assignment of the two of them, so it was done.

Ittai appeared. He glanced at Haven. "No offense, but I think you should change your hair style and don dowdier clothing. No sense tempting fate when you deliver the food to the prefect."

Haven was startled by the oblique compliment. "But what of the bed wench?"

"I haven't found him one yet. The city's fairest girls are all in hiding."

Oh. "I will change."

"And say nothing derogatory or personal in the presence of any Frank," Ittai continued. "Some of them grasp more Iberian than they pretend."

Fair warning, again. Iberian was a variant of Latin, and the Franks spoke another variant; Italics was another. "And what of Basque?" she asked in that language.

"I think none speak that," he replied. "But they would immediately suspect your origin if they heard it."

She changed to one of Flo's outfits, which hung loosely on her, and Flo helped her do her hair so that she looked relatively drab. "But you know," Flo murmured, "if he grabs you, you can't resist. It would get us all slaughtered."

Haven swallowed. "I know." She had had certain experience of this nature. She was married to Harbinger, who was a good man, but he had begun his courtship with a rape. Later another man, Bub, had pursued her, not caring about her marital state, until Rebel had intercepted him. But Rebel was not here in Pamplona.

Flo fixed an excellent platter, and Haven bore it up to the prefect's suite. The prefect had just bathed and changed into a robe for the evening, and looked much improved. In fact he was a handsome man.

"Thank you, woman," he said in Frankish.

Haven smiled ingratiatingly and backed away.

"No, wait a moment," he said in bad Iberian. "Your outfit does not do you justice."

"Thank you, sir," she said, dreading this. She had an eerie feeling of déjà vu, as if she had faced a situation like this before. How had she gotten out of it?

"There are dresses in the closet. Find one that fits you, and don it."

Worse. But she could afford neither to balk nor to annoy him. She went to the closet region, which was around a corner and out of sight of the main chamber, and found a number of lady's garments. These were surely Jes's, unused because they were too fancy for that woman's taste. She found one that was too large for slender Jes, and only slightly tight on Haven herself. She glanced back, saw that no one was spying on her, and with relief made a quick change. There were even matching slippers, loose enough so that she could use them.

There was a basin with water. She peered down into it, seeing her reflection. If she left her hair dowdy, the prefect might suspect she was trying to dissuade him, and that would be troublesome. So she combed out her hair and let it hang long and loose, fastened only with a wooden brooch. She now looked entirely too feminine.

If only Rebel were here! Rebel could make Haven look dowdy just by being near, and for once she would have appreciated it. Rebel also could have handled a situation like this, as she didn't mind with whom she had sex, as long as it was in some fashion by her choice. As it was, the prefect would surely find Haven appealing, and her friends were hostage to her behavior.

There was no help for it. She stepped out into the prefect's sight.

He was busily eating his dinner. He looked up. "Yes, that is a great improvement. You are a comely woman."

"Thank you, Prefect, sir," she said weakly.

"Call me Roland."

"Sir?"

"My given name. I think you and I should become better acquainted."

"Yes, sir, Roland." She was not the fainting type, but she felt faint.

"After all, it is not as if we are of different species. Franks and Iberians have interacted before."

He didn't realize that she was Basque, not Iberian. That was surely just as well.

"What is your name?"

"Haven, sir. Roland."

"And what is your background, Haven?"

He had asked, and she had to answer. But perhaps this gave her a way out. "I am Basque."

He snorted. "You can't be! They are rude, uncivilized primitives who live on acorn bread, clothe themselves in strips of woolen cloth, and are shod with boots of twisted hair."

"True, sir."

"You were not so garbed."

"I changed apparel, for fear a Basque woman would suffer roughness at the hands of civilized folk."

He laughed. "Well put, Haven! I see you have a mind as well as a body. I like that. What else is there about you I should know?"

She steeled herself and answered. "I am married."

He considered her thoughtfully. "And you are afraid that if you refuse me, I will have your husband killed."

That wasn't quite it, but was close enough. "Or my family, sir."

He nodded. "A legitimate concern. So it would be best not to refuse me. Is your husband close by?"

"No, sir. Not in this city."

"Roland. But family or friends are here?"

"Yes, Roland."

"As a married woman, you surely have an excellent notion how to please a man. No clumsy moves. No sloppy kisses or embarrassing messiness. No foolish screams or giggles."

She was silent. She did know these things.

"So there is something to be said for the married state. But also something to be said for innocence. I will make you this compromise: Be sure a suitable wench reports by dusk, or else come yourself, garbed as you are now. I think I would rather have you, with your experience, but I also prefer willing women. If you must come yourself, be willing."

"Yes, Roland." This was evidently a dismissal, so she backed away and out.

She realized that her heart was pounding. Roland had given her a chance to escape by being sure there was a wench. But if none could be found, she would have to report—and pretend to like it. He would know better, but since all he wanted was a good body, he didn't care. He was being reasonable, by his definition.

She had faced such a situation before, she was sure, though she couldn't remember it. There had to be some way out!

She returned to the kitchen. "Oops," Flo said, spying the change of clothing.

"He made me change. If there is no wench by dusk, he wants me."

Flo frowned. "Go tell Ittai. He may not realize the urgency."

Haven went to find Ittai. She found Jes instead.

"Don't tell me," the woman said. "Let me guess. The Frank made you get into one of my dresses."

"Yes. If there is no wench by dusk—"

"I will make sure there is. I wouldn't want my husband to see you in that outfit; he might lose interest in me." Then she smiled, showing that this was humor. "I'll bring a wench to the kitchen, and you can take her up."

"Thank you!" Haven said gratefully.

"We all know what's at stake here. These Franks are conquerors, primed for mayhem. We have to pacify them, so that they will move on and do their mischief somewhere else."

"Yes." Then Haven moved in and kissed Jes. She knew she had been rescued—again.

They had to make meals for a number of Roland's subofficers, and for their own household. Haven knew that all over the city, other households were performing similarly. No one wanted mayhem.

Just before dusk, Jes showed up with a lovely woman. "This is—"

"Sis!" Haven exclaimed, astonished. For this was Bub's sister.

"You had someone else in mind?" the woman inquired coolly.

"But your brother—" For suddenly it came back: Bub was the one who had pursued her.

"So maybe I owe you something for that."

"Owe me?"

"He tried to rape you, and almost killed your sister. Sometimes he gets a bit high-handed. I prefer gentler measures. I will make sure the prefect doesn't bother you."

"Thank you," Haven said, feeling faint again. Was it possible that Sis would make up for her brother's roguishness?

They went up to the prefect's suite. Haven entered first. He was resting on the bed. "Roland, sir, here is your wench," Haven said.

"Too bad," he replied.

Sis stepped forward. "Oh? What do you think of this?" She opened her robe, showing her breasts.

The Frank nodded. "You are evidently experienced."

"To be sure." Sis strode on up to the bed, disrobing as she moved.

Haven quietly departed. She hated to be beholden to Sis, of all people, but apparently she was.

She returned to the kitchen. "Never can tell how things will turn out," Flo remarked. "Bub raped me, long ago, before I started getting fat. Now his sister is saving you from similar."

"You?" Haven asked, surprised.

"It's his way. Maybe one day someone will kill him."

"That would be nice," Haven agreed bitterly.

The Franks did not depart immediately. Instead they remained in the city, and Haven and Keeper had to remain too, locked into their duties.

Then the reason came clear: the second Frank army had been forging through Barcelona, and now was coming to join this one, here in Pamplona. From here the unified forces would move on to Saragossa, which would become the provisional capital of the Frank conquest of Hispania.

In due course the armies did merge, and King Charles led his forces southeast toward Saragossa. The bulk of the Frank force moved out of Pamplona. But not Roland. He was in charge of the rear, securing the area so that no enemy could cut off the army's supply route. So Haven and Keeper still couldn't get away, much to their frustration.

Their work, however, was light. Roland was out much of the time, verifying local conditions. The fact was, the neighborhood was hostile to the Franks. The Basques were Christian, as were the Franks, but knew that north of the Pyrenees the Franks did not allow the Basques self-government, while south of the mountains the Moors were more tolerant. So just as some Moorish factions preferred to ally with the Franks rather than other Moors, the Basques preferred to remain in the territory of the Moors rather than that of the Franks. Any Frank forces that ranged too far out into the countryside risked attack. Haven had good sources of information, as messages were delivered constantly to Roland, and word spread privately among the Basques.

Roland had a simple way to handle the situation: he did not range too far out. As long as food and supplies continued to flow into the city, and from there on to the main army, he would not rouse himself to action. The citizens of Pamplona were not pleased with this burden, but were wise enough to avoid antagonizing the Franks; cooperation was good. There was no sense in stirring up the enemy pointlessly.

Not so for the main Frank army, however. There were skirmishes throughout its march toward Saragossa, and when it arrived, the city gates were locked against it. It seemed that the local commander of the city did not support al-Arabi's rebellion, so was supporting the other side. King Charles was furious, but there was not much he could do, as he had not brought siege equipment. This was supposed to be his base of operations, not a city to be conquered.

There were a number of inconclusive skirmishes. But the supply line was being increasingly squeezed, and hunger and discontent plagued the army. The Franks had expected to relax in Saragossa; instead they were stuck in the field unprepared. So Charles decided to give it up as a bad job, and the army returned to Pamplona.

Haven was relieved. Obviously the Franks would proceed directly to the pass at Roncevaux and be gone. Then life would return to normal, and she and Keeper could go home at last.

Her relief was mistaken. The Franks, angry at being balked, took it out on Pamplona. All the city's cooperation counted for nothing. It was thoroughly sacked.

Haven and Keeper were safe, as they were confined to the house. But they looked out to see the plundering proceeding. Every house was systematically stripped of its valuables. The Frankish soldiers broke into closed rooms, finding the hiding girls, and raped them along with their mothers. All food was taken, and what the invaders couldn't use, they piled in the streets and burned. To protest was to die—and many men were killed simply for being there. There was a pall of smoke from the destruction, which included many houses that hadn't yielded enough loot.

Haven was in tears as she brought dinner to Roland. He noticed; evidently Sis was out at the moment. "What seems to be the problem, Haven?"

"The needless destruction," she said. "We cooperated; we caused you no mischief. Now you are destroying us."

He shrugged. "This is the way of war."

"But we would have been as well off locking our gates against you."

"True. Perhaps better off, as is Saragossa. What is your point?"

She realized that this was hopeless. She set down his meal and departed before she said something to anger him.

She took food out to Keeper, at the stable, for he could not afford to leave the horses during this unrest. She stayed to talk with him. "The prefect doesn't care about the damage to the city," she said.

"Conquering armies don't."

"But we cooperated!"

"Only to avoid getting sacked before. But I think they would have let this city go, if Saragossa had been open to them. They are angry, and taking it out on us."

That was of course the case. "Still . . ." she started, and paused. Three Frank soldiers were entering the stable.

"Look here!" one exclaimed. Haven had picked up some of their language, so could follow common utterances. "Horses!"

"These belong to the prefect!" Keeper protested, stepping out to bar access to the animals.

The leaning soldier didn't even respond. He simply reached out and struck Keeper on the side of the head, knocking him down. The men grabbed for the bridles of the nearest horse.

"You can't do that!" Haven cried, appalled by the attack on her brother.

"And a woman!" All three Franks oriented on her.

Too late she realized that she should have kept her mouth shut and fled. Now she did, turning and running toward the house. The men pursued, but she had a head start, and managed to reach the door first. But as she opened it, one man caught her trailing arm, hauling her back.

"What's this?" a voice asked sharply. It was Roland, coming to the door.

"The horses!" Haven screamed, knowing that would concern the man more than any threat to her or Keeper.

"The horses!" Roland strode through the Franks, ignoring them. They faded back, realizing that they could be in trouble. In a moment they were gone.

Keeper was back on his feet, standing before the horses. A bruise was forming on the side of his forehead, and he looked unsteady.

"Any problem here?" Roland asked.

"No, sir," Keeper replied.

"Good." Roland made a military turn and strode back to the house. Haven followed, lest the soldiers return. They wouldn't touch the horses, now, but she had no such protection. As far as Haven could tell, the prefect hadn't even noticed Keeper's condition. The horses were all right; that was all he cared about. He wouldn't have cared if Haven had been caught and raped, or if Keeper had died. In that he was typical of the invading army, and of the ways of war.

When she was sure that the soldiers were not coming back, Haven went out to check on her brother. "I'm so sorry," she said, sponging off his bruise.

"You saved the horses," he said. "You distracted the Franks until the prefect came."

She hadn't seen it that way. Surely the horses were better off in the prefect's charge than as spoils of individual soldiers. But that was no praise for Roland; he was simply the lesser of evils.

The carnage continued, but didn't touch them directly again. Apparently most Franks did know that this was the prefect's residence. This was small relief, however, considering what was happening everywhere else.

Several days later the Frank army at last moved out, leaving Pamplona a wreckage. The citizens' only hope for survival was to go out into the countryside beyond the savaged region and hope for help from the folk who had resisted the intrusion of the Franks. Many of them were relatives or friends, so this was feasible, but it was sure to be an unkind winter.

Haven and Keeper finally were able to go home to the family. They had lost both their money and the supplies they had bought, but were otherwise not too much worse for wear. Most residents of the city had lost far more.

They avoided the army's rear guard, which was commanded by Roland, and went quickly into the trackless countryside. The army had the main road, but moved like a slow python, stretching out so that its vanguard was two days ahead of its rear guard. Haven and Keeper, afoot alone off the road, were able to move significantly more rapidly.

They reached their farm in the mountains and made a full report, confirming what observers had noted. The Franks were leaving, heading for the pass at Roncevaux with their plunder.

"They sacked a Basque city after it cooperated with them," Hero said grimly. "This is not to be tolerated."

"But we have no army that can withstand them," Haven reminded him unnecessarily. "Their forces are huge."

"Fifty thousand," Hero said. "But we may have a way. You say the tail end of it is dragging way out?"

"They have to wait for the main army to pass before they can move," Keeper agreed. "They are loaded down with their ill-gotten loot."

"Yes. Maybe we can relieve them of that."

They spread the word, and organized quickly. Armed Basques came from all around, and others went directly to the key pass, setting up for an ambush. Haven went too, because she knew the men were going to need to eat while they waited for their chance.

The vanguard of the Frank army was already through the pass, and the main army was filing through. The baggage train was as usual waiting its turn. The terrain was both steep and littered with boulders, making cavalry useless; in fact the Franks were leading their horses through.

A sizable force of warriors had assembled behind the peaks on either side of the pass. They had made no fires, and kept complete silence. Not that there was much danger of discovery; the Franks in their arrogance had not even posted sentries or outriders to check beyond the high slopes. They were just wending their slow way upward.

Haven took over the field mess camp. She organized the other women who had come, Rebel and Crenelle among them, and they made up hundreds of small acorn bread, goat cheese, and water-skin meals to hand out to the men.

The Frank caravan did not travel by night, and did post sentries then. So the Basques waited. When morning came the Franks resumed motion, their troops soon outstripping the heavy baggage train. The horses strained to pull the overloaded wagons up the steep slope, and there was constant cursing.

Keeper brought the dogs to her. "I'm going to try to rescue the enemy horses," he said. "You keep the dogs."

Haven wasn't easy with this. Keeper was not a warrior. But of course they wanted to save the horses, who could do good work on Basque farms. "I will keep the dogs," she agreed. She snapped her fingers, and the three dogs came to her, understanding that she was now the one in control.

It was time. Hero stepped up to the crest and lifted his right fist in a signal to the Basques on the far side. Immediately Craft pulled on a lever he had set up, and dislodged a great boulder. It started rolling slowly, gathered speed, and pounded other rocks into motion. In a moment a small avalanche was crashing down toward the Frankish column. Haven and the dogs peeked over the edge, watching the action from an excellent high vantage. She had no love for the Franks.

The avalanche was not great, but it did attract the attention of the troops below. Probably it looked much worse from that vantage; the defenders could not know how limited it was. They responded beautifully: they panicked. Men tried to flee up the opposite slope, or hide under the baggage carts. Any semblance of military formation vanished.

Then the Basques on both sides charged down the slopes. The main weapons they had were spears and clubs, buttressed by light leather armor. The Franks had superior weapons, but were disorganized, distracted by the descending stones, and caught completely by surprise. The Basques closed on them, striking with their spears and dispatching the soldiers almost before they knew they were under attack. Haven could not see the details, which was perhaps just as well as she had never been keen on human bloodshed, but made out the general pattern: Franks were falling and lying still.

She glanced at the higher pass. A contingent of Basques was there to make sure that no troops from the main Frank army came back to rescue their baggage train. The Basques would have no hope of defeating the main forces. But those forces were well along, going down the northern slopes, and perhaps did not even know their rear was under attack. If they tried to turn back, they would have trouble passing the Basque contingent before the job was done. Indeed, it seemed that no Frank troops were coming back.

Nevertheless, the Basques did not waste time. They rapidly

slaughtered the defending troops, closing in on the standard of the commander. Once he was taken out, there would be no remaining resistance.

Then Haven spied something that alarmed her. A Basque had been wounded—and he was familiar. It was Keeper, leading a panicky horse. He staggered and fell.

Suddenly she and the dogs were charging down the slope, heedless of cautioning calls. She couldn't let her brother die!

She was holding cloth for bandaging, but she needed her hands to brace against the slope and boulders so as to maintain her balance. So she stuffed the cloth down the front of her blouse, getting it out of her way.

Breathless, she circled horses and reached Keeper. There was an arrow in his leg, just below the leather. It looked like a flesh wound. She knew what to do. "Hold still and grit your teeth," she said.

"Haven! What are you doing here?"

"Saving you. Let me pull this arrow out." She took hold of it and yanked, hauling it out. Keeper's breath hissed through his teeth, but he did not scream.

Blood welled out. She hauled the cloth from her blouse and wrapped it around his leg, tying it tight to stifle the blood. The dogs crowded close, concerned.

Meanwhile, a man was coming for the horse. He was a Frank. He had evidently fought free of the attacking Basques and was about to try to escape on the horse. But the horse, spooked by the carnage, was shying away.

Then Haven recognized the Frank. "That's Roland!"

"The commander?" Keeper asked. "Where's my spear?"

"You can't fight him," she protested. "You're wounded."

Roland heard her. He turned to look. "The fair kitchen maid! You are helping these savages?" He drew his sword.

Haven realized they would both be dead in a moment if they didn't get away from there. She tried to haul Keeper to his feet. But it was too late; Roland was striding toward them, lifting his sword. "Death to traitors!" he shouted.

"We're not traitors!" she cried with useless defiance. "We never were your people." She overbalanced, trying to lift Keeper, and sank down to the ground with him.

Roland put both hands on his sword, about to slash it through both of them together. The dogs growled and leaped at him, but he ignored them; he had leather armor on his legs. Then he screamed and collapsed.

There was a spear through his back, hurled so hard that it had penetrated the armor. It must have reached his heart, for he was clearly dead. Hero came charging up. "Didn't anybody tell you to stay out of trouble?" he asked Haven.

She laughed, somewhat hysterically. "I forgot." She felt dizzy; in a few hours she knew she would be reacting with fear, horror, and other debilitating emotions, but right now she was reasonably steady.

The battle was over; Roland had been one of the last to be killed. Haven felt a tinge almost of regret. He had not been a bad man, merely arrogant and careless. If it had not been for him, she and Keeper might well have fared worse than they had.

But now it was time to tend to their remaining wounded. The other women were making their way down into the narrow valley that was the pass, carrying cloth to be torn into bandages. They would do what they could for whom they could.

Meanwhile, Craft was helping organize the plundering of the baggage wagons. Much of the ill-gotten Frank loot was useless to Basques, but much was good. Soon a line of men was proceeding downhill, loaded with their trophies. Surviving horses were turned around and hitched to reloaded wagons, which moved much better downhill than they had uphill. Before very long, the last of the Basques were departing, leaving only wreckage behind.

"As the Franks left Pamplona," Haven said with a certain grim satisfaction. Vengeance was complete.

•

Historically King Charles was far more successful elsewhere. In fact he fashioned one of the major empires of the time. He was known as Charlemagne. Frankish chronicles had little to say about the ignominious defeat of their rear guard in the pass of Roncevaux.

Roland was an officer of Charlemagne's court about whom little is known, but he does not seem to have been a figure of much distinction. He was the commander of the rear guard, who was careless about defending the baggage train, and paid for that neglect with his life. Thus he became a historical nonentity. However, several centuries later, he was the basis for a series of legends relating to Charlemagnian times, much as Sir Lancelot was for Arthurian times in England. Thus the drab historical prefect became the phenomenal legendary Roland, greatest of heroes. Why the mythmakers chose him for this undeserved honor we don't know; perhaps it was their need to explain away one of Charlemagne's ignominious moments. Roland's carelessness was mythically fashioned into a heroic effort to save the rest of Charlemagne's army from annihilation, at the sacrifice of his own life. In this manner the legend went greatly beyond the reality.

12

SPECIAL CHILD

After the decline of the Olmec culture in what is now southern Mexico, the Maya culture rose to prominence in the Yucatan area. This prominence can be considered as three six-hundred-year sequences: 300 BC to 300 AD was the Classic period; 300 to 900 was the Late Classic, and 900 to 1500 was Post Classic, or Florescent period. This was when the erection of stele and the use of hieroglyphs were abandoned. Block masonry was given up for pure concrete construction for walls and vaults, and surfaces were covered with a thin veneer of finely ground and meticulously squared and faced rectangular stone. The prior naturalistic design gave way to highly formalized geometric patterns. The orientation of buildings was changed. There were severe disruptions and population shifts between these periods, about which there has been much conjecture. For the purpose of this narrative, there is no mystery: climate was the root cause of the mischief. When intense, prolonged drought came, starvation followed, there was desperate war for diminishing resources, and the sophisticated religious and governmental structures collapsed in chaos. When and where the climate improved, the Maya rebuilt and flourished again—until the next drought.

But one area was largely free of this problem. This was a city now known as Dzibilchaltun, whose continuous occupancy may represent a New World record: perhaps 4,000 years. Much of that time it was a minor settlement, and though in Late Classic times it may have been the largest population center in the Yucatan, with anywhere up to 100,000 people by some estimates, but more likely in the 10,000 to 20,000 range, it remained politically minor. This may be because it was on the fringe, near the northern coast of the peninsula, away from the cultural center. Even its true name is lost to history; "Dzibilchaltun" translates to "place where there is writing on flat stones." But why did it remain so steadily occupied, when other cities rose and fell? Because in a region that had no rivers, it never succumbed to drought. It had about a hundred wells tapping into groundwater circulating four to five meters below the surface, with natural openings in the limestone cap providing ready access.

However, the city did suffer on occasion. The time is the year 1020.

•

The line of women seemed endless, and indeed it was: only nightfall would terminate it. Each bore a jug or heavy bag on her head, and walked steadily behind the one before her. Most were young, and many were attractive. Each approached the key station, and carefully dumped her load into the receptacle, before walking back the way she had come.

Keeper stood by the great stone tank, supervising the distribution of water. The men of the Xlacah army filed by its far end, each dipping his large cup in the water and carrying it carefully to a spot where he could drink it all unjostled. Water was the most precious supply of all, and none of it was wasted.

Actually the service of the women wasn't necessary; there was a corps of slaves to haul water and other necessaries. But women were restricted from this area, unless they had some particular task, so those who wished to be here arranged to have such a task. Keeper had set up the tank near a natural well that would provide all the water they needed, here in this dry terrain, but he did not make an issue of that. So the women came, some of them officers' wives who did not want to make their status obvious, this close to the enemy. Any woman was fair game for the enemy, especially a ranking one.

Keeper gazed out across the military formation. He knew what most of the troops did not: the outlook was not positive. The Toltec army was larger than their own, and more disciplined, and it had a reputation for barbarian savagery.

Xlacah, the "Old Town," had resisted the barbarian intrusion for decades, because it was large enough to defend itself, and could not be denied water by siege. But the Toltecs had gradually taken over the rest of the region, defeating the other cities one by one, and now had come for the last and largest. There had been brushes before, but nothing serious. The priest leaders had become perhaps too complacent, thinking the city invulnerable. But Hero, who had served in distant forces, had warned the family that this was not so. He believed that the time would come when Xlacah would be seriously attacked.

Now that time had come. The priests, too long neglectful of practical matters, organized for defense too late. The available soldiers were good, but there were too few. The levies for additional men were inadequate on short notice. So the city was in trouble, but didn't know it yet, because the priests would not admit any fault. They claimed that their human sacrifices ensured the favor of Itzamná, the Lizard God, the creator and patron of knowledge, and the similar favor of the powerful Death God who ruled the nine layered underworld from his Jaguar Throne. Mortal men could not stand against these; they would be obliterated if they tried.

However, the women of the water line were not blind. Their route was shielded from enemy territory, but they could catch glimpses, and they heard the mutterings of the men as they came for the water. Keeper knew they were carrying news back to their homes. Wealthy folk were quietly leaving. But the great majority had nowhere to go.

"Hello, brother," a woman murmured.

Keeper glanced up. It was Rebel, pouring her water jug into the tank. She was swathed against the heat of the sun, but this could not conceal her beauty of form and feature.

"Hello, Father." It was his daughter Allele, six years old.

"What are you doing here?" he asked, startled.

"You didn't come home."

So she had come out to see him. It made sense. But probably Crenelle wanted to organize for quick departure without alarming the child. So she had sent her out with Rebel, who could be trusted both to safeguard her and reassure her.

Actually, Allele was probably as safe here as at home. When the battle started, the women would expeditiously retreat, carrying what news of it they could. Meanwhile, many of them were moving on to the army campsite, to search out their men for liaisons. Some were merely prostitutes plying their trade. This sort of thing was officially frowned on, but unofficially encouraged; it made the men feel better and distracted them from the looming horror of battle.

Keeper embraced sister and daughter as they came to him. "Glad to see you both," he said.

"When is the battle?" Rebel asked.

"Tomorrow morning, we think. Depends when they attack. We are setting up defensive emplacements, because they outnumber us. It may get ugly. So you had better be far from here by then."

"We will be," Rebel agreed. "What word for home?" She was asking on behalf of Crenelle, obliquely.

"She should proceed with dispatch." Which was his way of saying the battle was likely to be lost.

She nodded. Then she glanced at Allele. "We have delivered our water; time to go on home."

"Awww." To the girl, this was an adventure. She knew about death, for she had seen some of the public human sacrifices, when the priests cut living human hearts out and held them high. But she had not seen the larger slaughter of war.

Keeper picked her up and kissed her. "Don't let your mother be lonely."

Craft approached, bearing his solid shield and bow, and with a huge claw-knife formed from a shell in reserve. Many Old Town soldiers disdained to use the bow, considering it a weapon limited to barbarians, but Craft knew better. The Toltecs had won battle after battle against the Maya because they were able to strike from much farther away than any spear-thrower could. He had argued for the use of it, and prevailed to an extent. His own bow was competent, for he had made it himself. But he was not actually a combatant, though he wore the headfeather of a lesser officer, as did Keeper. He was the supply technician, organizing the delivery and distribution of supplies, including weapons, food, and water. He looked grim. "Get the women out! Surprise attack." Then he saw Allele, and recognized Rebel. "You especially. I think they are trying to capture women."

No one needed to ask why. "On our way," Rebel said, herding Allele before her.

But it was already too late. A formation of Toltecs had broken through the Xlacah line, cutting off their escape. Their painted faces made them seem even more ferocious than they probably were. Women screamed, fleeing wildly.

"It's the water they want," Keeper said, catching on. Water was invaluable. "Rather than women." But they would take whatever offered.

"Both, surely," Rebel said tersely. "I think we had better stay right here."

"Why?" Allele asked, understanding at least part of the threat.

"Because your father and uncle can better protect us," Rebel told her. Then, to Craft: "What do you have for me?"

Wordlessly, he handed her a large obsidian knife. The blade was of course deadly sharp.

Several other women crowded in close, coming to a similar conclusion: they would be better off with two men than alone on the path.

"Get down behind the tank," Craft said to the women. "You too, Rebel." He raised his bow. He was not a warrior, but he was as good with a weapon as any man, because he had to understand a weapon in order to make it.

They ducked down. Keeper moved to stand beside his brother, holding his spear. The case looked hopeless, but they would do what they could.

The Toltec warriors intercepted the fleeing women. Then it was each man for himself, dragging away the woman of his choice, or merely raping her where she was. The women screamed but offered no resistance; helplessness would get them ravished but not killed right away.

But one contingent did not break ranks. It spread out to surround the water tank. Slowly it closed in. The men held bows or spears ready, the spearmen supporting heavy shields to protect the bowmen, but neither type fired or hurled. Keeper and Craft stood similarly, weapons ready but not yet used. It was clear that the moment they acted, they would be slaughtered; there were twenty warriors in the circle. But there was a Toltec officer with them, accounting for their discipline.

A woman screamed, lurched to her feet, raised her arms high, and dropped to her knees, facing out, arching her back to make her breasts stand out. She was surrendering. Others followed. It did not matter whether they were married or single; in war a woman had only one defense, and that was appeasement. Soon all except Rebel and Allele were offering themselves.

The Toltecs stopped moving. They were of course interested, as this was a recognized part of the spoils of war. Several glanced at the officer, who averted his gaze: leave to act on their own. Then one man gestured to one of the women. She got up and went to him. He led her out of the circle. Another man gestured to another woman, and she responded similarly. Soon all five of them were gone. They would give the soldiers not passion but nonresistance, and that should be enough. They would live as long as their appeal remained, so they would try to remain appealing.

Fifteen men still closed the circle. There was no escape in any direction. They did not advance. Probably the taking of the five women was intended as a demonstration for those who remained: surrender was feasible.

"You know what to do," Keeper said to Rebel. He kept his voice even, but he dreaded what was to happen. So suddenly, doom had come upon them.

"I'm sorry, dear," Rebel said to the girl as she rose to her feet and lifted her knife. "Stand before me."

Allele moved to stand before her. Rebel turned her by the shoulder, and put the deadly blade of the knife to the girl's throat, not quite touching. The child did not flinch. They faced out toward the enemy.

Craft stood to Rebel's right, and Keeper to her left, their weapons still poised. This was a deliberate pose, but no bluff. It was clear that the men would die fighting, while the woman would kill the girl and then herself before the enemy got them. There would be no easy takings here.

The leader of the Toltec contingent stepped forward, inside the circle, heedless of Craft's fully drawn bow. He was of high rank, for he wore a huge headdress of brightly colored parrot feathers, and a large jade-fragment necklace. He wore a thickly quilted cotton jacket for body protection, but carried no shield. He turned his back, showing his contempt for the defenders. He was not a large man, and probably owed his rank to wealth or influence rather than ability, but he had poise. He spoke a word of command. Every bow tilted to aim at the ground, and every spear went to the ready, no longer poised for throwing or stabbing.

The leader turned around again, to face the four. He ignored the arrow point that tracked his nose. "Serve me," he said.

The man's authority was so clear that Keeper had to fight the urge to obey. This was the time to stand firm, however difficult that was. None of them responded or moved.

"Then go." He signaled, and the circle opened, offering an avenue out.

They did not move. They knew that this was a trap; when their backs were turned, they would be shot down, the men at least, and woman and girl would become the unwilling playthings of the troops. If the females resisted, they would be beaten; if they bit, their teeth would be knocked out; if they scratched, their fingernails would be drawn out; and if they tried to flee, they would be hamstrung or blinded. If all else failed to make them amenable, they would be tied spread-eagled and naked in a position suitable for easy access, and a line of men would be formed to perform serial rape. Age did not matter, only gender. In war, public rape was a demonstration rather than passion, intended to destroy self image and resistance. The multiple rape of a child in front of her parent was a very effective ploy. So it would be better to cooperate—or to die first. That was why Allele had to be the first to die.

The leader signaled again. The bows and spears oriented, as one. "Yield, and you live," he said.

Still they did not move. This was a trial, and the outcome had not been determined.

"The child can go."

Allele shuddered, and Keeper knew that she was crying. She had been warned of the nature of war, and that it was better to die than fall into enemy hands, but she had never before experienced such a trial. Her courage was failing; her adventure had become more than unpleasant.

But she also knew that she would be helpless alone, and that there was still no guarantee. So she didn't move, though she knew Rebel would not cut her throat if she did move in this circumstance. Not unless the Toltecs attacked.

"You will not yield," the leader said, inviting their denial. But they were steadfast. This was not the occasion to evince any weakness at all.

The leader paced before them, seeming to be completely at ease despite the obvious threat to his life from Craft's drawn bow. He had the nerve of one who was quite sure of his power. Yet why was he toying with them?

They waited. The second stage was coming, and this was a positive sign. Keeper had expected to die, once they were surrounded; now he had hope.

The leader stopped, facing Keeper. "Will you trade?"

Now at last it was safe to answer. The offer had improved, indicating that they had won at least a measure of respect by their solidarity. Craft released the tension on his bowstring, without lowering the bow, and the Toltec warriors did the same. Violence could still erupt quickly, but this was a signal that it probably would not.

"For what?" Keeper asked. It was his prerogative, as this was his station; he was in charge here despite being younger than his brother and sister.

"Guard mine as you do your own."

This did not register. "Your what?"

The leader was pacing back and forth, not facing them. "My child."

All four of them must have shown their surprise, for there was a rumble of laughter around the circle. Surprise was, however, a tolerable weakness. The Toltecs knew something they did not. Even so, they would not have laughed had they not known that their leader permitted it.

"What child?" Keeper asked.

"My motherless daughter, the age of yours. I need a home for her, and that cannot be on the battlefield."

"For sure," Rebel muttered.

The officer heard her, but spoke to Keeper. "She is right. Your child is here because your wife would not leave her unguarded. But I have no wife."

Keeper realized that the man thought that Rebel was his wife, because she was the woman with the child. For the moment, that did not matter. "Hire a woman."

"I have done so. She does not care, and will not move. In any event, she cannot provide what my daughter needs. Very few can."

This was weird. This enemy warrior leader was talking family with him, in the guise of negotiation. "Move where?"

"To Xlacah."

It began to register. "You are to be garrison commander?"

"When the city falls, I will be one of the administrative officials. I must be there. I want my child with me, in a family. One with courage and caring." He paused, evidently troubled. "I am not yet ready to marry. My wife—her memory lingers. My daughter is all that remains of her. I must have her close and safe."

"But you cannot trust an enemy!" Keeper protested.

The officer shrugged. "Your brother could have shot me at any time."

Again they were startled. This man knew their relationship. That meant he had studied his enemy, targeting its commanders or key personnel. He had missed on Rebel, but that was understandable; he knew that Keeper was the married one. And it seemed that it had not been chance that had trapped them here.

"Your men would have killed us all," Craft said.

"Four captives, for one officer. An even trade?"

Point made. One commander was worth a hundred lesser men. An arrow could have reached Craft before he threw a spear, but instead he carried a good bow. At this point-blank range his arrow could penetrate the body armor. Most soldiers would have made the trade. "I would have killed you, had you attacked," Craft said.

"You would have been dead before you could strike back. You had to strike first. You knew that."

Craft nodded, yielding that point too. The man had almost dared them to strike first, killing him, and they hadn't done it. The man had known their nature. "This is embarrassing," Craft said.

"Not necessarily. You also knew I had something on my mind, or I would have had you killed without pause. So you waited to discover what that was." He glanced around. "All of you waited."

Indeed. "Why us?" Craft asked.

"My wife was Maya. Her matrilineal clan relates to yours. My daughter needs that support."

That explained much. The man wanted his child to have the association of her clan. Children who did not, could be cursed. Men were the leaders, but the power of the women was subtle and pervasive. Most of a girl's education was handled by her matrilineal clan relatives, especially the aspects relating to her status and marriage. So the man had searched out those relatives, however distant, and pounced when he found them within his grasp. This encounter was no coincidence.

"For the support of your daughter," Keeper said. "What price?"

"Safety of your household—because it would become hers. After hostilities cease."

"Our household includes warriors."

"Two, besides the two of you," the officer agreed. "They too will be spared."

"And you, sir," Rebel said, speaking directly to the officer for the first time. She included a signal of respect for his status that Keeper had not. Now that they were negotiating, this was appropriate. "You would be there with your child."

"When not in the field," the officer agreed again.

"What would you expect of the women of the house?"

"Of a married woman, only meals and domestic chores." He

glanced around. "The rules of war would not apply, even for one as lovely as you."

Meaning that sexual service was not required; he sought only compatible environment for his half-orphaned child. Considering that there would be chaos when Xlacah fell, such protection of their household would be more than welcome. Keeper glanced at Craft, then at Rebel, and then at Allele. They all understood; it was a generous offer, one that they could accept with honor. The fact that the officer evidently assumed that Rebel was Keeper's wife hardly mattered; relatives of favored captives normally shared privileges. His military research had evidently applied to warriors, ignoring women, who were beneath notice.

"Agreed, sir," Keeper said, setting aside his spear in a ritual token of peace. Craft set aside his bow, and Rebel put away her knife. Allele turned into her, sobbing, seeking comfort.

The circle of warriors turned their backs, signaling withdrawal of threat, and privacy for the dialogue to follow.

The officer nodded. "I am Tuho. My child is Tula, after our capital. She is unusual, as you will discover, but not difficult. You are now my guests. Your wife and child will be guided to my present home in Chichén Itzá to meet my daughter. You and your brother will acquaint me with the location and description of your home, so that I can protect it from the carnage to come."

Keeper nodded. They had in fact surrendered, but Tuho was being careful not to use the term "prisoner." He was guaranteeing their safety. "Agreed," Keeper said again.

"One detail, sir," Rebel said.

Tuho looked at her.

"I am not his wife. I am his unmarried sister. This girl is my niece." She squeezed Allele reassuringly.

The man was clearly taken aback. "I apologize. You will of course have similar status."

Keeper was surprised again. An officer, as a rule, did not apologize to a subordinate, and a man did not apologize to a woman. Unless he especially wanted her favor.

"Perhaps I will accept alternate status, sir, should it be proffered."

Tuho studied her, appreciating her meaning. She turned her profile to him and inhaled. It was a gesture she had always been good at; she had as fine a profile as any woman could desire. Keeper could not remember when any man had ever turned her down. "As you choose," he said. "It would be appreciated. Though temporary."

"Temporary," she agreed. She had just undertaken to become his mistress, for a while. Tuho had impressed her favorably. She would return the favor, in good measure. An affair with a ranking officer would have benefits well beyond that of mere survival, but this was more than that, because grace had already been granted. Rebel would give him passion. Now he had double incentive to see that they were treated well. Rebel normally had more than one reason for what she did.

Tuho signaled, and two men stepped forward. "Take this woman and this girl to my premises in Chichén Itzá. They will be guests there until return to their own home is feasible." He paused. "There will be no presumption as to their status. They are mine."

"Yes, sir." If any man touched woman or girl, or failed to safeguard her from molestation, he would incur the wrath of his commander, surely a lethal malady. The Toltecs had already demonstrated their discipline; the order would be obeyed.

Tuho signaled again. Two more men reported. "Ascertain the details of the home residence of these men, and arrange that it and its occupants be protected from molestation. See that these men are courteously treated; they are noncombatants, though they will not be disarmed." Which meant that they could keep their weapons. That was another generous gesture, for a man's weapons were valuable in more than the physical sense; they lent ongoing status, particularly in an enemy camp.

"Yes, sir." They focused on Keeper and Craft as the commander walked away.

The men guided them toward the rear of the battle area, but Keeper could see the action occurring. The surprise raid to intercept the water women had been only part of a general attack. The Xlacah troops were having the worst of it, having been caught out of position and unprepared. They would have lost anyway, being outnumbered and out-disciplined, but this was a rout. The end of Xlacah was late in coming, but certain.

Keeper and Craft gave the necessary detail, and the two Toltec soldiers departed. No one guarded the family or paid undue attention to them, though several glanced at their weapons. They were garbed as members of the Xlacah army, yet were obviously not prisoners. "It is almost as if we could just walk away," Keeper murmured.

"We would die if we did," Craft replied. "We are being watched. Tuho doesn't seem to leave anything to chance."

"A competent commander doesn't."

As dusk came, the battle concluded. Little quarter had been given; those Old Town soldiers who had not fled or surrendered had been slaughtered. Spear, arrow, or claw-knife—it hardly mattered as the blood flowed. Soon enough the way of it had become clear, and the surrendering had become general. Enslavement was after all better than death. High-ranking captives would be ransomed back to their families, in due course. Useful service personnel had of course been spared, such as the cooks, porters, and prostitutes. The Toltec army was set to march on Xlacah without further significant resistance.

Tuho returned. "If you will accompany me to the officers' mess, we will talk again," he said.

"Sir, if I may—" Keeper said.

"You may."

"My wife will be fleeing the house, fearing that we have died and that it will be savaged."

"A reasonable concern. But it would be difficult for you to cross the lines at this time, in order to reassure her. Our scouts pursue any strangers, and of course your own people are not necessarily friendly to any of ours caught alone."

"I am familiar with the terrain," Keeper said. "I could cross unobserved."

"Yes, I suppose you could. It is my hope that your facility with natural things can be turned to our advantage, once hostilities cease."

"I think so, then. But right now—"

"I appreciate your concern, and it is also my concern, as I want your household intact. I believe that your family is capable of providing what Tula needs. Very well; you will be released at a site of your choosing, and you and your family members will thereafter remain in your house until it has been secured. The troops will be perhaps exuberant when they first pass."

Meaning that they would be pillaging, raping, killing, and burning, in the manner of victorious savages. This was not official policy, but the tensions of recent battle had to be released. It would definitely not be safe outside the house.

"Your brother will remain with me, to make certain of the identity of the house as we approach."

Meaning that Craft would still be a prisoner, and would pay if there were any betrayal. Tuho was no fool, for all his indirection. He knew that they, as lesser officers, comprehended the nuances.

"Understood, sir."

The two soldiers who had interviewed them returned to take Keeper to the edge of the Toltec boundary. He chose his place, and slipped away. The two Toltecs neither spoke nor moved; they were guarding his rear, ensuring that there would be no pursuit. Not that that mattered. He understood the way of the natural land; no one would be aware of his passage.

Well before dawn, he reached the city. It was in a nervous state despite the hour, for news of the disaster in battle had spread. Families were already moving out, bearing their meager belongings on their backs. But not many, for most had nowhere else to go.

His house was near the central plaza, with its own internal well; that was the first detail Keeper had seen to, as he had a number of unusual plants that needed extra water. It would have been a shame to have to leave it, for the plants would soon die. Now, as much by happenstance as design, he would be able to remain.

His house was large, with many chambers, for the entire double family shared it, and they were well off. Around it were a number of much smaller round and rectangular homes belonging to poor families, for the neighborhood was mixed; there was no segregation by class. So the social levels were mixed, and neighbors did their best to ignore each other when their classes differed.

He used his secret entrance, then called out softly. "Crenelle."

She answered immediately. "Keeper! Where is Allele?"

"She and Rebel are safe. And Craft. We were taken by the Toltecs—"

"The Toltecs!"

"A surprise foray. They knew who we were. We will be protected. But we must take in boarders."

"Boarders!"

"The commander of the Toltec expedition, and his daughter. She is Allele's age, and needs a family."

"And what does he need?"

"Rebel will cover it."

Only then did she relax enough to embrace him. "Oh, Keeper, I was so worried. When Rebel and Allele didn't come home at dusk . . ."

He held her, and kissed her, and went into more detail about the events of the day. She was of course horrified by the slaughter, but relieved that those she loved were safe. "And this child—what do you know of her?"

"Nothing, except that she lost her mother. Her father is really concerned for her. Haven can surely see to her."

"Yes. It will be awkward having a Toltec in our house, but the child is surely a human being."

"She surely is." He was relieved; she was accepting it. "He suggested that this girl, Tula, is unusual, and that she has a special need, apart from the importance of association with members of her matrilineal clan."

Crenelle was concerned. "Is she ill?"

"I don't think so. Some special quality of character, perhaps."

"The daughter of a high chief is apt to be imperious. This we can endure, for she brings protection to all of us."

Keeper remained uncertain. "Would a chief notice such a quality in his child?"

"Maybe not. But whatever it is, we shall accommodate."

He nodded. They would *have* to accommodate. "Now we must tell Haven."

They did not need to wake Haven, who was completing preparations for fleeing the house; she showed up after giving them time to talk alone. Now it was her turn. She was relieved and intrigued by the news. But she had a question: "What of the temple guards?" For her husband Harbinger, and their brother Hero, were both palace guards.

Keeper shook his head. "They will be overwhelmed. The war is lost. Further fighting is pointless. We should bring them in."

"They won't desert their posts."

That was a problem. "I will talk to them before they go out," Keeper said. For the two men were at home, sleeping now; they were on the day shift.

Haven hugged him, then returned to her chamber. She had more confidence in him than he had in himself; he doubted that he could persuade his brother and brother-in-law to remain home in the palace's hour of need.

They settled down to sleep. Keeper thought Crenelle would be too stressed for passion, but she practically climbed on him, kissing and caressing. He was in her, and climaxing, and out of her almost before he knew it. Then she was sleeping against him, as if all were well. She too evidently had more confidence in him than was warranted.

They did not sleep long, for dawn was nigh, but the brief relaxation helped. Then they ate breadnut cakes, drank deeply of their sweet spring, and waited for what would come.

Hero and Harbinger got up and dressed, preparing for duty. Keeper intercepted them. "You must not go out today."

"Why not?" They knew, of course; Haven had acquainted them.

"The Toltec army will be investing the city today. They will slaughter all opposition. This house alone has protection."

"We must protect the palace," Hero said, touching his claw-knife.

"You can't protect the palace. Their force is overwhelming, and they will destroy all opposition. You must hide here, and give loyalty to the commander when he comes here."

Hero shook his head. "We are not ones to hide at the first sign of danger. Did you do so yesterday?"

"No." And that finished his argument. "Then let me go with you."

Hero considered. "How would that change anything?"

"Maybe I can still persuade you."

Both men shrugged.

They left the house together, following one of the raised causeways that connected the main groups of buildings. The old causeways were oriented east and west, while the newer ones were at the prescribed angle determined by the priests. Craft was the one who understood such orientation. Hero and Harbinger hardly cared; they merely protected what was there. The three of them crossed the central plaza. Large platforms surrounded the main city, and the most prominent buildings were here. The temple for Itzamná was here, normally active with priests and worshipers. But this morning it was quiet.

"Where are the priests?" Harbinger asked.

"Where do you think?" Keeper responded. "They know they'll be slaughtered, so they have gone."

They walked on to the palace to the south. This, too, was deserted. "How can we guard it, if there's nothing here to guard?" Harbinger asked.

"You can't," Keeper said. "All you can do is offer yourselves as sacrifices to the memory of the faithless priests who have fled."

They checked the residential quarters of the priests. They were empty.

"You're right," Hero said. "This is pointless."

"You can return after the Toltecs have restored city function," Keeper suggested. "They may dedicate our temples to different gods, but at least they will be functioning, and will need guarding."

"Let's get away from here before they come," Harbinger said.

Thus readily had Keeper won his point. He was relieved. If the priests had had some stamina or courage, there might have been a case, but as it was, there was indeed nothing to fight for. The priests plainly lacked the confidence in the gods that they had preached all their lives.

They hurried back to the house. They were in plenty of time; no Toltecs had shown up yet.

Keeper went back to bed; he had had little sleep the prior night. Crenelle joined him, he thought mainly as a courtesy, but then he realized that she had not slept either until he returned.

"Are you sure Allele is safe?" she asked him.

"Almost sure. A man with a lonely daughter—our household makes sense. She will not be lonely here."

"But there is much we don't know."

"Of course. But it does look good."

They slept some time, until nervousness about the situation outside rendered them unable. They got up and joined the others.

"It's happening," Haven said grimly. She was standing by the wall, peering out between strands of thatch that overlapped from the roof. Their house was solid stone only partway up; above it wooden supports led to the thick thatch roof. It was a good house, in a good location.

Except for one thing, now: the Toltec warriors were ravaging every house except theirs. Keeper could hear the nearest neighbor wife screaming as she got raped. He realized that she had better stop screaming soon, or she would suffer worse. Then, suddenly, she stopped—and he wasn't sure why.

He joined Haven, peering out. He saw flames starting at the next house. Then he knew why. The soldiers normally burned a house only after they had finished with it, and if they were annoyed because it had provided too little loot or entertainment. The woman had protested too much, so they had killed her and were going on to the next. This was their way of educating citizens to the new reality.

Except for this house. No soldier approached it. No soldier wanted his beating heart to be served up as the next holiday sacrifice. Tuho was being as good as his word. But that marked their house as one specially favored by the enemy; what would it mean when things settled down, and their neighbors remembered?

But as the awful day progressed, and the fires surrounded them, he realized that this would be no problem. There would *be* no neighbors. Those who weren't killed would be hauled away as slaves. His deal with Tuho had saved his family from likely extinction.

"Yet at what cost?" Haven asked, understanding his thought.

What cost, indeed! How could they take any pride in their salvation, knowing the cost to others? But the alternative would have been to have their own women raped, their men drafted into the Toltec army, their children perhaps enslaved. Unless they succeeded in escaping, as they had been planning to do. But the Toltecs controlled most of the rest of the region, so prospects would have been dim. They might have hidden until things settled down, then returned, but that had no certainty of success. So there really was no cost; they had simply found a better way to survive. Still, he felt ill.

It went on all afternoon, and into the night; the raiders simply burned houses to make light for their continued carnage. But it gradually diminished toward dawn; a man could rape only so many women before his lust lost potency, and ransack only so many houses before he tired of the sport.

Still, they did not leave the house. That would not be safe to do until Tuho gave them leave.

For three days they waited, as the fires died down. Fortunately they had supplies stored, and the water was of course no problem. They ate, and slept, and peered out, and repeated the process.

At last a party walked up to their house. Haven recognized Craft and gave a shriek of delight. She dashed out to hug him.

Keeper, more cautious, followed her out. There was Rebel, with two children. One of them was Allele, who leaped into his arms.

"That is Haven," Rebel said, speaking to the other child. "And that is Keeper, Allele's father."

"Where is Commander Tuho?" Keeper asked, looking around. For the man was not there.

"He felt it would be better for Tula to meet the family on her own," Rebel explained.

"Also, he's a very busy man at the moment," Craft added. "Collecting the scattered troops, assigning them occupation quarters, organizing food and refuse missions."

Now came the key introduction: Tula to Crenelle. Tula was a well-dressed girl, with valuable jade stones at her throat, and a fancy shell comb in her hair. Her gaze was clear, her little chin high, and her mouth was firm. She looked very much like the child of a chief.

Crenelle emerged from the house, smiling, but the girl, suddenly shy, clung to Rebel, the more familiar figure.

Crenelle backed off. "There is no need to hurry things," she said. But Keeper suspected she was hurt. Fortunately Allele took up the slack by hugging her.

They entered the house. They had prepared a chamber for Tuho, and made room for Tula by Allele's place, by Crenelle's bed. But they could be flexible.

As it turned out, they did need to be. Tula had known Rebel several days before she met Crenelle, and she wanted to stay with Rebel. Rebel, flattered, was not averse; she had no child of her own, and could have none. So Tula stayed with her for the night.

Next day Tula played with Allele, but was also interested in what the adults were doing. It was clear that she missed the family life she had lost when her mother died, and liked the returning feeling of it. But it was Rebel's chamber she shared.

The following morning Craft was home. Tula joined him; he, too, was more familiar, having traveled with her. She asked him questions about his work, and seemed interested in the answers. "She is a bright child," Craft confided to Keeper. "I saw that as we traveled. But there's something else about her."

"She seems normal, for a chief's daughter," Keeper said.

"She isn't. But I'm not sure how she differs."

In the afternoon, Craft went out. Now Tula oriented on Crenelle, as Keeper learned later from her. "She apologized for avoiding me, when we first met," Crenelle said, amazed. "She said the journey had made her tired and cross."

Keeper smiled. "That sounds like a rehearsed excuse."

"She seemed sincere. She stayed with me, and was interested in cooking and the washing."

"Maybe she hasn't seen much of those, being without a mother, so finds them intriguing."

"No, she has seen slaves do it. She even helped me." She smiled. "That made Allele jealous, so she helped too. Then they both went off to play."

"Normal children after all."

"I don't think so. It was almost as if Tula was humoring Allele, and when she saw her annoyed, catering to her."

"That's adult manipulation," Keeper said. "How could a child do it?"

"Tula is remarkably adult, in some ways. It's eerie." She paused, reconsidering. "But charming. I do like her."

Two days later, Tuho arrived. Tula hugged him and clung close. Soon she was showing him the house. She had learned a surprising amount about the house and its operations. She was plainly a very bright, attentive girl.

When Rebel joined the Toltec officer, Tula remained; it seemed she understood their relationship, and wanted to be part of it, in her way.

"I said there was something different about that child," Craft remarked privately. "I think I underestimated the case."

"Her father loved her mother," Haven murmured. "She likes the ambiance."

"But Rebel's his mistress, not his wife," Keeper protested.

"The child may not be clear on the distinction. Sex, love, family—all allied."

"And she already likes Rebel," Keeper agreed. "And Rebel likes her."

"This may become more than an affair," Craft pointed out.

"More," Keeper agreed, surprised.

"But I like Tula," Haven said. "She is like a daughter to me."

"How does your son Risk feel about that?" Craft asked her.

"He likes her too. She is like a little sister to him. She flatters him, and he blushes." Haven frowned. "She's as good at impressing a man as Rebel is, in her fashion."

"And impressing a woman," Craft said.

Haven nodded. "Rebel, Crenelle, me—we all find her charming. But I think Allele is becoming wary of her."

"Tula is taking my daughter's place as the girl of the family," Keeper said. "Some resentment is natural. I'll give Allele some time."

"And listen to her," Craft said. "Maybe she has fathomed the nature of the strangeness."

Keeper doubted it, but he did talk to his daughter. "Tula is new here, and so is interesting, but we have not forgotten you."

"She's strange," Allele said. "I don't understand her."

"She is the daughter of a high officer, and has no mother to mitigate his influence. So maybe she resembles a leader of men. But we must bear with her, for the safety of our family."

Allele laughed. "You think I'm jealous!"

Keeper gave her a careful rueful look, for it was indeed what he thought. "You're not?"

"No. She's not trying to take my place; she wants to be my sister. I like her."

"But you think she's strange."

"Yes. She's not like me."

"Maybe that's just as well," he said, hugging her.

There were other surprises. The two girls exchanged information, and Tuho approached Keeper. "We need the water secured for the continuing population. Some of the wells have been fouled."

"I will attend to it," Keeper agreed. "Craft will help me clean them out."

"Yes. Tula wishes to accompany you."

Keeper was taken aback. If the commander wanted his daughter to go out in the city with two men, it would have to be done, but it did not seem wise. "Sir, this may be ugly work. Some of those wells are clogged with bodies."

"She understands that. But if her presence makes you uncomfortable, there is no requirement. Your house has been good for her already."

No requirement—but not one to be lightly declined. "If she understands—"

"I will detail a slave to assist your work."

So Keeper and Craft went out to secure the water supply, and Tula went with them. The slave was named Kettle, and he answered to her; he was evidently trusted. He never spoke; he was, it seemed, mute, but he responded well in action. He had scars of the type obtained in war; perhaps he was a captive from a prior campaign. Slaves who could be trusted could be well treated, and given considerable responsibility.

They made a tour of the closest wells. The first was a crevice in the stone that dripped water from its sides, forming a pool in the base. It contained ashes and rubbish; the Toltec takeover had spread considerable debris. Keeper and Craft used a fine net to seine the water, clearing what they could.

"Why?" Tula inquired, interested.

"People must drink this water," Keeper explained, in the same manner he would have to his own daughter. "It needs to be clean."

Her face brightened, as if this were a wonderful discovery. Keeper felt a foolish thrill; it was nice to have his explanation appreciated. He reminded himself that she was this way with everyone, and wondered again where her true interest lay.

"Time and the spirits will make it pure," Craft remarked.

As they walked between wells, Tula addressed Craft. "What are Maya time and spirits?"

She was Toltec, and their concepts did not match. "This is complicated," Craft demurred.

"Make it simple."

Keeper had to smile, privately. This girl would not be diverted from her passing interest.

Craft tried. "Time is measurable, directional, and cyclical." He paused, realizing that this had to be way beyond the comprehension of a seven-year-old child. "You see how the days pass, and the seasons, and the years. In the old days we had an intricate calendar based on interacting cycles of set length." He paused again. "You know how there are special days, and holy days, and celebrations?" The girl nodded; those were things she understood. "We had a ritual almanac that counted off months of thirteen days, and twenty months, making a cycle of 260 days. But we also had a solar calendar of eighteen months of twenty days each, with five days added at the end, making a cycle of 365 days."

"Which is the right one?" she asked alertly.

"Both. They are just different systems. The way each child has a father and a mother; the two are different, yet they interact." He paused again, evidently realizing that this was a cruel analogy for a child without a mother. "I mean—"

"I know what you mean," Tula said sharply. "I had a mother. Now I need another."

"Yes. Now—"

"Why do you say you *had* these calendars? What happened to them?"

Keeper kept his face straight. The child was paying attention.

Craft took it in stride. "The calendars remain, but we have lost much of the use of them. Time and space are inseparable; the heavens and the underworld are bound together with the physical realm we know. Time is intricately linked with direction, and each major direction has its own color and tree, supporting the heavens. Our buildings were oriented with space and time in mind. But after the drought, a century ago, many cities lost the way, and so did our Xlacah. Our newer buildings are oriented at a different angle, and the old wisdom seems no longer to apply. I regret this; I believe the old system was the finest we could have."

"A father and a mother," she agreed.

"Yes. The beauty of it was the way the two calendars interacted. They were juxtaposed—" He paused, searching for a simpler term. "They were compared, and they matched every fifty-two years. That was the Calendar Round, a special cycle. Then the Long Count recorded the Great Cycle, to set events absolutely in time, even thousands of years."

"Is that how long it will take to make the well water pure?"

Craft laughed. "Not quite that long, I think."

"And what of the spirits?"

"Keeper can explain that better. He is the one in tune with the spirits."

But they were coming to a well, and had to break off, to Keeper's relief. Did the child really understand these complex concepts? If not, why did she pursue them so diligently?

The next two wells were clean. But the fourth was bad: there was a body in it. An old woman, who must have tried to resist the intruders, and been deemed unworthy of rape; it looked as if she had been bashed on the head and thrown here. Her head was facedown in the water, the gory back of her head showing. Her feet were out of the pool on the other side.

They assessed the best way to pull her out. She was fairly solid; both of them would have to haul, and she would drag.

"Maybe you should wait over there," Keeper suggested to the child, not wanting her to see the detail too clearly.

"But we can help," she protested.

"I don't think—"

"Kettle!" she called.

The slave stepped forward. He was a solid man, well muscled. He took hold of the feet and hauled. The body lurched as if alive. He braced and hauled again, dragging the head through the water.

Keeper and Craft jumped to catch hold of her flopping arms, adding their power to that of the slave. In a moment they had dragged her unceremoniously to a dry-land hollow some distance from the water.

"We had better bury her," Keeper said. "So she won't stink."

Kettle used his hands to scrape dirt over the body. This wasn't fast or elegant, but it was getting the job done. The slave did not seem to be bright, but he was a hard worker. Craft used his shell-claw to break the ground, freeing more dirt.

Keeper returned to the well. Tula was trying to use the seine on it, but lacked the size and reach to be effective. She was frustrated, and wore a villainous expression—which faded like morning mist the moment she spied Keeper. "Let me help you," Keeper said, catching hold of an end. She smiled up at him, agreeing.

They passed the net through the water, fetching out twigs and grass. But it remained cloudy. "I don't want to drink it," the girl said, wrinkling her nose.

"After a while, the water will clear," he explained. "It keeps flowing through, carrying the bad things away. Then people can drink it again."

"Oh, good." But her enthusiasm seemed less than complete. Keeper was privately glad to see her reacting normally. Then she reverted to her inquiring mode. "What of the spirits?"

"The Mayan gods appear in a host of guises and under many different names," he explained. "Most gods have a different aspect associated with each direction. Each also has contradictory traits, such as male and female, old and young, or good and evil. They guide the growing plants, and the stars in the sky, and the lives of mortal folk like us. For example, there is the Sun, who is bright in the sky by day, and by night rules the underworld as the Jaguar God. There is the Moon, also called Lady Rainbow, who presides over weaving, divination, childbirth, and medicine."

"Yes!" she agreed. "I want to know all about her."

He continued his explanations, and she seemed to understand, which was gratifying.

When they returned to the house, after clearing several wells, Keeper made it a point to compliment the child's efforts. "She really helped," he concluded. It was true, though most of it was because of the stout work of the slave, Kettle, there because of her.

After that, Tula went with him when he went out to work, accompanied by the slave. When she tired, or the pace was too fast for her, Kettle simply picked her up and carried her. The man never spoke, but it was clear that he, too, liked the child, and was glad to help her in any way.

One day they passed a field of maize. The plants were growing well, but were drying out. "I think the farmer is gone," Keeper said. "We should find someone to tend this garden, so the crop won't be lost."

"Why?" Tula asked.

"Because food is scarce, after the recent trouble. We need to salvage all we can. Soon these ears of maize will ripen, and then they will feed many people. If the plants get water." He looked around, and spied a bucket made from a large gourd. This was a dry patch; the farmer must have watered it frequently. "I see there's a well; maybe we can fetch some water."

Kettle went to the bucket, and took it to the well. He dipped it full, and carried it back to the garden. Keeper found another gourd, and Tula found a small one. She never shirked her share. The three of them carried water to splash on the garden until it was well soaked.

Keeper was getting to like the little girl despite his wariness about her motives. She was bright, and she liked to help. The slave, reflecting her wishes, was quite useful too. When they returned to the house, he let the others know.

"Wait till you learn what your daughter has been doing," Haven said.

"Allele?"

"She went out with Tuho. She has gotten interested in military things."

It was true. Tula was interested in nature, and avidly absorbed anything Keeper told her. Allele, impressed with the Toltec military formations, was similarly interested in the things Tuho had to tell her. "We seem to have exchanged children," Tuho remarked half ruefully.

"The attention of children is brief," Keeper said. "They will lose interest soon enough."

"Tula will not. But Allele—I think she views me as an emissary from the Death God, because of the scene on the battlefield. But I would never hurt a child."

"We did not know you then. Rebel would have killed her."

"And I respect Rebel for that. I would expect her to do the same for Tula, given a similar situation. But I want never to see that situation."

"Agreed, sir!" Then, venturing what might be a delicate matter: "Your daughter is special, but I don't think I quite understand her."

"I hardly understand her myself. She has a will of obsidian, but she masks it. Yet I am sure she likes your household, and wishes it no ill."

"She has impressed us all. Yet at times she hardly seems like a child."

"I think her loss of family toughened her. She didn't cry when her mother died, though I know she cared greatly. She has always been attentive to me, as if I am the one who needs care. That is why I wanted her in a complete, functional family: to learn the ways of it. Your family has exceeded my expectation in that respect; Tula is thriving."

"Yet in due course you will be moving on to another station. Then she will have to leave this family."

"This is a concern. But right now, it is well."

Allele did lose interest, and returned to her usual pursuits around the house and garden. But Tula did not. She stayed close to Rebel in the evening, and to Keeper in the daytime, being pleasant to the others but not devoted. At first this seemed natural, because her father was out most of the day, and she seemed uninterested in childish things; she wanted to be with a man.

"You are a father," Haven said. "When she's not with her own, she wants to be with another proven father."

"What of Harbinger?"

"You are the father of a girl like her."

Oh. At any rate, when Keeper went out, Tula always wanted to go with him, and usually she could, because his tasks were routine, not dangerous. The slave always came, and it was apparent that Kettle could and would protect her if so required. But apart from that, it was as if the slave did not exist; he was part of the background.

Tula eagerly listened to all that Keeper had to say about the growing for maize, beans, squash, peppers and other staples, and how water was vital to them all. "Drought is the terror," he explained. "Drought can destroy crops, and people too, for we can't live if we can't eat."

"Yes!" she agreed warmly. "The Old City survives because it has water."

"To a degree," he agreed.

"Why?" She meant that she wanted further explanation.

"Let me show you." They went to the central plaza, where the huge Ceremonies Complex dominated the landscape. The platform rose in three sloping terraces to four times the height of a tall man. The building on it was over a hundred paces long, with three huge vaulted chambers, and thirty-five doors facing north.

But people were living in those chambers now. "This is desecration," Keeper said. "Since the priests left, there is no one to enforce the sacred strictures, and refugees from the drought-struck region are taking up residence. See how little they care for it. There is garbage on the floor."

"Why did the priests go?"

"The city is under new administration. New people, who don't want the old ways followed."

He was afraid she would ask more specific questions, but perhaps she understood enough not to. Instead she changed the subject. "Promise me to answer."

"I always answer to the best of my ability."

Her gaze flashed. For a moment she looked like what she would one day become: a ranking Toltec woman. "Promise."

Keeper glanced at Kettle, uncertain what this meant, but there was no answer there. "I promise."

"Why did Rebel want to kill Allele?"

She had heard about the scene on the battlefield, when Rebel had held a knife to Allele's throat. Allele must have told her. "Rebel would never hurt Allele," he temporized.

She brushed this away like so much chaff. "You promised!"

So he had, and she would not be denied. "It is not good for a woman or a girl to be caught by enemy troops. It is better for her to die."

"Why?"

She wanted to know the detail. "This would be better for your father to explain."

"He won't."

So Tuho did deny his daughter in this respect. "That is because he doesn't want to hurt you."

"You promised!"

"I don't want to hurt you either."

"You told Rebel to do it! To kill her! Why?"

She would brook no evasion. She did indeed have a will of obsidian. "The soldiers would hurt a woman—or a girl—so bad, it's better for them to die first. Rebel would have killed Allele, and then herself, before the soldiers reached them. So they couldn't be hurt."

She pondered that. "You wanted it?"

"No. But I love them. I would rather see them dead, than tortured."

"But my father wasn't going to do that. He wanted me to live with you."

"We didn't know that, at the time."

"He said you have courage and honor."

"We did what we had to do."

"Yes."

"But I'm glad it turned out as it did. It is better for all of us."

"Yes."

She let the subject drop at last, but Keeper was left uneasy. The child had something on her mind, and he wasn't sure what it was.

Meanwhile, Rebel had a problem. She caught Keeper alone to discuss it. "I have talked with the others, and they don't know what to do. Maybe you do."

"Do? About what?"

"I think I am falling in love."

"With Tuho? That's not a problem."

"With Tula."

He stared at her. "I don't understand."

"I can never have a daughter of my own. Tula—she is such a darling. She wants me to marry her father."

"But it was agreed to be a temporary affair."

"Yes. When he goes to a new station, I will remain here."

"And be with Tula no more," he said, realizing the source of her distress. That much he could comprehend; he had felt the child's force of personality himself. He was coming to love Tula too, despite already having a wonderful daughter.

"Yes. I dread it."

"But you can marry him. You can make any man marry you, if you choose."

"Yes, but would it be right? To marry him for his child? So I could feel like a mother?"

Keeper considered. "Do you dislike him?"

"Oh, no, I like him. He's a good man. I could surely love him, if I let myself."

"Then why not let yourself?"

"Because the motive is wrong. It's the wrong reason."

He saw her point. Love with an unethical base was not wise. "Yet if it seems best, overall—"

"And Tula may not love me."

"But she does! She stays with you every night, instead of with Allele."

She shook her head. "She wants to make sure I marry her father. That's not the same thing."

"How can it not be?"

"I don't know. But it's not."

His sister shared the ambiguity they all did. Tula was wonderful, yet mysterious. None of them knew what was truly in her mind. "How can a child be planning something we don't understand?"

"I don't know. But I'm not easy."

That, added to his own doubt, made Keeper uneasy too. So next day he braced Tula. "What do you want with my sister Rebel?"

There was no evasion. "I want her to marry my father and make him happy."

"So you can have a mother?"

"No."

He was startled. "Then why?"

"A father."

"But you have a father!"

"Not like you."

"But—Rebel is my sister. She . . . I . . ." This was all confusing.

"Hug me," she said.

He glanced at Kettle, but the slave was as usual unresponsive. However, Keeper had learned to read him somewhat. If the man saw any threat to the girl, he acted. Had he seen a threat in such an action, he would have tensed. He was a slave, but no one would be wise to try to balk his protection of the child.

So Keeper kneeled and put his arms around Tula, hugging her. She hugged him back with an ardor almost like that of a woman. "I love you."

What did she mean by that? He tried to disengage, but she clung. "I want you to be my father."

That was too much of an answer. "But that can't be," he protested. "Tuho is your father."

"He doesn't have time for me."

And Keeper did. He was beginning to see that he had made a mistake. But he needed to know the whole of it. "I thought you were interested in water, in nature, as I am."

"Yes. Anything you do."

"Your father—Commander Tuho—is an important man. He must do his job, every day. He loves you, but can't be with you all the time. He brought you here so we could provide you with what you lacked."

"Yes. A family. I want it."

He was still floundering. "But you can have a family, if Rebel marries your father."

"Yes. I can be with you."

"I mean that Rebel can be your mother. She loves you."

"She is for my father."

"I don't understand." It was something of an understatement.

"He needs a woman in his life," she explained patiently. "When he has Rebel, he won't need me. I can be with you."

Her notion was coming clear at last. Tula wanted to provide for her father, so she could be free. She had been alienated by circumstance. Perhaps her mother, dying of disease, had told the child that she would have to take care of her father. Tula had taken it literally, and made an awesomely rational plan to fulfill the obligation. And to recover for herself what she most missed: a functioning family.

"What do you think your present father thinks of this?" he asked.

"He likes Rebel. A lot. She's very good for him. She's tough and she's pretty. When he saw her ready to kill Allele, he knew he liked her. She's very good at sex too. He'll be happy with her."

She had it all figured out. He tried another tack. "I already have a daughter."

"Yes. Allele. She's nice. I'll be her sister. The way Rebel's your sister. We'll stand by each other forever. A good family."

This was ridiculous, yet there was logic in it. He would not mind having a daughter like this, with no disparagement of Allele. But it could hardly be that simple.

"I am not sure about this," he said. "I will have to talk with Commander Tuho."

"Yes."

Their dialogue was done. He disengaged and glanced again at the slave. There was a trace of a smile on the man's face. What did it mean?

Tuho was away that day, but Keeper caught him next morning. "Sir, I need to say something."

"By all means."

"I fear you will not like it."

Tuho smiled. "Is my daughter becoming too much of a burden?"

"Not exactly. We get along well. Too well, perhaps."

Now Tuho frowned. "Be specific."

"Tula wants to join my family."

"She likes Rebel. So do I. Our arrangement is temporary, by mutual agreement, but I think I would like to make it permanent."

"To marry her?"

"Yes. That would make my daughter happy. In that way she can join your family."

"It is not that simple, sir. Tula wants to—to exchange Rebel for herself. To have Rebel join you, and Tula join us."

Anger showed. "How dare you presume!"

"I don't presume, sir. It was a surprise to me. I tried to explain, but she has her own mind. She—she doesn't seem to see you as a family. She wants ours. I thought you should know."

"If this is true, I shall have to take her away from here."

"I think so, sir. You wanted her to be with a good family. She wanted it too, too literally. We do like her; we all do. We would love to have her with us. But we never meant to take her from you."

Tuho nodded, making a key decision quickly, as a good commander did. "Will Rebel go with us?"

"Yes, I think so. We like Tula, Rebel loves her. She can't bear a child of her own."

"Arrange a meeting of the family, and we will settle this today."

"All of us? Surely a private dialogue would—"

"It must be accomplished openly, so my daughter understands."

Keeper nodded. "Perhaps so, sir. But this may not be easy."

"True."

It wasn't easy. Tuho spoke directly and plainly: "I must seek other quarters. My child and I will depart shortly. We—"

"No!" Tula cried, stricken.

He glanced down at her. "What is your concern?"

Tula knew better than to defy her father openly. Her plan was now transparent, but she did her best. "You must marry Rebel, and she will go with you."

"I would like that." He glanced at Rebel. "Will you accede to marriage, and to be this child's mother?"

Rebel was taken aback by the directness of the proposal. "I'm not sure this is wise."

"I do want you," Tuho said earnestly. "You are the best woman I have encountered, since my wife. Do you object to me as a husband?"

"No. But—"

"Do you dislike Tula?"

"No!"

"Then it seems sufficient. Will you marry me?"

"Yes," she agreed uncertainly.

"And I will stay here," Tula said, clapping her hands.

"No," Tuho said firmly. "You will come with us."

"But you have Rebel. You don't need me anymore."

He did not try to refute the girl's logic. "I need you both."

"But I need a family!"

"We will be your family," Rebel said. "I love you, Tula."

"But I love this family. Will you stay here?"

Rebel looked at Tuho. He shook his head. "No. We will go."

"Then I will stay here. With Keeper. And Craft."

Keeper closed his eyes. He couldn't respond.

Craft, similarly disturbed, did. "Sometimes two families intermarry, and stay together. Haven married Harbinger, and Keeper married Crenelle. But none of us are high officers like your father, Tula. He has responsibilities that take him many places. He is your blood father, and you must be with him."

"But I am giving him Rebel!"

Rebel spoke. "I think I can't marry you, Tuho."

"But you must!" the child cried.

Now Rebel did what she never did: she wept.

Tula turned to Keeper. "Why?"

This he could answer. "Rebel loves you, Tula. She wants to be with you, and be your mother. But if she marries your father, and you stay with us, she can't be with you. Your father loves you too, and if he marries Rebel, you say he can't be with you. So though they like each other, and want to marry each other, they can't, because they would be losing you. Unless you go with them."

"But I want to be with you," Tula said to Keeper. "Don't you want to be with me?"

How could he explain in a way the child would understand or accept? "Yes, I want to be with you, and have you for another daughter. But sometimes we must do things we don't like. Remember when Rebel was going to kill Allele?" Allele, sitting with Crenelle, flinched; she didn't like that memory. "She was ready to do it, because otherwise it could be worse."

Tula nodded. "Yes."

"Now Rebel is ready to give up your father, though she wants to marry him, because otherwise it will be worse."

"But you will not torture me."

"If I took you, it would torture your father. He needs you, Tula."

"But if he has Rebel—"

"He needs you more than he needs Rebel. You are all that remains of your mother." He paused, then tried another aspect. "Our cultures differ. We are Maya; you are Toltec. When we marry, the new couple spends seven years living with the bride's clan, paying off the debt to the bride's family. Then they move to the husband's family, or establish their own household. This is not the Toltec way, and your father is not able to do such a thing. We understand that, and Rebel is willing to forgo the way of our culture. But only if she can be with you; otherwise the sacrifice is too great. It would be similarly difficult for your father. Without you, it would not work well."

The child considered. She understood the importance of herself, though perhaps not in the way the adults did. She was accustomed to being the center of attention wherever she was—except when with her father. For a moment Keeper hoped she would yield to the ideal compromise, and agree to stay with Tuho and Rebel. But then she sighed, and walked back to her father. She had lost her ploy, but she wouldn't compromise. She was a warrior's child. She would leave without Rebel, rather than accept what she believed was the wrong family.

Beside her father, she turned. "This isn't over," she said grimly.

Keeper hoped she was right. But she was the one who would have to compromise.

•

The neglect of the temples and public buildings continued for centuries, and Xlacah decreased in size and importance. The squatters lived there for generations, leaving trash middens on the floors as deep as four feet. Yet the city was not dead; new buildings were constructed, and old ones renovated. One existing structure became the Temple of The Seven Dolls, but it's not clear what the purpose of the dolls was.

The Toltecs ruled for another two centuries, but then abandoned their Yucatan capital of Chichén Itzá. The Maya regained their power in the region, but lacked political unity.

13

PRINCESS

Through the centuries the fierce nomads of the Asian steppe made many inroads on the more civilized peoples to the south and west. China finally built a series of walls to try to fence them out, while Europeans tried to oppose them militarily. Neither policy was very effective.

The territory between the Black Sea and the Caspian Sea, dominated by the Caucasus Mountain range, was like a way station, at the edge of civilization as we understood it. Many tribes passed there on their way to Asia Minor and Europe. Circa 2,000 BC the Cimmerians held sway to the north, the Hittites and Egyptians to the south. By 800 BC the Cimmerians remained to the north, but the Assyrians dominated south. By 600 BC the Scythians had displaced the Cimmerians, while the Assyrians were giving way to the Babylonians. By 500 BC the Sarmatians, which may have been a branch of the Scythians, dominated the Caucasus region, while the Persian Empire prevailed south. This gave way to the Empire of Alexander, then to the Roman Empire.

Meanwhile the Sarmatians split into three groups, one of which was the Alani. The Alani were to settle in the Caucasus, with the Kingdom of Armenia immediately south. Neither was able to conquer the other, both being formidable powers in their own right for many centuries. They were neighbors for two thousand years. At first relations were hostile, but later there was amelioration and intermarriage.

Theoretically the Armenians were an outpost of civilization, while the Alani were barbarians. But this was always an oversimplification, if it ever was true. Sometimes they were destined to make common cause.

The setting is just south of the Caucasus, circa 1300 AD.

•

Craft saw that the situation was hopeless. The enemy, more numerous and better organized than his scouts had reported, and surely better led, had a commanding position. His soldiers were about to be slaughtered. They had already taken serious losses, and the wounded would die if not brought home immediately.

It was hunger that had done them in. They were well trained and disciplined, and had fought well in the past. But the enemy had laid waste the fields, filled in wells, and removed all stores of food. Foraging had become difficult, and as time passed, nigh impossible.

Oh, they had tried. They conserved water by pissing into sand-filled buckets and drinking the filtered liquid that dripped from holes in the bottom. It tasted foul, but was actually potable. They trapped rats and other rodents and roasted them as small delicacies. They made bread from anything handy, including trapped locusts, roaches, spiders, and other bugs. The vermin were dried before fires, and their dessicated bodies ground into flour which was then baked as bread. They ground up sticks of wood and baked it similarly. It was no pleasure to eat or to try to digest, but it was better than nothing. They even roasted animal dung.

But these were temporary measures, and there was no respite. Had there been rain to make seeds sprout—but the weather blessed the enemy with a drought.

Even retreat was not feasible. They could not travel. The men were simply too fatigued and ill with opportunistic diseases. A quarter of the army was lying on straw beds, dry heaving and awaiting the relief of unconsciousness and death.

The choices seemed to be cannibalism or capitulation. Craft did not like either. But neither did he prefer the likely doom of remaining inactive. So he did what he had to do.

"Fetch the white flag," he told his lieutenant.

"Sir!" the man protested.

"You can see as well as I can that we are in no condition to continue hostilities. We must cut our losses. I will proffer myself in lieu of my men. For food and water for them now, and forbearance from slaughter. You will see to their evacuation when I am taken hostage, when they are able to travel."

"But we can't trust the enemy commander!"

"We have no choice. I should be worth enough to make the exchange worth his while. He has losses of his own to attend to, and he won't want to be stuck with a field full of stinking bodies to bury. It is to his advantage to make the deal."

"I act under protest, sir." But the lieutenant fetched the flag. And balked again. "You must consult with your brother."

He was right. Hero was commanding the army, and this would have to be cleared with him. "Notify him of my intention."

The lieutenant galloped off on one of their few remaining healthy horses that had not yet been eaten, while Craft attended to matters of hygiene and sustenance. He could not be sure when the enemy would allow him to eat or piss again. Not that he had much to void; he had been on urine rations too.

Hero arrived shortly. "Have you gone crazy, brother?"

"You know the situation as well as I do, brother. We have to purchase respite for our troops, lest we make a bad situation worse than it needs to be."

"What will Crenelle say?"

That was a sharp cut. "I think I need to do it before she finds out."

"And if it goes bad, she'll be a widow."

Craft smiled grimly. "Then you'll have to marry her, Prince. It would not be an unkind chore."

Hero shook his head. "I'll make Keeper do it."

They were bantering, knowing the grimness of the situation. But it was true: Craft stood a fair chance of losing his life, and one of his brothers would then have to marry his widow, to protect his children. Both of Craft's brothers liked Crenelle, and she liked both, so it would work out. But Crenelle would never let Craft walk into such danger if she had a choice. As it was, she would blame Hero for not stopping him. So it would be Keeper she married. But the men knew that this was a necessary sacrifice.

Hero put his hand on Craft's shoulder. "Go with God, brother. I tried to stop you."

"You tried," Craft agreed. That was their cover story to satisfy Crenelle.

Craft mounted his steed, held the flag aloft on its short pole beside his royal banner, and rode out to meet the enemy. This was its own gamble, because they might elect simply to cut him down. But that would throw his less-wasted troops into a despairing fury that would pointlessly cost many more lives. What else would they have to lose? It was better for the enemy to parlay.

The enemy troops gave way before him, recognizing his banner. Then the enemy commander rode out to intercept him. Craft saw with surprise that the banner was royal. They had sent a baron out to parlay, an excellent signal.

Craft halted his horse and dismounted. He was putting himself at the mercy of the other, as he could readily be cut down before he could mount and escape.

The other dismounted and strode to face him, then waited for Craft to make his case.

"I am Baronet Craft. Our army is defeated. I proffer myself in lieu of the men, as hostage. Take me, and give them water and what food you care to spare. They will depart when they can travel."

"I am Baron Tuho. I accept your submission. Mount and accompany me to the city."

It was that simple. Craft remounted as Tuho did and guided his horse in the indicated direction. Tuho made a signal, and his troops started falling back, allowing Craft's troops respite. Serving women emerged from behind their ranks, carrying jugs and baskets. Water and food! Obviously they had been prepared for this situation. Craft himself would be captive, imprisoned, but his men would survive.

But Tuho did not guide him to a prison site. Instead they went to the palace. There royal servants helped Craft remove his armor and soiled clothing, washed him, and gave him a robe. They stored his sword and knife in a cabinet but did not lock them away. This was better treatment than he had anticipated. As a rule, royal hostages were not abused, but neither were they given much chance to make mischief.

When he was dressed, Tuho reappeared, similarly robed. "I thank you for courteous treatment," Craft said.

"We have long been neighbors. You are a man of honor. You will not abuse our hospitality."

"True. However—"

"You will meet my daughter," Tuho said. "The heiress Tula."

Craft paused, confused. "I don't understand."

"First, a bit of wine and bread. You look hungry."

"I am," Craft said. He smiled. "I will probably be worth more ransom healthy than failing."

Servants brought a jug and platter with flesh and bread. Craft looked at Tuho. "Eat, drink," the man said. "It would be pointless to poison you. But perhaps take them sparingly, until your system recovers."

Craft did so, taking a careful swig of the wine, which was excellent, and a piece of black bread. Tuho waited impassively.

When Craft had had a moderate meal, and was assured it would stay down, Tuho spoke again. "This way." The baron guided him to an ornate suite.

There they encountered an eight-year-old child. She was of course well dressed, with a female attendant, rather pretty in her features and poise. She bowed to Tuho, then turned to Craft. "Hello, Baronet Craft."

"Hello, Baroness Tula."

She giggled. "I'm not. Not yet. Let me touch you."

What was this? Craft glanced at Tuho, and was startled to find the man gone. So was the female attendant. He was alone with the little baroness, the baron's heir. Honor was honor, but this was a singular act of trust. He was an enemy commander fresh off the battlefield, and this was an innocent royal girl.

What could he do? Slowly he extended his right hand, open.

Tula took it, clasping it with both her own small hands. She remained that way for some time. What was she doing?

Then she spoke. "Your sister will come."

Craft smiled. "I think not. I have two sisters, both fair of feature, and neither would care to risk herself in an enemy city during wartime."

She finally released his hand. "She will come tomorrow."

This was curious, but evidently Baron Tuho wanted the two of them to become acquainted. "Why do you think so?"

"I had a dream."

Oh. Imagination. "Do you want her to come?"

"Yes. She will marry my father and maybe make him happy. Then I can be with Allele."

"With whom?"

"Your niece."

Her dream had gone wrong. "I have no niece. Only two sons."

She looked perplexed. "But your wife had her."

"My wife is Crenelle."

Then she looked really confused. "But she married your brother and bore Allele!"

Craft shook his head. "I think your dream got things mixed up. Crenelle was interested in all three of us brothers, but she married me."

"Something is strange. Where is Allele?"

"There is no Allele. Not in our family."

Her face crumpled. "But I like her. She's my age, almost."

Craft found himself holding her, comforting her. She was obviously mixed up, but sensitive. "I'm sorry."

"Maybe someone will have her later."

"Maybe," he agreed warily. Then he essayed a question of his own. "Why am I here with you, instead of in chains?"

"I told Father to bring you to me."

Surprises continued. "And he does what you tell him?"

"Yes."

He thought it best to let the matter drop, but curiosity overcame him. "Why did you want to be with Allele?"

"Because her family's better than mine. Father's a widower."

"That's why you want my sister to marry him?"

"Yes. When he's happy, he won't need me. Then I can go to a better family and be happy too."

This child seemed physically and mentally healthy, but she had a problem emotionally. Yet how did that relate to Craft's presence here? He decided not to ask.

In due course he was ushered to an adjacent bedroom. Was he to be this girl's guardian or companion? That hardly made sense. But now it was time to sleep. He could not be sure when this remarkably polite treatment would end.

"Craft."

He jumped. It was the child, in her nightclothes, standing by his bed. "Baroness, you should not be here."

She ignored that. "Are you sure you don't have a niece?"

"Sons only," he said.

She sighed. "I don't understand why my dream went wrong. But you will do." She climbed into bed with him.

"Baroness!" he protested, appalled.

"Call me Tula. Put your arm around me." She nestled close, as for sleep.

What could he say to her, that would not trespass on things no child was supposed to know? "Tula, you cannot be with a strange man! It would destroy your reputation."

"My reputation for being weird? Why do you think I made Father bring you to me?"

"*You* made him do it? Tula, I'm a hostage, not a companion."

"That, too," she agreed. "Now hold me, so I can sleep."

"Tula—"

"Be quiet, or I'll kiss you."

He started to laugh, weakly. Then she lurched forward and pressed her face into his, kissing him with surprising authority before withdrawing. She felt almost like a woman.

Was this a test of some kind? Were hidden servants watching? Well, he was at their mercy anyway. He put one arm around the girl, and let her snuggle close. She evidently wanted the comfort of an adult, and perhaps was accustomed to requiring a servant to do it. It seemed that her father was not the type, and where was her mother?

He closed his eyes, and slept surprisingly readily. It was oddly pleasant being close to this odd child. Could he have had a daughter or niece like this, had things been otherwise?

"She's coming!"

That jolted him awake. It was dawn, and Tula was sitting up. "She is?" he asked foggily. Who was "she"?

"Yes. I knew she would."

"Then perhaps you should get ready to meet her."

"I will." She bounced out of bed and ran to her own room.

That gave him a chance to see to his own morning details. He discovered a fresh robe on a chair beside the bed, so evidently a servant had been here in the night, seen them asleep embraced, and made no outcry. Which suggested that he had not trespassed in a way that could have gotten him summarily beheaded. Even the most innocent sleep, as this was, could have been lethal, otherwise.

Tula reappeared, freshly garbed, her hair neatly done. She was like a little princess. "This way," she said, excited. "We have to eat first."

Servants made them a meal for two. "Grape juice," Tula said. "Father won't let me have real wine. And poppy-seed bread."

"Poppy-seed!" Craft exclaimed. "This is humor?"

"No. It makes me feel giddy and I like it. I am less bored when I eat it."

Small wonder. Poppy seeds could be mind-bending, even hallucinogenic. But probably most of that was denatured by the baking process, so the effect was mostly imaginary.

He joined her in eating the bread. It was good enough. But soon he did feel slightly light-headed. Was it his imagination?

Again he wondered: was he being tested? Odd things kept happening.

Then Tula led him down to the presentation chamber, where Tuho awaited them. "She is now being admitted," he said.

Soon their visitor was ushered into the room, as the soldiers who had guarded her faded back. Only when he saw her did Craft remember: Tula had predicted that his sister would come. "Rebel!" he exclaimed.

She hurried to him and hugged him. "You are safe!" she said, relieved.

"Of course he is safe," Tula said. "I guarded him all night." She shot an imperious glare at her father.

Tuho looked abashed. "I wasn't really going to cast him into the dungeon," he protested. But his manner hinted that there could have been such a plan, foiled by the intercession of the child. Tula evidently had a fair notion what was what. So it had not been just her need for adult comfort that put her into Craft's bed and in close physical contact. She had stopped the men from coming for Craft after she was safely asleep.

"I made sure." Tula turned to Rebel. "You're pretty."

Indeed she was. Her fair hair and pale eyes made her stand out among ordinary women, and she had dressed to accentuate her female qualities. At age twenty-seven she was a stunning figure of a woman, and knew it. "Thank you." She did not seem to find it remarkable that a child was present and participating.

"What is your business here, Baroness?" Tuho asked Rebel, according her a title of honor that was barely technically accurate. Hero was the baron; his siblings were only relatives. Tuho's manner was controlled, but Craft knew he was taking in the qualities of body and bearing that Rebel was displaying. No man could do otherwise.

"I come to plead for the release of my brother. He is a family man; his wife and children need him." As she spoke she breathed a bit more deeply than she needed to, and angled her head prettily. She was exploiting her sex appeal. Her words were only a portion of the case she was making.

"Prince Craft is hostage for the safety of his troops," Tuho said. "They have been spared slaughter. They have been fed and watered. He must remain for ransom."

"Fed with poppy-seed bread!" she snapped.

"It is what we have to spare. It will make their condition more comfortable."

She evidently decided to let that pass. Any bread was better than none, and this was better than what they had been eating. "It has been a bad year. We don't have a lot for ransom."

"Then we shall be obliged to wait for a good year."

"But his family!" she protested.

"That is not my concern. I need resources for my own troops, and a fair ransom should help."

Rebel seemed about ready to cry. This was of course artifice, but just might be effective. "What can I do?"

"You can marry Father," Tula said.

All three adults were startled. "That is not the nature of this negotiation," Tuho informed his daughter.

"Yes it is," Tula insisted. "I saw it in my dream. That she would come here and marry you. You need a wife and she's pretty."

As if that was all there was to it. But the baroness was after all a child.

"I will consider it," Tuho said.

Rebel saw that her calculated physical appeal had gone too far. "You don't want me. I'm barren." She smiled with a tinge of bitterness. "A barren baroness."

"You can't be," Tula said. "Somebody has to have a daughter. I saw her in my dream."

Rebel shrugged. "It wasn't me." She turned back to Tuho. "I must return to my people. Maybe we can raise a sufficient ransom."

"I think not. You will remain here while I consider."

"You want a mistress, not a wife," Rebel flared. "I would not be suitable for either, unwilling."

"We shall see."

Rebel turned to go. Guards reappeared, blocking her way. She had been taken hostage too.

"She would not be good," Craft said, trying to save the situation. "She has a mind of her own."

Tuho's eyes narrowed. "How would you see it, Baroness, if your brother were put to the torture, pending your cooperation?"

"Don't threaten her, Father," Tula said. "She'll kill you. You can win her if you do it right."

The man eyed his daughter as if taking her seriously. "Is she worth winning?"

"Yes."

Tuho spread his hands. "I bow to my daughter's wisdom. Remain as my guest."

"But I do have to remain, regardless of my preference?" Rebel asked, unpleased.

The baron nodded.

So it was that Rebel moved in with Craft and Tula. She had tried to rescue him, and gotten herself captured too. She seemed to accept it, but Craft knew that Tuho's life would be in peril if he got close to her.

"Father is not a bad man," Tula said. "He does what he thinks he has to do. When you marry him, the ransom will be forgiven and you will be free to go home on occasion."

"*If* I marry him," Rebel said tightly.

"He's already smitten with you. He'd take you to bed today, if you let him."

"How nice to know," Rebel said wryly.

"You will like him, when you get to know him."

"You hope. Are you looking for a replacement mother?"

Now the girl seemed pensive. "Not exactly."

Rebel zeroed in. "*What,* exactly?"

"I want to be with Allele."

"Who?"

"She dreamed I had a daughter," Craft said, misspeaking.

"Not you, exactly," Tula said. "But somebody."

"Who is the mother of this Allele?" Rebel asked alertly.

The child struggled. "Nel . . . Nell—"

"Crenelle?"

"Yes! And—"

"Hero?"

"No."

"Keeper?"

"Yes!"

Rebel glanced at Craft. "If you die, Crenelle will marry Keeper, and maybe have that daughter. That's Tula's vision."

"But she's my age, almost," Tula said.

"Let's change the subject," Rebel said. "If I am to marry your father, I need to know more about you. What interests you, Tula?"

"Big stories. But we're out of new ones. That's why I eat the poppy seed. It keeps me from being bored."

Rebel considered only briefly. "We Alani have stories. Do you know of King Arthur?"

"No."

"Then let's get comfortable, and I'll tell you."

"Let me get some food," Tula said.

A servant appeared, and the girl gave the order: bread, jam, mead. Soon they were all seated on the bed, eating poppy-seed bread and drinking mildly alcoholic mead, and Rebel started in on the major Alan legend of King Arthur and his Round Table.

"Round?" Tula asked.

"Round. Because the king had many nobles, and they were all supposed to be even, and they could quarrel about which of them deserved to sit most royally, so they made the table round so that no one could sit above or below anyone else. It was a wonderful compromise."

"Oh," Tula agreed, fascinated.

"The story really begins when young Arthur pulled the sword from the stone."

Tula laughed. "Swords don't live in stones!"

"Yes, it was unusual. The sword had been plunged into the stone by the prior king, who said that the man who drew it out would be the next king. Everyone tried, but no one could do it. It was really wedged in tightly. Until Arthur, who was just a servant in a noble's estate, tried it. And the sword came out readily."

"That's crazy! Unless he was very strong."

"He wasn't. There's a different version, where Arthur was noble, destined to be king, but others weren't sure he had the discipline or power to handle it. He needed a persuasive sword. So the Lady of the Lake gave him her sword."

"Who?"

"Well, he never saw her. It was just this delicate hand emerging from the water, holding the sword. He took it, and after that others knew he deserved to be king."

"Ridiculous!" Tula said. "Tell me more."

Rebel did, evidently appreciating the audience. Craft appreciated it on two levels: it was a great old story, long told among Alani, and it was distracting the child from whatever other mischief she might otherwise come up with. It was also nice to see Rebel enjoying herself. For once she wasn't establishing her militant independence, but relaxing. That made her prettier than ever. Maybe the intoxicating bread and mead had something to do with it. Yet again Craft wondered exactly what was going on.

At length Rebel called a halt. "We have to sleep," she said diplomatically.

"That is unfortunate," Tuho said.

Rebel and Craft jumped; they had not known he was there. But Tula seemed unsurprised. "Can I stay up late, Father, to hear more?" she asked.

"No. You do need your sleep. Princess Rebel will be here tomorrow."

"I'm no princess," Rebel protested. "Not even a baroness."

"Yes you are," Tula said.

"Honorary title," Craft murmured, to stifle Rebel's rebellion.

"Which of us gets to sleep with her tonight?" Tula asked with a half-knowing smile.

Again, Tuho seemed to take her seriously. "She will choose."

Rebel considered. Craft knew what was in her mind: which one of the two could she better impress, and thus gain power over, in one night?

She decided. "Tula. Tonight."

Tuho was surely disappointed, but he accepted it with grace. It was evident that he already understood that Rebel had to be won her way. "There will be other nights."

"Perhaps," Rebel agreed.

She was definitely considering.

Tuho departed. "You will," Tula said confidently.

"Which?" Rebel asked.

"First a night, then marriage."

"How can you know?"

"I remember, from my dream."

Rebel glanced at Craft. "Should I?"

"Do you want to?"

"The night? Yes, it could be fun. But I don't like marrying under duress."

"You would never do that."

She nodded. "I will decide. I will probably do it for the right price."

"He'll meet it," Tula said. "He'll do anything for you."

"And this is what you want, Tula?"

Now the girl considered. "It will happen. Is that enough?"

"No."

"I thought you wanted it, Tula," Craft said, surprised.

"I do, if it's right." The child faced Rebel. "Will you leave your family?"

"No," Rebel said. "I will always be close to my family. Your father will have to accept that."

"Then it's right," Tula concluded.

"It's right?" Craft asked.

"I will join your family. That's what I want. Even if Allele's not there. I will be the only girl."

"So nice to have that settled," Rebel said with an irony Craft hoped escaped the child.

"Yes," Tula agreed. "Now hold me."

Rebel didn't even roll her eyes. She settled down on Tula's bed with her, leaving Craft to sleep alone.

That, he thought, was just as well. Tula had protected him by staying close, but there was more than a hint that she viewed him somewhat as Rebel viewed Tuho. That attitude, however far-fetched, could get him promptly tortured to death.

In the morning, after routine activities, Tuho joined them. "Tell us more about King Arthur," he said.

"Shall I hold you close so that you won't be frightened?" Rebel asked.

"By all means."

"Maybe later," she said with good humor.

She was definitely warming to him.

They settled down around the bedroom, with Tula nestling close to Rebel, and Rebel continued the story of King Arthur. Craft, listening to the familiar narrative, fell into a kind of daze or stupor, perhaps a dream. The food and drink were definitely intoxicating. He found himself in the role of King Arthur, taking the shining sword from the hand in the lake, which also seemed to be like glassy stone, and carrying it as his badge of legitimacy to govern his kingdom. Establishing the Table Round and summoning knights from across the land to help defend it from the invading hordes. Marrying a lovely princess for political reason, and falling in love with her. Only to have her attention stray. Finally betrayed by his illegitimate son and severely wounded in battle.

"You would not do that to me."

Craft came out of it with a start. It was Tuho speaking to Rebel. He was reacting to the legend of Arthur too.

"I would not," she agreed. "If you were mine, and you thought to stray, I'd kill you before you could sire an illegitimate son."

He was unperturbed. "I would not stray. There are similarities to our own legend of bold King Artashes."

"And lovely Satenik," Tula said rapturously. "It's so romantic!"

Of course the Armenians had legends too. "Similarities?" Craft asked.

"Artashes was a real king of Armenia, about fifteen hundred years ago," Tuho said. "Who became legendary. He did relate in part to the Alani."

"The Alani!" Rebel said, surprised.

"Tell us! Tell us!" Tula exclaimed.

"My daughter insists," Tuho said apologetically.

"Because the legend is like us," the girl said. "Like you and Rebel."

"*That's* what you dreamed!" Tuho said.

She nodded. "The legend foretold it. She is Satenik. Look at her wild fair hair and eyes, her imperious nature."

The baron glanced assessingly at Rebel, who stared back defiantly. She was exactly as the girl described. "Perhaps." Tuho settled back and began the narrative. And Craft soon found himself back in a vision.

The Alani, as seen in the Armenian legend, were a wild and powerful force, ranging down from the northlands. They brought sword, fire, and terror to the settled peoples they raided. They crossed the Caucasus mountain range and invaded Armenia. But King Artashes, intent on building the fair capital city of Artashat, rallied and defeated them. He drove them back across the river Kura, and in the process captured the Alani chief's son and heir. This was an impressive setback for the fierce warriors.

The Alani king sent an emissary with pleas to return his son. But Artashes kept him prisoner, concerned that only such a hostage would prevent the Alani from attacking again. He had beaten them this time, but they were too dangerous to leave to their own devices.

Then the Alani king's beautiful daughter Satenik came to plead. She stood at the riverbank and begged for the release of her brother. "O brave Artashes, conqueror of valiant Alani, hear the plea of a princess. Return my brother to the king, his father. 'Tis unworthy of heroes to enslave their prisoners, forever perpetuating the enmity 'twixt Great Armenia and the Alani."

She was bold and brave, and fair to behold. In fact she was absolutely beautiful in her person and her animation. She was also making sense. Artashes did not want perpetual hostility with his neighbors. He was, after all, trying to build a fabulous new city.

The king gazed upon her, hearing her words, pondering their import, and was overcome by passion for her. He made a decision. How better to nullify the thrust of these wild warriors, than to make an alliance by marriage?

So he rode his spirited steed across the stream, right toward the princess. Like an eagle on the wing he leaped across. He unleashed a rope from his saddle, a royal cord bejeweled with rings that flashed in the sun. He flung it out, and it circled her lithe waist and drew her to him. Her struggles were ineffective. He hauled her up onto his saddle, holding her before him, and bore her to his camp.

"Now you are mine, you comely creature!" he exclaimed jubilantly as his horse slowed.

"Am I?" she asked. She turned, caught hold of his head, and kissed him. Then the sun's motion stopped in the heavens, and all else faded away; there was only the divine contact of her precious lips. And in that moment he knew he was lost.

And so it was that they married, and fair Satenik governed Artashes's heart and his household, and peace was made with the Alani.

"She set a trap for him!" Rebel exclaimed. "She could have escaped him had she wanted to. Ineffective struggles indeed! She knew what she had to do."

"She dressed to be sure everything showed," Tula agreed. "Especially when he was looking down at her from his high horse. Big girls have things to be seen."

"Of course," Rebel agreed.

"She looked just like you."

Rebel smiled. "Well, I am Alani." She glanced sidelong at Tuho. "I did come to save my brother."

"You are playing the game she did," Tuho said. "With similar effect. I admit it." He took a breath. "Come with me now."

Rebel did not pretend to misunderstand. "Remember, I am barren."

"I already have a child."

"You will let my brother go."

"I will."

"There will be no ransom."

"No ransom."

She rose. "This won't take long."

"It's about time," Tula said.

"Time," Tuho agreed wryly.

Rebel left with Tuho. "She's already bound him," Tula said with satisfaction. "He is so desperate to clasp her willing he'll agree to anything she demands."

So it seemed. Big girls did have their ways. Rebel had succeeded in rescuing Craft, her way. Probably it was for the best.

Tula turned to Craft. "Did she really not know our legend?"

Craft laughed. "Dare I answer that?"

Now she laughed. They understood each other.

•

The legend of the captured princess is authentic; the Armenians have a collection of poems known as the Songs of Koghten *describing it in detail. There does seem to have been a battle and a capture, and certainly there was King Artashes. That Alan princess may have been the grandmother of the foremost early Armenian king, Tigran the Great, who ruled from 95 to 55 BC.*

The Arthurian legend's origin, in contrast, is shrouded. It has been thought to be based on a historical King Arthur, circa 410 AD when the Romans left Britain and the barbarians invaded, but there are no references at that time. Indeed, nothing stopped the invasions for long, and Britain was in time overrun by the Angles, the Saxons, and the Jutes. There seems to have been no hero to halt the process. Only more than a century later does the name start appearing, and it was several hundred years before the full flowering of the legend.

The indication is that there may have been a historic Arthur, but not in Britain. It was a legend of the Alani of Asia. How did it get to England? In the second century AD the Romans sent a garrison of 3,000 Sarmatian troops to Britain to help defend it, and they brought their legend with them. The Alani were Sarmatians. Some may have intermarried with natives and remained in Britain after the Romans withdrew. Their children learned the stories, and taught them to their children, and gradually it spread and amplified, becoming one of the major legends of Britain, Europe, and the world. Its true origin was lost, and assumed to be British. It seems that only the Alani know the truth.

But historical records are indicative. The Sarmatians worshiped a sword stuck in a stone. They fought under a wind sock–style banner shaped like a dragon and known as the Draco. It was said to roar when they rode into battle. They truly impressed the natives. They were commanded in England by a Roman officer named Lucius Artorius Castus. Legendary King Arthur was also known as Artorius. Even his weapon, the magic sword Excalibur, was first called Caliburn, meaning "white steel," deriving from the words chalybus (steel) and eburnus (white). There was a tribe of Sarmatian smiths known as the Kalybes, and such a sword could have been named for them.

The Alani may not have conquered the world physically, but perhaps they fared better mythologically.

14

HUNGER

Perhaps the most remarkable migration of Africa is that of the Bantu. They started west of the Niger River, apparently learned iron working from the Nok culture across the river, and with that advantage spread forcefully south and west. In the course of about two thousand years Bantu-speaking peoples colonized virtually the whole of Africa south of the Sahara Desert, largely displacing or absorbing the prior populations. In the process they expanded into many subcultures, bringing corn and millet agriculture, cattle herding, and iron working. This was not a conquest so much as a better way. Their successful lifestyle brought population growth, which in turn brought social and political stresses and the need for further emigration.

Then the land ran out. The tribes could no longer simply expand south to relieve the pressure of overpopulation. Warfare had been relatively minor, almost a pastime to settle incidental disputes. It became more serious business as the struggle for survival intensified. There was a revolution in military tactics, and unified, disciplined armies were formed. In due course these would discover a formidable new opponent: the incursions of the colonizing Europeans.

The Bantu vanguard became the Xhosa (pronounced KO-sa), finally settling in southeast Africa. But this did not mean that there were not serious issues farther north. The setting is the east coast of Central Africa, circa 1589.

•

They crested a ridge and came into sight of the fortified coastal village of Malindi. "Oh, no!" Tourette breathed. "Aren't those the cannibals?"

Hero shared his daughter's concern. It was evident that Malindi was under siege. They would not be able to get in now without risking the wrath of the besiegers. That would be worse than fatal.

"We need to consider," Hero said heavily.

"That is the understatement of the day," Keeper said.

"Is there a problem?" Tourette asked. "We don't have to visit that village, do we?"

Hero shook his head. "We do have to visit Malindi. But we dare not fall into the hands of the Zimba besiegers."

"But surely the Malindi exorcist is no better at casting out demons than any other."

Hero exchanged a glance with Keeper.

"It's time to tell her," Crenelle said.

"Tell me what?" Tourette demanded.

"There's a reason we came to this town at this time," Hero said. "It's ugly."

Tourette was catching on. "This is not about exorcism."

"Don't misunderstand," Hero said. "We value you above all else. But we don't believe you are haunted by demons."

"But my expressions! Something takes over and I can't stop it. Isn't that demons?"

"It is a problem," Hero said. "But we think it is something in your body or mind that goes wrong on occasion. It can't be demons. We don't really believe that demons exist. They are merely a way to try to explain things folk don't understand."

She considered that. She was a smart girl, and rational. Hero doubted that she had ever really believed in demons either, but she had gone along with it for the sake of harmony. "Then why have we been visiting so many healers?"

"To cover for our real mission. No one questions our desire to make you become marriageable, so we can travel widely without arousing suspicion."

She nodded. Ugly or defective girls were serious problems in the marriage market. She was far from being ugly, but her liability more than nullified her dawning beauty. She was also a realist. "And that mission is?"

"Goats," Keeper said.

Tourette paused, her mental processes threshing. "We have goats."

"This is a special breed that the Portuguese are rumored to have imported by sea. Very strong foragers, supremely hardy, especially during dry weather."

"They wouldn't die in the drought!" she exclaimed. "That would be valuable."

"Extremely," Keeper agreed. "But it was just a story. We need to ascertain whether it is true, and if so, we need to buy a breeding pair and take them home."

"Where we could breed a herd of them, and survive the next drought much better. But why the secrecy?"

"All tribes suffer from the drought," Keeper said. "Do you think we could bring such valuable goats through their territories without them being stolen?"

"Not if they knew," she agreed.

"We regret deceiving you," Crenelle said.

"Don't. I could have given it away without meaning to. In a fit."

The others nodded. "And you were an excellent cover," Hero said. "You have done your part."

Tourette smiled grimly. "By being what I am: haunted."

Crenelle hugged her. "By letting others think you're haunted."

"But you'll still have trouble making me marriageable."

"We'll find a man who understands," Crenelle assured her. "We wouldn't want any other kind." For marriage was a family matter.

Tourette returned to business. "So the goats are there, and if the Zimba capture that town, they'll eat them along with the people. So it's our problem."

"It's our problem," Hero agreed.

They retired to a secluded glade to hold a family conference. This time Tourette was allowed to participate. She was clearly thrilled with the recognition as a near adult, but also somewhat awed and nervous. The problem was serious.

"Here is the situation," Keeper said, filling in the rest of it for the girl. "We are not sure the goats are as great as rumored, but have to verify it in case they are, because of the great potential benefit to the Xhosa people. To keep the mission secret, it is limited to a single family unit, with a pretext to travel widely." He glanced at Tourette, who smiled.

Hero realized something he had somehow missed before: his younger brother liked his daughter, and she liked him. They were family, yes, but there was something almost flirtatious about their exchange of glances. That could become awkward.

"So we traveled," Keeper continued. "As rapidly as we could without overextending ourselves or revealing our true mission. We knew we had to reach Malindi before the Zimba did. But in the months we have been walking, the Zimba got to the town before we did. Now we have a difficult choice: give up our mission and go home, or find a way to get safely into that town. And out with the goats. I fear our journey has been wasted."

"May I?" Tourette asked thoughtfully.

"Speak," Hero said, curious as to what was on her mind.

"The Zimba. Weren't they peaceful farmers, until about ten years ago? When they suddenly turned cannibal and ate a whole village?"

"They were farmers and herders," Keeper agreed. He knew all about all things agricultural and pastoral. "But they were also experienced cannibals who did not hesitate to consume enemies killed in battle, or criminals. Cattle rustlers learned to respect their herds."

"The hard way," Tourette said, and they laughed together.

Hero glanced at Crenelle, but neither spoke.

"So when a bad drought came, depleting their herds," Keeper continued, "first they ate the dead cattle. Then they went after the town of Sena. It was a trading post doing business with the Portuguese, so they didn't like it anyway. They overwhelmed it and settled down to a huge feast. They consumed every man, woman, child, and animal in it, sparing only those who joined them as tribe members."

"That's what I heard," Tourette said, shuddering.

"When they had digested Sena, they went on to Tete, up the coast. They besieged it, and soon broke down its defenses and captured it. Then they systematically ate everything in it, as before. The surrounding tribes were horrified, but helpless to stop it. All they could do was flee."

"I can understand why," Tourette said.

"When we learned that this was happening, we knew we had to get those goats before the Zimba did," Keeper concluded. "But they moved faster than we expected. We thought they were still assimilating Kilwa, but it seems they finished with it. I dislike saying it, but I think our mission is already lost. There's no sense throwing our lives away at this point."

"They are going north?" Tourette asked.

"Town by town," Keeper agreed. "It takes them a while to finish a town, a year or two, but inevitably they march again, north."

"And who lives to the north?"

"The Segeju," Hero said. "They are fierce, but it is doubtful whether they could defeat the Zimba in open battle, and they seem reluctant to try."

"But if they're next to be eaten?"

"I suspect they prefer to believe that the threat is not immediate," Hero said.

"But if they found a way to defeat the Zimba, would they do it?"

"They might," Hero said. "But that doesn't matter, because I doubt there's a way. The Zimba are too strong."

Tourette was intent. "Suppose they came upon the Zimba by surprise? When they weren't ready?"

Hero shrugged. "Then they might. It would make long-term military sense."

"Such as when the Zimba are occupied attacking Malindi."

Hero considered. "As they are now. Maybe they would."

"Suppose we go to them and suggest it? That might save the town—and the goats."

Hero looked at Keeper. Could this possibly work? It would be dangerous, for a reason he did not care to voice. "What do you think?"

Keeper paused, evidently appreciating that danger, then nodded. "It's far-fetched, but at least it's a chance. We could ask them, if we decided to do that. At worst they would decline."

Crenelle spoke, her expression grim. "Since we have virtually no chance to save the goats otherwise, I believe we should try it. A small chance is better than none."

Hero looked again at Keeper, knowing how he would answer. "How do you see it?"

"I agree with Crenelle. At least it's a chance."

"Then let's get moving," Hero said. "We surely don't have much time before the Zimba breach the walls. Once they get into the town, all is lost."

They traveled north, avoiding the main routes, as they had all along. Smaller villages were easier to deal with, being less formal and more open to visitors.

As night approached, they came to a small agricultural village. They halted as the lookout spied them. They could communicate with other Bantu tribesmen, though the dialects differed.

"We are Xhosa, from far to the south," Hero explained. His knobkerrie, or wooden battle club, was hanging from his belt, obviously out of action. It was important to be nonthreatening. "Myself, my wife, my brother, and my daughter. We seek hospitality for the night, and a consultation with your healer."

"Healer? Why?"

"My child has an affliction. Maybe a demon possesses her. At times she acts crazy."

"Our healer can't handle that," the scout said. "What do you offer for the night?"

"We can perform our tribe's traditional song and dance. My wife remains shapely, and my daughter is dawning."

The scout looked at Crenelle, then at Tourette. He saw what any man would: a pretty woman and a pretty girl. That was viable currency anywhere, especially if they had any significant dancing talent. He nodded. "This way."

They followed him to the center of the village, where the local headman was waiting. Naturally the villagers had known of the approaching party long since, and probably had already known their mission. Also their entertainment capacity. Villages were in constant touch with each other, and always eager for diversion from the dull routine. The scout had been a formality of introduction.

Hero formally introduced their party. They were given a vacant hut, and a loaf of bread and some dried fruit. There was a cistern where they could wash.

As darkness closed, torches were ignited and mounted around the central circle. The villagers collected to see the performance. Such events, however minor they might be, always thrilled the children.

Hero took the stage. "We are Xhosa," he said. "Traveling to find help for our daughter, who is beset by a demon. If you see her doing something strange, do not be concerned; the demon afflicts only her, no one else, and usually quits soon. Meanwhile, here is our traditional dance."

Hero and Keeper sat on the ground. Hero brought out his stamping stick. This was a hollow length of wood that made a characteristic resonant sound when struck against the ground. Keeper had a small wood flute. Craft had made both instruments, and they were of fine quality though they looked ordinary.

Crenelle and Tourette took their places, standing, bare-breasted as were most women, their black skins shining. They wore beaded necklaces, brief skirts, and anklets of linked shells. Crenelle was well developed; Tourette was as yet undeveloped, a girl, but her aesthetic form suggested that soon enough she would be a woman to be reckoned with.

Hero struck the ground with his stamping stick. The sound rang out, commencing the dance. Keeper played his pipe, making a melodic tune. He was good at it, having trained since childhood, using the sounds to pacify animals.

Crenelle moved, swinging her hips grandly in the loose skirt. Tourette echoed her motion in a less pronounced manner, as though her slender body lacked the powers of expression of the older woman. They circled each other, their feet touching the beaten earth in time to the complicated cadence Hero set with his stick. There was an art to the beat of the stick, and now it showed.

Then Keeper played a sudden frill, and woman and girl leaped together as if startled, their necklaces lifting. Hero's stick thumped loudly as they landed. The village children laughed. But the adult men were watching closely, for Crenelle in musical motion was a sight to behold, and Tourette, even so young, almost matched her in appeal.

Their dance was genuinely appreciated, because the melody was catching, extremely well played, and perfectly coordinated. Many eyes were on Crenelle, of course, but Hero saw that almost as many were on Tourette. The girl was gaining, in appearance and grace, especially when dancing. Especially in the flickering torchlight, that made it easy to imagine that she was better endowed than she was.

They did several tunes, with several dances. Then the villagers joined in, with the support of their own musicians, especially the drummers. They were satisfied; the family had entertained them well enough. Hero was able to put away his stamping stick, his job done.

The village elder approached. "Yet she has a problem?" he inquired. "She looks quite appealing."

No need to inquire whom the elder meant. "When the fit comes on her, she twitches and makes weird sounds," Hero said. "It can be disconcerting. We need to get the demon out before she can marry."

"She could marry now," the elder said. "She is young, but her potential is manifest."

"Yes. But she could marry far more advantageously without the liability of the demon."

The elder nodded. "It does seem worth the effort." Then he changed the subject. "You know of the Zimba?"

"We are horrified by the Zimba," Hero said. "We were going to see the exorcist in Malindi, but the Zimba are besieging it."

"When they are done with Malindi, if they turn this way, we shall have to flee for our lives."

"What else can you do?" Hero asked sympathetically. He did not speak of the plan to enlist the help of the Segeju, lest there were a spy in the village who would relay the information to the Zimba. Extreme caution was best.

"Nothing, I fear," the elder said, and moved on.

In due course the party ended, and the family retired to the hut. They had once again found a comfortable rest for the night, as they had been doing throughout their journey.

In the morning they resumed their trek, with the good wishes of the villagers. It helped when they could entertain for their lodging. They had precious stones, garnets, that could be traded for accommodations, but they wanted to make those go as far as possible. Every night they didn't use one helped. They were hidden in the mouths of each of them, in tight little packets that in an emergency could be swallowed. Then they could be recovered when they cleared the digestive system. They were too valuable to risk being lost through robbery.

They traveled as rapidly as was feasible, knowing that the town of Malindi could fall at any time. On occasion Hero strung his bow and used it to bring down small game, so that they could eat without depending on villages. They were used to camping out, when they found suitable sleeping places. Often it had to be trees, for the ground could be dangerous at night. But trees, though relatively safe, were also relatively uncomfortable.

The Segeju were some distance up the coast. But travel was good, and they made it there in good time, considering. They were long-since hardened to the rigors of urgent marches. Even Tourette, despite her delicate appearance, kept the pace without difficulty.

They came to the southernmost Segeju outpost. The Segeju were savage tribesman from the north, not yet settled in. They remained on an essentially military footing, at least in this area. They were surely being cautious about their eventual encounter with the Zimba.

Alert scouts spotted and tracked the family for some time before challenging it. Hero realized that most people were on legitimate business, hunting or passing through, so they were merely watched until they lingered too long.

Three Segeju warriors barred their way. "What is your business here?" their leader demanded.

"We seek a healer," Hero said. He paused, for he was aware of something happening.

Now the tension set off Tourette, as sometimes happened, and she went into a series of grunts and wild facial expressions, while her limbs twitched uncontrollably. Her mouth opened and closed and her eyes rolled back. It was a siege, harmless, but frightening to those who did not understand. It did look as if a demon were fighting for possession of her body.

One of the guards nodded. "We have seen that before. Our healers can't cure it."

"Maybe in this case it would be possible," Hero said. "We would like to talk to your healer directly."

The leader shrugged. Tourette was after all a pretty girl, even in the throes of her fit.

The healer was an old woman, with lines of wisdom across her face. "We have seen this before," she said, confirming the scout's comment. "I doubt it's a demon, because exorcism has no effect. We can't help you."

"There is something else," Hero said.

"Oh?" She seemed not especially surprised.

"We needed a pretext to come to you, to talk with your headman."

Her mouth tightened. "If you waste his time, he'll rape your girl."

Tourette shrank back, knowing that this was not an empty threat. She knew she was attractive to men, especially those who liked their women young. But she was ready to risk it. They had discussed it before, to be sure.

"We will not waste his time," Hero said. This was the danger they had understood without discussion. Peaceful villages were one thing; warrior parties were another.

Before long they were before the local chief. "Your women are appealing," he remarked, his gaze passing openly across Crenelle and fixing on Tourette. He *did* like them young. It was a threat.

Hero quickly made the case, including their mission to get the goats. "You know you must encounter the Zimba sometime," he concluded. "This may be your best chance to defeat them. If you catch them at the right moment."

The chief squinted at him assessingly. "We are aware of the opportunity. But the Zimba are alert. Their scouts watch all approaches to Malindi, and they know our appearance. The moment one of us appears, they will sound that alarm and focus defensively, nullifying any possible advantage we might seek. Attack at this time is not feasible."

Hero saw the logic of it. The man was right. There was only one main access from the north, suitable for massed troops, and of course it would be watched. "It seems I did not think it through," he said heavily. "I thought we had a useful idea." Would Tourette pay for his mistake?

"However," the chief said.

So the man was playing a more complicated game. That explained why he had been willing to see them, despite guessing their mission.

Hero met his gaze. "There is a way?"

"You are not Segeju. The Zimba will not recognize Xhosa travelers as a threat. They will merely capture you, rape your women, and eat all four of you. Routine, for them."

Hero caught on. "You want us to distract them."

"So that we can secure their checkpoint and move our troops through efficiently before they know. Then much becomes possible." He eyed Hero. "You are a warrior. A good one. I know the signs. Your brother is not, but I suspect he can use a spear when he has to. And your women will have knives and courage. The four of you could surprise the Zimba warriors, who will have eyes mainly on the women. If you care to. What is your price?"

"The goats," Hero said immediately. "And safe passage out of the town."

"Agreed."

They were given nice food and lodging for the night. But Hero was cynical. "They saw us coming."

"Well, we weren't trying to hide from them," Tourette said.

"I mean that they anticipated our mission, and were prepared to use us, just as we want to use them. They needed nonlocal travelers to work their ruse. They are guesting us now so that they have time to organize for the attack."

Tourette considered. "So all that business about not wasting the chief's time, and how appealing our women are, was just a ruse, not a real threat?"

"No ruse," Hero said. "The threat is real. These people are as cynical and deadly as are the Zimba, apart from the cannibalism. We must perform as we have agreed, or pay the price."

"But the chief seemed so reasonable!"

"He is dealing from power. He knew that I, as a warrior, would understand. It is a fair deal."

She was outraged. "Fair? To risk rape of Mother and me, and who knows what else?"

"And death for Keeper and me."

She took stock. "Mother, you knew? Before we came here?"

"We knew," Crenelle agreed. "It is the only way to get those goats."

"Keeper?"

"Yes. I'm sorry."

She tried to retain her composure, but the tension got to her and she went into a fit of grimaces and grunts. They waited it out, then Crenelle put her arm around her daughter's shoulders. That was all.

Hero sighed inaudibly. An aspect of Tourette's innocence had been abated. Such insights were necessary but seldom pleasant.

"You could have told me," Tourette said accusingly to Keeper.

"I'm sorry," he repeated, pained.

That, too, was disturbing. The girl had a right to feel betrayed, but it was Keeper she chided, rather than her parents. As though she felt a closer connection to her uncle. And he had reacted as if the rebuke was personally deserved, when all he had done was go along with the decision of the family.

But such private interactions and their implications might be meaningless tomorrow. There truly was danger in their mission, as all of them appreciated. The Zimba were not patsies. If they, too, saw the family coming . . .

In the morning they set out south. It was a two-day walk to Malindi. The main access had a checkpoint manned by four warriors, day and night. The Segeju had timed their approach for the middle of a shift, so that help would not be coming soon. All they had to do was take out the four, or distract them long enough for the Segeju to do so. What kind of distraction would be effective? Screaming women being raped.

"Tourette," Hero said somberly as they camped beside the trail the night before the encounter.

"Yes, I have my knife," she replied, showing the iron blade where it was fastened inside her skirt. It was long enough to do the job.

"But can you use it effectively?"

"I know how."

That was not a sufficient answer. "You must not hesitate. Straight in the belly. Then as he folds over, across the neck. If you hesitate, he will disarm you. Then you will be finished."

"I know. I will not hesitate."

"Because you will have to do it alone. That is our strategy."

"Yes."

"Scream as he pursues you, so he believes you are helpless."

"I will, Father."

He kissed her on the forehead. "I love you, Tourette."

"She will do it," Crenelle murmured as he clasped her in the darkness. "So will I."

"You must scream too. They must not suspect."

"I will."

They spoke no more of the matter. They were prepared.

Next day they approached the checkpoint. There was no sign of the Segeju, but Hero knew their scouts were watching. The moment the Zimba guards were taken out, the Segeju would march in force, silently. Surprise was everything.

The guards spied them, and came out to surround them. They were armed with battle spears and long knives. "Who are you?" the leader demanded menacingly, glancing at Hero's knobkerrie and hunting spear with open contempt.

"I am Hero, a Xhosa traveler, with my brother, wife, and daughter. We have business in Malindi."

"You *did* have business there," the leader said, his gaze moving on to the woman and the girl. "Now you have business with us."

"Scatter!" Hero cried as the Zimba closed in, their weapons raised.

The four of them ran in four directions, as rehearsed. The Zimba, liking the sport, separated into four to pursue them. The leader went after Hero.

Hero circled a tree, spun about, drew his knobkerrie, and suddenly closed in on the Zimba. He swung the knob swiftly against the man's head. There was a thunk, and the man went down, his spear only half lifted.

Hero didn't even check on him. He knew the Zimba was dead. The man had seriously underestimated the potential of a warrior with a weapon he knew how to use.

Crenelle and Tourette were screaming, as they were supposed to. Hero oriented on Tourette, as the one more likely to need rescuing. But as he loped into sight of her, he saw her pursuer fall. She had stabbed him in the gut and jumped back. The Zimba was not dead, but he was seriously distracted by the wound.

"Good girl!" Hero said, swinging his knobkerrie down to club the man's head. *Now* he was dead.

Tourette fell into Hero's arms, sobbing. She had done what she knew she had to do, and now was reacting. He held her, comforting her, while looking around. Two down.

"Mother! Keeper!" Tourette exclaimed. "Are they—?"

"We'll see." Crenelle's screaming had stopped; that was probably a good sign, because had the warrior caught and disarmed her, he would be raping her, and she would still be screaming. But once she took him out, screaming would be pointless.

They found Crenelle standing over her antagonist, blood on her knife. "The fool," she said disparagingly. "He tried to grab me barehanded."

"Mother—there's blood on your skirt!"

"I couldn't step back in time." Crenelle wiped her soiled knife on the back of the fallen warrior, and sheathed it again under her skirt. "I'll have some washing to do."

Keeper appeared. There was no blood on him. He had his own knobkerrie. One advantage of that weapon was that it spattered less blood.

Their trap had worked. The way was now clear. "We must tell the Segeju," Keeper said.

"They already know," Hero replied.

Indeed, the scouts were hooting, signaling their people in a rapid relay. The troops would be marching in very short order, for the window of opportunity was only a few hours.

"Meanwhile their guardhouse is ours to ransack," Crenelle said. "We have earned our spoils."

Tourette shuddered, looking faint. She stepped into Keeper's embrace, needing more comfort.

Hero decided to let it be. He followed Crenelle to the guards' hut.

The moment they were out of sight of the others, Crenelle collapsed in tears. Hero held her, as he had held their daughter, supporting her physically and emotionally. "You were magnificent," he murmured, thinking of the way she had maintained her composure so that the others would not be alarmed.

"It was horrible," she sobbed. "I hate killing."

But soon enough she recovered. "We have goats to collect."

They took what few items interested them from the hut, but did not touch the haunch of meat. It looked human.

Now the Segeju were marching. The chief was talking with Keeper and Tourette. He smiled as Hero and Crenelle came up. "You did your part. You will have your goats. But you will have to wait until we reduce the enemy. You will stay with my personal retinue."

So it was that the family had an excellent view of that reduction. It was a literal massacre that made the women avert their gaze.

The Segeju caught the Zimba completely by surprise, just as they were breaching the town's defenses. They struck the Zimba down from behind, and routed them before they fully realized that they were themselves under attack. It was a strategic masterstroke.

"Maybe you had better get in there and see to your goats," the chief murmured to Hero. "My men may not distinguish between one breed or another. They are warriors, not goatkeepers." He laughed at his own witticism.

It was nevertheless a good suggestion. But Keeper would have to come along, to identify the goats. That would leave the women unguarded.

The chief smiled. "Fear not for your kin. I will personally guard them." His eyes surveyed them again as he licked his lips. "If you do not return, I will add them to my harem, as a favor. They well be safe."

That was exactly the kind of danger Hero feared. But in the situation, it was fair. If Hero and Keeper got killed, the women would be at the mercy of the Segeju. The chief's harem was probably their kindest alternative.

Hero, experienced in political machinations as well as combat, saw another aspect. The chief was attracted to the women, and wanted them, but couldn't take them without violating his deal with Hero. He did have his kind of honor, and appearances had to be maintained. So he was finding another way, by phrasing it as a favor. These were treacherous waters.

"Thank you." Hero glanced at Keeper. "Stay close to me; it's dangerous in there."

Keeper was surprised, but knew Hero had reason for his decision. He stood, holding his knobkerrie.

"We'll return soon," Hero told the women.

Crenelle nodded, understanding that there were more than goats at stake. Tourette looked suspicious, but quickly masked the expression.

They loped toward the wall, where the last of the Zimba were being efficiently dispatched. Keeper ran close. "What's your plan?" he puffed.

"I think there's an order out to kill us, and blame it on the confusion of the battle. Then the chief will take over the women as a kindness to the deceased."

"What must we do?"

"Avoid the Segeju warriors. If any pursue us, lead them into concealment, and take them out swiftly. We'll be like the women, seeming unaware. They aren't familiar with the knobkerrie either."

Keeper nodded. He was not a warrior, but could use his weapon, especially when buttressed by his big brother.

They found an opening and scrambled through, into the town. No one was in sight; the folk of Malindi were of course hiding, apart from their defending warriors, who had suffered severe attrition. At least there was no fire; the Segeju had come in time to prevent that.

"The goats should be in the central compound," Keeper said.

But as they headed for it, three Segeju warriors intercepted them. "You the Xhosa?" one asked. "Need help?"

"We are," Hero agreed. "We're fine, just looking for our goats."

"Good." The three raised their war spears.

Hero leaped to one side, Keeper to the other. Both swung their clubs in short swift arcs, catching two heads along the jaws. Without pausing Hero jumped at the third warrior, who barely had time to parry with his spear. Hero swept it aside, as the club was more massive, then reversed the swing and caught the man hard across the face.

None of the blows had been hard enough to kill. Hero remedied that by taking more time to strike each man again, hard enough. They could not afford to have the men report on this interaction. The chief would fathom what had happened, but be unable to make an issue of it. He had underestimated Hero's understanding, and his prowess, and his weapon. Warriors who specialized in iron tended to disparage wood. That was their mistake. In close quarters, the club was deadly.

They found the compound. It was empty, except for bones. "They slaughtered the goats!" Keeper said, horrified.

"They were hungry," Hero said. "Besieged, unable to forage outside. They had to eat what they had."

Keeper nodded unhappily. "I wish we had been a month earlier."

"They still might not have been special. It was only a story."

"Only a story," Keeper agreed grimly. "For which we risked our lives."

"We need to return," Hero said. "To fetch the girls, and trek south."

"Rapidly," Keeper agreed with a feral smile.

They made their way out of the town. The townspeople were appearing now, as news of their reprieve spread. They would welcome the Segeju, who had rescued them. Of course the Segeju had their own reason, but they had saved the town from a truly awful fate.

The chief seemed not completely surprised to see them. "No goats?"

"They got eaten during the siege," Keeper said. "But we thank you for your help, and will go home now."

"Of course," the chief agreed. Naturally he understood what had happened, and accepted it. They had won his respect. He would not connive further.

•

The Zimba were indeed thorough cannibals, as represented here. Presumably the drought destroyed their agriculture and herds, so they turned to the next convenient source of food: their neighbors. Until overwhelmed by the Segeju in 1589 as they were breaching the defenses of Malindi. That attack, coming as the attention of the Zimba was occupied by the siege of the town, was so perfectly timed it could hardly have been coincidence. The Segeju must have been watching, waiting for their opportunity.

Were there special goats? Unfortunately we will never know.

15

CITY ISLAND

The Spanish conquest of the Aztecs and Inca was swift, because they were centralized societies. The diseases, such as smallpox, the Spanish inadvertently brought surely made it possible, as they may have wiped out as much as 95 percent of the population, leaving a shambles of once-proud empires. But the Maya existed as several independent states, each of which had to be conquered separately, and the process took 170 years.

The last Maya holdout was the Itza, in the central lowlands of the Yucatan Peninsula, not far from the former splendor of Tikal. They had moved there from the north, perhaps circa 1200 AD, and lived in swampy jungle that the Spaniards found inhospitable. They lacked precious metals like gold and silver, other than those imported for royal ornamentation, so the Spaniards' greed for such things was not a motive. But as time passed the Spaniards did covet both the land and the potential slave labor there. Naturally they phrased their campaign as religious: to convert the heathen. The actual Yucatan campaign lasted about seventy years, with the Maya waging effective guerrilla warfare.

The setting is what is now northern Guatemala, by Lake Peten Itza. The time is 1697 AD.

Keeper gazed out across the water, where the Spanish fort was visible on the opposite shore. He was not a military man—far from it!—but this did not bode well. The Spanish were persistent and ruthless, and they were acting with sinister purpose. What did they have in mind?

"That is artillery," Craft explained. "Metal tubes that hurl metal balls with great force." He understood things that were made, including the devastating weapons of the invaders.

"But they are far across the lake," Keeper protested.

"Such weapons can hurl their balls across the lake to strike our walls and buildings. They have also built ships, one of which is large and has a cannon. Our arrows and spears will not stop it. I fear we will not be able to repulse this attack, when it comes. And it will come soon."

Keeper dreaded the news. "Is this then the end?"

"Hero fears it is. Every time K'atan 11 Ajaw comes, in our cyclical history, there are momentous consequences. We are in such a period now, and may be doomed."

Keeper grimaced. "Hero's our warrior. He surely has more practical reason for his concern."

"Yes. Our city Noh Petén is on a fortified island on a lake in the jungle in a swamp that has resisted all prior Spanish attacks. But this time they are making a supreme effort, and have formidable equipment. Hero says our best course is to flee."

Keeper glanced sidelong at his brother. "Is he speaking of our family, or of our culture?"

"Both. We shall have to act quickly when the time comes."

"I hate the thought. What of my maize fields, my bean stakes, my squash terraces? Without careful irrigation they will not endure."

Craft nodded with understanding. "Neither will your tame turkeys or little meat animals. But we can't take them along. This is a crisis."

Keeper knew it. His plants and creatures had fed the king and his staff for years, but they were not mobile. Would the Maize God ever forgive him?

Keeper turned to look across the city. They were standing on the upper deck of one of the twin ceremonial towers at the south side of the city, an excellent vantage. The towers were decorative rather than functional, providing the city an impressive outline from the lake. They had steep stone stairways that led to high temple doors that led nowhere. They were meant to be admired, rather than used. They certainly were impressive, standing some eight times the height of a man. All for show.

Except that in the event of attack from the lake, the towers and the wall between them would serve as a formidable defense. How could anyone approach, when lookouts stood on the towers and archers lined that wall? So there was a practical aspect to the decoration, as Craft had clarified for him in the past.

Actually, when it came to practical aspects, even the broad plaza of the central city had a special function. The seemingly level paved surfaces really were subtly graded to convey rainwater to the troughs that fed the city's reservoirs. True, this was an island in the lake. But if it were under siege, fetching water from the lake could be dangerous. So the rain was automatically collected, and the reservoirs kept as full as feasible. Keeper, who was in charge of the plants and animals that sustained the city, truly appreciated that most valuable resource, water. There was a large population to feed, and those plants and animals were a vital supplement to the supplies that were constantly imported from the cultivated mainland.

The rest of the city was similarly impressive, with its even higher sacrificial pyramid, and broad central plaza, and spreading temple. There was the king's palace, and the outlying residential buildings. And the terraced fields where there was room for them, mostly outside the walls. It had taken centuries for all the magnificent buildings to be built, but the result was grandeur and beauty. Raised causeways radiated from the plaza, connecting the rest of the island.

They made their way carefully down to the plaza, their spot reconnaissance done. Keeper had thought them safe from attack, but Craft's words left him shaken. If the walls were not proof against the Spaniards, what real defense did they have? Only the strength of their archers against the guns of the Spaniards. Keeper hoped that would be enough.

Keeper's wife Crenelle approached. She kissed him, then murmured, "Haven and I have special things to see to. Can you watch the children?"

He knew what she meant, and dreaded it. The women were preparing food and personal effects for emergency travel. "Already?"

"Haven says Harbinger says that the attack could come tomorrow. We must be ready to act without hesitation."

Keeper nodded. "I'll do it."

"Rebel will help." Crenelle departed.

Rebel was already helping. She had gathered the three children at Keeper's home: Haven's son Risk, twelve, Tuho's daughter Tula, ten, and Keeper and Crenelle's daughter Allele, nine. The boy was handsome, and the girls were on the verge of beautiful.

That was part of the problem. A noble who liked them young was casting a lecherous eye on both girls, and the family lacked the power to prevent him from acting. They would have left the town before, but the girls were being watched. They would be intercepted if they tried to leave the island. Yet that was not the worst.

Keeper was appalled by the prospect of having the barbarous Spaniards overrun the town. But he was also appalled by the threat to his daughter Allele. Yet maybe if the town was lost, they would be able to rescue the children. It was an ugly choice, but at least they might save something.

"Where's Mother?" Risk asked alertly.

"Haven and Crenelle are preparing a surprise," Rebel said a bit tightly. "Maybe for tomorrow. We have to stay out of their hair."

"What's going on?" Tula asked. She had always had an uncanny awareness of things.

Rebel glanced at Keeper, evidently trying to decide what to tell the children.

"The Spaniards are getting ready to attack," Keeper said. "Maybe tomorrow. It may be bad."

"But didn't we stop them before?" Tula demanded.

"Why do they keep coming?" Allele asked in turn.

Keeper exchanged another glance with Rebel. They were not going to be able to keep it from the children much longer. It was better to prepare them. In easy stages, if possible. "It will be worse this time," he said.

"Why?"

Rebel plunged in. She had always been militant, and had studied history. "Here is part of it. A hundred and seventy years ago the Spaniards first came to our land. They demanded that we swear loyalty to their king and give up our gods. We fought a battle and lost, but did not surrender, and finally drove them out."

"Yes!" Risk agreed.

"But a few years later they returned with more power, and captured some of our cities. We rose up against them and drove them out again. But some Maya sided with the Spaniards, and a few years after that they took most of our lands."

"Except for *our* land," Risk said.

"Yes. About seventy years ago the Spaniards marched on Noh Petén, but we killed them. Two years later they tried again, and we killed them again. That kept them away for sixty years."

"Yes!" This time the girls joined the boy in their appreciation.

Keeper winced. If only it were that simple.

Rebel continued grimly. "Two years ago a force of sixty Spanish soldiers and Maya allies attacked, but we beat them back. But that made them angry, and now they have come by the hundreds."

"So that's bad," Risk said.

"Very bad," Rebel agreed.

"They made a road through the jungle," Keeper said. "They brought equipment. They even brought a big boat in pieces, and put it together on the lake. They have weapons we have never faced before. It will be very hard to beat them back this time."

Now the children took it seriously. "Will we win again?" Risk asked.

Rebel shook her head. "No. Not unless they do something stupid."

"There's more," Tula said, looking truly frightened.

"We don't need to go into that," Keeper said quickly.

"What about the Long Calendar?" Risk asked. "What does it say?"

"That records significant events," Rebel said. "It doesn't predict future outcomes."

"Sometimes it does," Tula said. "Like Baktun 13."

"What is that?" Allele asked.

"That is too complicated to go into now," Rebel said.

All three children rebelled. "No it isn't," Allele said. "I want to know."

Well, it was a distraction when they needed it. Rebel gave them a simplified version. "The Long Calendar started many, many years ago, before the time of the Maya. It counts days, and it never repeats. Twenty days make a uinal, eighteen uinal make a tun, which is 360 days, and twenty tun make a katun, which is 7,200 days or about twenty years, and twenty katun make a baktun, which is 144,000 days or about 395 years. There are thirteen baktun in the Long Count. Baktun 12 started almost eighty years ago, and Baktun 13 will start 315 years from now. So it really isn't relevant to the present crisis."

"Don't the Spaniards have a different calendar?" Risk asked.

"Yes. But that doesn't relate well either."

"When is now on theirs?"

Keeper stepped in. "1697."

"Days?"

"Years."

Risk shook his head, not making sense of it. The Spanish had weird gods and weird dates.

"It's very bad," Tula said.

"That's why we oppose them," Rebel said. "We don't want to have to honor their mixed-up system."

Allele wasn't satisfied. "Our gods will help us. We can make a big sacrifice."

"Yes, the way we do for every big occasion," Risk agreed. "The bigger the sacrifice, the more the gods will help."

"Not this time," Keeper said. "This is beyond the gods."

"How can you say that?" Risk demanded. "The gods can do anything."

"We can't afford the sacrifice," Rebel said.

Tula screamed. Rebel quickly pulled her close, but the child was inconsolable.

Now Allele came alert. "She knows something! She always knows! What's so horrible?"

There was no help for it. "The priests did a reading," Keeper said heavily. "They concluded that there has to be an awful sacrifice to the Rain God."

"The Rain God!" Risk said. "So he'll make a storm and blow away or sink those boats!"

"But that's good, isn't it?" Allele asked.

"No," Rebel said grimly, still hugging Tula.

"But if the boats sink, they can't get here, can they?"

Tula screamed again.

Then Risk caught on. "Children! They sacrifice children to the Rain God!"

Allele paled. "And we're children. Fair ones."

"But not us," Risk said. "There are other children."

Keeper got out the rest of it. "A noble is interested in Tula and Allele. He . . . he asked to . . . to have both of you. We refused, of course."

Allele was not too young to miss the import. "I think I know who. His last mistress is getting too old. Thirteen."

"But that's not the same as sacrifice," Risk protested.

"When we told him no, he didn't like it," Keeper said. "Then the priest made his reading."

"Retaliation!" Risk said.

"Yes. Maybe if we change our minds, the priest will do a different reading."

"So it's him—or death," Allele said.

"Or escape," Rebel said. "We are making ready. Don't tell."

"That's what Haven and Crenelle are doing," Risk said. "Packing supplies."

"Without alerting the priests or nobles," Keeper agreed. "Hero and Harbinger are getting the boats ready. We have a secret place to go to. We'll leave tonight."

Tula screamed again.

Suddenly armed men filled the chamber. "But you'll do it without the children," the captain said.

They were helpless. Any attempt to resist would only get them killed. The priests and nobles had anticipated their attempt to escape, and struck when they had confirmation.

They carried the screaming children out. Keeper and Rebel were left alone. There was no need to arrest them; they were going nowhere without the children.

"It's my fault!" Keeper moaned. "I shouldn't have spoken."

"The children had to know," Rebel said. "They were catching on anyway. We were both careless."

She had spoken bravely enough, but now she dissolved into tears. Keeper tried to comfort his sister, but the horror was too big for comfort.

Yet how could they have allowed the girls to become the playthings of the corrupt noble?

At it turned out, the authorities were not so careless as to leave them long to their own treacherous devices. The warriors returned, and hauled the two of them roughly to a nether cell. There were the others, already rounded up: Hero, Craft, Haven, Crenelle, Harbinger, and Tuho. It was no glad encounter, and not just because it was crowded.

•

Next morning the news was that the Spaniards were assembling their boats, making obvious preparations for a massive attack. The warriors were at the ramparts, ready to repulse them. But Keeper knew it wouldn't be enough. The main boat was a small ship, with metal armor; arrows and spears would bounce off. That was the lesser threat.

"The artillery," Craft murmured. "That's what will destroy us."

"Surely a few hurled rocks won't hurt us," Keeper said. "Unless one happens to strike a person on the head."

Craft didn't answer. Keeper didn't have time to debate the point; he had been elected by the family to make a plea to the king. Only the king could overrule the priestly edict. But how was he to approach the king, when the guards wouldn't let any of them out of the crowded cell?

Then they were brought out, their hands bound behind them, and led to the temple. This was not promising.

But Keeper tried. "I must talk to the king," he said. "It is my right."

The guards consulted. They had been friends of the family, until this crisis, and surely did not approve of what was happening. But they would be sacrificed themselves if they did not obey orders. They sent one of their number to inquire.

King Canek was surely hard-pressed, but he granted Keeper a brief audience, because Keeper had done good work with animals and plants. Keeper was brought, bound, to see the king, who was garbed in his formal regalia for the sacrificial occasion. The king wore a large crown of pure gold, with a crest of gold, and his ears were covered with gold disks. The disks had hangings that shook and fell over his shoulders as he moved. On his arms were rings of pure gold. It was highly impressive, in part because Keeper knew that gold was exceedingly rare, and most of what existed in the city was what the king was wearing here. His tunic was pure white, copiously adorned with blue embroidery. He wore a broad black sash, signaling that he was also a priest of the Itza. His sandals were fashioned of blue thread with many gold jingles. It was his royal dress uniform, intended to be impressive, but Keeper couldn't help it: he was impressed.

"What is your concern?" the king inquired, as if he didn't know. There was that in his aspect that hinted he regretted the situation. Keeper had always gotten along well with him.

"My daughter, our children—the priests have taken them for the sacrifice," Keeper said. "I come to plead for their lives. They are innocent, and we love them."

The king gave him a serious look. "I understand. But we face incipient invasion, and our head priest knows best. I dare not overrule him, lest disaster befall us. I am sorry."

And that was that. The king had spoken. Keeper bowed and retreated. There was nothing else he could do. Nothing else the king could do. They were caught in the crisis, complicated as it was by the web of deceit concerning the children.

The sacrifice ceremony proceeded all too swiftly. There was music, dancing, and the burning of pom incense that Keeper himself had made from the resin of the copal tree. It was time for the bloodletting.

The priests brought out the three children, who had of course been drugged; they walked without animation, possessing no free will. They were placed before the sacrificial altar and tied there, their chests bared. There was chanting, the official offering of this blood to the Rain God. Then the head priest brought out the wicked obsidian sacrificial knife.

The priest was going to cut out their living hearts. And the family had to watch.

Crenelle sank to the floor. She had fainted, unable to bear the thought of seeing her daughter so cruelly murdered.

The guards hauled her roughly back to her feet. She was required to watch. But that gave Keeper an idea. If they could somehow stall the process, maybe there would come a chance to break it up. Their feet were free; he could lurch into the priest, maybe causing the man to drop the knife. It wasn't much of a hope, but any hope was better than none.

Suddenly there was a boom of thunder. The Rain God was answering, though there had been no sign of a storm before. The priest paused, perplexed. Any signal from the Rain God was important. What did this mean?

Something crashed into the wall of the building, smashing a hole in it.

They all looked, startled. The priest stood frozen, his blade uplifted. This was a remarkable response by the Rain God, considering that the offerings had not yet been made.

There was another boom, and another part of the wall was smashed open. This time part of the ceiling collapsed.

"The bombardment," Craft murmured.

Craft had been correct in his prediction: these were not pebbles, but solid metal balls that blasted apart what they struck. It was a devastating barrage.

A third boom and crash. Now the roof of the temple was cracking, and stones were falling to the floor.

Even the priest realized that this was no ordinary thunderstorm. He lowered the blade, dismayed. This did not seem like an expression of godly favor.

"The Rain God is angry!" Keeper shouted, surprising himself. "He wanted to save these children for his own purposes. Now we face his wrath!"

Panic erupted. They thought the Rain God was hurling thunderbolts. The musicians scrambled to get out of the temple, and the guards were as eager to escape as they were. Only the king paused, demonstrating his courage. He walked to Keeper, put his hands on his shoulders, turned him about, and pressed something into one of his bound hands. Then he moved on outside.

Keeper felt the object. It was cold and hard, a small stone. No—it was an obsidian knife!

"Hero!" Keeper said, turning his back to his warrior brother.

Hero caught on immediately. He came close, turned his own back, and his hands took the knife. In a moment he cut Keeper's bonds. Then Keeper took the knife and did the same for Hero.

Soon, as the bombardment continued, they were all free, including the three children. But the temple was collapsing around them.

"This way," Craft said.

The women guided the children, who were dazed but not unconscious. They followed Craft out of the temple. No one paid attention, because the bombardment was destroying walls and buildings alike. They still thought it was the wrath of the god.

They made their way through the confusion to the three canoes Haven and Crenelle had stocked. The men paddled, while the women and children sat in the centers.

Now they saw that others had the same idea. Many boats were fleeing the island. The people knew that the end had come. The last independent kingdom of the Maya was doomed.

But at least the children were safe.

A number were war canoes, not fleeing but paddling out to encounter the enemy. Their archers were braced, ready to loose their arrows.

But as they drew out from the harbor, they saw the Spanish fleet looming, led by a monstrous wooden ship with a metal-armored deck well above the water line. Its rail bristled with Spanish soldiers.

As soon as the Spaniards spied the canoes, they leveled their guns. There was a new, closer booming, and smoke puffed out.

The men aboard the leading war canoe cried out. Several had been wounded, and the canoe had been holed and was sinking. Their arrows had had no apparent effect. The guns of the Spanish were too much.

"Get out of here!" Hero called from his canoe.

They paddled rapidly away from the Spanish fleet. These were not even war canoes, and would have no chance against the Spanish. Their hope was that they would pass unnoticed, and not attract any fire.

They were not that lucky. One war canoe veered to follow them. The Spaniards were accompanied by Maya allies who fought beside them. Hero cursed them for traitors, but that hardly abated the threat they represented.

Keeper paddled desperately, as did his brothers and Rebel, but they could not outrace the war canoe. Steadily it overhauled them. Then it paused, merely keeping the pace.

"Surrender!" the war canoe commander called. "Agree to serve the new masters, and you will be spared."

"What of our women and girls?" Rebel called back.

"They are our property. They will be well treated if they behave."

That meant if they submitted to multiple rapes without resistance or attempts to kill themselves. If they made themselves useful as continuing mistresses, regardless of their ages.

"You are Maya," Keeper called. "How can you betray your own kind?"

"We are Christian Maya," the commander replied. "We have seen the light. You, too, must convert and worship the one true god."

Obviously that god did not object to the rape of children. "We can't do that," Keeper said.

"Then you die." The war canoe resumed its approach. It bristled with warriors. Soon it would grapple their canoes, one by one, and dispatch the fugitives.

Hero stood carefully in his canoe, orienting his bow. Immediately the opposing warriors dropped their paddles and scrambled for their bows. Hero did not wait. He loosed one arrow. It sailed high and long, and came down right in the chest of the commander. There was a cry as he fell, transfixed, and the boat ceased its pursuit.

Only Hero could have done it from that range, from such a precarious stance. He had always been the best shot. This time that ability had saved them.

They came to the shore and scrambled out of their canoes. They ran into the forest, the women dragging the recovering children by their hands. In moments they were shielded by the trees. The Spanish would not be able to catch them. They were not yet safe, but they had a good chance.

Yet Keeper was grief stricken by the fate of their people. The world they had known had been destroyed.

•

It was a remarkable effort by the Spaniards. They built a road through the jungle so that their mule train could transport supplies, artillery, and even a small dismantled warship they reassembled on Lake Peten. On the morning of March 13, 1697, they attacked, with Maya allies, and were victorious. They immediately set to work destroying the idolatrous idols and, indeed, any remaining civilization of the "barbarians." They burned the library of books containing what they called "lies of the devil." It was to take centuries to fathom the lost Mayan written language. Who, then, were really the barbarians?

The remnants of the Itza Maya fled into the surrounding jungle. They never regained their former prominence, and only a few hundred survived to the twentieth century. Conditions generally have been hostile to the several Maya tribes, with partly covert attempts to eradicate them.

Noh Petén, or Tayasal, was erased, and the modern city of Flores built over its ruins. The stones of the temple were taken for a Christian church. Today it is difficult to find traces of the original town; indeed, there is some question whether that really was its location.

It was, indeed, the end of a great culture. True, we of the modern world don't approve of human sacrifice. Yet we tolerate execution of those with whom we disagree, and make determined war on others whose religion differs from ours. Is this so much different?

The evidence suggests that the prior upheavals of the Maya were climatic in nature, with severe droughts stressing the population, bringing savage warfare. This time the worst enemy was probably disease, such as smallpox, decimating the population so that relatively small Spanish forces could overwhelm the natives, as mentioned in the forenote. Only the isolation of Noh Petén enabled it to survive as long as it did.

There were periodic rebellions by the Maya as time and oppression continued, but they remained a beaten people. Only relatively recently have the marvels of their calendar and cities been studied and appreciated. One can't help wishing that at least one of their cities had survived independently to the present day.

16

BOTANY BAY

Thanks to a spot of trouble in North America, which had ideas of independent nationhood, England was deprived of her convenient penal colonies there. But she still had convicts and London slum refuse to dispose of. Australia was wide open, unpopulated except for a few Aborigines that were of no account, according to the authorities. So arrangements were made to ship the refuse there. The idea was that they would found a colony and soon become self-sufficient, thus relieving the mother country of the burden of supporting them.

The First Fleet, consisting of eleven ships—two warships, six convict transports, and three supply ships—set sail May 13, 1787. There was no complete count, but the total number of personnel embarking was about 1,530, of which about 1,483 arrived at Botany Bay, because of deaths during the eight-month voyage. About one quarter of the almost 800 convicts shipped were female, including fourteen children. About 750 arrived, the children having increased to twenty-two because of births along the way. This was the nucleus of the new colony.

Of course, the Aboriginal natives had a different take on this enterprise. The place is the vicinity of what is now Sydney, Australia, but was then Botany Bay because of its variety of plants. The time is January 1788.

Rebel made her way to the hollow beside the water of the bay where the special herbs grew. She was the only one who knew their location, and she harvested them carefully, to be sure the cluster could regenerate. Herbs had to be treated with respect, or their magic lost effect.

As she moved, she pondered the question that was tormenting her increasingly. She was married to Harbinger, a fine man, and she knew she made him happy. But she was barren. Their people kept their numbers low, so as not to overburden the scant resources of the area. Young girls were first married to old men, so they would not conceive, and young boys were forbidden contact with girls or women until they navigated a complicated series of initiations. But that did not mean that there should not ever be children.

Harbinger was thirty-two, two years older than Rebel. It was time for him to start his family. But he couldn't start it with Rebel. They both knew that.

Her sister Haven was Harbinger's age, and near the end of her potential. She could give him a child—but it needed to be soon. Yet it couldn't happen as long as Rebel was in the way.

She had discussed this with Haven, but Haven would not agree to displace Rebel in this manner. So they were at an impasse.

But if Rebel took herself out of the picture, then Haven would do it. She would have no choice. Haven liked Harbinger well enough. She would have married him, had he gotten over a certain initial difficulty the two of them had had, and asked her. Rebel had gotten him almost by default.

There were certain herbs that would send a person to the spirit realm, swiftly and silently. Rebel knew where they grew. All she had to do was eat one. But if there was any suspicion that she had done it deliberately, neither Harbinger nor Haven would take advantage of their opportunity. It had to be by accident, and that was hard to arrange.

For one thing, Rebel didn't want to die. She wanted to live and love, to be happy and make a man happy. A man who didn't need children. But that would mean leaving the tribe, because there were no such men in her own tribe. She didn't want to do that; her ties with her siblings were too strong.

What, then, was she to do? That was the problem that balked her. There had to be an answer, but it eluded her.

O Spirits of the land, help me, she prayed silently.

There was a sound. She looked up, startled, and there was a strange man standing before her. He had hair on his face and oddly baggy clothing on his body, in contrast to her own loincloth. He was staring at her bare breasts.

Well, that suggested that he was of the mortal realm, because though her breasts were excellent, the spirits hardly cared about sex appeal. Who was he, and from what tribe? She had never seen his like. He was so pale in his face and hands! But it did seem that the spirits had answered her.

Then there was a sound behind her. She whirled, but too late to escape the second man. He grabbed her by the arms.

"Let me go!" she exclaimed. She could have disabled him with a knee, but preferred for the moment to play the role of the helpless girl. She wanted to learn more before she drew on her combat skill. It would be a rebuke to the spirits if she did not consider their offer carefully.

The man uttered something unintelligible. The other man responded. It seemed to be some sort of language, but like none she had heard. They must be from a very long way away.

The two men consulted. Then one produced some cord and bound her wrists behind her back. They were going to do something with her, or take her somewhere.

Rebel used the toes of one foot to catch the vine anklet on her other foot. It was an intricate anklet of her own design, identifying her immediately. She pushed it off and left it on the ground. That would show where she had been. Her brother Hero would come looking for her when she didn't return from her forage, and he would find it, and would know that something had happened to her.

Now the men walked, hauling her along with them. She had to walk, or fall; she chose to walk. Where were they taking her? This was seeming less like spirit intervention and more like something else.

They brought her to a busy camp beside the water. Beyond it were what looked like enormous canoes with treelike poles rising high above them. Rebel had never seen, dreamed, or even imagined such things. This must after all be the spirit realm!

As soon as they entered the camp, men clustered around, exclaiming in their spirit language and gazing at Rebel's breasts. She liked being admired, but this was more attention than she was comfortable with. All these men were oddly white-skinned, like her captors, with hair growing on their faces. All were similarly garbed. Evidently they didn't much like showing their bodies. If her body were as pale as theirs, she might be hesitant to show it too.

Her two captors took her to where a big structure was being put up. It looked like a kind of house, but was huge. There was a man in impressively strange clothing, evidently a leader, because they deferred to him.

The leader took a solid look at Rebel. He, oddly, did not seem to approve of her breasts. Then he said something. Immediately a man brought an armful of cloth. This turned out to be a set of clothing similar to what the men were wearing: a heavy shirt and trousers. They removed the cord binding her wrists so that her arms were free, and indicated that she should put on the clothing.

"I don't need stuff like that," Rebel protested. But then she saw one of the men watching her from across the compound. He looked vaguely familiar, or maybe it was just his manner. His eyes were fixed on her breasts and he was licking his lips. *All* these men seemed to be obsessed by breasts, one way or another, as if they were not perfectly natural and attractive accessories. He desired her—but she did not desire him. His stare made her feel like chattel. A man like that had raped her once, and bashed her on the head so that she lost her memory for a time. His name had been Bub, and he no longer existed, but she thought of this new man as another Bub. So she struggled into the shirt, but the trousers were so large and baggy that they covered her feet and dragged on the ground.

The men consulted, and decided that the shirt would do. Then the leader made a decision. He spoke curtly, and another man came up. This one was young and handsome; she liked his look despite his alien skin color and hairy face.

After further consultation, the young man approached her. He tapped himself on the chest. "George," he said.

He was introducing himself! She tapped herself on her voluminous new shirt. "Rebel."

"Revel," he repeated.

"Rebel."

"Rebel." This time he got it right.

She pointed to him, to show she understood. "George."

He smiled. He was really handsome then.

The leader spoke. The other men scattered back to whatever they were supposed to be doing. Then the leader went on about his own business. She was left with George.

He spoke to her, but of course she couldn't understand the words. So he took her by the hand and led her to the shelter of a tree at the fringe of their work area. He sat by the trunk and gestured her to do the same. She did so, sitting facing him with her knees bent before her so she could wrap her arms around them for support.

George blushed. That was interesting. It took her only a moment to fathom why: he had seen between her lifted thighs to her loincloth, the shirt out of the way. She had good legs, and they affected men, especially in this position. He desired her, and this time she was not concerned. She already knew he was no rapist. In fact, the chances were that he had never been with a woman, not having the courage to approach any sexually. That gave her control of the relationship.

She smiled at him. "I think we shall get along, George." But then she adjusted her legs to show less, because she wanted to know more about him than the state of his desire.

He got down to business. He tapped his chest again. "George." He indicated hers. "Rebel." Then he took the cloth of the shirt between thumb and fingers. "Shirt." He reached cautiously to touch hers. "Shirt."

"Shirt," she agreed, getting the word.

He touched his right hand with his left forefinger. "Hand." He touched hers. "Hand."

She took his hand in hers and squeezed it gently, causing him to blush again. "Hand," she agreed.

He touched his foot, which was covered by a heavy framework. "Foot," he said. Then he reconsidered. He took hold of the framework and pulled it off his foot. "Shoe." He touched his bare foot. "Foot."

Rebel wore no shoes. She lifted up one foot and touched it. "Foot." She smiled again.

George was blushing furiously. She had shown him more than her foot, in the process of lifting it. He had gotten the best glimpse yet. She was beginning to enjoy this.

They continued with words. Hand, Foot, Elbow, Arm, Knee, Leg, Head, Hair, Face, Eyes, Nose, Mouth. Rebel was good with words, when she tried, and she was trying now. She remembered each as it was introduced. Soon she knew a number of parts of the body, including "Breasts," gleaned via the worst-yet siege of blushing when she lifted her shirt clear to point them out.

Then they walked around the compound, and she learned Man, Spade, House, Tree, Flower, Woman. That last was not the best experience; the woman was old and seemed sickly, and she did not like the presence of young lush Rebel at all. Rebel, in turn, did not like the continuing stares of the man who was eying her. He was working, but orienting on her at every opportunity.

She needed to pee. But where? She did not want to do it in sight of these men. Men could react strongly to the sight of a woman peeing; she knew from experience. So she had to ask George, gesturing to the necessary anatomy.

He blushed again, naturally, but led her to the place set aside for such functions. She could tell by the smell. So she squatted and did it, while he faced away. That was interesting; he had the opportunity to see, but chose not to. She took that as further evidence of his niceness.

They returned to the main camp. There was the Bub man, staring, leering. He knew what she had been doing. *He* would have looked.

There was a sound. It was a Bell, rung by a Cook to summon the Men. They were serving Food, consisting of Bread, Cabbage, and Beer. That last turned out to be a foul-tasting but interesting liquid, being alcoholic. George cautioned her to drink it slowly, but she already knew its nature and could handle it. She knew all about fermenting berries.

They continued the word lesson, and as evening approached they were beginning to converse more meaningfully. She learned that this was a Colony, and the leader was Governor Phillip. But the Colonists were Convicts: people who had broken Laws—the precise meaning was vague, but it seemed they had acted badly—and been sent here on Ships—the monstrous canoes—to live so they wouldn't bother the people back in England. England was really obscure; it seemed it was an Island very far away across the Water where many many people lived.

Now there was a problem. "You are captive," George explained. "Can't let you go."

She understood about that. This was a foreign tribe, and they had caught her. What George did not understand was that she might be satisfied to remain a captive, because it would solve the problem of her marriage. So she was not about to try to flee, if that was his concern. For one thing, she knew that if she did, he would get the blame, and she didn't want that. She liked him, and knew that he liked her, or at least her body, as his blushes signaled.

The problem, it turned out, was that she needed a place to sleep here. George took her to the Female Compound, but the motley women protested vigorously. They did not want a (young, pretty) Savage among them. Rebel understood their case perfectly; she had that effect on ordinary women, and these ones were worse than ordinary. She made them look bad. But joining the Men in their Barracks was out of the question. Too many were clearly like Bub.

George consulted with Governor Phillip. Rebel couldn't follow all of the dialogue, but she understood more than the Governor thought. He didn't want to let her go, but understood why neither the men's nor women's barracks were suitable. It was his job to make decisions, and finally he made one: the Ship.

George was a Midshipman, someone who had some authority on the ship. He normally spent his nights there. So he would take Rebel there. She was somewhat in awe of that, because the idea of sleeping on a giant canoe was so new as to be daunting. But the notion also intrigued the adventurous side of her. What an experience!

They got in a truly canoe-sized boat, only this turned out to have

Oars, which were like paddles tied to its sides, and the oarsman pulled on them instead of pushing, so that he faced backward. But it moved along well enough, and soon they came to the Ship. There they caught on to ropes and were hauled to the Deck, which was well above the surface of the water. Then they went Belowdecks, into a cavelike labyrinth of narrow passages and Holds. It was dark, but George had a Lamp that was like a torch, with a small flame that burned steadily and gave off sufficient light.

They came to his Cabin, which was a section separated somewhat from the rest of the Hold. It had two Hammocks. He showed her how they worked: they were for sleeping in! Amazed, she got into one, and promptly spun over and fell on the deck. He had to show her how to stay safely within it.

But something else was wrong. She was feeling increasingly ill. In fact, she needed to vomit.

George caught on. "You're Seasick!" he exclaimed. "I should have realized."

"Sick," she agreed. Then she vomited into the wooden basin he fetched. After that she felt a bit better.

He explained, as well as he was able, and she followed most of it. People who were not used to ships were bothered by the way they rolled, especially when at anchor. It made them sick. Usually it passed in a few days.

"Days!" she exclaimed, appalled.

He spread his hands. There was nothing he could do. It was too late to return to land, and nowhere safe for her there. But if she closed her eyes and lay down, it should not be as bad.

She tried, but the hammock rolled her out again, and the next siege of sickness was building. That got to her; too much was new and strange, and she couldn't handle it. She started to cry, which annoyed her, because she preferred to be always strong and independent.

"I'm sorry," George said, and put his arms about her.

He was comforting her! This was ridiculous, but she really appreciated it.

She turned into him and kissed him. He fell back, embarrassed, but she stayed with him. She had already decided to seduce him, and this was a distraction she needed.

"Rebel," he protested. "I didn't bring you here to . . . to . . . I want you to be safe."

"I know," she said. And kissed him again.

After that, he was in her control. He was inexperienced, but more than willing, once he understood this was her intention. She got him out of his trousers, freeing his rampant member, and they did it on the tilting deck. In moments he was spurting within her. She did not have an equivalent climax, but that was not the point. She enjoyed making him hers.

"Oh Rebel!" he panted. "I think I love you!"

Which was part of the point. She wanted to bind him to her emotionally, and this was the most feasible way. Men did tend to foolishly love the women who seduced them. "Love," she agreed, kissing him once more.

They lay there a while, holding hands. Her sickness had faded; the distraction had been enough.

Then he tried again to show her how to sleep in the hammock, but she still did not feel comfortable there. Until he made the most persuasive argument.

"The sickness is from swaying. The hammock doesn't sway the same. You should not be sick in it."

She worked it out. "Hammock. No sick."

"Yes."

So she tried it again, and again, and finally caught the way of it, and was able to hang suspended in that narrow net. He was right: when she closed her eyes, it was like being in a tree, swaying slightly in the wind, a natural motion that did not make her ill. She was tired, and slept well enough.

In the dim morning she found him standing beside her hammock, gazing raptly on her. She knew that look.

She got out of the hammock as he steadied it for her, kissed him, and took him down to the floor for another round of sex. She knew he was thoroughly smitten with her, and this encouraged that. She did like him, though she had learned that he was only twenty, ten years younger than she. Did it matter? It was not as if they were going to start a family.

They went to the main deck, and then to the waiting boat that took them across the water to the camp. There they had the morning meal of gruel, which was a sort of grain soup. She could handle it.

The language lesson continued. George was clearly pleased by her ready progress. Of course it was more than that, but she knew better than to let anyone else know that she had seduced him. She learned that he was an artist. He sketched lifelike pictures with hard charcoal on parchment: the ships, the buildings, the trees, the people.

Then he got an idea. He had her stand beneath a tree while he sketched her. She looked at the result and shook her head. That huge clumsy shirt would never do. She took him by the hand and led him to a secluded nook. Then she took off the shirt and posed nude.

George was glad to oblige. He sketched her, and this time the picture was a flattering likeness. He made her even prettier than she was naturally. It was his love enhancing his art.

"So!" a man's voice exclaimed. "Getting a little, hey?"

They whirled. It was Bub Two, spying on them.

It turned out that George was an Officer, while Bub was a convict. George rapped out a few choice words, and Bub quickly departed. She understood the context: if Bub spoke disrespectfully to George, he would be punished. This rough crew surely had effective means of punishment. So he obeyed, but she knew he had not forgotten. Had she been alone, she would have had to fight for her body.

But thereafter she put the shirt back on, and they rejoined the main camp. George reported to the Governor, and had Rebel say a few words: "George. Rebel. Governor Phillip."

The Governor smiled, pleased by the progress. The native girl was being educated. "Carry on," he told George. That meant that George was supposed to keep doing whatever he had been doing. It seemed he needed such an order, to continue.

They carried on. Now they were allowed to depart the colony site, so she could show George the best scenic places to sketch. Naturally when they were suitably isolated she gave him sex again. Once a man got it from a woman, he craved more of it, and she intended to see that she was always protected by this man. She pretended delight in his prowess, though it was hardly special. His art was in sketching pictures; hers was in boosting the male ego.

She learned more about him. He was an upper-class youth—she wasn't clear on the concept of classes, but it seemed some were better than others—who wanted to be an artist, but was obliged to serve a tour as a low officer on a ship first. It seemed to be the English form of initiation. Fortunately for him, the Governor liked his sketches and encouraged them as a record of their accomplishments.

But why had he been assigned the chore of teaching her? For she knew it had been a chore, though he was now more than willing to pursue it. It turned out that officers were supposed to supervise rather than actually work, but he was not an effective supervisor. So the Governor needed to find some other work for him, and Rebel was it. As long as she behaved and showed improvement, she would remain his assignment. He hoped, blushing, she would continue.

Oh, she would, though it was now clear that if she chose to depart, George would not hinder her. He wanted her to be pleased with him, even if it meant losing her. If she remained a captive, Harbinger would be free to marry Haven and have a child. So it was a solution to her problem.

But, he protested, in time he would return to England. She would not want to go there.

No? She was increasingly curious about that island, and she couldn't return to Harbinger, as that would make her effort here pointless. Yet George was firm on this point: she would not like England. She would be a Freak there, a Savage, a Spectacle.

But suppose she married him?

That set him back. He loved her, but he couldn't marry her. His family would never allow it.

She dropped the matter. There was too much she did not yet understand.

So it continued for several more days, as the colony got built and the convicts settled into the routine. Rebel now had a fair vocabulary, but the way the words were put together was more of a challenge, and some of the background concepts, such as Class and Money were more difficult yet. But these challenges meant that she still required George's full attention. She gave him sex often, and was beginning to enjoy it herself, as she got to know and like him better. He was so very, very appreciative!

She learned that the Governor wanted her to become a liaison with her people, able to translate between the two languages. She was increasingly competent to do that. But what did the Governor want of her people? The two groups had little in common.

Then one day as she went alone to the lavatory trench, Bub sprang out and grabbed her. He had been lurking, waiting to catch her alone. He clapped a hand over her mouth to stop her from screaming. That was his mistake.

She bit the hand, hard. He let go, cursing. "God Damn!" They were not supposed to speak the name of their deity in a bad manner; that was why it was a curse.

Then he threw her to the ground. He drew a knife and menaced her with it. If she screamed or fought, he would kill her.

She did neither. Instead she scrambled to her feet and fled. Bub pursued. He was about to catch her, when he grunted and fell.

She turned. There was Hero, with a club. He had knocked Bub on the head, hard, and he was dead.

"I knew you were watching," she said.

"You left your anklet. So I checked. You seemed to be handling it, in your fashion."

"Yes. Harbinger should marry Haven, and get a child."

He nodded. "It is your choice."

Then another man appeared. Hero whirled, lifting his club.

"No!" Rebel cried. "That's George!"

"The man you're handling," he agreed. Of course he had seen their trysts too.

"He's nice. I'm learning their language. I'm hardly a captive anymore."

Then George came up. "What's this?" he demanded.

"This is my brother, Hero," Rebel said in his language. "Bub tried to rape me, so Hero killed him. Does this mean I must flee?"

George paused, assessing the situation. "Do you want to flee?"

"No."

"Then let's call it self-defense, or defense of you, a pardonable offense. The man was scum; the colony is better off without him. But your brother should disappear; he must remain unknown. And you must get away from here, quickly, so no one knows you were involved."

Rebel translated quickly for Hero. He nodded and faded into the brush. Then Rebel returned quietly to the main camp. George returned separately.

Soon thereafter the body was discovered by another convict. He raised a Hue and Cry, and many people came to see. They realized that a native, a Savage, must have done it. No one was very much grieved; Bub had not been popular.

Neither George nor Rebel said anything. The matter had been dealt with. But she gave him extra-special sex at the first opportunity thereafter.

Unfortunately that matter was not over. Soon the colonists realized that if one of their number could be killed by a native, others could follow. They did not realize that Bub had brought it on himself by trying to rape Rebel. They thought it was the beginning of a campaign against them. And neither Rebel nor George dared to set them straight, lest they bring suspicion on themselves.

Too soon it happened anyway. "That hussy Savage!" a women said. "She's one of them!"

"And George is keeping her company," a man agreed. "He's a savage-lover!"

Before long word reached the Governor. They were summoned to appear before him. "What do you know of this?" he demanded of George.

Rebel could have lied to the man. But George was young and innocent, and he feared the Governor. "Nothing," he said insincerely.

The Governor considered briefly. "You're a good man with the illustrations. I don't want to lose you. But I shall have to, if it turns out that you had anything to do with this. Anything at all."

George quailed visibly.

"So I shall address the woman," the Governor continued after a meaningful pause. "You, Rebel—you understand me well enough, don't you?"

She had to answer. "Yes, Governor."

"One of your countrymen did this thing."

If she lied, he would have it out of George instead. The Governor knew she understood that. "Yes."

"Why? Is it an attack?"

"No."

"Then why?"

He surely had already fathomed the answer. She had to tell. She knew she did not have perfect syntax, but she could put the words in place. "Man—Bub—try sex me. Me brother kill he."

The Governor nodded. "He was watching you. You are an attractive woman. He got what he deserved. But I am not in a position to publicize that. A man of my colony has been killed, and that cannot be countenanced."

Rebel looked blank. There were too many unfamiliar words.

The Governor glanced at George. George spoke, clarifying it by using words he knew she understood. "He know. But he leader. He must avenge dead tribe man."

Oh. That did make sense. Tribe came before all else. "Yes," she agreed, fearing what it meant.

The Governor almost smiled. "I want no war on my hands. We have other things to accomplish. Go tell your people to vacate the premises and not to harass us further. Rejoin your tribe; there is no place for you here, after this episode, much as I regret the loss of a potential translator."

George had to translate again. "Tell Family go away. You go too. No return."

"But I don't want to leave you!" she protested. It was not that she loved him, but he represented her best chance to do what she needed to do, and she did like him well enough, and was sure she could make him happy.

The Governor spoke to George. "I surely misheard. It can't be that she has any attachment to you, or you to her. She should be glad to return to her people."

Rebel suffered a flash of further understanding. The Governor knew how things were between them, and didn't like it. He wanted to get rid of her so that his illustrator would not be distracted. This was how.

Would George stand up to the Governor? If he did, she would stay with him, come what might. But she feared he would not.

She was right. "She . . . wants to be a translator," George said. "To learn more words. She can't do that if she leaves."

"Unfortunately that is no longer feasible. She must go. You will surely be grateful to be relieved of this chore, so you can return your full attention to your illustrations."

"Uh, yes," George agreed weakly.

He was simply not man enough to stand up for himself, even to secure the woman he loved. She had no choice but to do as the Governor wanted. That, at least, would leave George clear of this mess.

"I go," she agreed. She drew off her shirt, as it was really not hers, and stood bare-breasted. She was going native. Then she turned and walked away from them.

The men of the colony stared, but the governor snapped a warning that anchored them in place. All they could do was look. She made no effort to moderate her stride to reduce the bouncing of her breasts. Let them know what they were losing.

George made no protest. He *really* understood what he was losing.

When she was safely in the forest, Hero joined her. "They don't like their man getting killed," she explained. "But they will leave us alone if we go away and leave *them* alone."

"We can do that," he agreed. He knew, as she did, that they were nomadic. Traveling was their nature. Not only would it not be difficult to leave this hunting ground, it was natural. "But what of Harbinger?"

She sighed. "He is stuck with me a while longer."

"He will not be displeased."

Then they both laughed. It was not an ideal resolution, but it would have to do.

•

The colony near Botany Bay suffered lean times, as the terrain was not suitable for conventional farming despite an early report. Their cattle and sheep soon died. Their food had to be rationed. But they endured, and more convicts arrived year by year. Yes, there was an illustrator who was a midshipman named George, and the governor was Phillip.

There was indeed some trouble with the Aborigines, and a man was killed, though perhaps not for the reason described here. They also had trouble getting the convicts to work, as they were hardly motivated. The women had nothing to do, and existed at first in complete idleness. Somehow their clothing had been left behind, so they had to make do with substitutes. I doubt they were pleased. But in time the colony took hold and expanded. The natives were pushed back, and suffered grievously from the white man's diseases of smallpox, measles, and others. Their numbers were decimated. Their stone-age culture could not compete with modern organization and weapons.

The new nation continent of Australia was coming into being.

17

THE VISION

Times were hard for the Xhosa in the nineteenth century. They joined with their former enemies the Kat River Khoikhoi to rebel against the British. But in 1853 the British rallied and defeated the rebellion. In 1854 a disease spread through the Xhosa cattle, the "lung sickness," and they suspected it had started with cattle owned by European Settlers, or that it was caused by ubuthi, *or witchcraft. Either way, they wanted to be rid of the oppressive foreign presence.*

Then something amazing happened. The time is May 1856, by the mouth of the Gxarha River.

Hero knew immediately that the matter was serious. He had seldom seen Rebel as grave and doubtful as now. She was no fainting flower. So he set aside his incidental business and gave her his full attention. "What is it, my sister?"

"You will not like this," she said.

"Whatever it is you want, surely you can have it. I trust your judgment absolutely."

"It is not what I want," she said, frowning. At age thirty-one she remained a lovely woman, in significant part because she had never borne children or been tied to sedentary chores. Even her frowns were appealing.

"I want what you want: the greatest benefit for the family. We are doing well, considering these troubled times." Then he had an idea. "Are you going to leave us? Have you found a man to marry?" For she had liked Harbinger, but he had married her older sister Haven. Hero knew Rebel hurt because of that, yet supported it, because Haven was able to bear children.

She smiled, a trifle wearily. "No such fortune. This concerns our brother Keeper."

"He remains invaluable. He is the main reason we prosper: his expertise with cattle and crops. He wants to marry?"

"He should, but he won't. He still loves Crenelle."

Who was Hero's wife. That had always been a subtle difficulty between them, but Crenelle had chosen Hero, and Keeper honored that, just as Hero would have honored it had she chosen Craft or Keeper. So Keeper remained single, devoting himself to the welfare of the family. "I have no concern about my brother and my wife."

"Nor should you," she agreed. "But this also concerns your daughter."

"What does Tourette have to do with it?" he asked. That was the private name they called her, rather than her formal name Nongqawuse. It was part of the layered protection the family extended her, because of her malady. "She's a fine and lovely girl, even if I do let my pride show."

"Agreed. But a troubled one."

"There is nothing wrong with her that the right man could not fix. One who can accept her as she is."

"Exactly."

He gazed at her, confused. But already the matter was clarifying in an ugly manner. "Tourette . . . and Keeper," he said heavily.

"Yes. We have seen it coming. Now it must be dealt with."

He tried to dismiss it. "Because she flirts with her uncle? He's a responsible man."

"Indeed. That is why he came to me. We are close."

That was an understatement. Rebel loved her sister's husband, and Keeper loved his brother's wife. They had common emotional ground. Sometimes strangers had taken them for lovers rather than siblings, though there had never been anything like that between them. It was that they shared everything with each other, knowing their mutual understanding. "He came to you," Hero repeated.

"Try to understand, Hero. Tourette is vulnerable and impetuous and more than lovely. She turns male heads."

"She's a child!"

"She's a woman."

"She's only fifteen!"

"A young beauty. I could take any man I wanted; you know that."

"I know that," he agreed.

"So could she, and more readily, because she is younger and prettier. But she resembles me in a more subtle respect: she desires only one man, and he is not available."

"Keeper," he said. "But that crush will pass. She knows it is futile."

"She knows intellectually. He is Family. But she does not entirely accept it emotionally. He is her ideal."

"What are you saying?" he demanded, knowing well what it was, but wanting to make her say it—or back off. She had been correct when she said he would not like what she had to say.

"Understand, she is inexperienced, with strong emotion. She wants to love, to give herself to her ideal man, as any nascent woman does. And that man is Keeper." Rebel shook her head. "And were he not her uncle, he would indeed be perfect for her. He knows her fully, and likes her for what she is. He doesn't have to pretend not to notice her sieges." She gave Hero a serious look. "And that's the crux: they are right for each other, maybe regardless."

Hero was appalled. "You are speaking of incest!"

"I suppose I am. It is not unknown, when other factors are conducive. Which would be better, objectively: a perfect match within the Family, or imperfect matches outside it?"

"How can you even think of such a thing?"

"I had a Vision. It was vague, no specifics, just a feeling that there was a looming choice between a small evil and a great one. Tolerating a quiet affair was the small one."

"An affair!"

"What, really, would be wrong with it?"

"He's her uncle!"

"Apart from that?"

"There *is* no 'apart from that.' It can't be. And I'm sure Keeper knows it."

"He does. But he is under pressure."

He stared at her. "He can't be considering it!"

She sighed. "I see I must be more graphic. Here is what he told me. Picture it in your mind."

"Never!"

She put her hand on his arm. "Hero, please. You need to make the effort. Put yourself in his place. Feel his feelings."

This was unlike her. Rebel was well versed in sex, but had never urged anything like this before. What was truly on her mind? "I will try," he said gruffly.

Then she told him what their brother had told her.

•

They were in a secluded mountain pass, chill but bearable, camping for the night while the dogs made sure the cattle did not stray from the valley below. The grazing was good, and a few more days here would put some good weight on the cows. Tourette got along well with the dogs, and had been a real help moving the cattle here. Now they could rest.

Keeper tended to natural functions, then lay down, wrapped himself in his blanket, and settled for sleep, expecting Tourette to do the same nearby. Instead she joined him under his blanket. "What?" he asked, surprised.

"I had a dream," she said.

"A bad dream? Tell me, and that should deplete its power."

"A good dream. I seduced you."

Had he misheard? Oh, she must be teasing him, as sometimes she did, flirtatiously. "Never, you naughty girl."

She snuggled close, and he realized that she was naked. "Truly. Now I want to do it really."

This was more than flirtation. "Tourette—"

"I love you."

"And I love—but it's not the same. Don't think that—"

"I can keep a secret."

"That's not the point! You can't—"

"No one need ever know, but just the two of us. Our secret. Don't you find me interesting?"

"No! Not in that way."

She kissed him lingeringly. "Are you sure?"

"Yes I'm sure! I'm your uncle."

Her hand snaked into his trousers, finding his erect member. "Are you sure?" she asked again.

She had given him the lie. Her passion and her lovely body were arousing him. "Tourette, this can't be. You have to know that."

"I do know it," she agreed. "But my body doesn't."

"Go sleep by yourself. You are embarrassing me."

"Keeper, please! I love you. I know we can't marry. I know it must always be secret. But I beg you to take me. It is all I ever wanted."

"Tourette, I can't do it! It would violate our whole relationship."

"Please, I beg you," she said.

He steeled himself. "No."

She froze against him. "I'm so ashamed." She scrambled from under the blanket and hurled herself to her own blanket. "You must be revolted!"

He heard her quietly sobbing, and felt awful. Then he heard her yipping and snorting as the fit came on her. He couldn't let her go that way.

He got up, wearing the blanket like a cloak, and kneeled beside her. "Tourette, I'm not revolted. I know it's no demon in you, just a . . . a loose wheel in your body."

Her fit eased, as it normally did. "But suppose we did it, and it happened then? Wouldn't you be disgusted?"

He didn't know how to answer, and was silent.

"See—you would be. You can't risk it. I should have realized. I'm so sorry. I am humiliated."

"That's not it! It might even be intriguing." But he regretted it the moment he said it. He had spoken without thinking.

"Oh! I'm a freak!"

"No! I'm sorry I said it, but it's true. You are so lovely that I'd feel privileged to be . . . in you . . . when it happened. To possess you when you are naked, as it were." But he was horrified to hear himself talking like this, as though having sex with her were an option. "I shouldn't have said that either. I wish I could unsay all of it."

She paused briefly. "You *do* desire me."

"Yes, curse me! I do desire you. You are so much like your mother, whom I wish I could have married. But it is forbidden."

"So there's a chance."

"There's no chance!"

"Kiss me, and I will let you be."

It seemed a fair offer. He lay beside her and put his face to hers. She clasped him, half bestrode him, and kissed him with savage passion.

He knew then that if she tried to take it further, he would not be able to resist.

But after an eternal contact, she released him, settling for what he had offered. "Thank you, Keeper. I will always love you."

"And I you, I fear," he said. "But—"

"I understand." She closed her eyes. She was letting him be. He realized that she was not certain either, and needed some resolution of their problem.

But it was too late. He knew as he gathered the blanket about him again that he did love her as a woman, forbidden though she was. And that if she came to him again, he would succumb. He had always liked her, and now he loved her.

•

Hero shook his head. "That was too real."

"It is love denied," Rebel said. "But it will not be denied much longer unless firm action is taken. I repeat: My own Vision suggests that it would be better to let them do it. The alternative is worse."

"No! Nothing could be worse!"

She did not argue. "Then I think Keeper must go elsewhere, and soon."

"Our cousins could use his expertise. We can send him there."

"She might follow him. Her passion makes her headstrong."

"Then send him where nobody knows. Immediately."

She rose and departed without further word.

•

When Tourette discovered that Keeper was gone on private cattle business, she threw another kind of fit. But she was unable to express her reason, and no other member of the Family inquired. They all knew. It would just have to blow over in its own time and manner.

Hero was nevertheless nervous. Tourette's affliction could affect her in more than mere tics and sounds. She was not a vengeful person, but her mind could be devious. The way she had approached Keeper suggested that balking her illicit passion could be dangerous.

Yet what could she do? She was a fifteen-year-old girl, her prime destiny being marriage to a suitable man. She understood why they had sent Keeper away, even if her passion wished otherwise. Time would surely bring her emotional as well as her rational agreement.

Rebel caught his eye, and shook her head. She was nervous too.

Two days later Tourette had her Vision. She and her friend Nombanda had gone to fetch water from a pool near the mouth of the river. There she had met the spirits of three of her ancestors.

"They told me that the Xhosa people must destroy our crops and kill our cattle, the source of our food and wealth. In return the spirits will sweep the British settlers into the sea. They will replenish the granaries and fill the kraals with healthier and more beautiful cattle. No more lung sickness. It will happen on February 18, next year, when the sun will turn red, confirming the spirits' presence."

Hero didn't believe it. Oh, he suspected she had had a Vision, but that it derived in part from her malady and in part from her stress at losing access to Keeper. For one thing the date she named would be her sixteenth birthday, when by local tradition she would become adult and able to take charge of her own life and love. *That* was the fulfillment she craved, when the Family could no longer stop her from seeking her uncle.

If this was the worst result of the Family's action, they were reasonably well off.

But the Family consulted, and decided to let others dispose of the Prophecy. Just so they could not be accused of suppressing anything. There were those among their people who were credulous about such things. So Craft went to Chief Sarhili to repeat the prophecy.

And the chief, perhaps motivated by the need to do something about the cattle lung sickness and the detested presence of the British, did something astonishing. He ordered his followers to obey the Prophecy. To kill the cattle.

That launched another Family conference. "This is sheer folly!" Hero said. "The spirits have never interfered with mortal affairs to this extent before, and it doesn't make any sense anyway. Why should killing our cattle please the spirits?"

But Tourette was adamant. "My ancestors did not say why, just what. They must all be killed."

"And the chief believes this nonsense!" Craft said.

Tourette glanced sidelong at him, and Hero saw a flash of that compelling beauty Rebel had described. She had set her sights on Keeper, but had she oriented on Craft instead, she might have succeeded similarly. Yet that did not explain the action of the chief, who had not seen her, just heard the relayed prophecy. "Its not nonsense. It's a Vision. I saw it."

"Well, we're not doing it," Hero said decisively. "We need our cattle and crops to survive. We're not going to depend on magic or any other foolishness."

Tourette didn't respond. She never opposed her will directly to his. But obviously she still believed her Vision.

As it turned out, they did not have a choice. When they did not slaughter their own cattle, the chief sent a posse to do it for them. Suddenly all their cattle were dead.

Hero remembered what Rebel had said about the alternative being worse than the secret incest. This would not have happened if they had just let Tourette have her way with Keeper. Yet how could that ever have been justified?

The destruction of their crops followed. All the families were doing it, secure in their belief of reward from the spirits of the ancestors. At this point all Hero could hope for was that the Prophecy was correct, though he didn't believe it. He directed the Family to save all of the grain possible, and hide it, because he knew there would soon be desperate need.

The slaughter continued, spreading across the entire Xhosa nation, not just Chief Sarhili's clan. For a time there was feasting as the tribesmen consumed the flesh, but soon what was not eaten was rotting, and there was no more.

Now came the hunger. Their meager stock of grain diminished. Other families had already run out of food and were raiding their neighbors.

"Plan for defense," Hero said grimly. "We must keep a guard out always, especially at night."

They took turns, one Family member always alert. This paid off, for there were furtive attempts to sneak in and steal whatever was available.

But the bad siege occurred by daylight. A rogue posse charged the farm, six men running in tandem, brandishing spears.

They were ready. Haven, still a well favored woman, took her position, standing bare-breasted before the house as if caught unaware. Harbinger crouched behind her with his club.

Hero strode out toward them, pretending that he didn't know their business. "Hail, fellows!" he called. "What is the nature of this visit?"

They ignored him, charging on. So Hero became more assertive. He brandished one of his spears. "If you do not come in peace, we will smite you."

Still they charged, trying to get close enough to hurl their spears. Well, they had been given fair warning, and were obviously not going to be reasonable. Hero glanced meaningfully at Haven, who exaggerated her pose, turning to display herself more fully.

Craft had fashioned a small catapult that could place a stone with almost pinpoint accuracy. He oriented on the lead warrior and took him out with a stone to the chest. Then the second, closer. The raiders obviously had never seen such a device, and were heedless of it until too late. They continued their charge.

Now they were in Hero's spear range. He hurled his first spear before the third warrior got within his own range, and it transfixed the man, who had been foolishly distracted by Haven. Three down.

The fourth man had the sense to weave as he ran so that Hero could not be sure of accuracy. He reached Haven—only to be bashed as Harbinger sprang out from concealment, club swinging.

The fifth man, surprised, paused momentarily. That was enough; Hero got him with his second spear.

But the sixth man was right on his heels, bearing down on Craft while Hero and Harbinger were occupied. And Rebel sprang naked with a knife, and sliced his throat before he could react.

The first two warriors, bashed by Craft's stones, were stirring. They had been knocked out but not killed. Hero ran to dispatch them. But while he was spearing one, the other caught him about the legs, bringing him down. He had to twist around, get his hands on the man's throat, and throttle him to death. This took more time and was ugly to watch, and the man's blood from the stone strike smeared messily across them both. But in due course it was done.

They had won this battle. The six raiders were strewn across the landscape, dead and dying. But Hero knew it was just the beginning. Their real enemy was hunger.

"Harvest the two closest," he murmured to Craft. "Let the others lie as a warning to others."

Craft nodded. They had discussed this privately. He and Harbinger hauled each of the last two raiders into the house, after making sure they were dead. Hero maintained watch, in case another contingent attacked. Crenelle brought him a damp cloth to wipe the blood off.

No other attack came. In due course he turned the watch over to

Tourette, who had to take her turn as they all did. She had had the Vision, but she did not approve of being a patsy for criminal raids.

Rebel intercepted him. "Do we really have to do this?" she asked.

"Unless we prefer to starve, or become food for others."

She nodded. "We have no choice. But I hate it."

"So do I. So do we all. But this was perhaps inevitable the day Tourette decided to become a seeress."

"She couldn't help it, Hero."

He was struck by doubt. "Should I have let her be with my brother?"

"No, of course not." But her protest lacked conviction.

It was a lack Hero was coming increasingly to share. He had known his daughter was vulnerable, because of her malady. Because it robbed her of a normal life. And possibly it extended into her mind, and was responsible for the Vision. He should have known better than to force the issue. It wasn't as if incest, like cannibalism, wasn't known. The two would have been circumspect.

Rebel put her hand on his arm. "You did what you had to do. None of us anticipated what would happen. The chief should never have credited the Vision."

"He had his own reasons. We should have seen the politics of it."

"Easy to say now. But no one could have seen this particular awfulness coming."

He wasn't sure he agreed with her, but he appreciated her effort to console him. Not that this did any of them much good. "Let's get on with it," he said gruffly.

They joined Haven and Crenelle, who were carving the bodies. Both looked ill, but they too were doing what they had to. There simply was no other food available any more.

No one ate that night. They focused on getting the meat prepared and roasted so that it would keep longer. Craft kept a fire going in the cooking framework, and they scorched arms and legs as they severed them, and buried them in sand for storage. The sweetish smell of the singed flesh made more than one of them try to vomit, but fortunately their stomachs were empty.

In the morning the other four bodies were gone. Others had sneaked in by night and taken them. That was all right; the message would be spreading. It was not safe to raid this farm.

When the meat of the two bodies ran out, Hero and Rebel went out to find what else was available. They walked deliberately into an ambush, pretending ignorance, then reversed it, killing the attackers, who were weak from hunger. More meat.

So they survived, unpleasantly, while the majority of their neighbors fled the region or starved to death. Or ate the bodies.

The British came. It was not possible to fight them off; they were armed with guns, and were savvy about combat. So Hero did what he could, talking to them. "We survive as we have to," he said.

"To be sure," the British officer said. "We have come to arrest the perpetrator of this mischief, that idiot girl."

"Nongqawuse," Rebel said. "My niece."

"It's really for her own safety, as much as anything else," the officer said. "There are those who don't appreciate starving to death." Presumably that was British humor. "She will be given a fair trial."

And probably fed, and not raped. It was the best they could hope for. They had to let Tourette go. Had they resisted, they would have been exterminated in short order.

"The Xhosa tribe is finished," Rebel said grimly.

That about covered it.

Hero knew he could have avoided all this, by letting the willful girl have her way. Had it been worth it?

•

When the prophesied day came, the sun rose with its normal color, and the spirits delivered no replacement cattle or grain. The Prophecy was revealed as false. But the damage was done; the Xhosa were finished as an independent force, and their vacated land was resettled by Europeans. The Xhosa population of the area dropped from 105,000 to less than 27,000. It was regarded as one of the most remarkable instances of misplaced faith recorded in history. They had destroyed themselves by their eagerness to believe the Vision of a teenage girl.

The historical Nongqawuse survived the situation. After her release by the British she lived on a farm in the Alexandria district of the Cape, and died in 1898. What motivated her Vision, and the general acceptance of it, remains a subject of intense speculation.

18

•

SACRIFICE

The 50,000-plus-year history of the Australian Aborigines was drawing to a painful close. There might have been as many as a million of them at the time the European colonization began in 1788, subsisting across the continent as hunter/gatherers. But they were devastated by European diseases, deprivation of habitat, and the vicious nineteenth century policy of "pacification by force." In fact the British settlers seemed to be eager for pretexts to usher the natives into extinction. By the late nineteenth century this process was largely complete, and few independent Aborigines remained. Those remaining had to compromise desperately just to survive.

The place is the vicinity of Alice Springs, January 1, 1901. On that day Australia achieved independence from England. That freedom, ironically, did not extend to the natives.

•

Rebel returned from her gathering of tubers and berries to find the family grim. "What happened?" she asked Craft as she set the roots to bake in the hot ashes of the fire he had made, fearing his answer.

"A white family has been killed. We got the news from a child sent by a neighbor clan."

Rebel felt an ugly thrill of dread. "And they'll blame us. They always do."

"And it will be a pretext to go on a rampage and wipe us all out," he agreed grimly. "That's what they want. It could even be that one of them did it, to frame us."

"We've got to act, fast," she said. "We'll have to travel tonight, before they get organized."

"Hero says they've already got men with guns guarding the road. We're trapped."

"Then I'll have to go to George. You know what that means. I don't even know whether he'll be able to do anything. It has been only spot favors, before."

"It's our only chance," Craft said. "You'll have to beg." All the Family knew about George and what he expected of Rebel. They let it be, because they needed what she garnered in that manner. It was really another kind of foraging. They lived far from the shore, but via the white man they sometimes obtained seafood like crabs, clams, and fish.

"It's not that he won't," she said. "It's that I fear he can't. This may be too big."

"Go now. Try. Our lives depend on it."

"Tell Haven to take Harbinger tonight."

"I already have."

She looked sharply at her brother, but he wasn't smiling. He had known this was the only course. They all knew it. "Then I'm on my way."

She paused only long enough to put on her clean skirt and blouse, clothing the whites required of any natives who entered their domains, and to brush her hair neat. Then she kissed Craft quickly and hurried away. She hadn't eaten, but that didn't matter, because George would feed her. She also did not take her sleeping blanket, because George lived in a house that had a bed, and she would share it with him. She preferred the ground by the fire, as they traveled from place to place within their range, but could accommodate.

She had first encountered George two years before. He was then a stripling of twenty, a decade younger than she and impressionable. She had been gathering in the field, and he had been painting a picture of it. He had asked her to pose for a picture, offering a precious bag of sugar in exchange, and she, flattered, had agreed. She had kept her figure, but knew that age would inevitably make her fade, so this was a chance to be immortalized in her late prime. She was nude, as she normally was in summer, and saw that this aroused him, though he was too shy to make any advance. It was an effect she was pleased to have on him; it meant she still had her sex appeal.

The painting made her dynamic and beautiful, more so than she really was. George was a skilled artist who had fathomed her independent spirit and somehow captured it in paint. In the picture her hips were wider, her breasts firmer, and her eyes more piercing. She loved it. So she kissed him, and departed with the sugar, leaving him stunned.

Back with the Family, she related her encounter while they ate the baked opossum Keeper had speared. She learned that George was the son of an important person, the local governor. He was out of favor because all he wanted to do was paint pictures, instead of anything more productive. Because his family was wealthy he could get away with it, but he remained an embarrassment. They wanted him to get a trade, marry, and become a solid white citizen.

Several days later she had seen him again, painting a handsome tree. Rebel had not realized the tree was handsome until she saw his painting. He could fathom the inner spirit of a tree as he did that of a person, and render it on parchment. She smiled at him, and saw him melt. He was already smitten with her. She delighted again in having that effect on a young man. He was a White Settler, while she was just a tawny native girl, but in this respect she had power over him.

This time she proffered another kind of deal: language. She knew how to talk English, but also knew she was clumsy, with a strong "barbaric" accent. That made her an object of tacit ridicule when she had to interact with the white settlers. She wanted to do something about that.

She broached the matter directly. "Teach me to talk like an English Lady," she said. "I will give you this." She took his hand and set it on her bare breast.

George almost fainted, but soon enough the deal was made. She let him feel her all over as he drilled her on correct British pronunciation. She was an apt student, and within a year she could talk his language as well as anyone could, and he knew her body as well as any stranger could. He never tired of refreshing his awareness of it, however.

When hands were no longer enough, she let him use his mouth, kissing her lips, breasts, and buttocks. His stiff desire was almost painful for her to witness, but she pretended not to notice. They had come to know each other about as well as a white and a native could, considering that any such association was frowned on by both sides. They were, in their fashion, friends. And of course he was in love with her, though he knew she was older, and married, as well as being native. Hopeless in three ways.

But she no longer needed his lessons, so the deal was over. George was desperate. She was, it seemed, the only woman he had this sort of relationship with, or even wanted it with, and he didn't want to give it up. He knew she didn't love him, but that she would honor any deal she made. "What do you want?" he asked. "Anything! Please!"

She considered. This was not a contact or an offer to be lightly dismissed, and she did like him personally. Thus it was that their relationship advanced to the next level. In exchange for useful tools and supplies, she gave him sex, guiding him gently through his initial nervous clumsiness. She realized that this was a significant part of his attraction to her: she never misunderstood him, made fun of him, or denied him. He could do anything with her, and she accepted and encouraged it with grace in a manner she knew a white woman would not. She was not at all wary of an erect penis, or dismissive of one that was less turgid following orgasm. She did not protest when he buried his face in her cleft, sucked on her nipples, or poked his finger into her rectum. None of her orifices were forbidden to his exploration or possession.

He reveled in it, and she liked it well enough. He was so eager, so enthusiastic, so teachable. He soon learned how to arouse her, to make her climax by using his tongue, which was something her husband Harbinger seldom did. George was thrilled to make her react in this manner, knowing she was not pretending; it shifted some of the interactive power to him and simulated the love he truly desired from her. As affairs went, this was very good.

What, then, of Harbinger? That was another aspect of a more complicated situation. Rebel was sterile, and could not give him children. She felt guilty. At first it had not bothered him; affected as men were by her appearance, he had insisted on marrying her anyway, though her sister Haven was really a better match for him. But as time passed it bothered him more. She knew she would have to leave him, to free him to marry Haven and have a family. But he refused to hear of it.

Thus, slowly, had developed the tacit compromise. Rebel went shopping for things the Family really needed, paying for it in the way she had. When she did, Haven went to him, giving him what Rebel was taking elsewhere. He knew it, and was not entirely easy with it, but they did need the items, especially the tools and food, as drought and restriction to the worst lands made them hungry. It was not as if Haven was a bad exchange. She was full-fleshed and accommodating, and she genuinely liked him and would have married him had he not preferred Rebel. He had always liked her too, and this gave him access to both of them. He never would have done it, had they not been desperate, but it had its compensations.

There was nothing like going chronically hungry to adjust attitudes, even those relating to sex and marriage. Both women were skilled foragers, using their digging sticks to get many kinds of tubers, and picking many nuts, fruits and collecting seeds. But the drought made the pickings increasingly slim, and they had to compromise.

Now Rebel reached George's house. She checked to be sure no one was in the area, then knocked lightly at the rear door. Surely by this time George's family had caught on that he had a woman, but this was permissible providing he was discreet. It was the way of British men, and to this extent George was conforming to the pattern expected of him.

He heard her and opened the door immediately. She stepped into his glad embrace. "Oh, Rebel! I missed you so!"

"It has been only three days," she reminded him.

"I miss you when it's only three hours!" He kissed her hungrily.

"But why are you here? I wasn't expecting you until next week. I have no food." For normally she came to him once a fortnight, giving him a good evening.

"I'll explain in a moment," she said. She had decided that it would be better to handle the sex first, then discuss the problem when his mind was less distracted.

Soon she was naked and on his raised bed. The shorter time since their last connection did not seem to dampen his ardor at all. He licked her breasts and plunged into her, not trying to make her climax with him. It was a pattern they had discovered: his first exuberant effort warmed her up while taking off his desperate edge, and then the second or the third brought her to her own orgasm without stress. He loved all of it.

After he spent, and relaxed, and fetched her some of the white's bread and jam she liked, she broached it. "A white family has been killed. We didn't do it, but know we will be blamed. We'll be wiped out. Can you help?"

He was silent a moment, pondering. She knew why: if the Family got killed, she would be dead too, and he would have no lover anymore. He had strong personal motive to do something, if anything could be done.

"I must ask Father," he said. "I must tell him of you. He can act, if he chooses to."

"But does your father want to know about your connection to me?" she asked, sipping the ale he provided. It was strong stuff, making her dizzy, which was why she took it cautiously. She had to conduct business with a clear head. "I mean, surely he does know, but he wouldn't want it to be openly recognized. I'm native." As if he didn't know. It was simply a reminder that there were cautions about letting this personal association be more widely known.

"It's not that, exactly. Lots of men have native mistresses. The–the girls don't make demands."

And that was an advantage for a man, as well she understood. The native girls were compliant and obliging, knowing their place. Having no choice. "Unlike me," she said with irony.

He choked. "I didn't mean it like that! I love you!"

"I'm teasing," she said gently. "We have always understood the basis for our relationship."

"No we haven't."

She rained an eyebrow in the British manner she had learned. "Haven't?"

"I understand your basis," he said doggedly. "You need things. You pay for them. I love the way you pay for them. You'll do anything I ask, and some things I wouldn't dare ask, and some things I wouldn't even know to ask. You seem to exist to give me pleasure. Which is why I'm so thrilled when I somehow manage to give *you* pleasure. That gives me more joy than anything else. But you don't understand my basis."

He was evidently talking about something other than sex. This could be mischief. "And what is yours?"

"I want to marry you."

Mischief indeed. "George—"

"I know, I know! You're older, you're married, you're native. I don't care about any of that. You're the only woman I can relate to with comfort. I love you and I want to marry you."

"There is one more thing," she reminded him gently. "I'm barren."

"Yes. So you can be with me with no risk. I bless your barrenness."

This was new. She had assumed that he never thought about pregnancy or babies. Most men didn't, with mistresses. "So even if I were British and single and your age, I would not be suitable for you in that manner. Your family would never let you marry me."

"Maybe. Maybe not."

"I am not sure I understand."

"It's political. We just got our independence. Australia is now a Commonwealth nation, instead of a Territory. We'll be running our own affairs."

"Affairs," she agreed, smiling.

"I mean politically. It's not the same."

She kissed him. "I was teasing again. I know the language, thanks to you. But how does that relate to you and me? We remain in opposite camps."

"And our people mistreat yours horribly. I hate that. But we pretend it isn't so. That we treat you well."

She laughed. "Good luck making that case!"

"Father wants to make it. To show that we settlers are not the bigots the British are. He might let me marry you, to prove how well we treat you people. It's a lie, but truth hardly matters in politics."

That was something dramatically fresh and different. She needed to think about it. So she made time by distracting him with the second episode of sex. She kissed him and stroked him, wrapping her legs about him, and in due course had him worked up to another eruption within her. It wasn't as if he had any objection to her effort, whatever her reason.

"Oh, Rebel!" he gasped. "It's no lie that I love you!"

She needed to discuss this with her family. But first she had to get this quite clear. "George, would you marry me, if your father allowed it?"

"Yes! Oh, Rebel—"

"I have not said I would do it. I just want to know what the prospects are."

"*Would* you do it?"

"If that were the way to save my family, yes I would."

"Then I'll ask Father! To save your people, and to let me marry you."

"Tell me what he says." She kissed him again. "George, it seems unlikely that he will agree. Don't get your hope up."

"There's nowhere else for my hope to be. I know that to you it's just another payment for a service. I'm willing, nay, eager to have you on that basis. Rebel, Rebel, if I married you, maybe in time you would come to love me. Please say it's possible."

That much she could grant. "It's possible."

"I'm so happy!"

"You're welcome." She did fear that both of them were in for serious disappointment, for different reasons.

"But there's one thing."

"Oh?"

"Father might make demands."

"Fathers do," she agreed wryly.

"You would have to dress like us, stay in town, and not see your people."

"But you wouldn't tell if I sneaked out on occasion to see them."

"I wouldn't," he agreed. "But also—"

"What?"

He changed his mind. "Maybe not."

She didn't like this. "What?" she repeated.

He fidgeted. "Your religion, for one thing. You would have to be Christian."

"What is entailed?"

"Going to Church on Sundays. Believing in Jesus Christ our Savior. No more plant spirits and things."

"I would have to profess belief in your god in the sky," she said.

"Yes."

He had not picked up on the distinction between professing belief and actually believing. She knew just enough of the British religion to know that it had all kinds of strictures that they routinely ignored, like not killing, or lusting after a neighbor's wife, or taking their lord's name in vain, so she wasn't concerned. She could be that kind of hypocrite when she needed to be. But she had the feeling that this was not the whole of his concern. "What else?"

"Maybe I'm being paranoid. No need to speak of it."

So there was something, but he was extremely reluctant to express it. That was unusual, because she was the one to whom he expressed his deepest feelings most openly. She decided to let it pass. She would figure it out in due course. "No need," she agreed.

They made love again, and this time she climaxed with him, powerfully. That pleased them both. Then she dressed and departed, so that he could go immediately to his father. She was not sure what would come of this, but it wasn't as if she had a choice. If this worked, they would survive. It was in the end that simple.

•

"So George will brace his father, who can save us," Rebel concluded. "But I may have to marry him and separate from you, my family."

"Oh, Rebel," Craft said sympathetically.

"I would rather do that than have us all killed."

"It's a point," he agreed.

"So if I do that, Haven will have to marry Harbinger."

There was a brief silence. Then Haven spoke. "Maybe we can manage that."

So it was working out between them. "I will go in the morning to learn the decision," Rebel said. "I may not return."

"In that case you are mine tonight," Harbinger said.

She was. He had impassioned sex with her, but she had the impression it wasn't love. For one thing, it was all his, with no concern for her experience. When he was done he fell right to sleep. He had become reconciled to the inevitable. At the moment he was merely proving that he still desired her, for the record, as it were. So it did seem time. It was best for all of them, and not just because it enabled their survival. Or that Harbinger and Haven were falling in love. Or that George truly loved Rebel, and had become a better lover than Harbinger. These were all details in a larger picture.

In the morning she dressed well and walked to town. She tapped on George's door. He was ready. "He wants to see you," he said. "He's considering it."

Probably to be sure she wasn't a dirty bare creature speaking pidgin English. She could reassure him on that score. "I will see him," she agreed.

"Mother will dress you."

"Mother?"

"Yes, dear." It was an older woman, speaking from behind him. Rebel had not realized that he had company today. "You must be presentable."

Mother had come prepared. She garbed Rebel in underwear, chemise, and an uncomfortably tight corset, overset by a full-length dress. Rebel's breathing was restricted, but she didn't complain. She had more important concerns than this. "Thank you," she said faintly.

"You are a pretty one," Mother remarked as she combed and arranged Rebel's hair and fastened it in place with a number of little pins. "And you speak well. That's good."

"Thank you," Rebel repeated.

"You will be expected to mix socially, smiling and impressing others with your manner. You will warmly endorse the treatment your people are receiving. Do you understand?"

"Oh, yes," Rebel agreed. "I am a woman." She did not add that this meant she knew how to lie. It wasn't necessary.

"My husband has his little ways," the woman continued. "Accommodate them if you can, dear."

"I will do whatever I am supposed to do."

"Perhaps."

Rebel realized that she was missing something, again. What was it that they would not speak of directly?

The last things were a hat and shoes. Both were heavy and hot. The shoes had heels that were higher than the toes, forcing her to balance uncomfortably on them. Rebel felt as if she were confined in a portable cage. She reminded herself yet again that this was necessary to save her people. It wasn't as though she were alone; Mother wore a similar outfit.

George brought up a coach drawn by a horse. Mother guided Rebel into it. They sat inside its cramped compartment as it clattered along the road. Was this really worth it?

"It is only for formal occasions, dear," Mother said, evidently reading her expression. "At other times we wear comfortable clothing."

"Formal? But I thought he just wanted to see me, to be sure I'm not a savage."

"That too, dear."

They arrived at the governor's mansion, which was a larger house. Mother held Rebel's elbow firmly as they stepped down out of the coach. That was just as well, because Rebel was in danger of losing her balance.

The governor met them in what Rebel thought might be the drawing room, though she saw no drawings there. He was a hale man of some girth, with impressive sideburns, a daunting figure.

"Father, this is Rebel," George said. "The woman I would like to marry."

Rebel made a British curtsy. This was part of the language she had learned.

The governor looked Rebel over, and she realized he was seeing not the layers of clothing but the flesh beneath it. She had seen that kind of gaze before, many times. He was sizing her up as a sex object. Suddenly she understood what neither George nor his mother were speaking of directly. The man was a lecher, and he wanted a piece of her.

Well, if that were part of the price of saving her people, she could do it. Assuming George and his mother could handle it. It was an area she understood. The man would arrange private trysts with her, knowing that her barrenness eliminated most of the risk, and she would maintain his favor and the welfare of her people by obliging him. She would be discreet, never causing anyone embarrassment. In time—weeks, months, or years—his interest would move on to some newer, younger woman, and she would be free of him.

And he saw her understanding. "She'll do," the man said. He gave her one more glance and turned away. She had been dismissed.

Just like that. She had been accepted in more than one capacity.

They returned to George's house. "Will he act to save my people?" Rebel asked.

"He has already done it," Mother said as she helped extricate Rebel from the awful clothing. It was good to be able to breathe again! "The authorities have received a proclamation designating your range as a nature preserve. As long as your people stay within it, they can't be molested."

Just like that, again. She would marry George, not even needing to dissolve her marriage to Harbinger, because native marriages were not recognized by the colonists.

"There are things we do not speak of," Mother murmured. "We simply try to get along. Do you understand?"

Rebel gave her a straight look. "I do." Then, realizing how badly she would need an ally in this arena, she asked, "May we be friends in spite of it?"

The woman gazed at her. Rebel was surprised to see a tear in her eye. "We are all in the same situation," she said. "We must endure. We can do that better if we support each other."

Rebel spread her arms. Mother stepped into them, now sobbing openly. They were not so much high colonist and low native, so much as two women in a difficult position. Yes, they would be friends.

•

Some Aborigines survived, but their autonomy was finished and they were no longer a significant independent force. They had to work as laborers and servants, governed by the rules of the white man. At one point, thousands of their babies were taken and raised as whites, another effort to extirpate their culture. Today there are relatively few full-blooded natives left; the majority are mixed breeds. Many have lost touch with their original culture, eating Western foods. Those who still do hunt typically use guns rather than clubs or spears.

Among survivors, problems are rampant. Twenty-six times as many Aborigines develop dementia as whites. Up to ten times as many have circulatory diseases such as hypertension and rheumatic heart disease. Three to four times as many have type-two diabetes and the death rate is seven to ten times that of whites. And so on, with kidney disease, cancer, respiratory diseases. Communicable diseases are worse: tenfold in tuberculosis, Hepatitis B and C, twenty-fold in Chlamydia, forty-fold in dysentery and syphilis, and seventy-fold in gonorrhea. Threefold in suicide, two- to threefold in infant mortality. These are attributed to poverty, poor education, substance abuse, poor access to health services, and exposure to violence or other types of abuse. In sum: they are at the bottom of the totem, and suffer for it.

This is unfortunately typical of the peoples displaced by "modern" man, whether in America, Africa, or Australia. Efforts are being made today to redress some of the historic wrongs. But how can a vanished culture be renovated? An extinct language? A people whose numbers have been decimated, the survivors downtrodden? It seems that concern about justice comes only when the case is already lost. That's suspiciously convenient.

19

MUSA DAGH

We call them Armenians, but they called themselves Hai, and their country Haiastan. This perhaps typifies their status: they were an involuntary part of the Empire of the Ottoman Turks. They were restive late in the nineteenth century and early in the twentieth century.

To their north were the Alani or Ossetians, living in the Caucasian Mountain range between the Black Sea and the Caspian sea. They were hardly alone; the region has been a crossroads, and there may be as many as a hundred cultures there. Invaders had overrun them throughout history, and they had been divided between North Alania and South Alania, with the north annexed into the growing Russian empire. South Alania was smaller, with a different religion, but retained ties and hoped to be united with North Alania as a Soviet Republic.

World War I was commencing, and the Russians and the Turks hardly needed much incentive to fight. The Russians invaded November 1, 1914, but the Turks pushed them back a few days later. In January 1915 the Russians attacked again, this time with more force, scattering the Ottoman army. They had made a deal with the Hai: there would be an open Hai revolt coordinating with the Russian invasion. Turkey was in trouble.

The Ottomans decided to evacuate the entire Hai population from the area, settling them in Northern Iraq. That massive deportation started in May and was in full swing in June. It was not a gentle pro-

cess. The time is June 1, 1915; the place, South Alania and eastern Anatolia.

•

She was so worn and ragged that Craft hardly recognized her. Her horse was no better off, lathered and near collapse. "Rebel! Why are you here?"

"Tula," she gasped. "The Turks abducted her! They—" She stopped, running out of air.

His twin boys approached, aware that something interesting was occurring. "Dexter!" Craft snapped. "Fetch Aunt Rebel a drink. Sinister, take care of her horse."

The boys obeyed, glad to participate. Meanwhile their mother Crenelle arrived on the scene. She said nothing, merely took Rebel into her arms as she wavered, about to fall.

In minutes Rebel was better off, ensconced on a chair with plenty of water, her feet on a stool, her cooling body under a blanket. Now she was able to clarify her case.

"The Turks blame us, the Hai, for the mischief going on. My husband Tuho has been active in the resistance to the deportation. They know that, but didn't have proof. But now with the Russians invading, they don't need proof. They raided our house and took Tula. They are holding her at a military base. If Tuho doesn't turn himself in by the end of June, they will publicly rape and kill her. I can't let that happen! So I came to . . . to ask . . ." Rebel broke off, unable to continue. Crenelle took her hand.

Craft did a quick mental review. Rebel had met and married the Hai commander Tuho six years before, and adopted his daughter Tula, now fourteen. Girls were commonly betrothed at age twelve, but things were in such flux that this had not been feasible, so Tula remained home. Rebel could never have children of her own, and Tula truly became her child. Also, in a manner, did Allele, Tula's imaginary friend her age—and daughter of Keeper and Crenelle. Never mind that he, Craft had married Crenelle; Tula claimed that if Keeper had married her instead, Allele would be their child and Tula's virtual sister. Rebel had come to accept that as part of the price of Tula. She certainly cared.

Rebel had gone to live with her husband among the Hai, making annual fall visits to the home Family to stay in touch. But Haiastan was now a war zone as the Russians fought the Turks. The Alani were staying warily clear, though they favored the Russians. They had not liked the way the Ottoman forces had invaded the Caucasus region, requisitioning supplies by force. The Turks had hoped to inspire an uprising among local Muslim tribesman, but it didn't happen. Christians and Muslims got along well enough, in North and South Alania.

Then when the Russians invaded Anatolia, it did inspire a Hai revolt. Craft had not known that Tuho was an active revolutionary, but the news didn't surprise him. The Hai had always wanted to be independent, to have their own kingdom, as had been the case historically. The Ottoman Turks had other ideas, and the power to implement them. So resistance had been sporadic.

Until the Russians invaded. That changed everything. Under the Russians, the Hai could have their own semiautonomous state, and be free of the Turkish yoke at last. All they had to do was rebel at the propitious moment. That was the deal. A fortnight ago, according to scattered reports by refugees, a mixed force of Russians and Hai guerrillas had reached the city of Van, declared an independent Hai state, and set about massacring its Muslim population. Hai were flocking to the area, and its population was multiplying.

Craft and other members of the Family were not at all easy about that. The majority of people in the Ottoman Empire were Muslim, and there was bound to be savage retaliation. Already there was a report of a query by a conscientious officer where he was supposed to send a convoy of Hai. The response was, "The place they are being sent to is nowhere." In short, slaughter.

At the moment it was mostly chaos as the Russians and Turks fought each other, complicated by the forced evacuation of the Hai. Survival on those forced marches was slight; one report was that only 150 of 18,000 reached their destination in Syria. They might as well have been slaughtered. Craft had feared that Rebel and her family would be deported south with the others, facing similar odds. But this was worse, because it was more directly personal.

Soon Rebel resumed. "They are making her remove one item of clothing a day. Bracelets and beads count. But they are timing it carefully. In the last few days she will have nothing left but her dress and underwear. Then nothing at all, and she will be naked on the last day of the month. Meanwhile the soldiers are gambling and gaming to win the top places in the order. The top one will get to rape her on July first, and the second on the second, and so on. If Tuho doesn't come."

"And if he gives himself up?" Crenelle asked gently.

"Promises are worthless. They will kill him, before or after the trial. Then they will proceed with Tula until they tire of her."

That would be a while, Craft knew, for Tula was an eerily pretty girl. But even if she survived the ordeal, she would subsequently be almost worthless as a marriage prospect. She would be blamed for getting herself raped. It was the way of things in the Muslim realm. The Hai were Christian, but many of them had similar attitudes.

But it wasn't going to come to that. Rebel's plea could not be denied. Tula was Family. They had to rescue her.

Hero and Haven had been out, tending to business. As evening came, and Rebel got rest she desperately needed, they planned their mission.

They held a Family council. "We have to rescue her," Haven said. "She's Rebel's daughter."

"Adopted," Hero reminded her.

"Still Family."

Rebel stayed out of it. Craft cast the deciding vote. "Family." He had to support his sister. This was really ritual, rehearsing the reason for the action they all knew they were going to take.

"I will go," Hero said. "But I do not know that country well enough. I could not get horses."

"I do," Rebel said. "Tuho has connections I can use. They all know it's his daughter. There will be horses."

"A military base," Hero said. "I can direct a rescue raid, but I will need help. The Turks are not patsies."

"What of the Hai?"

"They don't dare," Rebel said. "Not openly. They are being deported, and the Turks are eager for a pretext to simply slaughter them. They have daughters too."

Clear enough. "But we are Alani," Craft said. "They can't get at our families. I will go also."

Hero shook his head. "Not enough. We will need a party of at least six, and even then it will be chancy."

"We have three," Rebel said. Indeed, she could do a man's work in combat, when she chose to. "And I will translate, and make the contacts." For in the Family, only she had become conversant with the Hai or Turk languages. The ability to communicate at need was vital.

Craft considered. "We can recruit three more."

"No you don't!" Crenelle snapped, reading his thought.

"They are of age for their manhood trial," Hero said.

"That's ritual," Crenelle said. "This is war."

"As if war is unknown to the Alani," Hero said with a grim smile.

Craft had to mediate again. "Maybe we should let them decide for themselves."

Crenelle looked grim, but did not speak. Haven went to fetch the boys.

In a moment they joined the Council. Risk, sixteen, Haven's son with Harbinger. Dexter and Sinister, Craft and Crenelle's twin boys, fifteen, mirror images of each other. All three were stout, vigorous lads, eager to prove their merit in any venue, so as to impress girls.

Craft summarized the situation for them. "So we need three more for a dangerous mission, from which not all may return," he concluded.

"Tula's our sister," Risk said, and the twins nodded. "We have to rescue her." Their visions of glory were almost tangible.

"The Turks will not release her lightly," Hero said. "We shall have to kill some of them. They will try to kill us in return. There will be blood."

"Blood!" the twins said together, not at all dismayed, while Crenelle winced. Hero had trained them in swordcraft, because guns were expensive and bullets were scarce, while a sword was always ready. In close quarters the swords would be deadly, but at any distance they would be prime targets for guns. That was just part of the danger.

Craft saw that the decision had already been made. The boys would have a harsh education coming, as their foolish notions of glory gave way to ugly reality, but it would indeed make men of them.

"If you go, I go," Haven told them firmly. "There will be discipline."

Not to mention food, Craft thought. Someone needed to attend to the dull details of routine management. She was not bluffing; she certainly knew how, and she could ride. "Who will take care of the home front?" he asked.

"Harbinger and Crenelle," Haven said. "And Keeper will see to the farm." They had a good commercial farm on the mountain, rising livestock, with some lumbering on the side, and traded with the valley settlers for fruit, wine, grain, cotton, and other staples. There was zinc mining nearby, with a prospect for more on their property; Harbinger was away, seeing to that. It was a going concern that should not be left unattended.

"Then it seems we are a party of seven," Hero said. "Six warriors and one commander." He glanced at Haven: she was being dubbed the commander.

They laughed. It had been decided.

•

They dressed in nondescript garb to mask the fact they were Alani, with fur caps, baggy trousers, and leather boots, and rode south toward Lake Van in the Ottoman territory. They avoided both the Russians and the Turks, because either side would quickly commandeer their horses and supplies for the war effort. They also tried to stay clear of the refugees fleeing northward, as there was nothing they could do for them.

Fortunately Rebel knew the back routes. It wasn't too bad near home, among friends, but there would be increasing danger as they progressed. They had planned for twelve days to make the three-hundred-mile journey, carrying essential supplies. Good, fresh horses were essential.

Craft was nervous, knowing how many things could go wrong. If a single horse went lame, they would suffer delay, and they lacked much of a margin. It had taken three days to organize for the trip, and they had to reach Theodosiopolis with enough time to scout the military camp, organize the raid, and accomplish the rescue. If there were any hitch there, Tula would be doomed, and some of them might die. But he would not speak of any of that.

They made good progress the first day, and camped in the forest near a stream. Haven supervised the boys caring for the horses, gathering wood, pitching a tent, and making a fire to cook dinner for them all. It was like an overnight picnic, so far. Hero, Craft, and Rebel reviewed the route for the morrow, which would be in unsettled territory. Russian and Turk patrols quested through it, looking for trouble, and had to be avoided.

"What are our chances?" Craft asked Hero privately.

"Even," his brother replied grimly. "They will improve if we can drill the boys effectively. We can't be sure how they will react to the first killing."

Craft nodded, knowing it was true.

They resumed travel early the next morning. The boys were tired from the hard day's riding, but did not complain. The party moved more slowly, watching more carefully for soldiers, so they could bypass them.

By evening they reached the first of the resistance camping points, the estate of a wealthy farmer. Rebel rode ahead alone to introduce herself, because the Hai would not admit to their role unless they were sure it wasn't a trap.

Soon she returned. "We can camp in the pasture, out of sight. They will provide fresh horses in the morning, and keep ours pending our return."

"Do they know we may return pursued?" Craft asked.

"They know. They trust us, now."

Craft realized that she had really good credits. Also, things were so generally unsettled that planning for the future beyond a few days was pointless. The horses might well be soon lost anyway. That made generosity easier.

They camped, and the farmer sent loaves of bread and skins of fresh milk to supplement their carried supplies. That was a blessing. Rebel took the boys and horses, so they could get to know the replacements. It would make a difference.

On the seventh day they reached a site in the mountains. "There is too much action here," their host said, as Rebel translated. "You will need to take the back route around the mountain. It is longer, but safer."

"What mountain is that?" Craft asked. Again, Rebel translated.

"Ararat."

"Mount Ararat!" Craft exclaimed. "Noah's Ark! It will be a privilege to see that."

The man smiled, needing no translation to appreciate his reaction. Then he spoke, and Rebel relayed it. "So you are a Jew or a Christian." It seemed it had been a kind of test.

"Christian," Craft agreed. "But the Muslims know of it also."

"But they don't consider it a holy place."

"Not as much," Craft agreed. "Is the trail sufficiently marked?"

"Not at all. That would give it away. But my daughter Fia will lead you."

"We appreciate that. My sister Haven will keep an eye on her."

"That may be difficult. She's fourteen and uncomfortably independent. We have had to hide her from the troops."

"Fourteen? Too bad we can't hide her from our teen boys."

The farmer smiled when he heard the translation, appreciating the half joke. Teens were teens all over, hard to manage.

The girl joined them in the morning, and Craft was relieved. Her face was plain, her body spare, and her hair was caught back in a messy knot. She wore a faded caftan-shaped robe and long soft trousers, with no decorations. She would be no magnet for the boys.

But as they started riding, and Fia led the way, Craft had cause to reconsider. The girl was a natural rider, clinging comfortably to her mount with no saddle or harness, her every movement competent and smooth. On horseback she was a beauty. And she knew it.

Worse, she had packed away her robe and trousers, and now wore a close–laced leather vest and short leather skirt. Craft realized they were for protection and comfort when riding through virtual wilderness, as she surely did a lot. There was no point in wearing her good clothes here. But the vest showed the outline of her nicely formed breasts as she leaned well forward, with a bit of flattened cleavage under the lacing, and the skirt showed her well-fleshed thighs. Especially when the passing breeze lifted the hem, flashing tantalizing glimpses of her taut bottom as it bounced with the gait of the horse.

The boys were staring. Craft could hardly blame them; he was staring himself. A girl who had seemed like nothing when standing still in traditional apparel was sheer dynamic sex appeal in motion on horseback. The boys were quietly vying to be first following Fia single file on the narrow sections of the trail.

Yet what could he say? The girl was doing nothing wrong, and they needed her guidance. So he pretended to be oblivious, both of the girl and of Haven's somewhat grim expression. She understood the voiceless dialogue all too well.

Near midday they broke for lunch. There was a small cold stream for water, by no accident; Fia knew the route. Haven shared out salted meat and dried fruit, including to the girl, and they took care of natural functions in the secluded brush. It was a pleasant location, cool because they were were well up on a mountain slope.

Fia perched on a convenient rock, loosened her hair, and leaned forward as she ate and talked. Her hair as it fell free was thick and flowing, and both breasts and thighs showed to advantage. The boys managed to find comfortable seats on the ground below her. They were rapt, pretending interest in her dialogue.

Craft glanced at Haven, but she gave no indication. Hero seemed not to be looking, but Craft knew he was; he was just better at masking it than most. Rebel was smiling faintly, well versed in the art of showing. It was Fia's stage.

"It is said that the ruin of Noah's Ark is near here," she said, as Rebel translated. "I have looked for it, but never found it. Only a few tattered planks."

"Planks?" Craft asked. He was actually interested in the subject. He had studied the specifications of Noah's Ark with an eye to possibly reproducing it, but had been too busy with other things to tackle such a giant project. And what would be the purpose? No serious flooding threatened.

"It has been more than a thousand years," Fia said. "Any original Ark wood would have rotted away to nothing long since. So these must have been from some more recent structure. Still . . ." She shrugged, her knees moving slightly apart.

Craft thought the boys were going to faint. Some things needed no translation.

"Probably they cannibalized the Ark to build new houses," Craft said. "So its wood might survive, but not in any recognizable state."

"That must be it!" Fia agreed. "So there's nothing remaining here."

"They might have saved some of it as a memento," Craft said. "Carefully covered and concealed, so that robbers wouldn't cart it away."

"Something still to find," Fia said dreamily. "I'll keep looking." Then she reconsidered. "Except that we're being deported. For our own safety, they say."

"You don't believe it?" Craft asked.

"There are too many stories of massacres. They march whole villages away, but we don't know whether they're really going to Mosul, or getting killed and buried. The Turks don't much like the Hai."

"Fia," Rebel said. "When's the deportation?" She spoke in Hai, but the essence was clear.

Now the girl's face clouded. "Tomorrow."

"Then how are we to return your horses?"

"You can't. They're lost anyway."

Craft was hardly surprised.

"And you," Rebel said. "What will you return to?"

Fia's face worked. "Nothing."

"Your father—he didn't send you just to guide us. It was to get you safely away from the family before the troops came." Rebel spoke in Hai, then in Alan.

Now tears started down the girl's face. "He took me aside. He said 'Fia, I love you. Don't come back.' I can't go back."

"And he trusted us because he had to. We're Family, and Christian. He knew we would not abuse you."

"Yes," the girl whispered. "He said to—to make the boys want me. So you wouldn't let me go. I am of age."

So the exposure hadn't been accidental, Craft realized. Fia had arranged to show her assets.

Rebel smiled. "And if we held a vote right now, whether to take you with us . . ." She glanced around, taking a silent survey.

"Yes!" Risk said immediately.

"Yes," Dex and Sin echoed together.

"Put your knees together," Haven said. "Of course we'll take you. But there will be rules."

Fia put them together even before the translation. "Yes."

"But we are going into danger," Craft protested, for the record.

"No worse than what she faces here," Rebel said. "We will not rape her and kill her."

"If the Turks catch us, we'll all be finished," Haven said. "Meanwhile she can be useful as a Hai contact. She knows the culture and the people, and she speaks the language."

"Yes," Fia agreed.

"You will night with me, not the boys," Haven said. "I will be your mother, and Risk your brother, and the twins your half brothers."

The three boys exchanged a glance, disappointed. They could no longer view Fia as a prospective romance. But they knew better than to protest.

They resumed their journey. Fia still led the way, but somehow now less of her flesh showed. She had vamped the boys by necessity, not preference. Or so it was convenient to believe. She was after all a teen, as they were.

The girl did turn out to be useful. She knew more contacts than Rebel did, could make herself more readily comprehended, and when the Hai understood that she had found an avenue to potential safety, they were generous in their assistance.

Risk was officially Fia's brother now, and he took his role seriously, staying close by her side. But it was evident that he was more than half smitten with her, and she was increasingly taken with him. They were working at learning each other's words. When this was over, if they both survived, there was likely to be a change in their relationship. Well, Rebel had married Tuho; such interculture liaisons were hardly unknown. Dex and Sin had already realized that they were out of it.

They arrived in the vicinity of Theodosiopolis, which the Turks had renamed Erzerum, a day ahead of schedule. Tuho was there, hale but drawn. He greeted them gladly. "She's down to basic apparel," he said.

"We will strike before she loses much more," Hero said.

Hero and Craft assessed the situation. There were a dozen Ottoman guards on duty in Tula's part of the compound. That was more than they had bargained on. "We need to get rid of half of them," Hero said grimly.

"We can take out several by ambushing them from a distance with our guns," Craft said. "But by no means all, and the others, alerted by the noise, will shortly overwhelm us."

"We need silence," Hero said. "We have only two pistols, and they should be saved for emergency. The swords will be relatively quiet, and they won't be expecting such weapons."

"I can help," Fia said.

"Not by getting gang-raped, which is what would happen if you show yourself there," Haven said.

"By distracting them," Fia said. "I am Tula's age and size. Suppose I dress like her, and show myself so it seems she is escaping?"

This was eerie. Almost as if Tula's imaginary half sister Allele had come to life.

"But she will be right there, in shackles," Craft protested. "They won't be fooled."

"If it happened at dusk, when it is harder to see?"

"They would quickly check."

"If I were naked?"

"Not safe," Rebel said, in both languages. "But it's a good idea. I'll do it."

"You're too old. And they need you for the raid."

"Fia—" Haven said.

"If I had a foolproof escape?"

They hashed it over, and concluded that it wasn't ideal, but that they did need to divert a number of troops. There was serious risk for all of them, but if it worked, they might even pull it off without losses.

First they had to make a deal with a local farmer, a secret member of the resistance. He had to cart food to the base on a daily basis, supplying the Turks free. The alternative would be to have his farm plundered and destroyed, and that might soon happen anyway. He was a reluctant supporter of the Ottomans. He agreed to help.

Then the boys sneaked into the unguarded supply depot, where there were only incidental things, like empty crates, brooms, and shoes. They stole several spare uniforms, such as they were. It was evident that this was a secondary outpost, starved of supplies. The "uniforms" were largely adapted from clothing looted from the local Hai, and were of mixed colors and types. But that would make it easier to masquerade as soldiers.

It was time: dusk. Fia took her place, hidden.

Hero, Craft, and the boys marched in toward the base, garbed as Turkish foot soldiers, complete with ceremonial scimitars. They had a prisoner with them: Rebel, in a torn dress, her hands bound but still resisting.

"Quiet, wench!" Hero said loudly in Turkish, two words Fia had drilled him in.

"Let me go, brute!" Rebel cried, struggling harder. She had learned four words, and of course had been exposed to the Ottoman environment for years. They spoke Turkish to be sure the guards would understand, and not think to question why a Hai captive would not be protesting in her own language.

The guards took an interest. They had not been expecting reinforcements, but various contingents were in the area, and sometimes different ones stopped by the base. Maybe these had come to share the captive, in exchange for some illicit wine. Muslims were not supposed to drink anything alcoholic, but this rule was widely flouted in the field.

Then Fia appeared beside a building, screaming. "Free! Free!" They had all learned that word, knowing she would use it.

The Turks did not even glance at the crate where Tula was imprisoned. It was obvious that she had somehow scrambled out of it. Four of them lurched unsteadily to their feet, shaking off the effect of the wine. They lumbered after the fleeing girl.

One guard was by the exit to the access road. He grabbed for the girl, catching her sleeve. But her shirt came off in his hand, leaving her bare-breasted. She was not as well-developed as Tula, but in the partial light and in motion the effect was good enough to fool the Turks. Her head remained covered by a tattered scarf like the one Tula had. They might not have cared much even if they knew she was different; she was a Hai girl for the taking.

The girl ran around the corner of the building and disappeared. The guards collided with each other in their eagerness to pursue her, and took moments to untangle and resume the chase. But as they did, a supply wagon came down the road, and the four guards almost collided with it.

There was a violent exchange of curses, by guards and the surly wagoner, as each sought the right of way in the narrow road. Then the guards squeezed past, resuming their pursuit though the girl was nowhere in sight, and the wagon rolled on into the compound and halted. "Help me unload, you loafers!" the driver called, or words to that effect.

But the four remaining guards refused. They were not day laborers, and they were on duty. The wagoner had to do it by himself, cursing steadily in a monotone.

Craft stifled a smile. If only they knew! Fia had disappeared not by fleeing down the road beyond the wagon, but by scrambling into the compartment in the bed of the wagon, under piled supplies. She was still there as the driver unloaded. She would remain there, silent, until the wagon trundled on out of the compound, empty.

Meanwhile the five men and one captive arrived at the other side of the compound. The guards stood, their eyes on Rebel, whose struggles had torn away her own shirt, though her hands remained bound before her.

"Take this spitfire," Hero said, using more rehearsed words. "Teach her manners." He shoved Rebel into the arms of the nearest guard.

The man gladly grabbed her and pulled her close. She came up against him, chest to chest. Then he groaned and collapsed. Blood welled from his chest where she had stabbed him with what turned out to be not a rope around her wrists, but a loose thong and knife.

The other three reacted quickly enough. But now Hero, Risk, and Dexter attacked them with swords. The Turks were caught by surprise, but they were trained soldiers, and in a moment were defending themselves with their own not entirely ceremonial swords. It seemed they lacked guns; maybe those were reserved for the front line.

Craft and Sinister ran for the crate. "Tula!" Craft called.

"Uncle!" she cried gladly, lifting her bound hands.

Craft used his knife to saw through the rope, while Sinister stood guard.

Meanwhile Hero quickly downed his man, but the other guards were driving Risk and Dexter back, being stouter and more experienced with the sword. Dexter cried out as he was wounded. Craft heard without seeing; he was focusing on the tough rope, making sure not to cut Tula's wrist along with it. Her hands came free, and she flung her arms around his neck, quickly kissing him in her relief at being rescued.

Craft heard a shot. Sinister screamed and fell. Now Craft had to look. There was a bullet hole in the boy's back, fired by a returning guard from the Fia chase. So there *were* some guns in service here, unfortunately. The wound had to be mortal.

Hero took on the guard who had wounded Dexter, and Dexter charged across the compound, his left arm dripping blood. He launched himself at the guard before the man could reload his archaic pistol, slashing viciously. He was the right-handed twin.

The guard dropped the pistol and drew his sword to defend himself, but Dexter, though inexperienced, had gone berserk. He slashed and slashed again, battering down the guard's defenses, and in moments wounded him on the arm, then on the neck, and finally in the chest. He went down, finished.

Hero and Risk had killed their men. "Get out of here!" Hero called. "The sound of the shot will bring every soldier in on the run."

"My brother!" Dexter cried.

"He's dead," Craft said. "We have to leave him." He hated to do it, because Sinister was his son, but he knew they would never be able to get away while dragging the body. They had to leave him so as not to lose more of their number.

Rebel crossed over to take Tula, who clung gladly to her. They were mother and daughter. Craft took Dexter by the arm and led him away. The boy was now like a zombie, his passion expended. They fled the compound, and soon were in the forest. They had escaped, for the moment.

Now there was time to unwind as they reverted to their own clothing. Rebel bound Dexter's wound; it was a bad cut on the arm, but not lethal. "You fought like a hero," she told him.

He refused to have it. "My brother!"

Tula tried to comfort him. "He was a hero. He died helping me and Allele escape." She still seemed to be half in shock herself, not having known she would be rescued. The Turks had made sure she understood what they had in store for her.

He would not be consoled. "He's dead!"

"He's dead," Craft agreed, stricken in his own way. "Make sure your mother does not lose you too."

That made the boy take notice. He was silent.

Craft was hurting, but what made it worse was thinking how he would have to tell his wife, Crenelle, Sinister's mother. She had been against letting the boys come.

They made their way to the rendezvous where Haven waited. She opened her arms to Dexter, and he fell into them, sobbing. She was not his mother, but she was well familiar with the role. She held him, wordlessly. Risk, her true son, nodded, understanding perfectly.

In due course Fia appeared, having made her way alone. That aspect of their ruse had succeeded splendidly.

Tula embraced her, having learned her identity and role during the wait. They were of even age and height, not otherwise similar, but in that moment they resembled sisters. They were after all both Hai, both Family.

Then they turned and closed on Risk, hugging him from either side. One was his sister, the other his girlfriend.

Tuho appeared. He clasped his daughter to him, and they both shed tears. The Family had come through. He kissed Rebel. They had been married six years and still seemed to be in love. Then he spoke.

"We can't stay here," Tuho said grimly. "The Turks are organizing to search the entire area, and they will torture anyone who they think has information. They have cut off the roads to Alania. There will be a cordon."

"So we will have to fight our way out?" Hero asked.

"We can't. They have overwhelming force. But there is a retreat."

"Ah," Hero said.

"It is just now being set up by refugees from Theodosiopolis and the surroundings. Hai who will be deported or massacred anyway. It is a mountain called Musa Dagh."

"Musa Dagh," Rebel repeated. "There's nothing there!"

"Not in the past," Tuho agreed. "But next month it will be a secret redoubt. They are ferrying supplies there now. We'll be safe there."

They traveled that night, tired and battered, but determined. They had no horses; those had been commandeered when discovered. They went by foot, carrying as much as they could.

They were joined by other Hai, similarly burdened. Tuho knew the way, and guided them all in the darkness. There was stumbling and muted cursing, but all of them were on a similar mission, facing similar peril.

The way became steep. Only the tenuous path led them through; the rest was impossible steepness and barren rock.

Finally by dawn, bone weary, they achieved the summit. It was a veritable fortress, spread across the top of the mountain, with stones being placed to shore up any likely routes from below. A small contingent could hold off an army here, indefinitely.

There was a tent for them. They wedged into it and slept as the day progressed. Tula lay between her parents, her hands tightly clasping theirs. She was still recovering. Risk managed to get a place beside Fia, with his arm around her, she nothing loathe. Craft saw Haven note it and fail to break it up. There was a death in the Family; she had evidently concluded that it was not worth sweating the small stuff. She lay beside Dexter, there if he required more comfort.

In the morning Hero and Craft were up, helping shore up the defenses, and Haven marshaled the girls and set about making a meal to feed all the troops. There were plenty of supplies, and they were still being ferried up.

There were also more people. What had been a group of several hundred soon became several thousand, and more kept piling in. All the Hai who were at risk of deportation or execution were coming here in a mass, with their families, and there were many of them. This was their sanctuary. There was a constant stream of supplies: all the food from the farms that were being taken over, including their animals, right here to be used.

And the Turks, it seemed, were ignoring them. No—it was that the Turks did not know of this retreat. They were scouring the area for the raiders who had freed Tula, and also doing battle with the Russians, and had no time for scouting isolated mountains. And no Hai breathed a word to them. No Hai who might betray them had been told; they knew whom they could trust. They simply faded out of their homes and jobs, to reappear here. It was a remarkable cooperative effort.

There was plenty of space on the mountain, but soon it was filled. An exact count was not feasible, but according to Tuho, their ranks had swelled to some fifty thousand people. The cooking enterprise had become massive, with hundreds of women and children working, and shifts throughout the day. Haven, having first organized it, and being the Family sister of Commander Tuho, became the mistress of it all, with Tula and Fia willing lieutenants who answered only to her. The men were quite satisfied to accept that.

But they were not satisfied to leave the Turks unchallenged. Now they organized as a military unit, and went down at night to harass the Turks and their German allies from the rear, so they couldn't focus fully on the Russians. Indeed, the Hai coordinated with the Russians, striking where most needed to facilitate the Russian invasion.

The Turks were clearly mystified. The Hai would attack, then disappear before there could be retaliation. The Hai were excellent guerrilla warriors, striking and hiding, leaving few traces aside from the dead Turks.

But it couldn't last forever. The Turks finally discovered Musa Dagh, and quickly organized to attack it. But their first onslaught failed, as the Hai drove them back with heavy losses. They had prepared well for this, knowing it must come. Knowing they had no choice but to fight, because loss would mean death for them all.

Yet Tuho seemed unperturbed. "We have supplies and ammunition for a month," he said.

"They won't give up in a month," Hero reminded him. But Tuho simply smiled.

The Turks tried again, and again. Each time they were thrown back by withering fire from above. They could not scale the rocky faces of the mountain without becoming targets for Hai snipers. Finally they conceded that the mountain fortress was unassailable.

So they laid siege to it, preventing any more supplies from being delivered. No one could leave, either, it seemed, unless to surrender. None did surrender.

"Now we're in for it," Haven muttered.

Tuho kissed her in a brotherly manner. "We truly hate to lose you and the girls, but it is time for you to go. I will follow later."

"Go where?" Haven demanded, unmollified.

"Down the back way," he said. "The one they don't know about."

"The back way!" Fia exclaimed, thrilled. "Like the way around Ararat."

"Like that," Tuho agreed. "The Turks don't know that their siege is incomplete. We have run no supplies along that route, to keep it secret."

But now Tula protested. "Father, you say you'll follow, but I know you. You'll fight them to the end, and die. Then I'll be fully orphaned."

Rebel kept silent. The girl had lost her natural mother long before; it was understandable that she did not want to lose her natural father too.

Tuho considered, then nodded. "I refused to lose you," he said. "Now you are refusing to lose me. I will come with you."

Tula hugged him. It seemed to Craft that the man had yielded with very little persuasion, as though he had planned on this anyway. Maybe he had simply been verifying his daughter's feeling.

They organized for the retreat. A carefully selected volunteer rear guard of five hundred men would remain to defend the fortress, which was so well situated that they could do so until they ran out of supplies. All others would quietly escape, in a steady stream through the secret route.

They made their way down in the dark, cautiously and quietly. There were guides who took their hands where required, conveying through through the more treacherous sections. All was accomplished in complete silence, so as not to alert the Turks, who were not far off.

At last they were down, and safely away from the mountain. Tuho talked quietly with their last guide, thanked him, and separated.

"Now we are on our own," he murmured. "The others are traveling to the Mediterranean, where British men-of-war ships are waiting to pick them up. But we shall go home to Alania."

"Alania," Craft agreed. They still had a considerable and dangerous trek, but with Rebel and Fia guiding them, they should make it through. Their mission was almost accomplished. If only Sinister hadn't died. But he stifled that thought. This was war, and losses occurred in war, painful as they were. For both sides.

"And we will remember," Fia said.

Craft had to agree. They would remember.

•

It was said that after a forty-day siege the Hai conceded defeat and laid down their arms. It was said that the Turks then massacred all 50,000 of them, leading off a general campaign of extirpation: the Armenian Genocide. That in the ensuing seven years as many as one and a half million Hai died, leaving their land depopulated: vengeance against a people who had sided with the Russians. That the Ottomans tried to cover it up, denying that there had been any such effort. That even today the Turkish government refuses to admit the truth. Today there are still meetings in South Alania memorializing that historical atrocity.

But the truth is murky. For one thing, if there was a massacre at Musa Dagh, it was of only 500, the rearguard that held the fortress. According to one account, all the others had disappeared down the other side of the mountain, traveling to the Mediterranean, where French and British men-of-war ships had been signaled. They picked up the main army and transported the soldiers to Alexandria, Egypt, which the British then controlled. But there were other centers of resistance, other fortresses, and they seem to have been mercilessly destroyed. So the area was depopulated, but perhaps not by deliberate organized genocide. By savagely forced migration. That suggests that the stories of a larger campaign of extermination may lack substance. But certainly entire communities of the Hai were wiped out.

Indeed there were massacres, but more Turks died than Hai. In the city of Van, when the Ottomans recaptured it and ended the brief Hai state, they butchered the men, robbed and raped the women, and left them to die. An American medical missionary on the scene reported that there were 55,000 Hai deaths. But the Russians and Hai guerrillas took a horrendous toll on the Ottomans too. At one point half the Ottoman army was tied down there, while the Allies took advantage of its weakness in the west. It was an ugly war, if that is not redundant. A war zone is no safe place for any residents, and emigration can be massive.

The British led an international war crimes tribunal on the island of Malta against 144 high Ottoman officials, of which fifty-six stood trial. But they concluded that there was not sufficient evidence for conviction, and all of the detainees were released. Now this could be considered a severe miscarriage of justice. But it could also be considered evidence that there had been no organized program of genocide, merely savage internecine war with related atrocities. The balance seems to favor the latter conclusion.

This was the beginning of World War I, that reshaped the political map of the world, resulting in the contemporary configuration of nations. Turkey had been a major power; thereafter it was a minor power. The climate of change here was not so much the weather, as the emergence of the modern world.

20

BOUNTY HUNT

The pressure of overpopulation intensified in the twenty-first century as the global total passed seven, then eight billion people. This had multiple effects, some beneficial, some ugly, even in the hinterlands. Another factor was global warming, which shut down the Gulf Stream, disrupted the North Atlantic oscillation, and changed weather patterns around the world, wreaking havoc with agriculture. This got the attention of Europe, which was threatened with prolonged cooling, possibly an ice age, while other parts of the world sweltered. Serious changes in the human mode of farming and energy use were urgently required. They occurred, perforce, rapidly and powerfully.

The place is the Basque Province of Zuberoa, formerly called Soule, in the united European state of Euskal Herria, its seven provinces once split between France and Spain. The emergence of the potent economic Common Market, with its Euro money, language, and culture, facilitated the political process, alleviating the unrest of the local people. Zuberoa, lost in the Pyrenees mountains of what was once southwest France, is generally considered to be the smallest and least significant province. The inhabitants are quite satisfied with that; unspoiled landscapes remain rare in the world. But there are other problems. The time is fall of the year 2050.

Haven brooded as she kneaded the bread in the evening, preparing it for the slow overnight baking in the stone oven. The house itself was massive stone, much like a fortress, with a steep snow roof. Stone was the building material of choice, high in the mountains, and the Basques were renowned stonecutters. This Family home was exactly typical, by no coincidence. At the moment her mood was similarly heavy.

She understood the problem well enough; what she lacked was an acceptable answer. She had reviewed it repeatedly, but it remained intractable. The Family had a serious cash-flow crisis, and would be lucky not to go broke.

Her mind drifted for a moment. They were Eskualdunak, the Sun people, or Basques to the rest of the world. It was said with some perverse pride that their language was one of the most obscure and difficult tongues in the world. Even apart from the problem of multiple dialects so diverse that sometimes two Basques could not understand each other, and had to converse instead in Euro. That the Red Master, known outside as the devil, seeking converts, had once come to their country to learn their language, but after seven years had gotten no further than Yes (Bai) and No (Ez), and gave it up in disgust. That it dated from biblical times, with Eve's name deriving from Eva, or Ez-ba, meaning No-Yes. Eve was all woman, surely to Adam's occasional frustration; she could change her mind. Adam's name meant "full of understanding," except when it came to Eve.

Haven paused to put away the *kaiku,* the slanted wooden container for milk, as she would not be needing it further tonight. Tourists tended to stare at it, thinking it was about to fall over, but it was as stable as the Basque culture. It was carved diagonally from a single tree trunk, perhaps in its way like the typical native.

Their Family farm was in the designated Pyrenees Wilderness Area, its technology limited to nineteenth century levels with certain significant exceptions. The big stone oven was no longer heated by wood fire, but by focused solar power, so as to be nonpolluting. The flour for the bread, whether grain or acorn, was ground by power from a windmill on windy days. Their water was heated by deep geothermal pipes and the waste water was circulated back into the ground so that the farm was net neutral on thermal pollution. Actually the farm was one of the few places that operated on natural water; most of the world now used desalinated water from the sea, processed by power from tides and currents in the ocean. And of course recycling gray water was mandatory, used largely for irrigation. Water from rain was a blessing when it came, but was unreliable.

As for power: they used harnessed horses for routine farm work; the girls were thrilled to supervise the animals. For travel thirty kilometers to the town of Soule they used an electric car, the power provided by the local spent-fuel nuclear plant, which "burned" rods formerly stored as dangerous nuclear waste. The internal combustion motor had been banned decades ago, except for carefully crafted nonpolluting versions. Not only did that significantly abate global warming, it freed the remaining oil to be converted to food, popularly dubbed oilfoo. But the farm looked primitive, as did their lifestyle, if not closely examined.

Hero entered the kitchen, which was traditionally the most important room of the farm. From time immemorial the life of the house centered there, because it was where the life-giving fire burned continuously. Now that was figurative rather than literal, but it remained the Family center. "You have time?" he asked politely in Basque. The Family clung consciously to the old tongue and the old ways, to whatever extent was feasible. It was a source of muted private pride to be able to speak in a language even the devil could not fathom, let alone tourists. Of course they spoke in Euro when dealing with outsiders.

Hero's approach meant there was something serious on his mind. He was asking if she could give him her full attention. He was not a subtle man. "Too much," she said, continuing her kneading. It was good to have her hands occupied when her mind was challenged.

Then she reconsidered, and paused to fetch them both small glasses of *txakolina*, the fruity young white wine they made from their own vineyard. It was best to relax when tackling serious matters. Artificial wine was far cheaper, even for them, and looked and tasted the same, but there was something about knowing it was natural that was appealing, almost comforting. It was one of their few food indulgences.

Hero knew her as well as she knew him. They were not man and woman, but brother and sister. They were both in their midthirties, both dedicated to the preservation of their culture. They discussed everything of any consequence, coming to Family decisions. "You have news."

"So do you," she agreed. "Tell me yours first."

"There is a meater in Soule."

That set her back. The meaters were criminals who poached people, usually tender children, to harvest for meat. "Anathema," she said. "Not the way I care to see the population reduced. You're sure?"

"Craft tracks them electronically. This one was operating in Pamplona. Then in San Sebastian on the coast. He figured the meater would move on into France, but the tag code he watched turned up in Soule this morning." He shook his head. "Heavy is the hand of foreigners." It was a Basque proverb relating to their traditional distrust of outsiders. Especially intruders of this variety.

"They have to keep moving," Haven said. "Unpredictably. Lest they be butchered and eaten by outraged locals."

Hero smiled, somewhat warily, appreciating her ugly joke: meaters ate people, so people might eat meaters. Actually the world was overwhelmingly vegetarian in practice if not appearance; the consumption of genuine meat had been outlawed decades ago. Only carnivores in zoos were entitled, and not all of them, depending on the supply of accidental kills. Most people would be appalled by the notion of eating real meat, let alone eating people meat. "There's an ad pitched to teens. We need to warn the girls."

"We do," she agreed grimly.

"What is your news?"

"We're in trouble. The drought damaged our crops, we're not allowed to irrigate with geothermal waste, our harvest suffered, we can't fill our orders, and we're running out of money. The forecast is for returning rain in spring, but we face a difficult winter. I can't find a way around it."

"Except by selling some of our land," he said.

"We can't spare anymore. We need it for the crops."

He didn't argue the case. He knew she had done a thorough review. "So we're desperate."

"Desperate," she agreed.

He pondered a moment. "Are we desperate enough?"

"Enough?"

"To go for the bounty."

"Bounty?" She had feared he would mention the black market for natural foods. She refused to compromise there; the Family was not criminal. Then she caught on. "Hero! You can't mean the meaters!"

"It would tide us through the winter."

"To spare," she agreed. "But those criminals are dangerous. That's why the bounty is so high. They only go after children."

"And succulent teen girls. We have three."

"Hero!" she exclaimed, appalled. But it was an uncomfortable truth: there was a sick hunger for real meat, and the animals of farms and protected wilderness areas were excruciatingly well guarded. So the meaters went after the most plentiful, least guarded prey: human beings. Children and girls did not have to be guarded sexually so much as for their flesh, literally. It was said that there was a special flavor to "long pig" and that there were those who cultivated it. Naturally fung-foo, the popular name for the alga produce, was not made in that flavor. It was bad enough that it was made in animal flavors, identical in taste, texture, and appearance to the real ones.

He sighed. "Bad idea. We dare not risk them."

That made her rebound, reconsidering. After all, they could not tolerate meaters in their area; *someone's* children would pay the price, if not their own. It would be a significant service to the community to rid it of these most unwelcome predators. "Could there be a way only to *seem* to risk them? As bait?"

"Bait?" he asked, frowning.

"For a honey pot."

He nodded, getting it. "Meaters normally don't slaughter their prey immediately. They drug them and ship them out of district, so that if they're caught in the act they can't be tried for murder. Once they're out, they're gone. They know how to evade the authorities. Then their prey is done for. So we'd have to see that they don't get the girls out. Risk knows how to pie a car."

"Wouldn't they use a copter?"

"Too obvious in the sky. All copters have their own registered tags that can be instantly tracked. They'll use a quiet, illicitly tagless car, losing it in traffic."

"But what about the personal human ID tags?" she asked. "They broadcast continuously."

"They'll cut them out and toss them into another passing car as a decoy. No hope there."

"Cut them out!" She was appalled anew. The tags were deeply embedded in flesh, so as to be difficult to remove without doing serious harm. Naturally the meaters didn't care about that; they would soon carve the rest of the body anyway.

"We're dealing with hardened butchers, remember."

She shuddered, remembering. "So if the meaters took the girls for innocents, and struck, we would rescue them before anything happened."

Now he reconsidered. "But there's always risk. The unexpected. We'd be up against experienced rogues."

"This terrifies me," Haven said. And realized that was because she had decided to do it.

"And me," he admitted. "There's too much danger."

"I will talk to the girls," she said. "It must be their choice."

"Of course," he agreed faintly. He had suggested the ploy, but obviously was not keen on it. Only their desperate need for legitimate money swayed him, as it did her. "I'll roust them out." He was letting her handle it alone, as was her right. She was the matriarch, the *etcheko primu*, the agreed heir of the house, empowered to make key decisions. She never did it carelessly.

Soon the three girls entered the kitchen. First was Hero's daughter Tourette, eighteen, and stunningly lovely. Only her syndrome prevented her from being married. That, and her passion for Keeper. Haven would have prevented the liaison, but had suffered a horrible Vision of the possible consequences, that could have wiped out her people, and relented. So it was only a vision, but Tula, who could be psychic, apart from her imaginary friend Allele, confirmed it. So Hero's daughter was having an affair with Hero's youngest brother.

That sent Haven into another spot review. The burgeoning population of the world had threatened to destroy it. Poverty and warfare were leading to starvation, yet the increase continued, worsening the situation. Something had to be done. The solution had been double: instead of raising birds, mammals and fish for meat, the world had shifted to harvesting insects. She remembered a figure from her days of school: it had taken almost nine hundred gallons of water to produce a third of a pound of beef for one person's meal. In contrast, a cup of water could do for a quarter pound of crickets. Caterpillars, ants, termites, roaches, flies, maggots—all were relatively efficient sources of protein and other essential nutrients. They were easy to raise and harvest, and wild ones did just as well. It had required some cultural adjustment in some parts of the world, notably North America, but in a generation what had been sickening became practical and tasty. Children loved bugfoo.

The other breakthrough related to primitive plants and fungus. Algae had been developed to produce raw food substance, that could be flavored and formed to emulate other foods, including meat. It was twenty times as efficient to eat grains directly, in the form of bread, cereal, pasta, and similar, as to feed it to animals for their meat. The alga was more efficient yet. So it became the ultimate affordable food, alleviating the word's hunger at one stroke. It was laced with antibiotics, anti-wild fungus, antivirus and other toxin nullifiers, and it also strenuously enhanced the immune system. Immunity on steroids, it was said, though steroids were not used. Thus a number of enduring plagues had been abated, including malaria, venereal diseases, the common cold, influenza, hepatitis, measles, mumps, tuberculosis, herpes, diseases like chicken pox, rabies, and even AIDS. And, perhaps most significantly, cancer, much of which was triggered by viruses. It was supremely healthy food.

But it had two liabilities: enhanced immune systems aggravated immune diseases like (here she mentally recited yet another school lesson) type-1 diabetes, Crohn's disease, glomerulonephritis (kidney disease), Guillain-Barré syndrome, juvenile arthritis, lupus, Multiple Sclerosis, psoriasis, Rheumatic fever, and ulcerative colitis. Those people had to have special counteractive medication.

It was also contraceptive. Those who ate it did not breed. Was that effect coincidental? The manufacturers claimed it was, a side effect of the enhanced immune response that made a woman's body reject foreign material like sperm, but most folk seriously doubted it. Yet it was quietly solving the problem of overpopulation. The birthrate had plunged, and only a few were able to get off the algae and generate children. There were contests with prizes of a month's "natural" food, so that people could become temporarily fertile again. So babies were still being born, but only desperately wanted ones.

The Family's livelihood related to this. They farmed the old-fashioned way, on the slopes and valleys, with natural sunlight and rainfall on natural soil, growing assorted grains with only limited fertilizer. Their goats grazed natural pastures, producing natural milk. Their hens produced natural eggs. There was an enduring market, because these were the foods that promoted human fertility. But all prices were controlled to prevent gouging, so while the farm normally did well, they were not rich. They had no truck with the black market as a moral issue and as a practical one: the authorities were watching. And they ate fungfoo, because their natural food was too important as a business to waste on themselves.

The sterility of fungfoo had another effect: since breeding was no longer the point of a social gender connection, and there was no danger of venereal disease, relationships had liberalized. Closely related people could have affairs if they chose, and age had ceased to be a barrier, so long as the sex was knowledgeable and consensual, and there were those who did have such affairs. Adultery was severely condemned among the Basques, but this was not that. Essentially, any breasted girl could indulge with any single man she chose, provided the choice truly was free. It was phenomenally liberating, and girls who might have been repressed formerly now evinced sexual urges parallel to those of men. Sex was power, youth was potent, and many an attractive young woman was eager to exploit it. Among them Tourette, with her uncle Keeper, whom she had long since wrapped around her little finger. Haven had had to approve it, as head of the family, and so no one else questioned it. By contemporary standards, it was acceptable, if not encouraged. Basques did not take readily to strangers, which made wider Family relations even more appealing.

Then came Rebel's adopted daughter Tula, fifteen, no wallflower herself. She had been taken hostage by a rival political faction, and threatened with rape and murder, until the Family had struck back with the aid of police and rescued her. And her invisible friend Allele, Tula insisted. The experience, while horrifying, had evidently impressed upon Tula the power her appearance could wield. She took after Rebel in that respect, and was already impressing boys and some who were more than boys.

And Fia, also fifteen, tacitly adopted by the Family when her own family was wiped out. She was like a sister to the others, but was unrelated. She was shapely in a lean athletic manner, but not pretty of face. That didn't matter to Risk, who had made his intention to marry her clear. They were indeed in love, and Haven had to pretend to ignore the fact that they now shared a bed. Risk could certainly have done worse.

Three schoolgirls, though soon Tourette would end that and assume the role of an adult woman. Would she marry Keeper? It was distinctly possible. Haven had spent her life as part of the new order, but her conservative heritage carried over, and she did have a private problem with the extent of contemporary sexual freedom. Yet above all else, she wanted the girls to be happy, and the Family united. This was part of the price of that.

"Girls," Haven said, "we have a problem. You may be able to help, if you choose to."

"Of course we volunteer," Tourette said immediately.

Haven silenced her with a raised hand. "Hear me out first. There is danger." Then she acquainted them with the situation, and their proposed honey trap. "The men will be watching via your broadcasting tags," she concluded. "So we should be able to accomplish it. But it *is* dangerous, and you need to consider carefully before volunteering. We'll try to ensure your safety, but there can never be a perfect guarantee."

"You let me be with Keeper," Tourette said. "Now I can repay you. I volunteer."

There was a certain logic there, and the girl knew what she was doing. "I thank you, Tour."

"You let me be with Risk," Fia said. "I volunteer too."

Logic there too, though Haven had not thought of it as any potential quid pro quo. "Thank you, Fia."

"And I will be with Craft," Tula said. "I volunteer. Allele doesn't mind."

Haven tried to stop her jaw from dropping. Her brother Craft was twenty years older than Tula. He had been the one to actually rescue her, in the Family effort, but Haven hadn't thought that had that much of an effect on her. Evidently she had been mistaken. True, they were unrelated by blood. Still, Tula was legally Family. Yet if she had set her cap for Craft, he was lost. She was, taken as a whole, some winsome girl, eerily prescient, with subtle nerves of steel.

"Fair is fair," Tourette said. "They're in love."

As if a fifteen-year-old really knew what love was. As if Craft's suppressed interest wasn't in Hero's wife Crenelle. Yet there was potential mischief there too. It might indeed be better to let him have the girl. Better the marginal legitimate interest, than the illegitimate one. Craft would never pine for Crenelle as long as Tula was in his bed.

"And well matched," Fia said. "She always liked him. Allele approves."

"You're in on this!" Haven exclaimed to them both. "You set it up!"

"We don't want them to have to sneak any more," Tourette said.

Any more? Haven had thought she was abreast of Family concerns. Evidently she has missed one. Maybe there had been hints, but she hadn't wanted to see it.

"Uncle Craft didn't want to upset you," Tourette said innocently.

Haven looked at Tula. "You are volunteering with the understanding that I will let you be with Craft."

Tula had the grace to blush affirmatively.

"And what of Allele, if you do that? Who will she have as her companion?"

"Sinister," she answered without hesitation. "He died saving her."

Haven was blank. "Who?"

"Craft's son with Crenelle. He's sixteen. Just right for Allele, and he understands her perfectly."

This was supremely curious. Allele was Crenelle's daughter by Keeper, and Sinister was her son by Craft? Just as if Crenelle hadn't always been married to Hero.

Then Haven had a revelation. "Alternate universes!" she exclaimed.

"Of course," Tula agreed. "I can see them."

And that suddenly made sense of much of Tula's mystery. She was attuned to what might have been, as well as to what really was. "But they're half-siblings."

"Yes," Tula agreed as if this were hardly relevant as an objection. "They are Family."

Haven threw up her hands, figuratively and literally. Tula and Craft would do what they would do, regardless. It was better to have it accepted. "Then so be it."

All three girls flocked to her, hugging her in thanks. Then they were gone, surely to tell Craft, and Tula would remain with him this night, no longer sneaking. Maybe it was all for the best.

•

They had it set up in detail by morning. The girls caught the electric helicopter school bus as usual. But when they got there, they sneaked out to answer an ad to taste test a new dessert made from fungus. The meaters' ad.

Meanwhile Hero, Craft, and Risk drove the car along the roundabout mountain roads to the town of Soule. They would park it inconspicuously and close in on the meaters' location, taking care to neutralize any spy beams that might spot them. Craft knew how to do that, of course.

Haven watched on the closed-circuit holo throughout. Tula's unit generated the picture via converging fields, showing what was in sight from a point just above her head. Fia's unit picked up the sound. Tourette's broadcast the two signals on a tight beam to Haven's receiver. It was a sophisticated nonstandard setup Craft had engineered that was quite likely to evade detection by the meaters.

The town was a miniature edition of a city, with its main population concentrated in multistory residential complexes, the limited manufacturing and services facilities close by, to reduce necessary transport. Covered walkways at several levels connected the buildings. Walking was encouraged; it was healthy and it saved energy.

The girls walked toward the address, which was a rented display shop on an upper floor near a car delivery access, and stopped outside, giggling conspiratorially. They even paused to do an impromptu little dance on the crowded street. Every Basque danced; it was in their blood, as were the lovely ancient folk songs and legends. They were being carefree girls, doing their own slightly naughty thing. One of the traditions that had faded in the liberalization of recent decades was the restriction against women participating in the Pastorales, the formal traditional dances. They even did the Sword Dance, concluding with the swords formed into an interwoven hexagon. The days of men dressing for female roles were gone. Now the genders could intermingle on stage as well as privately.

Others on the street smiled, their bodies faintly echoing the motions. What could be more delightful than young pretty girls being themselves? Basques were traditionally happy folk, forever joking and laughing despite being primitive. Haven counted on the meaters misjudging them as too ignorant to be anything other than easy prey.

There was a fair number of spectators, because off the farm, out of the wilderness preserve, the reality of the world was that it was thickly populated. The birthrate reduction policy had been in place only a generation, and there were still some eight billion people, most of whom were living longer than had been the case in past ages. In time the excess death rate would hasten depopulation, and when it got down to a single billion, arrangements would be made to increase the birthrate. Probably not in Haven's lifetime, though. Meanwhile every street was crowded, and privacy was largely limited to natural functions and small shuttered rooms at home. People were used to it, and took pains to get along. Tolerance helped.

"Let's do it," Tourette said, as if struck by a sudden wicked notion. They entered the shop.

Haven knew that the meaters were already verifying their identities via the tag broadcasts. No problem there: the three were exactly what they seemed to be, schoolgirls skipping school. Had they been anything else, such as undercover police, the meaters would have played it straight, giving them samples to taste and judge, thanking them for their participation, and letting them go. The meaters were not fools; they were careful. That was why they were so hard to catch.

"Your ad," Tourette said brightly in Euro. She wore a plain school dress that made her look two years younger but could not conceal her beauty. Not that it mattered; her tag established her age. "Dessert?"

The meater was a dapper-looking man with a badge indicating he was a specialty cook. "It's a new line of alga, grown in severely polluted waste water. Very efficient, especially considering that other strains of alga died. We are very proud of it. We think the taste is perfect. It has a special quality. But we want to verify that young citizens will like it." He was circumspect, but his pupils dilated as he surveyed Tourette. He was noticing.

"We do like desserts," Tula said. "But we've tried them all. Fungfoo gets dull. We're more adventurous."

The meater's eyes flicked to her. She had loosened her blouse to show a bit more flesh than would have been encouraged at school. She was an innocently flirtatious maiden. "This is not dull," he reassured her.

"Goody," Fia said. She was the plain girl of the trio, but she did have decent meat on her bones.

Haven saw the meater's masked assessment. These girls thought there was safety in numbers. That nothing bad could happen to them as long as they stayed together. They were naïve fools. Their tender flesh would soon fetch a good price on the underground meat market. But he covered it by seating them at a table and presenting them with three elegant desserts. "Taste as much as you want," he said encouragingly. "And give us your honest opinion. Will this do for a high-class restaurant?"

The three girls fell to, eagerly eating the desserts. And in seconds all three slumped forward, unconscious. Haven was surprised. She had known they would be drugged, but thought it would take minutes to take effect, so that their team could close in before the process was complete. Still, this would do. "Hero," she said, experiencing a small thrill of victory along with the danger. "They have struck." Because the meaters had to be caught in the act, to nail the bounty. Now they could be caught and turned in, dead or alive.

"On my way," he said. "Risk's got their van."

Then it started going wrong. It would take only two or three minutes for Hero to get there, as he had been staying clear so as not to risk alerting the meaters. But Dapper wasn't waiting. He swept around the table and put his hands on Tourette, literally ripping off her clothes.

"Hero, hurry!" Haven said tensely.

"Trying," he answered.

All Haven could do was watch as the man stripped Tourette and dragged her onto the floor. He opened his fly. His erect member sprang out. He was going to rape her!

On one level Haven knew this was folly, because the meaters needed to drag the girls into their van and depart as quickly as possible. On another she realized that the man wanted to rape a living girl, rather than a dead one, and he might not have a chance later in the process. So it made a kind of selfish sense. Still, it was a horror.

The man threw himself on her bare body and rammed into her, thrusting so hard her whole torso jumped. But that had an effect the meater evidently hadn't anticipated.

Tourette woke. Maybe it was because her nervous system was not quite normal. Maybe she hadn't eaten enough of the drugged pudding to be knocked all the way out for long. Maybe she simply didn't like getting raped. She was sexually experienced, but this was something else.

She struck that man on the side of his head with her wrist. It was no token blow. Tourette, like all Basque children, was an avid player of handball, pelote, their national game along with its cousin jai alai. Her wrists and hands were hardened from years' experience striking the hard little ball, and she had muscles where it counted. There would be a bruise.

Bruises. Tourette followed up with a flurry of blows by both hands, battering the man's ears painfully. He tried to jerk his head up and clear, but she followed him, now striking at his face. In a moment his nose was bleeding and his eyes were bloodshot. He lifted up off her—and she caught him with a knee. Where it counted.

Hero burst into the room. Now he saw his daughter savagely attacking the man, and realized at least part of what had happened. He clubbed the meater on the head with his own hardened fist, knocking him unconscious. Then he enfolded Tourette, who at last was able to relax and cry. She was going into a seizure, but at this point that hardly mattered.

Craft followed Hero in, and went immediately to the two girls, who were stirring. He enfolded Tula. So it truly was mutual, Haven noted; he did care about her. As if there could be any real doubt. Haven was already feeling better about it. The two really were, as Fia had said, well matched. The highly competent man and the brave and beautiful girl.

The rest was routine. Hero summoned the police, who took possession of the sadly battered meater and his partner in the van, whom Risk had conked on the head as he labored to start the pied motor. Both would be in need of the universal health-care treatment Euro provided, before they were put on trial. The police verified the identity of the meaters, who turned out to have a long record, and authorized the bounty.

The Family had done a public service. They had also secured their finances for the winter. They had paid a cruel price; Tourette would not recover her emotional balance for some time. Keeper would surely help her a lot.

It had been a rough day. But they had survived. That was what counted.

•

Whether there will be such a thing as fungfoo is questionable, but the problems of population and global warming are real. If there is not something of the sort, the near future will be much uglier than this. The twin pressures of the sheer numbers of people, and the loss of agricultural capacity will lead to wholesale starvation. People will not simply lie down and expire; there will be savage warfare for edible resources.

What of the Basques? How did they come to have such a difficult language, seemingly unrelated to any other? That is as yet unknown, as is their early history. It is theorized that they are a remnant of early peoples who were living in the area before the great expansion of the Indo-Europeans, managing to stave off the cultural onslaught, there in their mountain fastness. That their language was spoken there 5,000 years ago, before any of the contemporary people arrived on the scene. Cave art in the region dates back 15,000 years. Could that have been by the same people? But they do not seem to be significantly different from their neighbors in anything except language. The project to examine DNA around the world may in time determine whether they differ from the neighbors genetically as well as in language. Blood-typing suggests that they are indeed distinct from others in Europe. But there has surely been much physical admixture as well as cultural. They fought over the centuries to retain their independence, but with imperfect success. The later twentieth century saw the Basque Separatist Movement in Spain, an often ugly guerrilla campaign. But this may well have been justified by the cruelly repressive measures taken against them by the government, as was the case elsewhere with the Australian Aborigines, the Central American Maya, the African Xhosa, and the Armenian neighbors of the Alani. Brutality breeds brutality. At least, in this conjectured future, the Basques achieve independence.

AUTHOR'S NOTE

•

In 1966 my wife and I visited science fiction genre writer Keith Laumer. He was at that point a successful professional writer, readily able to sell what he wrote, who lived about forty miles north of us in Florida. I was a new writer, with about eight story sales to my credit, eager to get the word from an established one. It was a pleasant day-long visit, and I learned many things in the course of our discussion. In a subsequent year he had a stroke and became a mean man, and I never met him again thereafter. The stroke effectively cut off his writing and ended his marriage, until finally he died. It was a sad conclusion to a promising career.

But I inherited his reputation for being an ogre at conventions, though I had never attended one, and that was to dog me for decades. Apparently fans and other writers did not bother to distinguish between two genre writers living in west central Florida. I even wrote a novel in which an ogre was the hero, *Ogre, Ogre,* which became my first national bestseller, perhaps the first fantasy paperback original ever to do so. It didn't seem to matter in that respect. So my career flourished commercially, while my personal reputation remained low, though I have always treated both fans and other writers courteously, as those who have interacted with me directly know. Well, in fanzines—amateur magazines—when someone came at me with guns blazing or with a false accusation, I put him down; I never suffered fools or rascals gladly. Maybe that contributed to the determined effort of some to cast me as a talentless lowlife. So my life within the science fiction and fantasy genres has been anything but placid, and I owe organized fandom essentially nothing. And it all seemed to start with Keith Laumer.

But there is another connection to the man. In the course of our discussion I mentioned how I had aspirations to write ancient historical fiction, though I regretted not being able to take it back beyond historical times. He asked something like "Well, why *don't* you?" A simple question, and it made me realize that I was needlessly limiting myself. That was the point at which the GEODYSSEY series came into conceptual existence. I started collecting books on history, archaeology, anthropology, paleontology, and anything else relevant to the human condition as I wished to write about it. For a quarter century I built up my library, and pondered how to handle the huge project.

Finally in the early 1990s, my reputation secured by my fantasy sales, I started writing it, and the first four volumes are the result: *Isle of Woman*, *Shame of Man*, *Hope of Earth*, and *Muse of Art*. Big novels, ranging up to a quarter-million words long, and the subject barely touched. My early notion of having detailed progressive maps showing the changing extent of ancient empires faded as unworkable, and became simple spot maps to set the scenes. In this volume I don't even have that; I simply describe the locales.

My biggest problem was how to cover the whole of human history for several million years yet keep it intelligible and interesting to the average reader. Of course I had to sample it, as there is way too much to address fully. So I had a series of stories relating to breakthroughs in the human condition, such as the development of facile speech or the lockable knee. Stories, because the average reader does not relate well to anthropological lecturing. He needs to identify with a character and see the world through those eyes, feeling the character's feelings. In short, a soft touch. I saved the lecturing for the italicized notes surrounding the stories, which readers could skip if so inclined. No lists of kings and dates here; I prefer the feel of the times, especially for the common man.

Even so, it wasn't enough. I did not want my narrative to fall apart into many loosely connected episodes. I needed to unify it. This brought me to perhaps my single most significant device: having a single small cast of characters per novel, experiencing life as it was ten million years ago, one million years ago, a hundred thousand, five thousand, one thousand, five hundred, and so on right up to the present and the near future. But not science fiction, not time travel. I did it by having them be different people, of different periods, but similar in character and relationships and names. In this novel, Hero is actually twenty different people; the name is a mere fictive convenience. He always has two younger brothers and two younger sisters, similarly aged and named, whatever their race or situation. We are all ordinary people, regardless of our appearance or circumstance. Hero always is interested in a woman named Crenelle, regardless of whether he marries her. I let the reader, knowing that, suspend his disbelief and see Hero and his siblings as the same people. That lends personal unity to the whole, despite widely changing times and places and cultures. A few characters originated in prior volumes, but they have the framework of this novel when visiting here.

All went reasonably well for four volumes, and I was satisfied to continue writing them indefinitely. I had hired a researcher, Alan Riggs, who was marvelous in delving into arcane references and coming up with the information I needed. Yes, I had my library of about 3,000 selected volumes, but I figured it would have taken me a year or more to write each volume, doing my own research, and I couldn't afford that. Because I earned my living through funny fantasy, not historical fiction, and I needed to maintain my income so that I could afford to take the time for history. My frivolous fantasy was my serious business, while my serious historical fiction was my less commercial preference. That's the way it is, in the inverted realm of publishing. As it turned out, each volume still took me half a year, compared to the three months or less each fantasy novel took.

Then I lost my market for historical fiction. Details are complicated, but the essence is that my publisher mismarketed it as dark fantasy, which it wasn't, so that readers of historical fiction didn't know about it, and readers of fantasy weren't much interested. It was a shame. Publishers can be idiots, but they control the money and marketing, sometimes to the detriment of their authors. So sales declined, and the publisher lost interest. Deprived of my market, I let my researcher go and stopped work on the novel. *Climate of Change* was two-thirds completed, but there it stopped. I wrote fantasy instead. I am, after all, a commercial writer; if I can't sell it, I hesitate to write it.

Thus it remained for a decade. In the interim several things happened. I became a decade older, now in my seventies, and increasingly conscious that I risked leaving several projects unfinished when I died, and that bothered me. So I started completing novels and series, tying up loose ends. One of them was *Climate of Change*. But of course my researcher was long since gone, and I still didn't want to take a full year or more for a single novel. Still, I should be able to finish a third of a novel in half a year, using my accumulated library; that seemed a fair compromise.

My wife's strength declined mysteriously, until she could no longer walk or even stand and was confined to the wheelchair. She could not move it herself, because her arms weakened the same way her legs did. I took over the household chores, meals, dishes, shopping, etc., and had to heave her in and out of the wheelchair. My writing plummeted as my working time diminished. This also affected my appearance: for decades we had exchanged haircuts, but she could no longer do mine, so I started growing my hair long. Now I wear it in a ponytail and I'm satisfied. I like to say that I never knew what beautiful hair I had until after I turned seventy. Then at last we got a diagnosis: CIDP, or Chronic Inflammatory, Demyelating Polyneuropathy. In English, that means that her immune system was attacking and stripping the myelin insulation around her nerves, so that they were in effect shorting out. The signals her brain sent to her limbs didn't get there, and her muscles were atrophying for lack of use. It is related to Lou Gehrig's disease and other wasting diseases. After taking out the arms and legs it can progress to the lungs, and that is the end. Fortunately for us this variant was treatable. It required four-hour infusions of IVIg every five or six weeks. Each treatment cost $3,000, and for a time we had to pay it ourselves, after Congress changed the reimbursement rate to make it unfeasible for hospitals. We were lucky we could manage it, because others who could not were dying. But the treatments are effective, and she was able to learn to walk again, painfully, and now is securely back on her feet. She can't walk far, but she can function well enough. This year we had our fifty-second anniversary; death has not yet us parted. She took back some of the household chores, and my writing time increased, though not to what it had been before. It was another reminder of mortality, however. We never know what the future holds. It was time to get this project done.

In that interim the Internet expanded to prominence, and with it came services like e-mail, search engines, and online data bases. I discovered that Google and Wikipedia were fine research tools, effectively replacing my human researcher. Modern technology was coming to my rescue. It wasn't perfect, but the combination of my library and the Internet enabled me to complete the novel on my schedule.

Meanwhile human history continues. In that intervening decade the United States manufactured a pretext to invade and occupy another nation, leading to incalculable financial, human, and moral costs. Population continued its devastating increase, leading to widespread poverty and starvation. The scourge of AIDS became globally prominent, worse because whole nations are trying to pretend it doesn't exist. The cost of energy, notably oil, is increasing horrendously. And the climate, of course—global warming is now recognized, and is helping drive plant and animal species toward extinction. The change of climate is increasingly dominating public awareness.

I discovered something as I returned to historical research and writing. My writing and reading tastes have been warped by my success in fantasy. I once thrilled to research ancient cultures and events; now they are less compelling. Oh, it was great fathoming how the Alani princess was captured and married by the Armenian king, discovering how the Zimba of Africa ate entire towns, how the Spaniards destroyed the last independent Maya state, how the first British colony of Australia was founded, how the Xhosa torpedoed themselves by believing a teen girl's vision, investigating the notorious Armenian genocide—yes indeed, it all is fascinating. But not as much so as it was for me before. I regret that on one level, but must recognize its reality. I have been corrupted by the ease and wonder of fantasy.

Still, I'm glad to finally complete this novel, and hope that readers like it. So has my negative impression of the direction our species is taking ameliorated? Not at all. This novel suggests a positive outcome to the several trends that can destroy us, but I'm not at all sure such necessary policies will be implemented. I fear we will continue with the ecological disaster we call agriculture, with outrageous pollution, and to breed and consume wastefully until we crash, leaving a devastated remnant reverting to savagery. With luck, I won't live to see that, but I'm afraid my children will. I wish it were otherwise.

I hope I am wrong.